Sons of Toil

Also in Century by Margaret Sunley

Fields in the Sun
The Quiet Earth

SONS OF TOIL

Margaret Sunley

C

CENTURY

LONDON SYDNEY AUCKLAND JOHANNESBURG

First published in Great Britain in 1992 by
Random Century Group
20 Vauxhall Bridge Road
London SW1V 2SA

Random Century Australia (Pty) Ltd
20 Alfred Street, Milsons Point, Sydney, NSW 2061
Australia

Random Century South Africa (Pty) Ltd
PO Box 337, Bergvlei 21012
South Africa

Random Century New Zealand Ltd
PO Box 40–086, Glenfield, Auckland 10
New Zealand

The catalogue data record for this book is available from the British Library

ISBN 0 7126 4691 4

Phototypeset by Intype, London
Printed in Great Britain by
Mackays of Chatham PLC, Chatham, Kent

Chapter One

As the farrier released the big grey mare's leg and straightened his back, Jonadab Oaks consulted a heavy turnip watch which he fished from deep in an inner pocket.

'About noon, Jeth,' he announced. 'We'll knock off for dinner.'

As he rose stiffly from the bench where he had been watching the blacksmith at work, he glanced round with pride at the little forge; it had been created from one of the loose boxes surrounding his stableyard.

'It were a good idea o' mine to mek this forge,' he said complacently. 'It's better for thoo to give me a day every few weeks, instead of us trailin' all t'hosses up t'village every time.'

'Aye.' As the lad led the horse out, Jethro Brown wiped his dripping forehead with a large red and white kerchief. He smiled inwardly to hear Jonadab congratulate himself on the idea of having his own blacksmith's forge at Aumery Park Farm. Jethro knew that the idea had stemmed from George Oaks, Jonadab's second eldest son. Before putting the proposal to his father, George had gone up to Fadmoor and discussed it with the local farrier.

Over the previous twenty years, Jonadab had built up a good business breeding heavy horses for use by the breweries, railways and even the army. Although George had foreseen the convenience of fitting out a small forge at their own farm, he knew from experience that his father must be approached with the utmost tact where any innovation on the farm was concerned.

Jonadab had the dourness of the true north-Yorkshireman. His life was lived within rigid constraints so that, for him, conduct was strictly divided between good and evil, black and white. Life held no grey areas for Jonadab Oaks. For almost fifty years he had struggled to mould and guide his family by his own strict moral standards and when one of them 'fell by the wayside', as he phrased it, he took it as a personal affront.

'T'missus'll have plenty to spare, if thoo wants to join us for dinner.' The invitation was perfunctory, rather than pressing. Jonadab knew, and Jethro knew that he knew, that the farrier would have brought his own snack to eat at midday.

As he made his way back to the farmhouse, Jonadab looked round with satisfaction. He loved the farm, tucked away in the remote valley of Sleightholmedale. Here he had been born, seventy years before, and here his forbears had tilled the land and tended their stock for as far back as anyone knew. Although only a tenant-farmer, he loved this land with a fierce pride.

It was almost the end of October; the sky was cloudless and the air crisp and clear. The trees of the broad-leafed woodland that clothed the sheltering hills, glowed in the light of the sun in a tapestry of rich autumn colours.

As he leaned on his walking-stick and surveyed his fields, Jonadab's eye was caught by a movement along the road. Half-closing his eyes, he squinted against the sun to see more clearly. Two riders were approaching and, after a few moments, he recognised his daughter, Tamar Lassiter and her twelve-year-old son, Hilary.

'Aah hopes as 'ow there's plenty, Mother,' he said, upon entering the kitchen. 'Our Tamar's just coming down t'road wi' yon lad of hers.' Annie's face broke into a delighted beam.

'By, that's grand!' she exclaimed. 'It's not often she brings young Hilary.'

'He's riding an' all – not in a carriage,' answered Jonadab. 'Aah do feel she meks him a namby-pamby.'

'Nay, Jonadab,' remonstrated his wife. 'He's a delicate lad and she has to look after him.' Her husband's only reply was a grunt as he drew his Windsor chair up to the huge, well-scrubbed deal table which almost filled the cosy kitchen.

Martha, their youngest daughter, bustled about, setting

two extra places at the table and putting two more plates to warm on the hob. Although married to Jonadab's shepherd, Bob Lamb, and the mother of a young girl, she and her husband still lived at the family farm with her parents.

Annie Oaks rose stiffly from her rocking-chair next to the fire. She had become rather rheumaticky of late and spent her days by the warmth of the range, knitting innumerable pairs of woollen socks for the men of the family. As she went to take her place at the other end of the long table, the door opened and the kitchen suddenly seemed to be full.

The first to enter the kitchen was Tamar, and at the sight of her daughter Annie wondered, not by any means for the first time, how she had managed to produce such a beautiful and vivacious woman. Although she was now turned forty-one, Tamar Lassiter's looks were unfaded. The dark sheen of her black hair was, as yet, untouched with grey and although the unusual amber eyes had darkened slightly to a light hazel, they were still shot with golden lights and fringed by sooty lashes. She crossed quickly to her mother and, as she bent to kiss her cheek, Annie caught the whiff of rose-scented perfume which always surrounded Tamar.

'Kiss Gran, Hilary,' she instructed, as she drew off her gloves. The boy who came forward, rather diffidently, was tall for his age but slightly built. His hair was of an incredible silvery fairness, adding to his appearance of fragility. He had been a sickly child, susceptible to chest infections, but now seemed at last to be developing a stronger constitution.

'I rode all the way here,' he told the assembled family proudly. 'It's the longest journey I've ever made on horseback.'

'Well done, lad,' replied Annie.

'Aye,' rejoined his grandfather, thankful for any sign of manliness in what he considered to be a puny weakling.

Tamar and Hilary's entrance had coincided with that of her brother George and Martha's husband, Bob. Although George Oaks lived at Cherry Tree Farm, just over a mile further down the little valley, the two farms were worked together and he took his midday meal at whichever was the closest to his work.

He and Bob Lamb had attended to Tamar's horses and while they were washing their hands at the kitchen sink, Martha was busy placing the dishes on the table.

'There, this'll stick to your ribs Hilary,' she laughed, as she carried a huge steak and kidney pudding to place it before her father.

Once the food was served, not a word was spoken. Jonadab's opinion, that good food should be given the attention it deserved rather than be eaten to the accompaniment of conversation, had been drilled into them too deeply to question his authority.

He fully realised that there was a purpose behind Tamar's visit. Both she and Hilary had an air of suppressed excitement, but Jonadab applied himself to his meal, refusing to be hurried. Tamar helped her sister to clear the table, a fact which gave her father grim satisfaction. She had married above her class, and was the wife of Sir Stephen Lassiter, a wealthy landowner. Although she had adapted successfully to her new station in life, her father took care, whenever she came back to the Dale, to ensure that she did not forget her humble origins.

When they were all served with pint pots of tea, Jonadab's piercing blue eyes shafted towards his daughter.

'Well?' The word was almost barked at her. Tamar, however, was her father's daughter. He had kept her waiting when her news was eager to burst out. Now he must wait!

Taking a deep draught of the tea, she surveyed him over the rim, eyes wide with affected innocence.

'Yes, Father?' Her demure tone, however, did not deceive Jonadab.

'Come now,' he answered, glancing at the long-case clock that stood in the corner of the room. 'It's obvious thoo've summat to say, so spit it out. I haven't all afternoon to waste.'

Tamar looked round the table to make sure that she had everyone's attention.

'Victoria's coming home from Canada next week.' She

paused for a moment so that her next statement would make its full impact. 'Our Joe and Mary are coming with her.' The excitement among her listeners was proof of the shock resulting from her announcement.

'Oh, oh!' Annie could say no more for a few moments. Tears coursed down her face as she lifted up her pinafore and dabbed at her cheeks.

Even George, normally undemonstrative, felt his face break into a grin.

'Our Joe coming back? By gum, that's grand,' he said.

Tamar was bombarded with questions. Laughingly she held up a hand.

'Just a minute!' she protested. 'I've no idea how long they intend to stay, nor even if they're eventually going back to Canada at all.'

This last statement caused another spate of questions. George glanced at Bob Lamb.

'You'll be wondering what's up,' he said. 'It's over twenty years since our Joe and his wife went to live in Canada. We never expected to see 'em again.'

'Oh, the Lord be praised.' Annie's hands were clasped together while her face shone with joy.

Jonadab's voice suddenly cut through the babble.

'So!' Although the tone was quiet, he stilled the excited clamour which surrounded the table. 'We're expected to kill the fatted calf because the prodigal son is returning, are we?'

The voices died away as the rest eyed him uncertainly.

'Nay, Jonadab! Surely you're pleased that they're coming back?' Annie's tone was disbelieving. She looked for some softening of her husband's expression, but there was none. He sat upright, one hand clasping each of the chair arms. His eyes glared out from under the jutting eyebrows like shafts of ice blue.

Annie eyed him with apprehension. He was even more short-tempered nowadays than he had been in his youth and she knew from long experience that he needed careful handling. She felt, however, that on this issue she must stand firm.

'He's your eldest son,' she protested. 'You must be glad that we sh'll see him again.' She had feared that she would reach the end of her life without this longed-for reunion and could not accept that Jonadab did not share the joyous exultation which flooded the whole of her being.

'Nay. He's no eldest son to me,' came back the reply. Slowly Jonadab pushed back his chair and rose to his feet. Placing his hands on the table, he leaned forward and looked round the family. 'An eldest son's place is by his father's side, working his family's land,' he stated flatly. 'Joseph gave up that privilege when he chose to leave this Dale.'

Before he could go on, he was interrupted by George. 'I can't believe what I'm hearing, Faither! Our Joe has been lost to us for over twenty years and you're casting a shadow over his homecoming. Surely you'll be glad to see them?'

All in the room seemed to hold their breath while they waited for his answer. He sighed deeply.

'Aah sh'll be glad to see them,' he acknowledged, at last. The admission brought a sigh of relief from his wife. He continued to speak, however, struggling to make them comprehend the emotions which the news had raised in him.

'We're told they may not go back. On what terms are they coming, then? 'E can't expect to come back 'ere and take our George's place.' His eyes dwelt for a moment on George, registering the look on his son's face. 'Oh, aye! That 'adn't occurred to thoo, 'ad it?' he said dryly. 'Mebbe thoo've forgotten as 'ow he deserted us when we were struggling to build this farm up. Now we're successful, back 'e comes – and for why, might I ask?'

George's face mirrored a variety of emotions as he considered the implications of what his father had said. His happiness at the prospect of seeing Joe again was now clouded with doubt.

Tamar studied their father. She recognised with a sinking heart the tell-tale signs of rising anger. The vivid blue eyes, undimmed by age, glowed out from beneath brows that were still black, in contrast with his iron-grey hair. The slightly flared nostrils were white with anger and his lips were compressed into a hard, thin line.

Little Maria Lamb, sensing the tense atmosphere, clambered up on to her mother's lap, burying her head in Martha's bosom.

'Hilary, take Maria out to see the horses.' Tamar spoke quietly, but firmly. Hilary's bottom lip protruded in a slight pout but, catching his mother's eye, he thought the better of a protest. Rising from his chair, he held out his hand to his little cousin, who ran to him eagerly, anxious for his attention. When the door closed upon them, Tamar addressed her father.

'When Joe and Mary went to Canada, they hadn't much option,' she pointed out. 'There was no room for them to live here and life was not made easy for them up at the Butlers' farm.' Turning to her brother, she added, 'I'm sorry George, but you know it's true.'

George nodded. Joseph's mother-in-law, Ann Butler, was his mother-in-law also and had lived in his home for several years. She had been a hard and domineering woman when younger, but was mellowed by age. He realised that the fact that she lived in his house had changed her attitude from when Joe had lived beneath her roof.

Martha Lamb's gaze shifted from one to the other. She had been a child when Joseph and Mary had emigrated, but vaguely remembered her eldest brother as a pleasant, easy-going young man – very similar, indeed, to George. The reason for his departure had not been discussed openly at the time, so she was disturbed to discover that his return was not an event of unalloyed happiness to all the family.

Tamar again looked across the table at her father, who had sunk back into his chair.

'*I* shall be happy to see them again, Father.' Her tone held a slight defiance. 'They have been very kind in allowing Victoria to stay with them for a year.' Before she could continue, however, Jonadab was on his feet again.

'Aye! And that was a lot o' daft!' he exclaimed. 'Why should she be sent to Canada – and in such a rush an' all?'

Tamar bit her lip in vexation. Her father always managed

to seize upon items she was not prepared to discuss. After the merest hint of hesitation, she replied, 'Victoria had been disappointed in love and I felt that she needed a change.'

Her father's grunt of derision was expressive enough to need no words, but nevertheless he followed it up.

'Plenty of lasses are disappointed in love, as you call it. They 'as to get over it as best they can. She's lucky Stephen has t'money to pay for trips overseas.'

There had been times in Tamar's life when, if not actually hating her father, she had felt extreme dislike. Now, although she tried to quell it for her mother's sake, she felt that feeling rising once more within her.

She and Jonadab were like setting a spark to tinder, she thought ruefully. They could not be together for very long before the flame of disagreement flared up.

Looking to where her mother sat at the foot of the table, she noted how crumpled and wizened Annie's rosy face had become. It was brought home to Tamar, suddenly and unexpectedly, that her mother was an old woman. Going to Annie's side, she put an arm round her shoulders and pressed her cheek against the older woman's.

'Come on! Cheer up, Mam,' she murmured. 'It'll be all right, you'll see. We're all delighted that Joe and Mary are coming back and we shall have a grand family reunion.'

Jonadab's chair scraped on the flagged floor as he rose from the table.

'There's too much to do for us to sit 'ere gossiping,' he said. 'Come on lads; come back to work.'

He allowed his son and son-in-law to go out first, then stood in the doorway, looking back at his wife.

'No doubt you'll be putting t'flags out and mekking a fuss when they comes,' he said, 'but mark my words; there's none so blind as them as can't see.'

Chapter Two

As Jonadab was making his cynical prophesy, the ship carrying the members of his family was already approaching Liverpool.

Victoria Lassiter shivered and drew her cloak more closely round her. Peer as she might, she was unable to penetrate the dense fog through which the ship nosed its way.

She had stood by the rail, straining for her first sight of England, until the fog that enshrouded the River Mersey had chilled her to the bone. Men's voices, calling instructions, drifted eerily through the mist like disembodied spirits and, with a sigh of disappointment, she turned to go down below.

The fog had thickened since she had come up on deck and she paused to get her bearings. As she did so, her uncle's voice came to her. Although he sounded quite close, she was unable to see him through the swirling veil.

'Victoria, are you there?' He sounded anxious, and she was quick to reassure him, calling out as she moved towards him.

'Here, Uncle.'

As they met, he took her arm and together they went towards the companion-way.

'This is a fine homecoming,' he smiled. 'A real pea-souper to greet us.'

'Mmm, yes,' Victoria answered almost absentmindedly. Glancing sideways, she studied her uncle.

Physically, he was obviously her Uncle George's brother, although there the similarity ended. Over the past year, during her stay in Canada she had often tried to assess how he would fit in with his family in England.

It was over twenty years since Joseph and Mary had emigrated and she was aware that they could have no idea of how far they had drifted from those they had left behind. What her Grandad Oaks would make of his eldest son when they were reunited she could not envisage.

Jonadab was a strict and unyielding man. This she knew, but she acknowledged also that he tried to be scrupulously fair. In contrast, Joseph's hardness crossed the bounds at times and became vicious and then he in no way resembled the Joe talked of with such affection by his family.

She was bound to acknowledge that her uncle and aunt had made her welcome in their home. A year ago her lover, Thomas Forster, had been killed in a riding accident, leaving her pregnant, and she had been packed off to Joseph's farm in the Northern Province of Canada before anyone at home could learn of her condition.

Victoria nibbled her bottom lip and swallowed hard as she thought of her baby, Tommy, left behind. Resolutely she pushed the thought to the back of her mind. Victoria had inherited from Tamar not only her stunning beauty, but the ability to concentrate her mind on those things that were important at the time, while tidying away into its deepest recesses anything that she felt unable to face.

Tommy was secure in the charge of her maid Gertie, who had married in Canada and taken Victoria's child as her own. She tried to turn her thoughts now to her homecoming to Thorsbury Manor, where she would take up the threads of her life again with no taint of scandal to blemish her name.

Mary Oaks looked up as they entered the cabin. She had obviously been pretty in her youth, thought Victoria, but middle age had faded her looks and petulant lines were etched from her nose to the down-turned lips.

'Will the fog delay our landing?' she queried. 'I'm dying to get on dry land and walk on firm ground again.'

Joe shook his head. 'We've taken a pilot aboard and those chaps know the river like the back of their hands, even in the fog. It shouldn't be long before we're ashore.'

When they did eventually disembark it was too late to continue their journey, so Joseph called a cab and asked the driver to take them to an hotel near the station.

With the coming of dawn the fog lifted and so did their spirits as they started out on the last leg of their journey to York. The outlook, as far as Normanton, was depressing, being mainly through congested urban scenery. Mary wrinkled her nose in disgust as the train passed mills, factories and streets of mean little houses.

'Has England grown into one big town?' she asked pettishly.

'No, Auntie Mary. It's lovely at Thorsbury, where we live,' answered Victoria. 'I'm sure too, that you'll see very little difference in Kirkbymoorside since you left. Of course, Sleightholmedale never changes.' She smiled as she added the last sentence. She could not imagine Grandad Oaks allowing anything to change, down in the Dale.

Now that she was once more in England, Victoria was impatient for the journey to be over. She was longing to see her parents, whom she knew would be staying in York for a few days, to await their arrival. Victoria was more homesick now, on this last leg, than she had been during her whole year in Canada.

Once they left the little mining town of Normanton behind, the train ran into open country. Mary leaned forward and looked out of the window with mounting excitement. She took in the varied chequerboard of the fields, Some were of green pastureland while those bordering were either the rich brown of newly-ploughed earth, or the stubble of the recent harvest, bleached almost cream by the action of rain and sun. The scene mirrored the picture of the Home Country that she had carried in her mind throughout the long years of her exile. The small groups of trees and denser patches of woodland, clad in a variety of autumn shades, were suddenly both welcoming and comforting to her.

Sinking back into her seat, she closed her eyes against the unexpected prick of tears. Although her children and more than twenty years of her life were back in Canada, she had an overwhelming sense of having come home.

Opening her eyes, she glanced from Joe to Victoria.'Don't the fields and trees and hedges look lovely after the great expanses of the prairie?' she exclaimed. Before Victoria had time to express her wholehearted agreement, however, Joe answered his wife.

'They're old-fashioned and impractical,' he said. 'I don't suppose that Father's farming methods have changed in all the years we've been away.' He looked across at Victoria, questioningly.

She thought of the valley, with its even pace of life; of the cosy farmhouse nestling deep in the Dale, protected by the steep wooded hills on the one side and the majestic sweep of the moors on the other. She smiled.

'Grandad isn't one for great change,' she answered, 'although Uncle George more or less runs the farm now, because Jonadab's more interested in his horses. Anyway, I don't think you'll find things much different from when you left.'

Mary's face was clouded. 'Things'll be different for me,' she said sadly. 'Father and Elizabeth have both died and my old home is sold. At least I shall see Mother again.'

The group fell silent, chastened by Mary's sorrow. Joseph felt a mixture of emotions. Although he had agreed to accompany his wife on the trip and was anxious about leaving his own farm in Canada in the hands of his son, Georgie, he also felt an overwhelming sense of homecoming. The unrelenting toil of building up his own spread had taken its toll on him and he felt much older than his forty-four years. The thought of returning to the peaceful valley of his youth was tinged with nostalgia and a yearning for the quiet life, as he remembered it. With his wife's reminder of her loss, he now felt guilty that in his eagerness to see his former home and his family again, he had overlooked the fact that Mary's return would be less happy. He fell into a sullen mood.

Victoria was seated facing the engine and was the first to break the silence.

'Oh, look,' she cried excitedly. 'York Minster!'

Her uncle and aunt rose and went to the window, looking ahead to follow her pointing finger. They had never visited the city before and found the sweep of the medieval walls, leading towards the twin towers of the great cathedral, an impressive sight.

'My word, but it's a grand view,' was all that Joe could say before they were pulling into the station and all was bustle as they prepared to leave the train.

Catching a porter's eye, Joe soon had them and their luggage into one of the cabs that were lined up outside the station.

'Young's Hotel,' ordered Joseph, as they settled back.

'It isn't fair,' remarked Victoria. 'I do hope Mama and Papa are there already. I'm dying to see them.'

'Well, the ship did make good time,' her uncle replied. 'I do hope we haven't taken them unawares.'

As the cab turned into High Petergate, Mary and Joe gazed in awe at the size and grandeur of the Minster, now seen at close quarters.

'I'd like to go in if we're here long enough,' remarked Mary.

Joe hesitated. 'I feel that we should press on and get home as soon as possible,' he protested. The nearer he got to his childhood home, the more impatient he felt for the long journey to be at an end. And, although he would not admit such a motive to the others, he was also keen to receive the letter from Georgie that he was certain would be waiting for him on his arrival at Sleightholmedale.

By the time the cab drew up outside the Hotel, Victoria was almost breathless with excitement at the thought of seeing her parents again. While the Hotel porter organised the luggage and her uncle paid off the cab, she hurried through the doors and up to the reception desk.

'Are my parents, Sir Stephen and Lady Lassiter in the Hotel?' she asked.

'Lady Lassiter has booked in, but has gone out to do some shopping, madam. I don't think she expected you until tomorrow.'

Victoria's face fell and she turned back to her aunt, her whole attitude mirroring the keen disappointment which engulfed her.

Joseph joined them, to find them standing in silence, aimlessly gazing around the foyer.

'What's up?' His tone was testy. He had expected Tamar to be awaiting their arrival, ready to set out on the journey to Thorsbury Manor. They were staying there overnight before carrying on to the family home, down in Sleightholmedale.

'We've taken Mama by surprise,' explained Victoria. 'She didn't expect us until tomorrow.' She paused for a moment, considering and then went on, 'I wonder why Papa hasn't come?'

Feeling a draught, she turned and saw her mother entering the Hotel.

'Mama!' She hurried forward, throwing herself into her mother's arms.

Joseph and Mary were speechless as they took in Tamar's appearance. Although Victoria had taken photographs of her family to Canada, Tamar's portrait had failed to convey her vibrant beauty.

Recalling the Tamar of twenty years ago – rebellious, turbulent and inclined to pertness, Joe found it hard to believe that this composed and elegant woman was indeed his sister. The hair, which had once tangled about her face, framing it in an unruly mass, was now dressed and coiffed in fashionable curls; she seemed to be taller but this, he realised, was her deportment – that of a woman confident in her beauty and also, of her status. Tamar had developed into a lady: not merely through her title but far more subtly, through her self-assurance and deportment.

Looking over Victoria's shoulder, her eyes found them, standing a little apart, unsure and uncomfortable.

'Joe! Mary!' She swept forward, arm outstretched, smiling with delight. 'Oh, how lovely to see you again after all these years.' Suddenly everything was all right. This was the old Tamar, bubbling over with pleasure in the meeting.

Automatically, she took charge. Their luggage was transferred to their rooms, while they were whisked into the dining room. The staff obviously knew her and she received their obsequious attention as though born to it.

During lunch she explained that they were to stay overnight in York. Stephen was on business in the West Riding, where he owned woollen mills, and would come by train from Leeds the next morning.

Victoria was disappointed not to see him immediately, while Joe was frustrated by the enforced delay. Only Mary was pleased. Now she would have the opportunity to visit the Minster and explore the city.

While they ate, Tamar studied her daughter. Although there was no let-up in her conversation with Mary and Joe, asking about their children Georgie and Jeanette, and bringing them up-to-date with family news, her eyes constantly strayed to Victoria.

She was relieved to see that the pregnancy and birth seemed to have had no ill-effects upon the girl's appearance. Victoria was as lovely as ever – a little fuller in the bust, perhaps but that was an advantage, she decided.

Both mother and daughter were eager to be alone. There were so many questions to be asked and answered on both sides that they were anxious to be rid of Mary and Joseph's company for a time.

'Did I hear you say that you'd like to go round the Minster, Mary?' Tamar smiled at her sister-in-law. 'It's only round the corner, so perhaps you'd like to go there this afternoon. We shall be leaving for home as soon as Stephen arrives in the morning so it may be your only chance.'

Although Joe was not particularly keen to visit the Minster, he reluctantly gave in to Mary's persuasion and, after arranging that they should all meet for dinner, the pair set out.

Tamar led the way upstairs to her bedroom. As the door closed, Victoria burst into tears.

'Oh, I've missed you all so much, Mama,' she wept. 'Even Hilary, although I know I sometimes used to get impatient with him when he teased me.'

Tamar sat on the bed, holding Victoria and gently rocking her until her sobs subsided and, giving a shaky smile, she dabbed her eyes and blew her nose.

'What about the baby?' Tamar asked, after a brief hesitation. She was reluctant to say anything which would undermine her daughter's self-control again, and yet the child was her grandson and she was curious and anxious to hear about him.

Victoria's eyes misted over again, but she managed to maintain her composure.

'He's lovely.' She paused for a moment, her gaze far away. 'I didn't want to leave him. It broke my heart, Mama.' Her lower lip trembled, but she swallowed hard, rose from the bed and went to her valise, which she had placed just inside the door. Taking a photograph from it, she passed it to her mother.

Looking fondly at the picture of the baby in the arms of Gertie, Victoria's maid, Tamar was relieved to see no obvious resemblance to her daughter in the child's face.

'I would have liked a portrait of myself holding him,' Victoria said wistfully, 'but I thought it better to have him taken with Gertie, since he's supposed to be her child.'

Tamar was pensive for a moment, moved to see her daughter's suffering. However, she believed in the adage that time was a great healer. Gertie was illiterate so that Victoria would probably never hear any more news of the child whom she had to leave in a far-off land.

'He'll be well looked after, darling,' she said. 'Gertie will love him as her own.' Then she rose from the bed and addressed Victoria briskly. 'Put on your cloak and bonnet and let's go out and see what we can find in the way of new clothes for you.'

It was the best thing she could think of to cheer up her daughter: and it worked. The rest of the afternoon was spent happily on a shopping spree, so that over the evening meal, both groups were animated, the conversation full of their activities.

During their exploration of the Minister and the quaint, narrow streets of the city, then in their bedroom later that evening, Mary and Joseph had discussed Tamar at some length.

Although they and their families at home were able to

write, their efforts were laboured so that letters were necessarily brief, starkly setting out essential news. Thus, although they had been aware that Tamar had married above her station and that her husband had inherited a baronetcy, they had not fully realised quite how large a gap had been opened up between Tamar and the rest of the Oaks family, including themselves.

Joseph could not help but feel rather piqued. As the owner of two thousand acres of prairie, he had expected to come back to England and impress his family and those of the neighbouring farms, with the way he had got on in the world.

Although he and his partner, Mary's brother Jack Butler, had amassed what seemed to be a great deal of land, the prairielands of the North West Territory were only just becoming established as wheat-growing areas. So it was that their years in Canada had been a time of toil and struggle. Jack preferred the solitary life of a trapper and it was his fur-trading that had provided the steady income to sustain Joe's family during the early years of their voluntary exile.

Until Victoria's arrival in Canada, he had expected to be able to keep up the pretence which his letters home conveyed. He and Mary had been overwhelmed when their niece came, accompanied by a maid and obviously unused to housework.

Since their arrival in York, it had been brought doubly home to them that the Lassiters' circumstances in life were far beyond their own. The Hotel and its furbishments were of such a high standard that they felt ill-at-ease and even inferior. Yet Tamar was obviously quite relaxed in the surroundings and accepted the staff deference as her due.

'I can't get over our Tamar,' Joe remarked, as he and Mary undressed that night. 'She's like a different lass from when she was young.' He smiled at his memories of life down in Sleightholmedale.

'She was a bit of a handful,' he reminisced. 'More than a match for our mam. Mind you,' he chuckled, 'Faither could always tame her.'

He and Mary were unaware that Victoria had been born

before Tamar's marriage and that Stephen Lassiter was not her real father. So Jonadab had not, in fact, managed to tame his wild and wilful daughter . . .

Stephen Lassiter arrived soon after breakfast the following morning. Joseph was on his way downstairs when he saw the hall-porter open the main door. Recognising the man who strode into the reception hall with such assurance, he paused halfway down the stairs and drew into the shadows to study his brother-in-law. The photograph carried by Victoria made him easily recognisable, but what had not been apparent was his unusual fairness.

Although Joe knew that Stephen was in his mid-forties, his hair was of such a silvery sheen that he appeared, at first sight, to be prematurely white. His voice, low and well-modulated as it was, carried clearly as he asked for a page to be sent to tell Tamar of his arrival.

Turning on his heel, Joe took to the stairs, two at a time, and went back to join Mary in their room.

'What's up?' she asked. 'I thought you were going down to sit and read a paper until Stephen arrived.'

'He's just come,' Joe answered, then paused. He had developed self-confidence, even cocksuredness, during his years abroad and was unsure how to put into words his diffidence in approaching Stephen. In a new country, where everyone started out equal, he felt as good as any man – 'and better than most' – as he often bragged. At the sight of Stephen Lassiter, however, he had been swept back into his youth, when members of the 'Quality' caused him to feel abashed and inadequate.

Mary regarded him with curiosity. 'Didn't you speak to him, then?' she enquired.

'No. He was busy at the desk, so I thought I'd wait till Tamar was with us, to introduce us,' he answered. As he spoke, there was a rap on the door, and Victoria's voice came to them.

'Uncle, Auntie!' she called, in excitement. 'Papa's here. Are you ready?'

As they joined her on the landing, Mary found the girl's

enthusiasm infectious. They would not be travelling to Sleightholmedale until the following day, it seemed, but even Thorsbury Manor after weeks of hotels and travel would be a relief.

They went downstairs to where Tamar and her husband were standing amid a flurry of hotel staff, who were busily engaged in bringing down their luggage and stacking it in the hall.

'What time is your man due, Sir Stephen?' the head porter enquired, as they approached.

Stephen consulted his watch, flicking open the case with an immaculately manicured nail. 'He was told to be here at ten, so he should be along any time now,' was his reply.

At that moment, Tamar turned and caught sight of them. 'Here are Joe and Mary,' she smiled, placing a hand on her husband's arm to draw his attention. As Joseph walked forward, Stephen's eyes seemed to assess him shrewdly, before his face broke into a smile and he stepped to close the gap between them, hand extended.

'How good to see you at last!' he exclaimed, seizing Joe's hand in a firm grasp. As he greeted Mary, equally warmly, the porter came to tell them that the coachman had arrived.

The fact that Mary and Joseph passed the journey in comparative silence went unnoticed owing to Victoria's incessant chatter.

During her stay with them, they had found her withdrawn, aloof even and knew that their children had considered her unfriendly – indeed, stuck up! Now, asking eagerly for news of friends, neighbours and employees, they saw a vivacity at which they could not have guessed.

For their part, Joe and his wife were overwhelmed by the obvious wealth of the Lassiters. To be conveyed in the travelling coach, manned by their very own coachman was impressive enough, but Stephen's comment as he leaned to look from the window: 'This is where my estate begins,' reduced them to complete silence.

The coach trundled on through mile upon mile of rich, well-tended farmland. When at last they crossed over a four-arched bridge, approaching wrought-iron gates guarded by twin lodges, Victoria cried, 'Oh, please tell Robert to go down the village, Papa!'

Here was even more to add to their astonishment. Passing the lodge gates, the coach mounted a hill and went through some trees, before turning left to go down the village street.

On the right-hand side snuggled cottages of honey-coloured stone, topped by roofs of weathered, rusty-hued pantiles. Although small, the cottages were neat and tidy and their good state of repair bespoke a caring landlord. Down the opposite side of the village, behind a wooden fence which ran the whole length of the street, was a fairly narrow strip of dense woodland.

Victoria leaned forward to look at the trees. 'Those are the Walks,' she told her uncle and aunt. 'In spring and summer they are the loveliest place you can imagine – like a fairyland of flowers.'

'Why are they called the Walks?' asked Mary.

'Because that's where we walk.' Victoria had lived at Thorsbury for as long as she could remember and accepted as normal the fact that part of the estate was private, for the sole use of the family at the Manor.

'Can't you walk anywhere you want to, then?' Her uncle was intrigued.

'Of course, but the Walks are specially for us. The estate-workers don't go there – except the gardeners, of course.'

'What if they did?' Joe pressed on. He had forgotten the almost feudal relationship between master and man, back in England.

Tamar laughed. 'They wouldn't dream of going into the Walks, so the question never arises.'

Before the topic could be pursued, they reached the bottom of the village and Thorsbury Manor was revealed to a stunned Joe and Mary.

In the pale autumn sunlight, the south front of the mansion seemed to shine with an almost airy lightness. 'Magnificent' was the word which sprang to Joseph's mind, as he gazed incredulously at his sister's home. Although Thorsbury Manor was far larger than he had ever imagined, the whiteness of the stone and the innumerable windows, all reflecting the sun's rays, gave the building an insubstantial quality, almost like a mirage.

On the right they passed a great stable block built of brick, and then the coach drew up before the portico. The double doors were opened by a butler, and Tamar ushered them inside.

'Have luncheon served, please Hodgetts, when you've shown Mr and Mrs Oaks to their room.'

'Certainly, m'Lady,' was his reply. Then turning to Joseph and Mary, he said, 'This way, if you please sir, madam.'

Once in the privacy of their bedroom, Joe looked at Mary with an expression of near-bewilderment on his face.

'To think we'd no idea of all this,' he said, in amazement. 'Nobody gave us any indication that Tamar's husband was as rich as this. I expected the Manor to be just an extra-big farmhouse, but this is like a palace. Did you see the size of all them stables round that courtyard that we passed?'

'He seems to own the whole village, as well as several farms,' Mary rejoined. 'I wonder what Victoria thought of our place, when she's used to luxury like this.'

'Whatever she thought, she was glad enough to come to us,' Joseph answered, 'and don't you forget it. For all their money and position it was us they turned to when trouble struck.'

Chapter Three

Joseph Oaks was no longer the patient easy-going man he had been in his youth. Twenty years in a new country had made him sharper. The necessity to beat his rivals in an effort to acquire land had changed him. He was now harder and less tolerant than the young man who had sailed trustingly into a new life, all those years ago.

Consequently, he took no pains to hide his disappointment when he learnt that they were not after all, to proceed on to Sleightholmedale the following day.

'Don't spoil Mother's day,' Tamar remonstrated. 'She's getting as many of the family together on Sunday as she possibly can. You're a farmer yourself, and must realise that Sunday is the only day they can come.'

Catching his wife's eye, Joe forced a grin. 'Aye. I expect our Mam'll be putting on a fine spread,' he conceded. He was irritated by Tamar's use of the word 'Mother'. Annie Oaks had always been 'our Mam' to her children and he considered that his sister put on too many fine airs and graces. Unaware that a different life-style had changed him, he failed to appreciate that Tamar's altered life-style had forced her to change from the girl he remembered.

Sensing his brother-in-law's impatience, Stephen made every effort to keep his time at Thorsbury full of interest. While Tamar chatted to Mary, bringing her up-to-date on family news, Stephen showed Joe the stable block and the horses. Here Joe learned that his father had not only made a reputation for himself as a breeder of fine shire-horses, but that he specialised in greys.

'It's so useful to be able to pick them out at a distance,' said Stephen. 'The men don't slack when they know that the horses can be clearly seen moving against the brown of the soil.' He smiled reflectively. 'Your father gave me that tip,' he said.

Joe felt a sense of surprise. He had automatically assumed, perhaps because of Stephen's accent and his gentlemanly bearing, that Tamar's husband would consider himself to be above the Oaks. Joe's recollections of his father had not been of a man to inspire affection. Respect, yes. Affection? Not really.

As they went round the buildings, it was brought home to Joe that Stephen knew every man and every horse by name. He enquired about families and the men answered him with a friendly deference, obviously holding him in high esteem.

The more Joe was shown, the more he realised that Tamar's husband was a far wealthier man than he could have believed. He had no way of knowing that when Stephen had inherited the estate, some fifteen years earlier, it been in a run-down condition. His father's ill-health over many years had meant a great deal of hard work on Stephen's part, to pull the estate round.

Once the stables and horses had been inspected, the two men mounted up and Stephen took Joe on a tour of his lands. From the pretty little village, to the extensive woodlands and the farms, all Joe saw gave more evidence of Stephen's care and firm control.

'You should see it,' he told Mary that night. 'Nothing second-rate. Everything stinks of money, and all handed to him on a plate. When I think of how we've had to work and scrimp and scrape for what we've got, it doesn't seem fair.'

Mary was perturbed by Joe's bitterness. She was enjoying the novelty of their stay in the Lassiters' luxurious home. She found both Tamar and Stephen pleasant company and was at a loss to understand her husband's attitude.

'He seems very nice,' she pointed out.

'Anybody can be nice, with what he's got,' was Joe's uncompromising answer.

'Anyway, he's made Tamar happy. She's settled down and seems really content.'

'Of course she's content! Wouldn't you be, in her shoes?'

He was determined not to bend, even a little, in his resentment of Lassiter.

As he climbed into bed, he gave a sigh of satisfaction. 'Anyroad,' he said, 'I can best him for youngsters. Their Victoria's no better than she should be and that Hilary's a pasty-looking namby-pamby: not a man like our Georgie.'

Mary's patience was at an end.

'We're the last to criticize Victoria,' she said sharply. 'Have you forgotten that Georgie was on the way when we got married? Anyway, we gave our word not to breathe a word about Victoria's baby, so don't forget.' There was no reply from her husband as he blew out the light.

Although chilly, the weather remained dry and clear, with no trace of the fogs which had heralded their arrival in Liverpool. The party set off for Sleightholmedale immediately after Sunday breakfast, Tamar and Mary travelling in the coach with Victoria and Hilary, while Stephen and Joseph accompanied them on horseback.

'I thought you would see more this way than from inside the coach,' Stephen remarked and despite himself, Joseph appreciated his brother-in-law's thoughtfulness.

As they rode through the Vale of Pickering, Joseph gazed avidly round, drinking in the scenery. He still considered that the small fields, split up by hedges or patches of woodland and coppices were wasteful and out-of-date, but he had to admit to himself that they possessed a beauty that was lacking in the wide expanses of the prairies.

When they rode up the steep, cobbled main street of the little town of Kirkbymoorside, he was surprised and relieved to see that the last twenty years appeared to have left it unaltered. It could have been only a week or so since his last visit, so little had it changed.

His excitement mounted as they left the town and, still climbing, made for the spot where the road branched, the left-hand turn leading to the little Dale which had been his home for half his life. The lumbering coach had slowed to walking pace and Joe felt like surging ahead, so eager was he to reach the family farm and see his parents again. He curbed his impatience, however, and eventually they reached the top of the steep hill which led down into the valley.

Although many of the trees were already bare, the branches interlaced overhead, so that they appeared to be entering a tunnel. The road, which snaked down the side of the escarpment, was tricky to negotiate, being carpeted with fallen leaves. The layer beneath was damp and slippery, but the covering that overlaid it was dry and brittle, making the surface deceptive, so that the horses placed their hooves gingerly.

Once they emerged into the sunlight at the bottom of the hill, the sight of his family home made Joe's throat constrict and his eyes filled with tears.

The long, low farmhouse, nestling under its roof of thatch, was just as he had pictured it in his mind. The duckpond appeared smaller than his memory had portrayed it but, on the opposite side of the road, the sparkling spring which chuckled down the hillside to fill the mossy stone trough was unchanged. He smiled as he recalled how he and his siblings' daily task had been to fill the water-barrels for household use.

They had reached the door and, as Joe dismounted, it was opened by his brother George, who stood there smiling rather self-consciously. His hand came out to shake Joe's but suddenly they were embracing, slapping each other's shoulders, and twenty years were swept away.

Once inside the kitchen, Joe's breath caught in his throat to see the way that his mother had aged. His father appeared little different. His hair was tinged with grey but, despite his slight limp, his stance was as upright as ever, and the piercing blue eyes were as challenging. Categorized by her husband, in her youth, as a 'fine figure of a woman', Annie Oaks seemed to Joe to have shrunk. Instead of spilling out of her rocking-chair, as he remembered, there was room enough and to spare. Her cheeks were still rosy, but wrinkled and wizened, like an apple stored too long. She rose slowly and stiffly to her feet and then held out her arms. Once clutched close to her, Joe felt like a lost child who had come home, at long last.

After the emotional reunion with his mother, Joe shook his father's hand.

'Thoo's back, then.' Jonadab's statement was as matter-of-fact as if Joseph had just returned from a trip into town. No one could guess the depth of his feelings to see his eldest son once more in what Jonadab regarded as his rightful place.

Once they were all squashed in round the huge deal table, Joseph gave a sigh of satisfaction and looked about him. The kitchen had not changed. He could swear that even the crockery was the same as in his youth. The tall water-barrels still stood by the shallow stone sink. Whose job was it to fill them now, he wondered. Sniffing appreciatively, he decided that the kitchen even smelt the same. The appetising aroma of dinner mingled with the pungent scent of the herbs hanging in bunches from the rafters to dry.

Once they were at the table, Joe could study his family in more detail. George seemed little different. He was broader and his face had lost the vulnerability of youth, but the two of them were still, obviously, brothers. His sister Martha had been a child of eight when they had emigrated and was now a married woman, with a toddler and another on the way, by the look of it. Her husband, Bob Lamb, seemed a nice enough chap, he thought.

Ann Butler, his mother-in-law, had mellowed with the coming of old age, he decided. Gone was the domineering woman who had driven him and Mary to emigrate. She was more subdued and seemed to devote her attention to her grandchildren. Edward was George's son by his first wife Elizabeth, and Annie was the daughter of his second wife Sarah. Both of George's wives were Mary's sisters, so that his mother-in-law was also George's mother-in-law. He had never thought the relationship complicated until now, looking at them anew.

Sarah provided the greatest surprise. She had been only a child when they had left. Now, in adulthood, she had grown so much like her sister, Elizabeth, that the resemblance was uncanny. Upon comparing notes later, both Mary and Joseph agreed that it was as though Elizabeth had never died. Was this, they wondered, the reason for George's marriage to Sarah?

Once the meal was over, Mary went to sit in the parlour with her mother and Sarah. Now that she was back in England, she felt the death of her father even more keenly than when she had first received the news. With a stab of guilt, she heard her mother's voice.

'It was the shock of our Jack going off to join you and Joe in Canada that caused his heart attack. If Jack had only talked to us, Father would have taken it better, but just disappearing and leaving a note made him very bitter.' Mary could not tell her that it was Jack's fear of his parents which had caused him to keep his departure secret. He had dreaded the scene that would have ensued, had he been open.

Seeing the sadness on their faces Sarah broke in, 'The rest of the Oaks will arrive this afternoon, but our Jane's living in Middlesborough and couldn't come. Christy's expecting at any time, but wants you and Joe to go and stay with her and her husband in Leeds for a week.' Mary produced photographs of Georgie and Jeanette, and the talk became a bridging of the twenty-year gap.

As Jonadab took up his walking-stick and led the men outside, Joe was surprised to see Tamar and Victoria don aprons and begin to clear the table, along with Martha and the maid, Lydia. Upon seeing his expression, Tamar glanced towards the door. Seeing that her husband had left the kitchen, she lapsed into the dialect of their childhood.

'Faither sees Aah dissent get too big for mi boots,' she laughed. Joe joined in the laughter. Perhaps she hadn't really changed, despite the rise in her fortunes.

Joe had been right in one assessment of his father. His farming methods had not altered. The fields were exactly the same size and bore the same names as when he had worked them.

As they strolled round the familiar landscape, Joe wallowed in feelings of nostalgia. He forgot the harshness of life in the Dale; the severe winters and unremitting toil were superseded by memories of the cosiness of family life and the companionship of working with his brothers. He thought of the life he had led here, in the tranquil valley, compared to his present life on the prairies and his mind went to his son.

'Has a letter arrived for me, Father? From Canada?' he asked nonchalantly, trying to conceal his anxiety.

'A letter? For thoo – 'ere?' Jonadab looked at him suspiciously. 'Why should thoo be getting letters 'ere?'

'I told our Georgie to write and keep me up-to-date, that's all. But it's early days yet. It takes a while for the mail to get through. I expect he'll be writing soon.' Joe tried to make light of the matter, reasoning that it was, indeed, too early for his son to have much to report, but inwardly he fretted.

Jonadab grunted a noncommittal response while mentally querying his eldest son's reply. Was there, as he suspected, an ulterior motive for Joseph's return? He walked on in silence.

As they passed the foreman's house on their way back to the buildings, the door opened and a burly man crossed slowly to the neatly-stacked pile of sawn logs. Upon seeing the group, he raised a hand to Jonadab.

'Afternoon, gaffer,' he muttered and, after a nod, seized a couple of logs and went back into the cottage.

'Who's that?' Joe asked his father.

'Toby, Lydia's husband,' was the answer. 'We've had 'em both since they were bairns. Aah took 'em from t'workhouse.'

'What happened to Bert Weald?' Joe wanted to know. He had liked and respected his father's foreman.

'Dorcas caught pneumonia and died,' explained George, 'so Bert retired and went to live with his daughter and her husband at Appleton. We sometimes see him in Kirkby on market days.'

When they eventually reached the buildings, Joe's opinion of his father's reluctance to move with the times underwent a revision. He knew from Stephen that Jonadab had become a well-known horse-breeder. Indeed, the first two grey mares had been bought while Joe was still living at home and he could recall the excitement created by the purchase of the pair.

Now, it seemed to Joe, the whole farm was geared mainly to the raising and schooling of heavy draught-horses. The dairy herd was reduced to just two house-cows and not only were all the old buildings used for the stabling of horses, but a whole new range of stables and loose boxes had been constructed, surrounding a covered yard. Far from being the old stick-in-the-mud that Joe had presumed, Jonadab had branched out into an entirely different type of farming, and it had obviously paid off. The surrounding moorlands still supported flocks of sheep but down in the valley, the heavy horse reigned supreme.

'Aah've even got mi own smithy,' boasted Jonadab, showing off his latest venture with pride.

Not for the first time, Joseph wondered how much their father was worth. 'Not that we'll ever know – not till he's six foot under,' he thought. His father still ruled with a rod of iron, he could see, and kept his business to himself.

Upon returning to the house, they found that the rest of the Oaks family had begun to arrive. He had vaguely known his sister Beth's husband, John Smithson, as a young man living in Gillamoor, before he and Mary had left for Canada. He seemed to be quiet and unassuming and Beth appeared happy enough. She had always been more placid that the fiery Tamar, who would never have settled into the life of a farmer's wife.

His eldest sister, Ann Waind, arrived from Bransdale with her husband John. Joseph had always liked the dependable and steady John and was pleased to find that he was now a respected cattle-breeder and a judge at Agricultural Shows.

The whole house was filled with a laughing chattering throng, all happy to welcome Joseph and Mary. When everybody was supplied with food, Jonadab tapped his mug with his spoon, to gain their attention.

As the talk died away and all eyes turned to him, he stood up and looked round the room.

'While thoo's all here, Aah've summat ti say,' he

announced. Knowing his fondness for springing surprises, all his family eyed him with apprehension. What was he up to now?

Satisfied that all eyes were focused on him, he paused for a few seconds, to give more impact to what he had to say.

'As thoo knows, Aah'm seventy now, and t'time's come for me ti retire.' This was the last thing that any of them had expected. Jonadab was as dominant and strong-willed as he had ever been and the idea of him relinquishing the reins seemed unthinkable.

George's heart raced. Had his brother Joe's return to his native land given their father the idea of reinstating him to his position as the eldest son, despite all that he had said? He felt sick at the thought. His whole life had been devoted to this farm and he loved the little Dale in all its aspects. In the spring, when the hedges were clothed with perfumed drifts of May-blossom and the grass was starred with the gold of celandines and carpeted with blue speedwell, his heart lifted with joy. Now, in October, when the trees flaunted the myriad fiery shades of autumn and the purple of the moors was dimmed to a more sable hue, he felt at peace with the mellow mood of the countryside. His life had been dedicated to this land. Surely his father would not pass him over, even though Joseph was the eldest son.

Joe's mind was running along similar lines. Why had his father chosen this particular time to make an announcement? Faced with the possibility that his father could, perhaps, name him as his successor, Joe wondered whether or not he would wish to take over Aumery Park Farm. He knew that Mary would probably like to stay in England, but he had a lot of hard work and money invested in Canada and was not sure that his son and daughter would want to leave their home.

Only the youngest son, Jonadab Junior, was unaware of the undercurrents rife in the room. He had been only twelve when Joseph and Mary had left England and he had grown into a true son of his father. While Joseph and George took after their mother's side, being just over medium height and stocky of build, Jonna was tall and lean, having inherited their father's rangy build. The two elder sons had their mother's velvety brown eyes and hair of almost chestnut brown, while Jonna's startling blue eyes contrasted sharply with his black hair. His wife, Maisie, was the only child of a wealthy farmer in the neighbouring village of Skiplam and Jonna's future was mapped out securely. He would inherit his father-in-law's farm and had no real interest in what became of Aumery Park Farm.

Jonadab was enjoying himself. His clear blue gaze seemed to George to be looking into his mind and reading the hopes and doubts which tussled there.

No sooner had his thoughts been mirrored in his open expressive face, than George was put out of his misery. As though from a distance, he heard his father's voice.

'Aah've had a word with Sir James and he's agreeable for George ti tek over t'tenancy.'

Not until then had he realised that he had been holding his breath. Now, as he let it out in an almost-silent sigh, he caught Joe's eye. The look of disappointment crossed his brother's face so swiftly, that George was not even sure that it had ever been there. It was replaced by a broad grin, as Joe seized his hand in congratulations.

Jonadab had still more to say, however. 'Oor George and Sarah'll move up here this next week; Mrs Butler an' all, of course,' he added, turning to her. He did not ask her, everybody noticed. He told her. 'Oor Martha and Bob will go ti live at Cherry Tree Farm,' he continued. Then, turning to Joseph. 'There'll be no room here, so thoo and Mary will 'ave ti stop at Cherry Tree wi' Martha and Bob while you're in England.'

The smile disappeared from Joe's face as though it had been wiped off. He had envisaged their stay being in the cosy, thatched farmhouse which had been his boyhood home. He had pictured them sitting round the fire in the evenings, while he impressed his father with accounts of the vastness of his lands and the huge amounts of corn produced there. Now he was to be packed off a mile down the Dale, to a farm which had not been rented by the Oaks, when he had left. Martha was like a stranger, having been a mere child at the time of his emigration, while her husband Bob was a complete stranger – and yet it was with them that he and Mary were to be lodged during their holiday.

Looking across, he saw his father's sardonic gaze fixed on him. As his brown eyes met the piercing blue ones he knew, with certainty, that Jonadab had organised this deliberately: he did not want him and Mary with them at Aumery Park Farm.

George was equally taken aback at his father's suggestion – nay, it was an order – that he and his family should move into the main house. For a moment he was dismayed but then he caught sight of Sarah's face as she sat by the window, nursing their daughter. It was suddenly transformed as though illuminated from within. Since her marriage to George three years earlier, she had felt that she lived in her dead sister's shadow. She knew only too well how striking was her resemblance to her eldest sister.

'As like as two peas in a pod,' her mother often told her, little knowing how demoralising Sarah found the statement. She never felt totally sure that George really loved her, or whether she was merely a substitute for Elizabeth, in his eyes. Living in the house which had been his and Elizabeth's marital home, surrounded by furniture for the most part chosen by her sister, she often expected her husband to actually address her as 'Elizabeth'. Now she was to be given the chance to move out – into a house which bore no trace of George's first wife. The only memories here for George were childhood memories. To Sarah, it seemed like the answer to her prayers and she looked across towards her father-in-law, eyes shining and lips parted in a smile.

George had expected to meet some resistance from Sarah, but she was so obviously delighted at the thought of the move that he felt relieved. He knew that his mother-in-law, Ann Butler, would enjoy his mother's company so he supposed his father had pleased more folk that he'd upset, with his unexpected decision.

So engrossed was George with his own thoughts, that he

missed Martha's gasp. Jonadab caught it, however, and swivelled his attention to her, in time to see the little gesture of pleading as she looked towards her mother.

'It'll do oor Martha good, an' all, to run her own home. She can't be tied ti her mother's apron strings all her wedded life.'

Annie was fair flummoxed, as she would have put it. She knew that she was becoming frail and depended upon Martha to run the home as she, herself, had always run it. Martha followed Annie's recipes – made the butter and cheese following her mother's directions exactly. She knew how to make Annie's special beeswax polish, which kept the rich patina on the old oak furniture. For some reason known only to himself, Jonadab had arranged this series of moves, like a calculated game of musical chairs. Who was to be pushed out and why, she had no way of knowing – all she knew was that her home would be dominated by Sarah and Ann Butler.

'They'll bring their ways 'ere,' she thought. 'Aah'll be overcome wi' Butlers. Aah'll drown in a sea o' Butlers.'

Jonadab had timed his thunderbolt so that there was no chance of any discussion. He had announced his decision and would brook no debate on it. Those of his children who had moved away were suddenly thankful that they were far beyond his jurisdiction.

They began the flurry of donning coats: the men went to bring the pony traps from the yard. Ann and Beth instructed their children to 'kiss Gran and Grandad' while they issued invitations to Joe and Mary.

Tamar managed to buttonhole George during the bustle. Guiding him into a corner, as far from their father as possible, she hissed into his ear, 'What's all this in aid of, then?'

'I've no idea. It's the first I've heard of it,' was his reply.

'He's up to something,' Tamar mused, glancing across the room to where Jonadab stood, drinking in the various reactions to his announcement. Catching her eye, he pushed his way over to them.

'Stirring things again ist thoo, Tamar?' There was a half-smile on his lips as he continued, 'Thi mother allus said that, given a stick, thoo could stir mud up in t'clearest pool.'

'No, Father. I was only wondering what *you* are stirring up,' she replied, lifting her chin slightly in a haughty gesture.

'Them as lives t'longest, 'll see t'most,' was his only answer as he followed her to the door, to wave to those of his family who were going home.

Chapter Four

If anyone had asked Jonadab Oaks why he had so upset his immediate family, he could not have told them. Part of the reason was that his own father had handed over the running of the farm to him, long before the age of seventy. George, however, could have run the whole holding from Cherry Tree Farm without moving up to the old farmhouse.

When a querulous Annie had asked why he intended to change the routine and move them all round, his answer had been, 'It does no 'arm ti keep 'em on their toes.' He was forced to admit to himself, though, that in some way, the whole thing was directed at Joseph. He did not want Joe and Mary to get too cosy in Joe's boyhood home.

Although Jonadab was a regular chapelgoer who would never question his Lord's ways, he had always felt a degree of sympathy for the prodigal son's elder brother. He considered that the son who had stayed at home and worked hard for his father deserved more consideration than he had apparently received. He was determined to show George that his commitment to the family farm was appreciated. He was relieved and pleased to see his eldest son again, but it must be made clear to Joe that he was only a visitor. Joseph's visit should not be made so comfortable that he would want to stay permanently.

Yet Jonadab was to be frustrated, for the changeover could not take place immediately. The Martinmas Hirings in Kirkbymoorside were to take place the Wednesday after he had set the cat among the pigeons, as he termed it.

It was the custom for Jonadab to call the men into the parlour and pay their annual wags at noon on the day of the Hirings. Whether they replied 'Aye' or 'Nay' to his question, 'Is thoo stopping?' they had the rest of the day off, to spend at leisure. In the same way, whether or not there were new men or maids to hire, the farming families also went to the Hirings, where there were stalls, jugglers, sometimes wild-beast shows and all manner of entertainment.

On that Wednesday, George left his work a few minutes early and strode into his mother's kitchen just before noon. 'Where's Faither?' he asked, looking round. Martha nodded towards the parlour. When George entered, Jonadab was just placing a huge ledger on the table.

'Thanks,' said George, pulling out a chair and seating himself before the ledger. 'Could you pass me the money-bag, please, Faither?'

Jonadab stopped in mid-movement and stood in disbelieving silence for a few seconds. '*What?*' The jutting brows shot together over the blue eyes while Jonadab's brows corrugated in question.

'I'll pay the wages, if you'll pass me the brass.' Although George's voice was even, inside he was trembling. It was not the first time in his life that he had steeled himself to defy his father, but this time he was well aware that his whole future depended upon his success.

''As thoo gone mad?' Jonadab plonked the leather money-bag on the table and, placing his hands palms down on the polished surface, leaned forward, glaring down into George's upraised face.

'Nay, Faither. I'm the boss now, or have you forgotten? In my book, it's the boss who pays the wages.'

While his father digested this statement, George opened the ledger and, running his finger down the sheet, appeared to be concentrating on the names and figures. In reality, he could see nothing written on the page. His eyes were blurred and he could feel the perspiration beading his top lip. Determined to stand his ground, he braced himself to meet the fury which he knew would break over him at any moment. He heard the long intake of breath as his father prepared to deal with this insurrection, for this is how it would appear to Jonadab, he knew. His father was an absolute monarch on his own domain.

When it came, however, Jonadab's voice did not emerge

in the roar expected by his son. In a tone hardly above a whisper, yet as cold as ice, he spoke slowly.

'*Get – out – of – my – chair!*'

George took a deep breath to steady himself, and then replied just as firmly, 'No!'

Raising his eyes, he saw the veins in Jonadab's neck begin to throb and swell, while the tell-tale tic in his forehead denoted the rising of his temper.

George rose to his feet. 'Listen to me, Faither.' He was desperate to have his say before his father's rage erupted.

'It was only Sunday when you said, before all t'family, that you'd retired and I was to be the boss. Well, as I've just said – the master is the one that pays the wages. It's my job now, and you must leave me to it.'

Jonadab's mind raced to counteract his ploy. 'These wages is for t'year that's gone. Aah was maister for that year, and Aah should pay t'workers off at t'end of it.'

George's mouth fell agape. This argument had not occurred to him. Taking another deep breath, however, he held his ground. If he allowed his father to best him in this, he would never be acknowledged as master by the workforce.

'That makes no matter, Faither.' There was desperation in the pleading look which he gave him. 'If you do the paying out, the men will think you don't trust me to handle the money. I'll not have their respect, and I can't run t'farm without it, as you full well know.'

Jonadab cogitated for a few moments. It was difficult for him to back down, but George's face had hardened. The look of entreaty had been replaced by an expression of mulish determination. Then George shrugged and pushed back his chair.

'Right! I know where I stand now. Anyroad, I've put enough away to get a farm of my own, and enough stock to get started, so it looks as if this is where we part company.'

From the set of George's face, it was driven home to his father that, at long last, he had pushed him too far.

'Come, lad. Don't be hasty,' he said placatingly. 'Aah'm sure we can come ti some agreement.'

George made no reply. As he turned to leave the parlour, there came the first tentative knock on the door. He turned and his eyes locked with Jonadab's for what seemed a long moment.

'There thoo is, then.' His father pushed the bag of money across the table and swung on his heel to make for the door.

'Come in,' he said to those who queued outside. 'T'maister's ready ti pay out.'

George heaved a sigh of relief as he retook his place at the table and opened the drawstring bag. In reply to his query, 'Are you staying?' he found to his surprise that all the men answered, 'Aye.' He had heard rumours and hints that at least two had intended to stand at the Hirings for new jobs. Their minds had obviously been changed by the fact that he had succeeded his father as the boss.

Although Jonadab Oaks was well-respected and a scrupulously fair man, his workers found him a hard task-master. In his youth it had been his boast that he would ask no man to do anything which he himself could not do better or quicker. He had grown too old still to make the claim but he drove his men hard. George had a different approach – he requested, rather than ordered, but the men would work just as hard for him as for his father.

He saw no more of Jonadab until late afternoon. All but Annie had gone up into the little market-town which was teeming with those attending the Hirings. The day was typical of November, with wispy tendrils of damp mist lingering in the valley. While not actually raining, the air was heavy with a dampness which seemed to seep insidiously into the bones. There had been no frosts nor gales as yet to strip the trees of the last of their leaves, which hung bedraggled and soft-hued. All the autumn flame was faded and the trees seemed clothed in muted scraps and tatters.

Mary and Joseph found the dampness more penetrating than the crisp dry air of Canada, which was, they said, a healthier type of coldness. Before the day was over, George and Sarah were heartily sick of their shivers and grumbles.

The afternoon set out, however, with them all in good

spirits. The children, Edward and Annie, were round-eyed with wonder as they took in the coconut-shies, roundabouts and swingboats. George and Joe took them on some of the rides, accompanied by squeals of excitement. To Sarah's surprise, Mary was almost as excited as the children to see all the confusion and jostling crowds.

'Canada is so big,' she commented, 'that this must seem very tame by comparison.'

Her sister's tone was quite bitter when she answered, 'Tame? This is wildly thrilling, Sarah, compared with our life at home. We are miles from anywhere and the nearest settlement, Portage la Prairie, is nowhere near the size of Kirkby.'

Sarah was intrigued. She had not had a great deal of time to question Mary about their life in Canada, presuming it to be similar to her own, but on a grander scale.

Mary soon enlightened her.

'When we had saved enough money to go west and establish our own farm, the only way to travel there was by Red River ox-wagon. Everything we had was packed into it and we travelled over a thousand miles, until we reached Portage la Prairie. I stayed at the fort there for over two years, while Joe and our Jack went out to stake their claim on the land and build a house.

'Well,' she paused and sighed, 'it was really just a log-cabin at the beginning, but it is a house now. They've extended it and improved it so that it's a lovely big house now.'

Sarah looked at her sister with new respect. 'You must have had it rough,' she sympathised. 'We'd no idea.'

Mary shrugged. 'You know how proud the Oaks are. Joe would have died rather than let his father know how hard the life was.' She hesitated and turned to her youngest sister. 'Don't say anything to George. If Joe wants their dad to know, let him tell him himself. We've a lot of land and he's gradually getting it under cultivation, so before long we shall be truly rich – provided our Georgie keeps things under control while we're over here. I wish he'd write. Joe doesn't say much, but I know he's worried. It was all my idea to come over, now the farm's finally started to pay its way. Up to now, we've been very dependent on what our Jack earns. Furs are like gold and Jack loves the life of a trapper. He speaks Cree like an Indian and is a very successful fur-trader.'

Sarah found it difficult to take in all these revelations – a far cry from what she had imagined.

'Oh, George!' Sarah smiled. 'What a mess they look.' Both children were clutching toffee apples, faces liberally coated with the sticky mess.

'Can we go to the circus, Mammy?' Young Edward was dancing up and down, holding Joe's hand, while little Annie was held safely above the throng in George's arms.

Before Sarah had time to reply, Jonadab's voice interrupted.

'Is t'maister havin' a good time, then?' The voice held a trace of sarcasm, but the blue eyes twinkled. George hitched the baby higher on his shoulders, while his eyes met his father's.

'Now then, Faither,' he said.

''As thoo set on any new men?' his father demanded.

'No, Faither. Nobody left. They're all stopping on for another year.' George made the statement matter-of-factly, but his heart swelled with pride as he said the words.

Jonadab's brows drew together. 'Nobody?' He seemed disbelieving. George could not remember a year when not a single worker had left the farm at Martinmas. He was only too pleased that his father seemed to hold no grudge over their confrontation of the morning.

Jonadab's expression was quizzical as his eyes held George's, over little Annie's curly head.

'Aye. I'm enjoying misself, thank you Faither,' was his reply to the original question.

'Aah'll be getting back down ti Mother,' said Jonadab, as he turned away.

Realising that the rest of the party had no notion of the battle for control that had taken place that morning, George watched his father's departure and then, with a smile which was rather forced, said, 'Come on, then, if we're going to see that circus.'

He had no way of knowing that, as Jonadab rode back down into the valley, he was going over the morning's events in his mind and what had originally been annoyance at George's stand against him, gradually turned into admiration. By the time he and Annie retired to bed, George's stubbornness had now become a commendable determination.

'A chip off t'owd block, oor George is,' he told his wife, although no word passed his lips about the scene in the parlour earlier in the day. ''E was a real boss when 'e paid t'wages out. Aah'm glad Aah've retired and put 'im in charge.' If there was any credit to be claimed, then claim it Jonadab would.

Annie smiled as she agreed with her husband. She had not been married to Jonadab for almost fifty years, without acquiring a thorough insight into his character. Even though he thought that he meant it, she knew that he could not entirely relinquish the reins as long as there was breath in his body.

When George and Sarah went to bed, it was the first chance he had had to pour out what had happened in the parlour.

'What a blessing you stuck up to him,' she commented. 'Once he'd named you as the master, he'd no right to interfere.'

'I had to best him,' George agreed. 'I'd made up my mind that if I was to be boss in name only, there was no point in staying here. I'd have left.'

Sarah sat up in bed, eyes wide and questioning. 'Left? What do you mean, left? Where would we have gone?'

'I'd have taken a farm of my own and started out afresh,' was his uncompromising reply.

Sarah was speechless. She loved George with unquestioning devotion and would follow wherever he chose to go, but to give up the right to an established and successful farm and start again from scratch seemed to her the height of folly. At any rate, it had not come to that, she thought with relief.

'Your father won't let it rest at that,' she warned. 'Although he said that you're to be the boss, he'll question every decision you make.'

'Aye.' George sat on the bed with a thoughtful expression. 'I'll have to play it clever. I'll have a talk and suggest he looks after t'horse business, while I look after the farming side. That should keep him happy.'

'You'll need to sort out the money part of it,' she pressed. 'Most of the crops are grown for the horses. There must be some agreement about finances. Really, you should take full control of that now.'

George paused in the act of climbing into the high bed beside her.

'I never thought of that,' he said in a surprised tone. 'If I'm to run t'farm, I suppose I should handle t'brass.' He snuggled down into the warm billows of the goose-down mattress. 'Nobody knows how much he's got,' he said reflectively. 'Not even our mam. He'll never tell me.'

'He must,' Sarah persisted. 'If you're to run the farm properly, you must be in charge of the accounts. How can you know what and when to buy and sell, if you don't know how much money is at your disposal?'

'Aye.' His reply was half-hearted. After the episode of the morning, he could not bring himself to think of facing up to his father again. With a deep sigh, he kissed Sarah and immediately fell into a dreamless sleep.

The change-over of houses took place at the end of the week. There was no great upheaval, as only personal belongings were moved. The two houses were already fully furnished and equipped, so that only clothing, bed and table-linen were to go, in addition to ornaments, pictures and other treasured possessions. George packed these on to a flat cart, helped by Kitty, the little girl who had been employed to help George's first wife Elizabeth, with young Edward. On his tenth birthday, her younger brother Freddie had also been taken from the workhouse by George in order to keep them together. Now they scuttled backwards and forwards, humping huge bundles and slinging them on to the cart. Little Edward ran to and fro with them, following his idol, Freddie.

Once everything of weight or value was stowed on the cart, George whistled for his dog, Meg, and taking his crook, made his way round the back of the farm. Anyone seeing him cross the moss-covered stepping stones over Hodge Beck and strike up to the moor would have been justified in thinking that he was going to check his sheep. When he reached the moor edge, however, George turned and sat on an outcrop of rock, looking down on the home he was soon to leave.

Cherry Tree Farm was a sturdy building of mellow stone, facing four square to the south. The farm buildings surrounded an open yard to the rear and, on the north side of the holding, a straggle of Scots pine offered protection from the winds, leaning away from them in twisted postures.

George felt in melancholy mood as he looked at the garden which fronted the house. He enjoyed his garden and had taken a pride in its cultivation. He smiled slightly, remembering his father's advice when he and Elizabeth had first come to live there.

'One year's seeding means seven years' weeding.' Well, he'd heeded the exhortation and, even after a week of hoeing in the fields, had picked up his hoe on a Saturday afternoon to keep his garden trim and weed-free. Now the flowers were faded and gone, while a few rows of sprouts and cabbages stood forlornly in the autumn gloom. Even the stream, which in summer chuckled happily over its stony bed through the valley bottom, now slid greyly between its banks, reflecting the leaden skies which echoed his mood.

Unlike Sarah, George could not look forward with enthusiasm to the move. When he had been a youth at home, there had been Joe and young Jonadab, his brothers, and his father's brother, Uncle George, to engage Jonadab's attention after work. His heart sank as he contemplated the long winter evenings ahead, when his father would dominate the conversation round the table. Still, if he was indeed to be boss, George supposed there would have to be some drawbacks.

Casting his eye back to the farmyard, he noticed that Kitty and Freddie seemed to have come to a halt. The cart was evidently loaded. Clicking his tongue to the dog, who lolled at his feet, he seized the crook and strode rapidly down from the moor. What had to be done would be done, he supposed, but it was with a heavy heart that he'd be flitting.

Leaving Sarah to follow in the pony trap with her mother and baby, he lifted Edward up to sit beside him while Kitty and Freddie scrambled up on the load. As the cart trundled up the lane between the farms, he wondered, not for the first time, what was behind this apparent whim of his father's. He knew that neither his mother nor Martha wanted the upheaval. Annie would feel bereft when her daughter left, this he knew.

When he reached his father's farm, for he could not think of it as his, Martha's red-rimmed eyes and pinched nose were proof of her feelings. She and Bob had carried their belongings out to the lane, where they were placed next to Joe and Mary's luggage. Kitty lifted Edward down from the cart and gave him two patchwork cushions to carry.

'Go ask your Grandma Oaks where they've ti go,' she instructed, as Joseph came out to give George a hand.

'I've brought my own Windsor chair and Sarah's rocker,' said George. 'Faither took over Grandad's when he took over t'farm, but I can't see me ever sitting in his.'

'The whole thing's bloody daft,' Joe answered. George could not believe his ears. That one of Jonadab's offspring should swear was inconceivable. Seeing his shocked look, Joe laughed. 'You've worked with him till you're as narrow-minded as he is,' he challenged.

'That's as may be,' George replied, 'but I don't want that sort of language used in front of my children or my wife.'

Joe shrugged. 'Your outlook would 'ave been broadened if you'd got out of this Dale when you were younger. You're as set in your ways as the old man.'

There was no reply from George as he began to carry

things from the cart to the house. Eventually the change-over was completed and the cart was reloaded with Martha and Bob's belongings. Annie clung to her youngest child, reluctant for her to leave, until Jonadab said sharply, 'Come now, Mother. It'll do t'lass good ti stand on her own two feet. She's been cosseted long enough.'

Annie Oaks rarely retaliated, but she was stung to retort, 'Cosseted? Thoo doesn't know t'meaning of t'word. There's nobody cosseted 'ereabouts, but thoo.'

When the evening meal was over, those now ensconced in the farmhouse at Aumery Park, settled down round the fire. George pretended to be immersed in the *Malton Messenger*, but his eyes continually strayed towards his father. Sarah could see that he was steeling himself to tackle Jonadab about the financial side of running the farm.

'Come along,' she said, putting down her sewing. 'Let's have you lot up to bed.' Freddie was to sleep in the room reached by a ladder from the kitchen, while Kitty was to share a room with her charges. She picked up little Annie and held out her hand to Edward. 'Come on,' she instructed.

The little boy drew back. 'No! I want to sleep in t'lads' room with Freddie,' he protested.

The lads' room, as it was known, had been occupied by his father and uncles from boyhood until their marriages, and he had expected to sleep up there. He glowered round at the adults and his bottom lip stuck out with determination.

'I'm not a baby. I'm turned five and I don't want to sleep with them,' nodding towards Kitty and his little sister. 'I', a lad and I want to sleep in t'lads' room.'

George's patience was running out. Sitting by the fireside with the conversation dominated by his father, he suddenly realised what he had lost. He was no longer master in his own home: indeed, he was not *in* his own home.

'Stop crying, Edward, and go up to bed,' he ordered, more sharply than he had intended.

The boy's eyes were suddenly brimming. He dashed away the tears as he followed Kitty. 'Now look what you've done!

You've made my eyes go juicy,' he cried accusingly, blinking rapidly to contain the flow.

Even his Grandad smiled as the boy trailed off through the door which led towards the stairs, via the parlour. George's face, however, did not even soften. As soon as the children had left the room, he turned to his father.

'I'd like a word, Faither, if you don't mind.'

'Goo on then, spit it out,' was the rejoinder, as Jonadab settled back in his chair and looked across at him.

Although George was willing to tackle his father in front of Sarah, he was loth to do so before his mother and mother-in-law.

'In private,' was his answer. Jonadab's eyebrows rose.

'There's nowt private amongst us,' was the uncompromising reply. 'We're all family. What concerns one, concerns us all.'

'No! This only concerns you and me.' George, bending to the fire, lit a spill, rose, opened the parlour door and stood holding the knob, looking back into the kitchen.

'It'll only take a minute,' he persisted. 'But it's summat I want to sort out.' With that he crossed and lit the oil lamp which stood on the parlour table. There was never a fire, except on Sundays and at Christmas, so that he shivered, partly with anxiety at the scene which was to come. He bent to adjust the flame, straightening up as his father entered the parlour.

'Noo then, what's up? Say what thoo's got to say – it's nobbut cold in 'ere.' Jonadab sounded truculent, annoyed at having to leave the warmth of the kitchen.

'We must sort out about the money, Faither.' George made the mistake of sounding apologetic; almost diffident at bringing up the subject.

'Money? What money?' Jonadab was not feigning his puzzlement. He was genuinely at a loss to know what George was getting at.

George sighed. 'I'm supposed to be running this farm and I know nowt about the financial situation. I must know how we stand and I must have access to the money, Faither.'

As Jonadab told Annie later that night, he was dumbfounded.

'Am Aah ti take it that thoo expects me, me who's worked and sweated and laboured ti build up a bit of capital, ti hand it ti thoo on a plate? Nay! Aah'll not 'ave that. Aah 'asn't sweated mi guts out, all mi life, just ti give it away.' George did not answer immediately. He waited until his father had sat down and pulled out his handkerchief to mop his brow.

'Faither.' He spoke quietly and soothingly, hoping to stem the tide of anger before it reached full flow. 'When you took over from Grandad Oaks, you must have taken charge of everything.'

'There was nowt to tek charge of,' his father replied bitterly. 'It was a poor moor-end farm, more bracken than pasture and little stock, apart from sheep. Your Grandad was hard put to make enough to live on. Times were rough and he was glad enough for me to tek over.'

'Well, you're obviously not glad for me to take charge, Faither. In fact I don't know why you ever said it.' George was resentful. His father seemed to give with one hand and take away with the other.

Jonadab made no answer for a moment. He himself still could not say why he had made the surprise announcement of his retirement. Having thought about it since, although he would never admit the fact even to his wife, he bitterly regretted his decision. Looking across at his son, he began to speak, his thoughts far away.

'Aah'm the one who's built this farm up. Aah'm the one who's rented more land and had the foresight to go into t'heavy hoss business. It's taken years of struggle and the fact that it's succeeded is all due to me. Thoo can't expect me to give it all up.'

George was exasperated. 'Nonsense!' he retorted. Before Jonadab could open his mouth he swept on, 'You might have made the decisions, but you had three sons and a brother who worked unstintingly for no wages. And a wife and daughters,' he added, 'who stood the market with what they could make, grow and gather, so that you hadn't the responsibility of clothing them. You may have been the brains behind this farm, Faither, but it was the rest of us that did the hard graft – and don't you forget it!'

The three women, who sat round the fire in the kitchen, jumped when Jonadab got his breath back and answered the challenge.

'*What?*' he roared, in a voice that could be heard throughout the house.

In the kitchen, Ann Butler gasped, 'Whatever's going on?'

Annie Oaks fanned herself with the corner of her apron. 'It's not good for Jonadab to lose 'is temper,' she said uneasily. ''E gets terrible headaches.'

Sarah said nothing. She knew what George was saying to his father and awaited the outcome with anxiety.

'What?' Jonadab repeated hoarsely, in disbelief at this ingratitude.

George now warmed to his theme. 'How often, Faither, admit it, have you left us working and ridden off "on business"? Did any of us know where you'd gone, or what this business was? No, we didn't! You've always been too secretive about your affairs, wanting to appear so clever to the rest of us poor mugs. Well, I've sweated and toiled my guts out for this farm, as much as you and more than t'rest. Our Joe and Jonna upped sticks and left when summat better was offered, but I've been daft. Anyroad, I'm not so daft now. You can get Joe to run t'farm for you; he'll grab at t'chance.'

His father looked at him, his brows drawn in surprise.

George gave a hard laugh. 'Oh, aye! Things aren't as good for him over yonder as he'd have you believe. Things Mary told Sarah would open your eyes. Anyroad,' he concluded, rising to his feet, 'that's how it stands. I sh'll look for a farm of my own to go into on Lady Day.'

With this statement, he left the parlour and returned to the questioning looks of the women round the fire. Refusing to enlighten them as to what had gone on, he addressed himself to his wife.

'Mash a pot of tea, will you, Sarah love?' he suggested,

resuming his seat. He sat sipping his tea staring into the fire, while his father wrestled with his thoughts in the parlour.

Eventually the door opened and Jonadab came in and sat down in his chair. Holding out his hand to the flames, he looked across at George.

'We'll ride up ti t'bank and t'lawyer's in t'morning,' he said, as he picked up his mug of tea.

George heaved a sigh of relief, as he looked across at Sarah.

Chapter Five

The following morning saw George and his father riding up into Kirkbymoorside. Jonadab was morose and uncommunicative, deep in his thoughts and obviously regretting what he considered to be his surrender to George. On the other hand George was exultant. Not only had he triumphed over his father – one of the few times in his life – but when, at bed-time, he had tried to tell Sarah all that had passed between his father and him, she had laid a finger across his lips.

Holding out her arms she whispered, 'Never mind all that, George, come to bed. You know what they say – "New house, new baby"!' The lovemaking that followed had been more abandoned and passionate than George had ever experienced.

He was still smiling in reminiscence when they arrived at the York Union Bank, but there a shock was awaiting George. There was no wonder that the manager had ushered Jonadab in as though he were a privileged customer, for when they settled down to make arrangements for George to have access to the farm accounts, he was shattered to find that there was well in excess of a thousand pounds in the bank. 'No wonder the crafty old beggar didn't want any of us to know,' he thought. 'Our Mam's scrimped and scraped all her married life and he's sitting on a fortune.'

This was in actual cash, too, in addition to the value of all the horses and the remainder of the live and dead stock at Aumery Park. George was, as he told Sarah later, utterly gobsmacked.

He came out of his daze, though, when he heard the bank manager say, 'So we shall make it that both signatures are necessary for any transactions to be made, shall we, Mr Oaks?'

'Aye, that's the measure of it,' said Jonadab. George's feeling of smugness vanished when he realised that he would be unable to do any deals unless they met with his father's approval. No sooner had this thought occurred to him, however, than he was struck by another. 'But he won't be able to act without my say-so.'

Glancing towards his father, he felt, by the sardonic twist to the older man's lips, that his open face had betrayed his thoughts.

Upon leaving the bank, they strode across the market-place without speaking. Their heads were bent against the keen wind which drove a fine drizzle towards them. The road was glistening under the rain and the main street of the little town was deserted. When they reached the solicitor's office, George felt a wave of disappointment to find that a deed of partnership was to be drawn up. So he was not to be sole boss, then. He heard his father's voice explaining the situation to the solicitor.

'It's best that we work in double harness, till t'lad gets the 'ang of things.' George bridled at hearing himself referred to as 't'lad'. He was now turned forty and had worked on the farm all his life, but still his father could not accept him as a responsible adult.

'Congratulations, Mr George. You're a very lucky man to get the partnership of such a successful farm.' Mr Hugill smiled as he shook George's hand. Pressing his hand in return, George looked at his position afresh. He supposed that he was, indeed, fortunate. His father need not have taken this step and if he hadn't done so. George expected that on his death, everything would have had to be sold or divided with Joe and Jonna.

He was not too sure how the law worked and had no time to reflect further, as Mr Hugill followed up his congratulations by asking, 'And how are Sir Stephen Lassiter and your daughter, Lady Lassiter? Stephen was a great loss to our profession when he inherited his father's estate and left his law practice in Helmsley.'

Jonadab always felt secretly gratified when people knew

that he was the father-in-law of a baronet, although he would never have acknowledged the fact.

'They were well, last time I saw them,' was his reply. Then, wanting to impress the solicitor further, he continued, 'Their daughter has been over to Canada visiting my eldest son, Joseph and his wife. They brought 'er back and are staying over for a few months. You may remember Joe – he married one of John Butler's lasses. He's got over two thousand acres of wheat farm, over yonder.'

Mr Hugill was suitably impressed and Jonadab, at least, left the lawyer's office in a glow of satisfaction.

Contrary to what Jonadab had supposed, things were not going well for the Lassiters. Victoria was glad to be back in her own home, but although she tried to appear happy and carefree for her parents' sake, it was often a vain attempt. Her thoughts constantly strayed to the child she had left behind and she would fall into bouts of deep despondency. Remembering that Gertie was unable to read and write, she knew that she would probably never hear any more of Tommy. Despite Tamar and Stephen's efforts, she often appeared lost in a miasma of depression – unspeaking, unheeding, deep in a morass of desolation.

Her young brother Hilary was now away at school, so that at least her parents were spared the necessity of trying to explain her behaviour to him.

'I'm at my wit's end,' Tamar confided to her husband one morning as Victoria drifted away from the breakfast table. 'She seemed all right when she first came back but the longer time goes on, the worse she gets. She rarely speaks of the baby, but seems to dwell on him more and more.'

'Send for the dressmaker and get Victoria interested in some new gowns. The pre-Christmas round of parties and balls will be upon us before long and new clothes and a bit of excitement should soon perk her up,' was his response.

Although Tamar agreed, deep in her heart she was not too sure. Remembering her own determination never to be parted from Victoria, albeit faced with her father's condemnation and rage, her heart bled for her daughter. She realised how fortunate she had been, not only to keep her child but also to find a loving and caring husband – indeed, a wealthy one. Taking Stephen's advice, she sent for the dressmaker to come from Malton and the next few days were spent poring over pattern books and swatches of material.

'You're a little fuller in the bust, Miss Lassiter,' observed Madame Rose, 'otherwise your measurements are just about the same.' Tamar's eyes met Victoria's over her head, but no comment was made.

Flying in the face of convention, which decreed virginal white or the palest pastels for young unmarried women, Tamar had ordered the most expensive of Victoria's ballgowns to be made in a heavy amber silk. She had never forgotten the first gown that Stephen had bought for her. This was upon their betrothal, while she was still his housekeeper. Victoria had inherited her mother's wild tangle of rippling curls and tawny, almost golden eyes, and Tamar knew that the colour would suit the girl to perfection, just as that earlier gown had brought out in herself a sensual beauty which she scarcely knew that she possessed. So it was with Victoria, when Madame Rose came with the completed gowns. Tamar left what she thought of as 'the gold one', until last. This was partly because she felt that the others might be an anti-climax, and partly because she was half-afraid that the impact would not be as striking as she had hoped.

Her fears were without foundation. When the dressmaker slipped the gown over Victoria's head, the face which emerged from the tawny folds was bewitchingly transformed by the hues of the silk. Her large expressive eyes shone with an amber light, shot with flecks of gold, while her complexion, in sharp contrast to the fashionable pink and white, was a pale, velvety bronze.

Tamar and Tempy, her maid, as well as Madame Rose stood in silence, speechless at the vision.

'What's wrong? Doesn't the colour suit me?' Victoria pirouetted anxiously in front of the cheval-mirror, trying to see all sides at the same time. She knew that this gown had cost far more than all the others and was afraid that it was a disappointment.

'No, darling. It's perfect,' Tamar was quick to reassure her. 'It's just so different from anything you've ever worn before, that we were surprised at how well it looks.'

Once it became known among the county families that Victoria had returned from her visit to Canada, the invitations began to arrive. Her days became filled with discussing them with Tamar and deciding which to accept. Tamar was adamant that Victoria's re-entry into society should be at some outstanding event and that, to attend, she would wear the gold gown. Stephen was not too sure about the colour.

'Her looks are sufficiently striking to make her stand out above the rest.' He was proud of Victoria. 'It isn't a girl's colour,' he protested. Neither Tamar nor Victoria, however, could be dissuaded.

While Victoria had been in Canada, Tamar had written to tell her of Francis Sturdy's plea to be allowed to pay court to her, once she had recovered from her grief at his cousin Thomas Forster's death.

Consequently, during her year at Joe and Mary's home. Victoria's thoughts had often strayed to Francis. Once her torrential grief at the loss of Thomas had been replaced by a deep sadness and a dull ache, she discovered that she was looking forward to seeing Francis Sturdy again. Although she still mourned her lost love, Francis was a tangible link between them. Not only was he Thomas' cousin, but he was the one who had known of their secret meetings and had provided alibis for Thomas at these times.

While out visiting with her mother one day, Victoria had heard that Francis was due back from his Grand Tour in early December. Although she hid her excitement, she waited eagerly for him to call on her and was disappointed at his non-appearance. However, no actual date for his return had been mentioned, so she curbed her impatience and looked forward to the busy social season that lay ahead.

Tamar decided to relaunch her daughter into society at

a grand ball, to be held in the second week of December at Dumcombe Park, the home of the Earl of Feversham.

As she opened Victoria's bedroom door on the evening of the ball, she heard her daughter humming a light-hearted little tune as she surveyed her appearance in the long mirror.

'Thank God,' whispered Tamar. She had almost abandoned hope of seeing her daughter happy again but, at long last, she appeared to be clawing her way out of the pit of despondency into which she had sunk. The face which she turned towards her mother, as she came into the room, was radiant. The gown was all that Tamar had hoped. As Victoria spun towards her, the heavy gold silk caught the light from the lamps, enhancing the blackness of her hair and filling her strange, tawny eyes with fiery lights.

'I've brought my topaz necklace and earrings for you to wear,' Tamar said, handing the jewelcase to Tempy.

Tempy had been the little maid at Stephen's house in Helmsley, when Tamar had first gone to be his housekeeper. She was one of the very few people who knew, or still remembered, that Victoria was not Stephen Lassiter's natural child. When he had inherited his father's title and estates, Tamar had brought Tempy to Thorsbury, ostensibly to act as her lady's maid but, in effect, as an ally in a strange world. Although Tempy had later married an estate-worker, her two boys were now in their teens and working so she was, once again, Tamar's maid and confidante.

Fastening the jewels round Victoria's neck and into her ears, Tempy stood back.

'There!' she said with satisfaction, her head cocked to one side to take in Victoria's appearance. 'Thoo'll knock 'em out tonight, Miss, make no mistake.'

Tamar sighed. Almost twenty years of tuition had failed to make Tempy act or speak like a proper lady's maid. However, she wouldn't change her for the most experienced French maid in the country, she thought with affection.

Victoria's excitement was effervescent. After a year of almost Spartan existence at her uncle's home in Canada, she was at last subjugating her grief and revelling in her new clothes and the start of the party season. She had tried to describe to her parents the dreariness of life over at Joe and Mary's home.

'Georgie and Jeanette have no fun,' she had told them. 'Only things like Church socials and Church picnics. They never go to balls or dances. There's practically nothing to do there.'

Tamar had merely smiled indulgently. Victoria had been in no state to go partying and had obviously been homesick. Joe was wealthy. He owned vast tracts of land and she imagined his life to be similar to hers and Stephen's.

When their coach arrived at Dumcombe Park, Victoria leaned to look from the window as they made their way up the long drive. The house stood above them, a mass of lights shining from every window. She knew that she had lived in Helmsley when she was a small child, but could remember nothing of that period of her life.

As they walked up the magnificent flight of stone balustraded steps which led to the great front door, Victoria's excitement mounted. When they entered the hall, she was awestruck by the grandeur of her surroundings. The walls appeared to rise to an incredible height, supported by giant Corinthian pilasters. The surfaces were richly decorated with classical figures apparently carved in stone and there was a cheerful log fire burning in a huge, ornate fireplace.

Their cloaks were taken and Tamar gave Victoria's gown a twitch to spread the skirt, and teased her hair so that the ringlets and curls were at their most becoming. Stephen smiled with approval. There would be few here tonight who could match his two women for beauty, he thought proudly.

As they were announced, they entered the saloon through heavy double doors. There they paused for a moment, Tamar and Victoria overwhelmed by the opulence of the huge room which was lined with oak panelling, heavily enriched with gilding. At either end of the long room was a pair of carved wooden pillars, graceful despite their great height.

The room was thronging with people but although Victoria looked around anxiously, she could not see Francis Sturdy. She was, however, immediately surrounded by admirers, eager to put their initials on her dance programme. Not wishing to have every dance earmarked, she held back one or two including the last dance of the evening, for when Francis arrived. Surely he must be invited, she thought, trying to appear at ease while she laughed and chatted about her stay in Canada.

Giving her one last glance, before she and Stephen joined in the dancing, Tamar congratulated herself again on her choice of material for the gown. Victoria's vivid beauty was emphasised and her eyes, framed in thick, black lashes, appeared lighter and more golden than their usual amber shade.

The room was warm, with two fires blazing, so that at the end of the second dance, Victoria sank on to one of the window seats with her fan while her partner left her to fetch a cool drink. Through the hum of conversation around her, she suddenly heard the announcement of the name 'Sturdy' and, looking towards the doorway from the entrance hall, saw Francis with his parents and sister. He looked quickly round the gathering and then, with a wave to his family, began to make his way purposefully across the room in her direction.

As he approached, she studied him over her fan. He had broadened out since she had last seen him over a year ago and his blunt features were more handsome than she remembered. Greater maturity and his travels abroad had increased his self-confidence and, in place of the different youth it was now an assured young man who threaded his way through the groups which stood around the dance floor.

Victoria snapped her fan shut and her lips parted in a welcoming smile, before the realisation dawned upon her that Francis' eyes had not once met hers.

He was making his way instead towards a group seated on an ornate, gilt-framed sofa, a little to her right. She had attracted enough admiring glances and requests for dances to know that she was looking her best, so that it was an extra blow to recognise that Francis had not even noticed her.

Quickly raising her fan once more to her face she watched as Francis reached his objective.

'Caroline.' His ardour was obvious in his tone, as he bent over the hand of the girl who rose to meet him.

Victoria flushed, swept through by humiliation and disbelief. Because her thoughts, during her stay in Canada waiting for the birth of her child, had often been centred upon Francis, she could not believe that his declared love for her had faded.

She stared at the girl at whom he was gazing with adoration. She looked no more than seventeen and had the pink and white prettiness of a doll. Her corn-gold hair was drawn back from her face, hanging in ringlets at the back and above her ears.

In her imagination Victoria had built up her reunion with Francis and dwelt on it so frequently in the last few days, that her disappointment was all the harder to bear. She felt the brimming of tears in her eyes. To the astonishment of her partner, who was on his way back with her drink, she rose swiftly to her feet and, brushing past him, eyes unseeing, hurried down the saloon.

It was during a pause in the dancing so that Tamar, who was standing chatting to a group of acquaintances, saw the headlong rush as, her skirts rustling like wind through dry bracken and her fan fluttering at a furious pace, Victoria made for the withdrawing-room which opened off the far end of the saloon.

The fan paused in its oscillation as she surveyed the room from the doorway. All the groups of chairs were occupied, mostly by dowagers and other chaperons passing the hours in desultory conversation. She threaded her way through them, heading for one of the window seats. Determined to keep her tears of disappointment in check, she stared out of the window, blinking rapidly.

Slowly, the pressure of tears subsided and was replaced by a nursing rage. Who did Francis Sturdy think he was, she demanded of herself. After Thomas was killed, he'd practically begged her parents for her hand and now here he was making a fool of himself over that vapid chit straight from the schoolroom.

'I'll show him!' she muttered, and returned to the dance floor and her waiting partner.

'I'm so sorry.' Her smile was radiant and the young man was won over into adoring subservience. From that moment, she threw herself into enjoying the rest of the evening. Every dance was now spoken for and, whenever she paused for a rest, she was surrounded by five or six young men, all obviously infatuated.

When eventually Francis tore his eyes away from Caroline to see who was at the centre of the laughing group nearby, his heart lurched to recognise Victoria. She was lovelier than he had recalled, darkly vibrant, making Caroline appear rather insipid. Catching his eye she nodded and smiled. He heard her throaty laughter, low and seductive, in answer to some witticism from one of her admirers and Caroline's sweet tinkling laugh, which until now he had considered so musical, suddenly seemed quite shrill.

As she laid a hand on his arm and raised her limpid, forget-me-not blue eyes to his, he was overcome by a feeling of guilt. He could not decide, however, whether this was through having let Victoria down in some way, or because of his comparison between the two girls – in which Caroline was definitely found wanting. As he spotted Mrs Chelton, Caroline's mother, bearing down upon them like a ship in full sail, he turned away with a sick feeling that he had made a great mistake. 'I should have waited until she came back from Canada, before even looking at anyone else,' he thought. Just then, however, Victoria swirled past, smiling up at her partner and Francis had to admit to himself that she did not appear to be particularly affected by his neglect, if it could be socalled.

'It was a marvellous evening. I enjoyed every minute of it,' she told her parents airily at luncheon the next day.

'I thought it was odd, to say the least, to see young Sturdy so wrapped up in the Chelton girl,' observed Stephen. 'He did ask for our consent to call on you upon your return from Canada, yet no sooner is he back from Europe than he's taken up with someone else.'

'I understand he met her in Paris and, spotting him as eligible, her mama got her hooks into him before he knew what was happening,' commented Tamar. 'I doubt if she's any more than sixteen and, I would have thought, too empty-headed for Francis. He may have proved unreliable, but he did seem to be a very thoughtful and sensitive young man.' She was thinking of the way he had ridden over to Thorsbury, determined to be the one to bring the news of his cousin Thomas' death to Victoria.

The toss of her daughter's head was a little too forced to be carefree.

'He can please himself,' she said shortly. 'There are plenty more pebbles on the beach for a girl to choose.'

Yet Tamar was conscious of the tell-tale patches of colour which flooded her daughter's cheeks, and she knew that Victoria was more hurt by Francis Sturdy's conduct than she would admit.

She was perturbed too, as the season progressed, to note that, though pursued by many eligible men, Victoria's fancy didn't settle on any one of them in particular.

Chapter Six

Down in Sleightholmedale, life was not progressing smoothly, for Jonadab's capricious alterations to the lives of his family had caused undercurrents of resentment and frustration.

For Annie Oaks, it was the loss of Martha's ministrations that caused the most distress. Sarah did her best, she supposed, but it wasn't like having one of your own. One small irritation was that she *would* grate nutmeg over the deep-dish custard tart. While this was one of Jonadab's favourite foods, he disliked the flavour of nutmeg. As yet, he'd made no comment, but she knew that the day was not far off.

What was more upsetting was the care of her feet. Every Thursday afternoon Martha would bring a bowl of warm water and place it on the clip-rug by Annie's chair. Once Annie's boots and woollen stockings were removed, she would heave a sigh of contentment as her poor old aching feet luxuriated in the soothing warmth of the water. After rubbing the callouses on the heels with a pumice stone. Martha dried her mother's feet, gently cut her nails and then trimmed her corns with a cut-throat razor, before replacing her boots over clean stockings.

This was one of the small comforts of Annie's life, and it had ceased with Martha's removal to Cherry Tree Farm. Lydia had offered to undertake the task, but Annie was reluctant to receive such intimate attention in front of 't'Butlers', as she called Sarah and her mother. Consequently, the whole treatment was shifted to the chill of the bedroom, instead of the cosiness of the fireside. Lydia was not as confident nor as adept with the razor as Martha, so that the whole business had become an unpleasant chore rather than a welcome hour of pampering.

Martha, wrenched suddenly from the security of what had always been her home, felt estranged and lonely at

Cherry Tree Farm. Once Bob had left for work, her day stretched before her with only her sister-in-law Mary for adult company. She worried about her forthcoming confinement. Her mother had acted as midwife for little Maria, and she was afraid that there would be no time to fetch Annie when her labour started. When she tentatively broached the subject to Mary, her sister-in-law tried to reassure her.

'Don't worry,' she consoled. 'I'm perfectly capable of delivering it. After all, I was midwife to Vic . . .' She clapped a hand over her mouth and looked at Martha's shocked face, above her fingers. Martha plonked the flat-iron down on its stand.

'Go on!' she challenged.

'It's somebody who lives near us in Canada,' answered Mary, refusing to meet her sister-in-law's eye.

'From what you've told me, nobody lives near you.' persisted Martha. 'You can't mean our Victoria, surely?'

'Oh, my God!' Mary was embarrassed and confused. 'I've opened my big mouth and put my foot in it, good and proper. Your Tamar'll kill me if she ever finds out.'

Swearing Martha to secrecy, she confided the whole story of why Victoria had been sent to them in Canada. Martha left the ironing and made a pot of tea. Sitting by the fire, she heard the whole tale in shocked silence. More than any of her brothers and sisters, she had lived her life under her father's influence and had adopted his standards. She had even felt disapproval at Mary's exclamation, which in her eyes was blasphemous. The story which followed, however, shattered her illusions about her glamorous niece.

With Tamar's marriage and rise in the world, Martha had pushed to the back of her mind the circumstances of Victoria's birth. She knew that none of the family had revealed in their letters to Joe and Mary the fact that Tamar had had an illegitimate child, and was now tempted to pour out the whole tale in exchange for Mary's disclosures. She pulled herself up in time, however, and returned to the ironing, wishing that Mary had kept the secret. She felt uneasy with her newfound knowledge and wondered how it might affect her attitude towards Tamar and Victoria, when next they met.

Looking up from the sheet over which she had absent-mindedly run the iron back and forth, until that particular part was as stiff and smooth as a piece of glass, she suddenly broke the silence which had fallen between them.

'What about the baby – did it live? If so, where is it now? What happened to it?'

'Aye, he lived,' sighed Mary. 'A grand little lad he was. Gertie married a chap in Portage la Prairie and took him as her own. He'll be well looked after, don't fret.'

'I just didn't fancy one of ours – our flesh and blood – being sent into an orphanage.' Martha was relieved that the baby had not gone to strangers. Being an open, guileless girl, she felt the burden of the secret almost too much to bear. However, she had given her word and must try to be more discreet than Mary had been.

By now, Joe as well as Mary was feeling keen disappointment at the way the visit had worked out, while the lack of correspondence from his son was a constant source of irritation.

'What's our Georgie think 'e's playing at?' he complained to his wife. 'I told him to keep me informed. I knew we should never have come. It's obvious we're not wanted here.'

'Nay, Joe. No news is good news,' Mary said placatingly. 'I'm sure we would've heard if anything was amiss.'

'If it wasn't for the fact that I'm obviously a thorn in the old fool's side, I'd feel like packing up and going back now,' Joe sneered, deriving a perverse sense of satisfaction at being such an irritation to his father.

When they had first arrived, Joe had harboured an idealised dream of working alongside George and his father, as in the old days. He had foolishly believed that he would slip into his old place on the farm, as though the intervening years had been wiped away. Instead he discovered that the routine of the farm rolled smoothly. Every man had his jobs and every job had its full complement of workers. When Joseph turned up at Aumery Park Farm, more often than not he found himself in the way, or hanging about his mother's kitchen.

Consequently, he took over Martha's tasks at Cherry Tree. A woman's work, he told himself bitterly as he collected the eggs, milked the housecow or fed and cleaned out the pigs.

As November crept inexorably on towards winter, the mists which clung to the valley seemed to seep into his very bones, so that in addition to a persistent shivering chill which he felt unable to shake off unless crouched over the fire, his joints acquired a dull, rheumatic ache.

As much as they had looked forward to seeing Joe and Mary, certainly Martha and Bob were not the only ones to wish their visit was over.

The valley was so sheltered and remote that it teemed with wildlife. But apart from shooting wood-pigeons once a week in February, as a means of culling the pests, neither George nor his father did much shooting. Food was plentiful and they saw no sport in the destruction of beautiful creatures just for the sake of it.

The morning that Georgie's letter finally arrived, telling his father that everything was indeed running smoothly, Joe, filled with a renewed sense of wellbeing, sighted a cock pheasant strutting down the lane outside Aumery Park Farm where he had called in to collect the letter. He was filled with excitement. 'I'd forgotten about pheasants,' he announced eagerly. 'Can I borrow your shotgun, Father? I'll look after it.'

'Aye, and thoo'll buy thi own cartridges,' his father observed. 'They cost too much for me ti provide 'em.'

'I'll ride up to Kirkby and get some this afternoon,' Joe said. 'I could just fancy a bit of pheasant.'

Although, later that afternoon, the sound of the gun was frequently heard, when he dropped a couple of brace off at his mother's before going on to Cherry Tree with another four birds. Joe seemed to have failed to get the pleasure he'd expected.

'No sport,' he said grudgingly. 'They're like sitting ducks

– they nearly come and ask to be shot. Anyway, they'll make a change for tomorrow's dinner.'

What Joe had also brought back from Kirkbymoorside and what he had no intention of telling the rest of the family about, was a supply of whisky. Since returning to England, he had missed his regular evening tipple, being reluctant for his father to discover that he enjoyed a drink. He knew from his youth Jonadab's opinion of those who 'supped with the Devil', as he put it.

When they all settled down by the fire that evening, he brought out a bottle and poured himself a generous helping. Bob Lamb looked across with interest.

'What's that?' he enquired. Joe held the glass up to the oil lamp, so that the light glowed through the amber liquid.

'Golden nectar,' he smiled. 'Get a glass and have a drop.'

Bob hesitated and Martha broke in, 'No, I don't think so. Bob's teetotal.'

Her brother turned towards her. 'Bob's also a fool, if he lets his wife dictate what he can do.' Looking back at Bob, he went on almost pleadingly. 'When a man works hard, especially in cold weather, he needs a drop of something to make the life stir in his veins. This is really a medicine and it'll do you good. Bob.' Joe was anxious not to drink alone and yet, the sight and smell of whisky had set his taste buds tingling. He'd almost forgotten what it felt like; first the sharpness of it in his throat, followed by the warm glow which reached the whole of his body. His tongue ran round his lips in anticipation, but he delayed the pleasure which awaited him, rising instead to fetch a second glass, into which he poured a fair amount, though less than his own.

'Go on, lad!' he urged, slapping his brother-in-law on the back. 'This'll put hairs on your chest; it separates the men from the boys.'

Bob took a tentative sip. He drew in a sharp breath, but held back the cough that tried to follow.

'It's . . .' he paused '. . . unusual,' he managed to get out at last.

Joe held his first sip in his mouth for a moment and then let it slowly trickle down his throat in a fiery stream. After a long sigh, he smiled and relaxed back into his chair, twisting the glass in his hand.

'Grand,' he said.

Martha looked anxiously towards Mary but she merely smiled across and went on with her knitting.

After the first shock, Bob began to feel elated. It did perk him up and warm him through. Joe was right – it was a medicine. When Martha placed a cup of cocoa before him, he looked up at her with a bleary smile.

'Thanks, love,' he beamed, 'but I'll just have another glass of Joe's medicine before I tackle that.'

Joe was only too willing to oblige and, by the time Martha poured away Bob's cold cocoa and announced that it was bedtime, most of the bottle had been consumed.

'Come on, Bob,' she insisted. 'You've to be up early tomorrow, to start bringing t'sheep down to t'lower pastures.'

'Don't nag,' her brother intervened.

'It'll be Father who's nagging, if Bob's late for work,' she snapped.

The reminder of his father-in-law brought Bob to his feet. He was too far gone, however, to make his way up the stairs unaided. To Martha's mortification, he swayed back and forth, a foolish grin on his face, unable to put one foot before the other. As she grabbed his arm, his legs buckled and he ended up in a giggling heap on the floor.

Eventually, with Joe's help, Martha managed to bundle him upstairs. No sooner had the door closed than Bob let out a low moan and clutched his stomach. Martha was only just in time with the chamber-pot, as he began to retch and vomit, all the while groaning and clutching his head.

After a sleepless night, during which Bob was convinced that he had been poisoned, he eventually fell into a fitful sleep in the early hours. When, however, Martha shook him into wakefulness, he was soaked in sweat and his head was pounding so hard that it was painful even to rest it on the pillow.

'You can't go to work,' insisted Martha.

'I must.' He tried to struggle out of bed, but fell back

against the pillow, his face waxen, his eyes pink-rimmed. 'I'll never touch another drop as long as I live,' he vowed.

'Well, at least that's something,' she retorted as she hurried into her clothes. 'If our Joe's as bad as you, I don't know who'll ride down to tell 'em you're too poorly to go to work.'

By the time she had used the bellows to stir the sleeping fire into a blaze, Joe had come downstairs, chirpier than he had been for some days.

'Now then,' he greeted her, rubbing his hands. 'Where's Bob?'

'You may well ask,' she answered bitterly. 'He's been up all night and isn't fit for work. You'll have to ride down and tell our George as soon as you've finished,' she said, banging his breakfast down on the table. 'And don't you let our Dad find out what's up wi' him,' she added.

'Don't worry, I won't split,' he grinned.

George called in on his way up to the high moor, to bring the first flock of sheep down to the lower pastures before winter closed its grip on the little Dale.

'How's Bob? What's up with him?' he demanded.

Martha glanced at Mary, who was dressing Maria by the warmth of the fire. 'Come up and have a look at him,' she urged her brother. He followed her upstairs and, once on the landing out of earshot, she poured out the whole sorry tale.

'It was drink,' she half-whispered.

George was incredulous. 'Drink?' he echoed.

'Our Joe brought some whisky back from town and persuaded Bob to have some. He's been bad all night. In fact, I thought he was dying. I didn't know what to do.' She looked at him pleadingly. 'You won't tell Mam and Dad, will you?'

'Nay, don't be daft. I don't know what Father would do, if he knew our Joe drank. 'E doesn't reckon much to t'way he's turned out, as it is.'

Entering the bedroom, he looked down at Bob Lamb. When Bob had first come to work for them as a shepherd, George had been drawn to him because he had reminded him of his brother, Joe. As he looked at Bob's sleeping face, good-natured and with a half-smile despite his pallor, he thought of the sharp eyes and hard mouth that characterised Joe's face nowadays. He felt that he'd insulted Bob ever to compare him with Joe.

His life in Canada had forced Joe into a different mould. Although he curbed his language before the family, George had heard the oaths he used to the men and knew that his father would send him packing if he heard them – and now drink! With a worried sigh, he turned from the room.

'Let him sleep it off,' he advised his sister. 'I'll see to the sheep today and he should be all right tomorrow.'

Rounding up the sheep, even with two good dogs, gave him little time for thought, but he was sure that Bob's evening's carousal had been a temporary lapse, egged on by Joe.

Whether or not Joe felt ashamed about the affair, George did not know; neither he nor Bob ever discussed it with him. Certainly Joe's attitude seemed to improve and he ceased his constant carping and criticism of what he called their outdated farming methods.

One morning, early in December, he watched two of the farmworkers at Aumery Park threshing the day's allowance of oats, with flails. The crops were spread on the floor of the barn between two doors, and the grain was separated from the husks and straw by being beaten with wooden flails. It was a time-consuming task which needed to be done most days. Once threshed, shovelfuls were thrown into the air, so that the draught between the doors blew away the chaff, while the heavier grain fell to the floor, between the thresholds.

When his father and George came in for dinner, Joe addressed Sarah.

'I'll stay for a bite of dinner, if you don't mind.'

'Of course – there's plenty.' George had confided the story of the night that Joe had got Bob Lamb drunk. Consequently, he had gone down in Sarah's estimation and she was barely civil. Luckily George and his father came in then, so that she had no need for any further conversation.

While the men washed their hands at the sink, her mother and Annie Oaks took their places and Kitty got the two children settled.

When all were at the table, and Jonadab had said Grace, they tackled the heaped plates in silence. Even Edward and little Annie knew that Grandad did not allow conversation at mealtimes. If any voice broke the silence, predictably it was his own.

'We sh'll 'ave ti buy some more hay,' he remarked to George. 'Thoo can come wi' me tomorrow ti look at a stack. Thoo might as well learn ti judge one.'

Judging a stack was a highly-skilled job and Jonadab was an expert. First the hay was tested by the insertion of a hay-needle: a long metal rod with a barb at the end. This pulled out a wisp from the very centre of the stack to be tested for sweetness and ripeness and also, to see that the stack was not over-heating in the middle. Once satisfied, the weight of hay in the stack was calculated and a valuation made. When the deal was struck, the buyer sent one of his workers whenever the hay was needed. This was cut with a hay-spade, in slabs and tied into manageable bales to take back.

George's mouth was full, so he just nodded. Since the partnership, his father had shared decisions with him and involved him in any buying or selling. He felt that he was finally being groomed to take over the farm.

As most plates were now empty, Joe looked down the table towards his father.

'I'm surprised to see that you're still using flails for threshing, Father,' he said. Jonadab's brows drew together in a frown.

'What else would you suggest?' he enquired.

'Doesn't anybody hereabouts run a threshing machine?'

'Well, there was one at t'Great Yorkshire Show, last summer – a smelly, noisy, dangerous-looking contraption, if thoo asks me.'

'Efficient, though,' Joe spoke decisively. 'We couldn't manage any other way, given all the grain we grow on the prairies. We'd be flailing from now until Domesday, and never get threshed.'

George leaned forward. He had been impressed by the threshing machine at the show, but his father had dug his heels in and refused to discuss them.

'All right. You have hundreds of acres of wheat, but what advantage would there be for us? We thresh what we need, as we need it.'

Seeing that both his father and brother were listening. Joe warmed to his subject. 'Using a thresher, your grain is a lot cleaner. The grain, chaff and straw are separated for you and, once it's bagged, you know exactly how much you've got to see you through the year. Your oats run at twelve stones to the bag; barley sixteen and wheat eighteen stone. The way you go about it here, you're halfway through the winter when you find out you're not going to have enough to last. If you buy in late, you've to take what's left on offer.'

Jonadab's eyes were thoughtful as he drained his mug of tea. He wiped his hand across his mouth, then scraped his chair back on the flagged floor and rose to his feet.

'There might be summat in what thoo says. Aah'll think on it,' he said, as he lifted his overcoat from the back of the door. Pulling it on, he went from the kitchen leaving George looking crestfallen.

'You wouldn't believe it,' he said to the room in general. 'I've been nattering at him to hire a threshing machine since first I read about 'em. Would he listen? Not 'im! He turned pig-headed and wouldn't even talk about it.'

Joe grinned cockily. 'You don't know how to handle the old man, little brother,' he rejoined. With a disgruntled 'Humph,' George followed his father out of the kitchen.

Sarah looked at Joe. He went further down in her estimation every day that dawned, she decided. Thinking back, she remembered when he had come to live with the Butlers, upon his marriage to Mary. Although she had only been a child, she recalled him as steady and good-natured, much as George still was.

Looking across at him, she wondered what his life in Canada had been like, to change him so drastically. His eyes, though the same brown as her husband's, were cold and inscrutable, lacking the spaniel-like warmth of George's. As he finished his mug of tea and pushed it across the table towards her, his lips curled in a self-satisfied smile.

The thought flashed across Sarah's mind that Joe was up to something, though for the life of her she could not imagine what. He'd spoilt her day, she thought crossly, clearing the table noisily, with much banging and clattering. She knew with certainty that her laughing remark to George about, 'New house, new baby,' had borne fruit and she was going to tell her mother and mother-in-law that she was pregnant again, once the menfolk had left the house. Now, for some indefinable reason, the pleasure in her announcement was gone, superseded by her unease over Joe.

'Eeh, lass! We shan't 'ave a pot left.' Her mother-in-law's gentle chiding interrupted her reverie.

'I'm sorry, Ma.' She was instantly contrite. 'I was miles away.'

'What's up, love?' asked Ann Butler.

'Nothing, Mam,' Sarah reassured her.

Joe followed his father and brother from the kitchen, whistling as he went. He was not yet sure, himself, what he was up to. He certainly had no wish to stay in England, but he objected to George inheriting all that their father left. No amount of fishing had led George to divulge how much was in the bank, but Joe could assess for himself the value of the live and dead stock, particularly the horseflesh.

'There's more ways of killing a cat than choking it with butter,' he told himself. He was satisfied for the moment to ingratiate himself with his father, if possible at George's expense.

'I'm his eldest son and should have my fair share,' he told Mary frequently, and she was in full agreement.

Chapter Seven

'Tamar wants us all to go ti Thorsbury for Christmas dinner,' announced Jonadab, looking up from the letter he was reading. 'Thoo an' all, o' course, Mrs Butler,' he added, with a nod towards Ann Butler. Although she now lived with them, it was unthinkable to either side that they should use the familiarity of Christian names. She inclined her head, slightly.

'Thank you, Mr Oaks,' she replied, wondering inwardly how she could get out of the invitation. She had not really settled at Aumery Park Farm and now bitterly regretted not buying a little home of her own after her husband's death. She felt that she could not face the idea of a day surrounded by even more of the Oaks family and wondered if she could stand the journey to one of her other daughters, in either Leeds or Middlesborough. An easier way out was to present itself, however.

Martha had called in with the letter, which she had collected from the Post Office on her weekly visit to Kirkbymoorside.

'I'm not going,' she announced flatly. She had no wish to meet Victoria again, as yet. She was only too afraid that her attitude towards her niece might betray what she knew.

'Nay, lass,' her mother remonstrated. 'Thoo must come. It wouldn't be like Christmas without you and Bob – and little Maria, of course,' she added.

Inspiration suddenly struck Martha. 'It's the baby. It's due just after Christmas and all that jogging about on t'journey might bring it on early. After all, I wouldn't want to 'ave it by t'roadside,' she grinned.

Annie's relief was only too evident. She had not visited Thorsbury Manor very often, but always felt intimidated and uncomfortable in front of the servants. 'That settles it,' she declared. 'Aah'd forgot about t'baby being so near. Aah'll stop at Cherry Tree wi' Martha and Bob.'

Jonadab's steely eyes met the velvety brown ones. Ignoring the pleading in his wife's face, he spoke firmly.

'No thoo won't, Mother. It's a chance, while Joe and Mary are still with us, for us to 'ave a real, good family Christmas. Aah can see it might be unwise for oor Martha ti go, but thoo must. There's nowt more ti say on t'matter.'

Seizing her chance, Ann Butler broke in. 'I'll stay with Martha. In the unlikely chance of the baby coming early, I've had plenty of experience with my own girls and can deliver it.'

Lydia looked up from the sink where she was washing up.

'Kitty and Freddie can spend t'day wi' me and Toby. Christmas is nowt wi' no bairns of your own, so we'll be glad ti 'ave 'em.'

So it was settled, though not to everybody's satisfaction. Annie saw her youngest daughter only about once a week nowadays. Though she lived only down the valley, she was too busy with her dairy-work, pigs and hens to visit her mother very often. Sarah too, would have preferred to spend Christmas with her own mother, but was intrigued at the thought of Christmas dinner at Thorsbury, with no cooking to do and servants to wait on them.

Winter had been slow coming to the valley. Apart from one light snow shower in late November, there had been no appreciable fall. Just before Christmas, however, the temperature plummeted, making the ground iron-hard. All the sheep were now down from the high moor, safely gathered into lower pastures, where they were more easily accessible for feeding. Nevertheless, the menfolk studied the sky with great regularity, anxiously on the lookout for snow-clouds. A heavy snowfall would not only imprison them in the valley, perhaps for several weeks, but could even block the road which led down to Cherry Tree Farm.

Christmas morning brought a hoar frost, so that when the weak December sun made its appearance, the whole valley sparkled; every blade of grass was clearly edged with an outline of rime and the ruts in the road had hardened into solid ridges, demanding caution by iron-shod hooves. The outlook was breathtakingly lovely. The hedgerows and trees, albeit bare of leaves, were picture-like in their icy beauty.

Tamar had sent a messenger a day or two before to say that she would send down the Lassiter travelling coach, for the women and children. The men would accompany them on horseback.

After breakfast, Bob Lamb brought Maria up in the pony and trap, and took Ann Butler back down with him. By the time Edward, Annie and Maria were warmly wrapped up for the journey, the coach had arrived and Robert the coachman tucked warm travelling rugs round the occupants, before setting out for Thorsbury.

Annie Oaks dozed in a corner of the coach most of the way, but Sarah had her hands full entertaining the children during, what seemed to them, a long and tiring journey. The novelty of being in the coach soon wore off and Edward became fretful that Freddie had not come with them, considering himself too grown-up to play babyish games with his little sister and cousin.

When, however, Sarah looked out as they turned in at the wrought-iron gates, which were already opened for them and said, 'Here we are. This is Thorsbury,' the children crowded excitedly at the window.

Edward was wide-eyed. 'It's a castle!' he exclaimed.

Sarah smiled. It did look like a castle, she was bound to admit, with its light stone walls rising to crenellated splendour.

The coach drew to a stop outside the imposing double doors and Robert helped them down, while a group of lads ran from the stable block to take the men's horses.

When they entered the Great Hall, they were overwhelmed by the scene. The sum total of the Christmas decorations in their homes was a sprig or two of holly on top of the pictures. Here, the pillars which rose to the ceiling were swathed with ivy and other greenery and even the mantelpiece had swags and drapes of holly and myrtle, interspersed with shining baubles which reflected the fire-light with a myriad of colours.

The children were spellbound, gazing around in wide-eyed silence. Maria pointed excitedly to the other end of the hall, where a fir tree stood in an oak tub, bright with decorations and tiny candles clipped to the branch-tips. Even the adults were impressed, never having seen a Christmas tree before.

'The Queen can't have much grander,' Joe whispered to George. 'He must have a gold-mine in yon woods.'

Before George could make any response, Tamar came eagerly into the hall, hands outstretched and face alight.

'Oh, how lovely to see you all,' she greeted them. 'Where are the others?'

'Oor Martha felt that it's too near 'er time, love. She couldn't risk it,' Annie Oaks explained. 'And Mrs Butler's stopped with 'er – just ti be on t'safe side.'

The meal that followed exceeded their wildest expectations. Goose and plum pudding were customary fare at their Christmas dinners at home, but set before them now were garnishes, accompaniments and courses that left them impressed and slightly uncomfortable.

Although Stephen struggled to keep the conversation flowing with talk of horses and farming, all but Jonadab felt constrained by the silent watchfulness of the servants, who stood around, ever attentive.

Tamar thanked her lucky stars that she had decided to allow the three little ones to eat with them, instead of providing a separate meal in the old nursery. Once settled at the table, they were completely unabashed. Their Grandad was not the boss here, Edward had decided, so his demands that children should be seen and not heard, particularly at the table, did not apply. Egged on by his example, the two little girls also chattered incessantly, so that the silences between the adults were less noticeable.

Once the protracted luncheon, as Tamar called it, was over, they all returned to the Great Hall, Sarah giving a glance back at the table. Down at home, the Oaks women would have to face the clearing away and washing up and she was enjoying the novelty of walking away from the table, with no more to do.

Once they were seated Tamar gave an apologetic glance towards her father. 'Perhaps Stephen, you'd give out the presents,' she said. Knowing how prickly Jonadab could be about anything that he saw as charity, a great deal of thought had gone into the choosing of the gifts.

With Victoria and Hilary at his side to take the boxes, Stephen quickly glanced at the labels, to ensure that the excited children were the first to be served. Maria and little Annie carefully unwrapped their parcels and then opened the boxes to reveal identical dolls, one dressed in pink and the other in blue.

'What do you say then?' their grandmother gently prompted.

'Thank you, Auntie Tamar and Uncle Stephen,' they chorused, almost in unison, and then drew away from the adults to occupy themselves in some mysterious childhood occupation with their toys. Edward was already tearing impatiently at his paper, casting the pieces around him on the carpet, oblivious to his grandfather's frowns. At home, every piece of wrapping paper was carefully straightened, folded and put away for future use. Brown paper was prized especially highly, and some women produced their children on mattresses swathed in brown paper, to avoid the soiling of sheets.

When eventually the box was revealed and its lid cast aside, Edward's eyes shone with delight to see a beautifully painted wooden engine, with two carriages to hook on behind. Once the children were engrossed with their possessions, it was the turn of the adults. George put into words what they were all thinking.

'We didn't expect presents,' he said, a slight resentment in his tone. 'At home, it's only t'bairns as gets 'em.'

'I know, I know.' Tamar spoke hurriedly and placatingly. 'It's just that, with Joe and Mary being here, I wanted this Christmas to be special – something we'd all remember.'

For Mary and Sarah there were Paisley shawls, and one each also for Ann Butler and Martha. For her brothers and brother-in-law she had chosen gloves and scarves. 'Sufficiently useful and uninteresting to meet with Father's approval,' she had explained to Stephen. 'You know how insistent he is that everything should be serviceable!'

Her own mother's shawl was a warm and cosy plaid. 'Just like the Queen's so fond of,' Tamar assured her. Annie's eyes swam when she unwrapped an extra present – a pair of soft velvet slippers with quilted soles. Nobody but Martha knew how she suffered with her feet, she had thought, and could imagine the bliss of unlacing her boots and slipping her feet into them, after tea.

Jonadab curbed the exclamation that rose to his lips. It was typical of their Tamar to buy such things, he considered, 'Nowt but flimflams', was how he dubbed them in his mind.

Now it was his turn. Hilary carried over to him a long, slim parcel. Obviously a walking-stick, he thought, without enthusiasm. He already possessed a thumbstick to help him around the farm and a good, solid stick for market days and other visits to town. When he unwrapped the silver-headed cane, however, he was momentarily at a loss to know what to say. Nobody could call this ultilitarian; indeed, the only ones he had seen to equal it had been carried by the gentry. His family watched the varying emotions which chased across his face and then relaxed, as pride won and he smiled.

'By gum, Father! Every man a guinea!' exclaimed Joe, as Jonadab stood up and tested the height and strength of the stick.

'Thank thoo! It's champion,' he said, retaking his seat. Tamar had been correct in her assessment of him. 'He already thinks he's better than everybody else,' she had told Stephen. 'Now he can show them all that he's as good as the best of them.'

Hilary had been at school when Joe and Mary had stayed at Thorsbury on their way from Liverpool. Now he avidly questioned Joe about life in Canada.

'What about the Red Indians, Uncle?' he asked, eyes shining. 'Are they fierce?'

Joe laughed. 'No. The ones where we live are Crees. They're very friendly. In fact, Aunt Mary's brother Jack works with them. He traps wild animals and speaks the Cree language.'

Hilary was even more impressed. 'I shall go to Canada when I grow up.' His eyes swept the room, as he made the boast.

The sun was dipping beneath the trees which surrounded Thorsbury village when they piled into the coach, clutching the treasured presents. George went round for a word with the coachman.

'I know that you've been down it many a time, Robert, but the hill down to Aumery Park Farm will be dangerous in t'dark and with a frost. When you reach t'top, I'll walk between your horses and guide 'em down.'

'Very good, sir.' Robert touched his hat with his whip and clicking his tongue to his team, moved off.

'Aah wonders what sort of a day t'others 'as 'ad?' murmured Annie Oaks, as she rested her head back on the upholstery of the coach.

'Quieter than ours,' smiled Mary. After the handing out of the gifts, the afternoon had become animated and lively. The men had gone for a stroll round the stables, while Victoria had played the piano for the children to sing and play musical games. The womenfolk just sat and chatted, watching the children indulgently. It was a pleasure just to do nothing but talk, Sarah thought ruefully. Jonadab made it only too plain that he disapproved of idle hands.

The morning had begun quietly enough at Cherry Tree Farm. By the time Ann Butler arrived, the goose was already in the oven and the pudding was steaming merrily away. The older woman sniffed appreciatively.

'It's a good smell you've got,' she smiled. 'Is there anything you'd like me to do?'

'I've done the sprouts, but I'm ready for a sit down, if you wouldn't mind peeling the potatoes for me?' Martha felt rather diffident at asking Mrs Butler for help. Somehow she always seemed rather aloof, but Martha had not felt too well of late. Her ankles were swollen and there was a constant dull ache in the small of her back.

As she sank into a chair by the fire, Ann Butler eyed her. 'How long have you to go?' she enquired.

'Nearly a month,' came the reply.

Ann was surprised. 'It looks to have dropped,' she observed. Martha made no answer. Bob had just passed the window and she rose to her feet to tip the contents of the big iron kettle, which hung on a hook above the fire, into the brown tea-pot which sat waiting on the hob.

Smiling at her husband, she remarked, 'There, you'll be ready for that. Is it cold outside?'

Bob blew on his hands and held them out towards the fire. 'Aye, it is an' all. Too cold for snow, in fact.'

Silence reigned for a few minutes, while they all sipped the hot tea appreciatively. Martha glanced towards Bob. 'I'd go and get changed if I were you. After all, it is Christmas Day,' she smiled.

He rose to his feet. 'Aye. I'll make an effort,' he said.

The black iron pan of potatoes was now boiling on the hob, with the trimmed sprouts waiting to take their place when they were cooked.

'I'll lay the table,' Ann Butler offered, 'if you'll tell me where you keep the cloth.'

'In the sideboard drawer, in the parlour.' Martha was back on her feet. 'I'll just give the goose one last basting, and then we shall only be waiting for the sprouts to cook, while I'm mashing the potatoes and making the sauce for the pudding.'

Taking the piece of washed sacking, which served as an oven-cloth, she carefully lifted the heavy meat tin from the oven. Balancing it precariously on the oven plate, she endeavoured to tip it gently away from her, her right hand poised with the ladle with which to scoop up the fat.

Just as Ann came back with the table-cloth, Martha gasped, as the heavy tin tipped forward, splashing the hot fat over her shins and on to the fire. Shrieking with the pain of the scalding fat, she let the whole lot, roasting tin and goose, fall on to the hearth. The fat showered out, splashing her apron and causing a sheet of flame to shoot from the grate and envelop her. Before Ann Butler could reach her, she was in a screaming heap on the hearthrug, her apron on fire and her body writhing in fear and agony.

'Bob! Bob!' Ann's voice came out as a hoarse croak: her throat felt paralysed. Rushing to the water butt, she plunged the washing up bowl into it, and emptied it onto the distraught girl.

The searing flames were immediately doused, but Martha's cries and sobs were in no way diminished.

'My legs! Oh, my legs,' were the only words Ann could distinguish in the incoherent yelping and whimpering given vent to by Martha as she continued to roll about on the rug.

'My God! What's happened?' Alarmed by the noise from the kitchen, Bob ran in, hooking his braces over his shoulders.

Ann quickly explained and added, 'The burns look bad. We must get her stockings off.'

Bob ran to the table drawer and, returning with a pair of scissors, cut Martha's woollen stockings up the back, from the ankle. Tenderly, he tried to lift them from her shins, only to find that the wool had melted on to the skin and there was no way he could remove them.

'What's to be done?' Martha was now in a dead faint and, at last, still and quiet. 'Should we lather 'em wi' butter?' It was the only thing he could think of for burns.

'No!' On this point Ann Butler was definite. 'It's fat that's caused the scald. It wants no more fat. Where's she keep the bicarb?'

Martha had a stock of home-made nappies, carefully hemmed from old soft sheeting, so they soaked two and plastered them with bicarbonate of soda and gently wrapped the poor, blistered legs. Fortunately, the bowl of water had done its work, before the serge of her dress could be set alight by the burning pinafore. Ann plastered a paste of bicarb and water under her chin where the skin was scorched, but still Martha showed no signs of recovering consciousness.

'Can you carry her up to bed, before she comes round?' Ann was trembling as the reaction set in, but her dominance was beginning to reassert itself. She had always been at her best when faced with a crisis.

Bob aimed a boot at the cat, which was gingerly tearing at the goose skin. Bending down, he picked up his unconscious wife and made for the stairs, with Ann Butler following. As he carefully placed her on the bed, he looked down at the red stain on his sleeve. Their eyes met, in disquiet.

'What's wrong? What is it?' Bob gasped hoarsely.

'She's bleeding. The shock must have brought her on early.' Ann Butler paused for a second or two. 'Go and see that the kettle's filled up, Bob. I'll be down in a minute to wash my hands.'

Upon his departure, she turned back to the bed. Her worst fears were confirmed. Martha had without doubt gone into premature labour and was haemorrhaging severely. Ann's heart sank. She had never helped at anything more than the most straightforward birth.

Without another look at the still-unconscious girl, she hurried down to Bob, panting both from exertion and fear. Standing by the sink, vigorously soaping her hands, she spoke over her shoulder.

'You'll have to ride up to the cottage and bring Lydia,' she instructed. 'I sh'll need another woman. In fact – ' Drying her hands, she turned to face him. 'How are you fixed for brass, Bob?'

'Brass?' For the life of him, he could not see what his finances had to do with Martha's condition.

'Can you afford the doctor? T'isn't a straightforward birth and her legs are badly burnt.'

Bob's face was desperate. 'If she needs a doctor, a doctor she shall 'ave. I took 'er in sickness and in health and she must 'ave t'best I can do.'

'Right. I'll get back up to her. Let Lydia ride the pony back and you borrow one of Mr Oaks' horses. You'll get up to Kirkby faster.'

Bob hesitated by the door. 'It's Christmas Day. Will t'doctor come?'

She set her lips. 'He'd better,' she retorted. 'Tell him it's a matter of life and death.'

Tears welled up in Bob's eyes as he ran from the house, leaving Ann Butler to return to her patient. In her brief periods of awareness, Martha constantly screamed with the pain which racked her body and seemed to bore into the very bones of her tortured legs. For the most part, however, she tossed on the bed, lost in delirium, unable to respond to the older woman's instructions. And still the blood seeped inexorably away.

'Mrs Butler! Mrs Butler!' came Lydia's voice from the kitchen.

'Come on up, lass. Quick!' she urged.

Lydia approached the bed, her face filled with horror as she took in the bloodstained bedding.

'Oh, my God!' she whispered.

'I can't stop t'bleeding. Run down and fetch me summat to prop the bedfoot up. Books – stones – anything!' As Lydia's boots clattered on the stairs she shouted after her, 'And some cold water an' all.'

'Cold? Don't you mean 'ot?'

'No! Cold!' Ann's face was grim. How long would the doctor be, she wondered. When Lydia returned, two large stones cradled in her apron, the two of them heaved up the foot of the bed and used the stones to keep it propped up.

'There! That'll raise her feet and should help,' Ann panted, as she wrung out a cloth in cold water and placed it on Martha's distended body.

'What will that do?' Lydia asked.

'I hope it'll help staunch the flow. She can't go on losing like this.'

When, eventually, the baby put in its appearance, it was obvious that nothing could be done to help it. Although Ann swung it by its heels and blew between the pale lips, there was no way the little lungs could be coaxed into breath.

By the time Lydia had wrapped the pathetic body in a towel, they could hear the sound of hooves outside in the yard.

'That'll be the doctor,' Ann gasped. 'Thank the Lord! Give me a hand to strip this bottom sheet and put a clean one on, before he comes up.'

'You've done a good job, Mrs Butler,' remarked the doctor, when he finished his examination of Martha. 'Nothing could have saved the child, but raising the foot of the bed and the use of cold compresses has gone a long way to check the haemorrhage.'

Martha's eyes flicked open and she looked wildly round. 'Oh, my legs,' she groaned.

'It's all right, Mrs Lamb. I'm just going to give you a whiff of something to put you to sleep, while I dress them.' The doctor's voice was soothing, as he bent over her.

When they returned to the kitchen, he gave Ann Butler a small phial. 'What I have given her should keep her sleeping peacefully all night,' he said. 'She's lost a lot of blood and needs building up, so give her beef tea, liver, good broth. If the legs are too painful to bear, give her three drops of this in water.' Turning to Bob, he said solicitously, 'Your wife has had a bad time, Mr Lamb. I'm afraid the child was stillborn, but you've Mrs Butler to thank that Martha is still alive. But for her prompt actions, we might have lost the mother, too. I shall come back the day after tomorrow, but if you are at all worried, don't hesitate to come for me.'

Bob nodded speechlessly and it was left to Ann to thank the doctor and ask if he would give Lydia a lift back to the Oaks' farm.

'I know you've Toby waiting at home, Lydia,' she said, 'as well as Kitty and Freddie, but I want you to be there to tell Mr and Mrs Oaks what's happened, as soon as they get back.'

'Aye. Aah will an' all, Mrs Butler,' Lydia assured her, as she ran to get into the doctor's gig.

When the rest of the family reached the top of the hill leading down into the Dale, George dismounted and handed his reins to Joe. Although the full moon was high in the sky, giving a silvery clearness almost as bright as daylight, the hill was treacherous at any time, and he knew that under the interlaced branches, the road would be cast into shadowy gloom.

Taking his place between the two coach-horses, holding a bridle in each hand, he led them at a slow pace down the long and tortuous road to the valley bottom. As he remounted, he glanced towards his father.

'That's funny,' he remarked. 'As I looked across towards home, it seemed as though there was a light on.'

'It 'ud be t'moon, shining on t'glass,' Jonadab answered.

George was not convinced. 'It was more yellowy than moonlight,' he persisted.

True enough, when they arrived, there was lamplight shining from the window. Jonadab dismounted and, striding to the door, threw it open.

Lydia awoke with a start and raised her tear-stained face from where it had been resting on her arms, upon the table.

'What's up?' Jonadab barked, glancing swiftly round to see that she was alone. ''As summat 'appened?'

By now, the rest of them had pressed in at the door and the kitchen was full, everyone talking at once; all wanting to know what was amiss.

Sobbing noisily, Lydia gulped out the whole tale, her listeners growing silent as she poured out the details.

Annie Oaks sank into her rocking chair, her face convulsed with grief. As yet, she was too stunned to cry.

'Martha burnt and t'baby dead?' she whispered almost uncomprehendingly. 'Aah should nivver 'ave gone, Aah knew it.' She was sure that, had she been there, none of it would have happened. Lydia, however, rubbed salt into the wound with her next remark.

'T'doctor says it's due to Mrs Butler that Martha's alive. If it 'adn't been for 'er, she would 'ave died.'

Chapter Eight

Tamar had wanted a Christmas they would not forget and, undeniably, the memory of this one would stay with them for ever. Although Annie Oaks broodingly told herself that, somehow, both the scalding of Martha's legs and the loss of the baby could have been averted had she only stayed with her daughter, she was forced to acknowledge the debt they owed to Ann Butler. Undoubtedly, her care of Martha had stopped the haemorrhage which could easily have cost the girl's life.

Annie was eager to move down to Cherry Tree Farm and nurse her daughter, but Mrs Butler would have none of it. When Annie drove down, full of maternal concern, she was bound to admit that things were under control. Ann had arranged the fireguard to hold the bedclothes away from Martha's legs, which she dressed regularly, and Annie was relieved to see her daughter looking better than she had hoped, although obviously in severe pain and saddened by the loss of her baby.

'It were a little lad, Mam.' Martha's cornflower blue eyes, so like her father's, were awash with tears. 'Bob wanted a son!'

'There'll be other bairns and other sons, lass,' comforted her mother. 'Just thoo set thi mind ti getting strong again.'

'Mrs Butler's been so kind,' Martha continued. 'She saved my life of that I'm sure.'

Annie sighed. 'Aye. We sh'll allus be in 'er debt,' she agreed.

When she went downstairs, there was a mug of tea waiting on the hob.

'She seems to be coming along all right, don't you think?' Ann Butler asked. 'And I'm only too pleased to stay down here and look after her till she's back on her feet.'

Annie tried to put into words the gratitude she felt, but Ann brushed the faltering thanks aside.

'It's a blessing I knew what to do. Don't you worry, I'll look after her.'

If the truth were told, she was happy to be back in the house which had been her home since the death of her husband. She had never felt really comfortable at Aumery Park Farm. Just as Annie Oaks had felt uncomfortable being surrounded by Butlers, for her part Ann felt overwhelmed by Oaks. Down here, she was in familiar surroundings, with Mary for company. She longed to hear about the life in Canada and about Georgie and Jeanette, her grandchildren. This was the first privacy she had enjoyed with her daughter, since the couple's return from overseas.

The ultimate satisfaction for her, however, was that she felt needed. During the months at Aumery Park Farm she had felt superfluous. Although little jobs were found for her attention, there were too many women in the house. Here, with Martha in bed, she took charge and worked in harmony with her daughter, Mary.

The gloom of the homecoming had soon erased the glow brought about by their day in the luxury of Thorsbury Manor, from the minds of the rest of the family. Their mood was reflected in the weather. It was a common country saying that three hoar frosts were followed by rain, and so it proved to be. In the weeks after Christmas, the skies wept as though to reflect their own misery. The rain swept over the valley in curtains from lowering leaden skies.

The washing that was draped from lines in the wash-house spilled over into the kitchen, where sheets hung limply round the fire on the clothes horse, filling the house with sudsy steam. Wet washdays were a bugbear to Jonadab, upsetting his routine and keeping him from his seat by the fire. Consequently he absented himself from the house, except at meal-times, when he made his disapproval clear by sighs, puffs and constant rubbing of the steamed-up magnifying glass, as he tried to peer at his newspaper.

Tempers became frayed and only the children were happy. Maria had remained with her grandparents until

Martha recovered and she and little Annie played contentedly with their dolls. Edward was still entranced by the novelty of his train and, if that palled, was happy to be in the stables trailing round after Freddie.

'We could do with a load of yon 'ay Aah bought, bringing down from Gillamore,' announced Jonadab, when the rain eventually stopped.

'I'll go if you like,' offered Joe. He had begun to wish that they had sent Victoria back alone and delayed their own visit until the summer. The valley, which could be enchanting in the sunshine, was narrow and claustrophobic under heavy skies, with the darkness of the moors seeming to press in on all sides. Joe had forgotten how restricted were the views in the valley.

After more than twenty years living on the wide expanses of the prairie, with its boundless horizons, the little Dale depressed him. He chafed, too, against Jonadab's attitude. On his own land, he was used to giving the orders and woe betide any man who was tardy in carrying them out. What he regarded as his father's arrogance irked him, although he did his best to hide his feelings.

Now that the chance to escape for two or three hours offered itself, he was quick to seize it. Besides, there was an inn at Gillamore.

Jonadab agreed and, with a call at the inn at the back of his mind, and someone needed to mind the load while he indulged his thirst, Joe announced, 'Freddie can come with me. There's no heavy work and he can learn to tie a load.'

'Can I come, too, Uncle Joe?' Edward tugged at Joe's coat, anxious for his attention. 'If Freddie's going, can I come?'

Joe looked across at Sarah. 'Well, it's very cold,' she said reflectively. 'You must be well wrapped up.'

While Joe took himself off to the buildings, to yoke up his team and collect Freddie, Sarah bundled Edward into his overcoat and, wrapping a warm woollen muffler round his neck, she crossed it over his chest, pinning it at the back with a large safety pin.

'There you are,' she said, pulling his cap on to his head. 'Do as you're told and don't get in Uncle Joe's way!'

Joe collected the ham sandwiches that had been hurriedly made by Annie and lifted Edward to sit between him and Freddie. A crack of the whip caused the two horses to amble slowly forward.

'Bring as much as thoo can manage,' Jonadab called from the yard. 'It's turning colder; we might 'ave snow later.'

Without turning, Joe raised his whip to show that he'd heard. The old man couldn't leave anybody to do even a simple job without sticking his oar in, he thought, giving the team a vicious flick with the whip.

When they reached Gillamore, Joe had a word with the farmer whose stack his father had bought, and then set to work quickly and efficiently. The hay was nicely compacted and the hay-spade sliced into the stack crisply and cleanly.

When he had enough to make a bale, he showed Freddie how to tie it firmly, with one of the straw ropes they had brought with them. When he was satisfied that, with Edward's help, the bales could be firmly tied, he returned to the cutting, leaving the boys to judge and tie the bales. The best way to teach them, he considered, was to let them get on with the job.

When they had cut enough hay to make a good load, they sat with their backs to the fragrant stack and demolished the ham sandwiches, together with a bottle of cold tea, which they passed companionably from one to the other. Freddie and even Edward had the heady feeling that they had achieved the status of manhood: doing men's work and eating men's food.

Joe loaded up the wagon, while the two boys tied up the last of the bales. He fastened the first rope across the load, showing Freddie how to pull it tight and make it fast. Leaving the two boys to do the rest, he made his way to the farmhouse for a word with Albert Simpson, the farmer.

Whistling tunefully, he strode back towards the wagon, consulting his watch. Good. He'd worked well and would have time to spend an hour at the inn, before making for home. While Freddie scrambled up on to the far side, he lifted Edward up.

'Come on, lads,' he said. 'Let's be off.' To their surprise, however, not far along the main street, he drew the horses to a halt and jumped down. 'I shan't be a minute,' he said, crossing the wide grass verge and entering a long low building.

Freddie had been brought up in the workhouse and Edward in a remote valley; neither knew the meaning of the sign hanging over the door. At first they were quite happy to sit and chat. Then Freddie found a piece of string in his pocket and they played cat's cradle. It was a girl's game, but there was no one to see them engaged in such an unmanly pursuit.

Gradually, the temperature dropped and a wind began to rise. Fitful at first, it was not long before its icy fingers began to pluck at their clothes and the two boys leaned together trying to draw warmth from each other.

'Whose house is it, anyway?' Edward was shivering and his tone was surly.

'Dunno. Shall Aah go and look for 'im?'

'Yes. Tell 'im I'm cold,' Edward instructed.

When Freddie knocked on the door, there was no reply but he could hear the sound of men's voices inside. Cautiously, he opened the door and peered round, to be met by the delicious warmth which emanated from the large log fire in the grate.

''Ere, clear off!' The landlord glowered at him from behind the bar. Upon seeing him, Joe rose to his feet, glancing at the clock.

'I'm coming, lad. Out you go,' he said shortly, turning towards the bar to buy a bottle for his pocket.

Edward was beginning to regret coming on the trip. He was chilled through and wanted to be home. He longed to climb up on his Grandma's knee and be cuddled in front of the fire.

When they reached the top of the precipitous hill which led down into Sleightholmedale, Joe halted the horses and jumped down. Deep inside, he felt a trifle shamefaced that he had stayed so long at the inn, as both boys were obviously chilled to the bone.

'Now, you two, sit still while I put the clogs on the back wheels,' he instructed the boys, explaining what he was about to do. 'The wheels fit into these things,' he said as he released one of the chains which held the iron shoe to the bottom of the wagon. 'When we go down a steep hill they stop the back wheels turning so that the waggon can't gather speed and go so fast that the horse can't control it.'

Young as they were, the boys probably knew as much about the fitting of shoes on to carts as did Joe himself, but he felt that he must go on talking to keep them cheerful. Far from perking up, though, they showed no interest in what he was doing or saying.

The wind was whipping through the trees, moaning and howling, reflecting their forlorn mood. They were only too thankful when Joe resumed his seat.

'Cheer up, lads. We'll soon be home,' he cajoled, as he began to guide his team carefully down the track.

As they reached the steepest part of the hill, to Joe's unease he felt the load shift. He had failed to check the ropes after the boys had tightened them and now the badly secured bales were slipping off to one side. Sensing the sway, the horses leaned back into the britchings trying to adjust to the strain. Joe prayed that the harness would hold. The weight of the hay was dragging the wagon over to the left, where there was a sheer drop, steep as a cliffside.

As the load swayed perilously, the horses, eyes wild with fear, began to whinny and edge backwards. Frantically Joe pulled on the reins. 'Whoah! Whoah!' he cried, but the hay slewed further to the left as the load began to jack-knife. Grabbing Edward, he pulled the boy towards him and released the reins, ready to leap to safety. At that moment, the load began to topple and the two horses bolted.

'Jump, Freddie!' he urged hoarsely. 'The whole lot's going to go!' Clutching his nephew to his chest, he hurled himself sideways off the wagon, landing in a heap at the side of the track.

Joe set Edward on his feet but the child was shaking uncontrollably and weeping in great, gulping sobs.

'Are you all right?' Joe demanded, giving him a shake. There was no answer. The little boy was too distraught to speak.

'Stop 'ere. I must calm them 'orses,' Joe insisted. However, he felt a trickle down his leg and, upon investigating, found that the whisky bottle was smashed and had gashed his thigh badly. He tied his neckerchief round the leg and peered over into the crevace at the other side of the road. He could see no sign of Freddie.

Picking up the sobbing Edward, Joe limped down to where the horses had stopped, just round the corner. The iron shoes on the back wheels had checked their progress so that they stood, heads down, trembling and sweating with fear. Joe lifted Edward up on the wagon and then went to soothe the two great shires.

Eventually, stroking and murmuring to them, he managed to steady them. He glanced towards Edward, who was sobbing with his eyes hidden in the crook of his arm. Hurriedly, Joe went towards the back of the wagon and emptied the remains of the broken bottle into a tuft of grass by the side of the track. Then, after removing the shoes from the back wheels, he climbed up beside Edward and, with a click of his tongue and a jerk on the reins, set off again.

Further along the valley, George and two of the farmworkers were busy digging out the roadside ditch. This was one of the most boring of the winter jobs and they said very little as they shovelled out the sludge and piled it on the bank.

'What's that?' George suddenly exclaimed, upon hearing shouts and the sound of hooves from the direction of the entrance to the little Dale. As they paused, the sound of commotion became clearer and louder.

'Whoah! Whoah!' Joe's voice echoed panic: then came silence.

Throwing down their shovels, George and his companions broke into as fast a run as their heavy boots would allow. Before they had covered much more than half a mile, however, the wagon lumbered into view. The only signs of the load of hay were a few wisps and strands, caught here and there on the wheels. Joe held the reins tautly, while little Edward leaned against his uncle, gripping tightly on to his coat.

Although the men faltered, George still ran towards the vehicle, his eyes focused on his son's white and tear-stained face.

'What's up? What's happened?' As Joe drew the horses to a halt, George lifted Edward into his arms, whereupon the boy immediately began to cry once more.

'Oh, Dad, Dad,' he wailed. 'I'm so cold and frightened. Where's Freddie?'

George's eyes scoured the woods looking for the child, then his shocked eyes met those of his brother. 'Where *is* Freddie?' he demanded.

Joe's eyes shifted away uneasily. 'He jumped, when the load slipped. He's probably down in the woods, below the road.'

'Jumped!' George raged. 'You let a little lad jump off a moving wagon into that?' He flung his arm wildly towards the woodland which tumbled down into the valley. 'Why, thoo blitherin' idiot! If owt's 'appened to t'lad, on your conscience be it!'

Guilt and anger conspired together to contort Joe's face into a sardonic sneer. 'Who the hell do you think you are, little brother, to pass judgement on me? You don't even know what happened yet.' He glared down from his elevated position on the wagon.

Incensed now, George reached up, intending to drag his brother to the ground. 'No, I don't know what happened, so I suggest you tell me. And if you use the Devil's language in front of my bairn again, I'll knock your foul words out of your mouth!' He grabbed the leg of Joe's breeches to pull him off the wagon, then drew back, looking with horror at his own wet hand. Wrinkling his nose, he sniffed in disbelief.

'You've been drinking,' he accused, his voice now lowered into a menacing whisper.

A dull flush suffused Joe's cheeks. He had always blushed easily, right from childhood and now, as hard a man as he seemed to be, the tell-tale colour flooded his face.

George's eyes blazed and his normally placid nature erupted in blind rage. 'You've risked my lad's life, and that of little Freddie, for the sake of a glass of whisky!' he almost hurled at his brother. 'You – !' Jumping up beside his brother, George raised a clenched fist to strike him.

'No, Dad!' Edward let out a terrified whimper at the unaccustomed outburst from his father.

Grudgingly, George lowered his arm and took the reins from Joe's hands. Without looking at his brother, he spoke more calmly to Edward. 'Come on, lad, let's get you home, near a warm fire.' George placed his son on the wagon and sat down beside him. 'Move over if you want a lift.' He still felt unable to look at Joe, but kept his voice level for Edward's sake. 'Whatever Faither'll say, I don't know. It's bad enough you've lost t'load and upset a pair of valuable 'orses, but if you've any sense left in that wooden head of yours, you'll keep out of his way and not let him smell the liquor. Although why I should try to protect you, I don't know.' Casting his eyes around one last time, he sighed. 'And Heaven help you if owt's 'appened to Freddie.'

Joe moved across to the passenger side. 'He'll have made his way downwards, instead of climbing up,' he replied, as though addressing a rather slow child. 'As soon as I felt the load shift, I shouted to him to jump.'

George raised his eyebrows. 'Didn't you fasten it tight enough?' he asked bitterly. 'If you'd forgotten how to do t'job, you shouldn't have offered.'

Before Joe could answer, however, Edward squinted up at George. 'Me an' Freddie tied it, Dad,' he said, with a mixture of pride and doubt. 'Was it done wrong?'

George kept his eyes fixed grimly ahead, but could make no response. The more he heard of the afternoon's events, the more he despised his brother.

Upon reaching the farmhouse, he handed the horses and

wagon to the third man, or thoddy, who came running in answer to his call.

'They're upset. Give 'em a good rub down and some oats,' he instructed, 'and check that wagon,' he called, as it trundled away.

When he strode into the kitchen, still carrying Edward, with Joe following behind, his parents were seated at each side of the fire and Sarah was nowhere to be seen.

Annie laid aside her darning. 'Whatever's up?' she cried, holding out her arms for the boy.

'Give him a basin of broth, Mam,' said George. 'He's frozen stiff.'

Annie sat the child down on the hearthrug. 'Stay there, while I get you some nice hot broth.' Turning to Kitty, who was laying the table for tea, she said, 'Pass a basin and spoon, lass.' And, turning back to the fire, she ladled the soup from the cauldron which, filled with nourishing broth, hung above the fire all winter. Constantly replenished, it was always simmering, ready for those who came in chilled from their work.

Jonadab looked from one son to the other, conscious of the tension between them. Joe hovered by the door, reluctant to move within smelling range of his father, in case the odour of alcohol should be detected.

'What's 'appened?' Although the words were quietly spoken, they carried all the old man's authority, and his eyes moved from one to the other, questioningly.

George did not answer. Inside he was seething with bitterness towards his brother. 'And anyroad,' as he said afterwards to Sarah, 'I wanted to see how he wriggled out of it.'

With a quick glance at George, Joe gave a self-conscious half-laugh. 'Just at t'steepest bit, t'load slipped. It only moved a bit at first, but the shifting of weight caused t'wagon to begin to slew. I could tell the lot was going over, so I grabbed Edward and jumped.' He looked towards his father at last, to find the blue eyes boring into his soul.

Before Jonadab could speak, Joe continued hurriedly, 'I'm afraid the hay's scattered, but the horses and wagon are safe.'

George shot him a look of condemnation. 'And t'rest,' he prompted. 'Tell 'im about Freddie.'

Kitty had stopped setting the table and stood, a bundle of cutlery in her hands and her eyes fixed on Joe. Her face was pale and her eyes apprehensive.

'Please, Mr Joe, sir. Where is oor Freddie?' There was a slight quaver to her voice, as she looked from one to the other.

Jonadab rose to his feet. 'Aye. What's 'appened ti t'lad?' His brows were drawn and the words almost barked at Joseph who looked anxiously around.

'I thought he'd 'ave been here by now.' He suddenly felt worried. 'As soon as I felt t'load shift, I shouted to 'im to jump. I expected he'd landed well down from t'road and it would be easier for him to go on downwards and come along t'valley bottom, rather than climb back up and come by t'road.'

'In other words, thoo didn't look for t'lad?' Jonadab's face was one of disbelief. 'He could 'ave broken a leg and be lying there and thoo nivver bothered ti look.'

Turning to George, he ordered, 'Get t'men rounded up wi' lanterns. It'll be dark soon and we can't 'ave an injured bairn lying out in t'woods all night . . . specially in January.'

As the three men moved out, Annie noticed Joe's torn clothing and the makeshift tourniquet over his bloodstained breeches.

'What's thoo done to thi leg, son?' she asked anxiously.

'It's nowt, Mam. I tore it on summat when I landed,' he said as he slammed the door behind him.

Kitty had carefully placed the cutlery around the table and now came to the fireside, where she sat down on the rug, her arms round Edward. Annie looked at that girl's face which was pale and anxious.

'Go upstairs, Kitty, and tell Edward's mother that there's been a little mishap and 'e needs 'is mammy,' she said. 'She's putting t'ironing away in t'linen closet.'

Sarah came running into the kitchen and gathered Edward into her arms. Although in reality her sister's child, he was as dear to her as her own little Annie and she never thought of him as anything other than her own.

'Whatever is it, little pet?' she crooned. Eventually, between hiccups and sobs, the tale was told: how Uncle Joe had taught him and Freddie how to tie the load; how they had been left on the wagon, to become chilled, until Freddie had gone to a man's house and got Uncle Joe out; and finally, how the load had slipped and Uncle Joe had grabbed him and jumped off the wagon, shouting to Freddie to throw himself off the other side.

When it was all out, he leaned against Sarah and closed his eyes, totally exhausted.

'There, there, pet,' she soothed. 'It's over now, and Daddy and Grandad'll soon find Freddie, you'll see.' Then turning to Kitty, she said, 'Go and waken little Annie, please, and wash her hands and face ready for tea.' Sarah was anxious to keep the girl busy, during the waiting period.

Darkness was upon them, before the searchers found Freddie. While half the men had followed the road, the others had chosen a footpath which ran along the bottom of the escarpment, hoping to meet him making his way towards home.

Jonadab, on horseback, accompanied the group on the road, his temper becoming shorter as he saw his valuable hay strewn on the road and caught among the trees and undergrowth.

'Little of that can be saved,' he grunted, 'but then, it's matterless compared with finding Freddie.'

Where the boy had hurled himself from the load, as it teetered on the edge of the track, was the place where the ground fell away most steeply. Although sheer, it was tree-clad and fairly thick with brushwood, so that Freddie's body had hit one obstacle after another.

The men scrambled precariously down, lanterns in one hand and clinging desperately with the other to any tuft of grass or scrubby twigs, until they reached the spot where the poor mangled body lay. There was no way they could carry him back up to the road. Indeed, to descend to the bottom of the scarp was difficult to manage.

It was big, clumsy Tobias who gathered the broken remains into his arms. Coming from the workhouse himself, he had always had a soft spot for Freddie.

''E's 'ere, maister,' he called up.

''Ow 'is 'e?' came back Jonadab's voice.

''E's dead, maister.' Slow-witted Toby knew of no way of softening the blow.

The two groups met at the bottom of the hill and made their way back in silent procession. Freddie had been popular with all the men. He had been chirpily cheerful, eager to please and had brought a little merriment into the unremitting toil of their days. Joe could feel the hostility which emanated from them as they made their way homeward. He was left in no doubt that the workforce placed the blame for Freddie's death squarely upon him.

When the stunned and speechless group arrived at the farmhouse, Joe made to carry on to the stables.

'I'll get off down to Cherry Tree and get my leg seen to,' he said, never even pausing in his stride.

'Thoo'll come wi' us,' his father replied.

Joe hesitated, obviously ill-at-ease. 'My leg's hurting. I'd like Mary to dress it.'

Jonadab swung round. ''Ave Aah bred a coward, as well as a fool?' he demanded heavily.

Joe flushed and stood uncertainly in the road. Jonadab had, by now, dismounted and passed his horse to one of the men. Turning to Tobias, he placed a hand on his arm.

'Wait 'ere, lad, for a minute.' He spoke gently, conscious of Toby's distress. 'Give me a chance to break it to 'em, afore thoo brings 'im in.'

When he entered the kitchen, Sarah glanced up. 'Thank goodness, Pa. Have you found him?'

'Where's t'lass?' he answered brusquely, looking round the kitchen.

'In the dairy. Why? Is he hurt?' Sarah and Annie exchanged worried looks.

At that moment Kitty came through into the kitchen. 'Oh, maister!' she exclaimed. 'Is Freddie with you?'

'Thoo must be a brave lass, Kitty.' Jonadab spoke sadly. 'Aah'm afraid Freddie's gone from us.'

Even as he spoke the door opened and Tobias entered, carrying his pathetic bundle, closely followed by George and Joe.

Kitty burst into a paroxysm of frenzied sobs. Catching sight of Joe, she screamed at him, 'Murderer! Thoo killed oor Freddie! Thoo's a wicked, wicked man!'

Chapter Nine

Freddie's violent and untimely death had deeply affected all the inhabitants of the two farms. Jonadab and Annie Oaks relived, with anguish, the death of their own ten-year-old daughter, Maria, who had been drowned in Hodge Beck over twenty years before. Jonadab was adamant that Freddie should not have a pauper's funeral and himself paid for the boy to be buried as though he had been one of the family.

George felt a deep bitterness against his brother. 'It could have been our Edward,' he constantly reminded Sarah. 'Our Joe stank of drink when I first met him, up t'hill.'

'I can't believe the change in him,' was her reply. 'When he first married our Mary and they lived with us in Fadmoor, he was a grand lad. I was only little, but I can remember how kind he was. What's altered him?'

George had no answer. 'They're different in foreign parts,' was all he could think of to say. 'Life's hard and men 'as to be hard to stick it out.'

He blamed himself for bringing Freddie from the workhouse. 'If I'd left him for somebody else to take, he'd still be alive,' he brooded.

Sarah, however, was more philosophical. 'He could have met with an accident on any farm,' she argued. 'As it was, he and Kitty had more than two happy years together. She would have lost track of him if they'd been separated.'

Both Kitty and Edward were devastated. The small boy could hardly remember the time before Freddie had lived with them and was like a little lost soul, wandering round, dry-eyed but pale-faced. He despised his sister Annie and cousin Maria, considering it beneath his dignity to play with them. The whole incident, culminating in the death of his constant companion, had had a profound effect upon him, making him withdrawn and introspective, a far cry from the happy little boy he had been.

'Oor George should 'ave let t'New Year in,' grumbled Annie. 'We've allus 'ad a good year when 'e's been t'First Footer. Aah felt uneasy when oor Joe was so set on doing it.' Although Annie was as fervent a chapel-goer as her husband, she tended to play safe and was steeped in superstition. Now she was gloomy. 'It bodes ill for t'rest o' t'year,' she forecast.

Joe felt uncomfortable under the accusing stares, whenever he visited Aumery Park Farm. His own family tried to be natural in their dealings with him, but the farm men were surly and uncommunicative. Whenever he entered his mother's kitchen – for none of them could think of it as Sarah's – he could feel Kitty's accusing eyes fixed upon him. Her cheery little face was now pinched and white and the hatred she felt for him was starkly obvious. Joe began to find jobs to occupy himself down at Cherry Tree Farm.

'I'm not going to be treated like muck,' he told Mary. 'I'm sorry about the lad, but it was an accident.' Nevertheless, he felt uncomfortable and made arrangements to stay for a few days at Thorsbury Manor and then go on to Mary's sister, Christiana, who lived in Leeds.

'I shan't be sorry if they're snowed in down here and we can't get back for a while,' he told Mary.

'I can't help thinking that you're making a mountain out of a molehill,' was her reply. 'Nobody can blame you.'

Once Joseph and Mary left, the atmosphere lightened. Martha was now up and about, although her legs were badly scarred. She was grateful for Ann Butler's company and the older woman felt more comfortable down at Cherry Tree Farm, so by mutual agreement, she made her home with Martha and Bob.

Although there were snow flurries, there was no heavy fall, keeping open access to and from Sleightholmedale. The ground was iron-hard, so that both men and horses toiled to turn the soil, their days cold and gloomy with not even a fitful ray of sunshine to lighten the bleakness.

Joseph and Mary extended their absence. After a week with Tamar and Stephen, they moved on to Leeds and then went to Middlesborough, to visit Mary's sister Jane.

Jonadab and Annie received no word from them and had no idea when they intended to return. However, even his mother was forced to admit that the atmosphere on the farm was easier without Joe.

''E's not t'lad 'e was,' she complained, with the fretfulness of old age. She had been so excited by Joseph and Mary's return that her disappointment in the way her eldest son had developed was a sore blow. In his absence, she had thought fondly of him and his family, remembering him in her nightly prayers and recalling little anecdotes of their doings and sayings with fond remembrance. Now she was puzzled and distressed to find the hard and uncompassionate man that Joe had become. Mary had always been sweet-natured and was still so, as far as her mother-in-law could tell. ''Ow she puts up with 'im, Aah don't know,' she said.

George and Bob Lamb often discussed Joe's drinking, as they worked together among the sheep. Neither had said anything to Jonadab about it and Bob was terrified that his employer would find out about his own solitary lapse. Despite being his father-in-law, Jonadab was a strict employer and would tolerate no strong drink, tobacco nor card-playing on his farms. 'The Devil's instruments,' he was wont to call them.

The third week in February brought a dramatic change in the weather. The frost broke and with the thaw came torrential rain.

'February fill dykes, living up to 'er name,' Jonadab remarked, as he swathed himself in washed sacks before venturing out. There was always a plentiful supply of these, and the men wrapped them round their legs, cross-gartering them with pieces of string, as protection from rain, snow or cold. Other sacks covered heads and hung down over the shoulders, like cloaks, whenever they had need to face the elements. For the most part, George found the men work in the buildings, mending and patching harness, bagging up flailed corn or repairing woodwork and machinery.

The whole valley was awash as tiny trickles and runnels of water surged down from the drab moors, swelling Hodge

Beck into a foaming torrent which splashed and swirled its way through the valley.

On the third day of the deluge, a trap drew up at the door of Aumery Park Farm and Mary ran into the kitchen, bonnet, hair and cloak soaked and running with water.

'Oh!' she exclaimed, taking off her bonnet and shaking it. 'I hope it isn't ruined. I've only just bought it in Middlesborough.'

Sarah passed her a towel. 'Dry your hair and give me your cloak,' she urged, pushing her sister towards the fire. 'Why didn't you let us know you were coming? Mam may not have your bed aired.'

'It was Joe,' replied Mary. 'He just took it into his head that he wanted to come back. I wanted to stay until the weather picked up, but he didn't seem to hit it off with our Jane's husband, Dick.'

Before either Sarah or Annie could comment on this, the door was flung open again and Joe panted into the room. 'God! It's turned to hail, now!' he cried, shaking the hailstones from his hair on to the clean, flagged floor.

'Joe!' Annie's face was shocked at what she considered to be blasphemy.

'Sorry, Mam.' He was instantly contrite. 'But it is the last straw. We've had a terrible journey over t'moors in this downpour and now it's hailing; stones as big as marbles they are, an' all.'

They joined the rest of the family for tea, while their clothes dried and they waited for the storm to abate a little, before continuing on to Cherry Tree Farm. After the meal, conversation was almost as easy as it used to be. Only Kitty was silent, sitting on her stool, helping little Annie with the last of her tea and trying not to look at Joe. Edward was sullen and would not smile in answer to Joe's cajolery, not even when his uncle produced a wooden Noah's Ark, complete with animals, together with a doll's cradle for little Annie.

'What do you say, Edward?' Sarah spoke sharply, but the child paused and eyed Joe almost insolently before uttering a grudging, 'Thank you,' and laying the toy aside.

After an awkward pause, Jonadab took up the conversation.

'Aah've been in touch wi' a chap that 'as a threshing set and when t'weather improves, 'e's going ti give me a day.'

George was flabbergasted. The thought that his father could make such an arrangement at Joe's instigation and without consulting him, was like gall. He rose from the table, his normally equable temper rising.

'It's nice to know who's t'maister, then!' he threw accusingly at his father.

Jonadab looked across at him and held him, momentarily, with his eyes. 'As Aah remembers it, Aah made thoo a partner,' he said in a tone intended to brook no contradiction.

'Aye, well. Partners should consult with partners,' George answered bitterly. 'You're fond of quoting the Lord's word to us, Faither. Doesn't the Bible tell us, "No man can serve two masters"? Well, you expect all on this farm to do just that!' With which he stormed out into the night, slamming the door behind him.

Sarah half-rose, but her father-in-law's upraised hand checked her. 'Leave 'im be, lass. This weather'll cool 'is 'ot temper soon enough.'

She, however, knew the pride which had filled George when he had thought that his father was retiring in his favour, and she also knew the depth of his humiliation when the deed of partnership had been signed and it appeared that Jonadab had no faith in his ability to run the farm. Although she retook her seat, she looked steadily at the old man.

'One day you'll push him too far,' she said warningly.

Once February had gone March came in, more like a lamb than a lion. Although the sun had no power, it shone palely most days from clear blue skies and, in the fresh breezes which caressed the land, the soil began to dry and the hazel catkins to dance.

Joe surprised Mary with the announcement that he intended to ride over to Skiplam to see his brother, Jonna.

'Why?' she asked. 'You haven't a lot in common.'

'We've more than you think,' he retorted. 'For instance – we share the same father.'

'You share the same mother, too,' she laughed, 'but I wouldn't say you're very much alike.'

'I didn't say we're alike,' came his answer, 'but we do have things in common: things to discuss.'

She could get no more from him, and though she puzzled over it with both her mother and Martha, they could think of no reason for what Joe had suddenly found to discuss with Jonna.

Upon his return, he appeared well satisfied with whatever had transpired and whistled about the farm, apparently more cheerful than he had been since Freddie's death.

'I'm off up to Aumery Park,' he called up to Mary the next morning, as she was busy making their bed.

Satisfied that the ice had been broken by their sudden return to his father's home during the hail-storm, Mary was pleased that things seemed to be on the mend between Joe and his family. They planned to return to Canada in late April and, although anxious to get back to her home and children, Mary knew that she would not see her mother again.

She spent long hours talking to the older woman, feeding her every detail of their life since they had left England. In her turn, she was storing up memories to take back and pass on.

When they had first arrived, Jonadab had lent a riding horse for Joe's use. While he saddled up, he broke into snatches of song and seemed in high spirits. Mary well knew that he had not touched a drop of whisky since Freddie's death and was delighted to hear him so happy, without the aid of alcohol.

Upon arriving at Aumery Park Farm, he passed the horse to the charge of one of the men and went looking for Jonadab. To his satisfaction, the old man was alone in the tack-room, inspecting the harness that had been repaired during the spell of bad weather.

'Ah, Father. Here you are.'

Jonadab looked up. 'Aye. 'Ere Aah am,' he retorted laconically.

Joe sat beside him on the bench. 'Since I came back, I've thought a lot about the situation here,' he began.

Jonadab eyed him quizzically. 'What situation's this, then?' he enquired.

His son hesitated fractionally and then, with a sideways glance, proceeded. 'Living with our Mam every day, as you do, you won't have noticed how much she's aged.' He paused, choosing his words carefully, but Jonadab interrupted.

'O' course she's aged – and so 'ave Aah. We're in us seventies, not spring chickens.'

Joe pressed on. 'That's just the point. You both should be taking it easy. When we first came back, you said you'd retire, but you still do a full day's work. Why don't you really retire and, perhaps, buy a little cottage in Kirkby?'

Jonadab was too astounded to speak for a moment. 'Spend mi hard-earned brass on a cottage, when Aah've a perfectly good 'ome 'ere?' He was incredulous. Before Joe could make any reply, however, he continued, in full flow, 'Besides, what would Aah do all day? Thoo must be daft.'

Joe at last managed to get a word in. 'I'm thinking of our Mam, as well. She'd like to be near to the shops.'

'Shops be blowed! They're a temptation ti spend money. The further away from shops women live, the better.' A sudden suspicion dawned on Jonadab's face. 'Oor George's put thoo up ti tis. Sarah warned mi Aah'd push 'im too far and now 'e wants rid of mi.' He took a deep breath. 'It's a bad day when a son that's been treated as Aah've treated 'im, goes behind 'is faither and stabs 'im in t'back.'

Joe broke in. 'No, Father. I've not discussed it with George. It's me and our Jonna. We feel you should take things easy.'

'Jonna?' Jonadab was taken aback. Although his youngest son lived just across the moor, they rarely met. Two or three times a year, visits were exchanged and they occasionally encountered each other on market days, but ordinary farming families lacked both the time and inclination for much social life. It was sufficient for Jonadab and Annie to know that Jonna was there, within contact if need be.

'Yes. He's as worried about you and Mam as I am.' Joe's voice was solicitous.

His father sat and cogitated for a moment. He was offended to think that his family considered him to be too old and decrepit to do a full day's work. He admitted to himself that he tired more easily than in his prime, but the reason for that, of course, was his gammy leg, from when his thigh had been broken.

'And what are we supposed ti live on, might Aah ask?' he enquired, at length.

Joe relaxed. The first hurdle was over. The old man was willing to consider his proposition.

'Well, Jonna and I have discussed it and agreed that the sensible thing would be to auction the live and dead stock and share out the proceeds four ways. George already has this farm: Jonna will inherit Maisie's Dad's place and I've got my spread over in Canada. An injection of cash would be a boon to us all and would still leave enough for you and Mam to live on for the rest of your days.'

He sat back. There: his plan was out. He had been bitterly resentful when it seemed as though the lot would go to George, the second son, and Jonna had taken little persuasion to fall in with the scheme.

During his days at home, the youngest son had always felt that he lived in George's shadow, nursing a brooding jealousy which he now had a chance to appease.

Joe eyed his father anxiously. Jonadab sat, staring unseeingly ahead, trying to marshal his thoughts. At last he spoke.

'My life 'as been spent in this Dale, working this land. 'Ere Aah was born and 'ere Aah shall die. Thoo obviously can't understand the way Aah feels, but George knows. 'E feels t'same.' He sighed heavily, and regarded Joe with a look, half-scorn, half-pity. 'What contribution 'as thoo made ti this farm? Thi brother, George, 'as given 'is life ti this land.' As Joseph took a breath, Jonadab held up his hand. 'Mek no mistake, 'e's got enough brass laid by ti tek on another place. Elizabeth worked every way she knew, when she were alive, poor lass, ti raise money ti set 'im on 'is feet. She stood t'market, ran a tea stall and scrimped and scraped for a farm of their own, but whenever it came to it, oor George wouldn't leave us. 'E feels for this land as Aah do and 'e shall 'ave 'is reward, when Aah've gone.'

Realising that he had failed, Joe gave a bitter laugh. 'You mean he knows which side his bread's buttered,' he sneered. 'You don't think he'd have spent his life down in this dreary hole, working his heart out for an old skinflint like you, if he hadn't had an eye on the main chance, do you?'

Jonadab's patience was at an end. Worse than that, he felt a sense of sick disappointment in this eldest son of his. What kind of life could he have lived to change him from a sensitive and thoughtful man into one who was so hard and grasping, he wondered.

'Enough's been said.' The deep sadness he felt was reflected in his voice. 'When thoo went ti t'Canadas, Aah thought as 'ow thoo was lost ti us. Aah nivver expected ti see thoo again.' His piercing blue eyes looked straight into Joe's, but Joe refused to meet them, his eyes swivelling away.

Jonadab sighed. 'It would 'ave been better if thoo'd nivver come back. Yon bairn would still be alive and me and thi mother could remember the man thoo was, not seeing the man thoo's become.'

There was a long silence. Joe felt robbed. He had not only thrown away his chance of any of Jonadab's money, but for some reason unfathomable to him, his father's esteem. He held out his hands in a pleading gesture.

'Nay, Faither. Don't take on so. Me and Jonna only had your own good in mind: yours and Mam's.'

'Stuff and nonsense!' Jonadab had had enough. 'Thi mother lives like a queen, waited on hand and foot, in the house that's been hers since our marriage. She's got her children and grandchildren round 'er and thoo would wrest 'er from it all and put 'er in a cottage in Kirkby? Thoo dissent understand us at all.'

Joe stood up. 'Oh, all right. Have it your own way. I just thought it would make life easier for you both.'

'Thoo just thought it would mek thi own pocket fuller,' came the reply.

Joe realised, ruefully, that he had gone too far. 'Fair enough, Faither. If you want to die in harness, it's up to you,' he said.

Jonadab rose as well. 'Aah can think of no better way ti go,' was his answer.

As Joe turned to leave the tack-room, his father spoke again.

''Ow long were you and Mary planning to stay?' he asked.

'We thought we'd leave it till the end of April; see the countryside at its best.' Joe felt relieved that the expected outburst from his father had not materialised.

'If Aah was thoo, Aah'd mek it sooner, rather than later.' Jonadab's voice was calm as he delivered his ultimatum. 'Aah'm sorry, Joseph' The depth of his emotion was shown in the use of his son's full name. 'Aah think it's for t'best if thoo goes 'ome now, or finds somewhere else ti stop. Thoo's turned out ti be t'serpent in our Eden and it's best for us all if thoo leaves.'

Chapter Ten

Two years had passed since Joseph and Mary's departure; although Sarah received letters from Mary, the only person Joseph communicated with was Tamar. Not only were her title and life-style something to boast about, now he was at home once more, but he had hopes that she would invite Georgie and Jeanette over to Thorsbury in recompense for Victoria's visit to Canada.

Victoria remained unmarried. Since Francis Sturdy's apparent rejection of her, she had discouraged any other admirers and refused several offers of marriage. Despite Tamar's pleas, she was adamant.

'I don't want to get married just for the sake of it,' she stated. 'I want a good marriage, like yours and Papa's. Yours is the happiest and strongest marriage that I've seen.'

Tamar felt a sharp pang of guilt. Only she knew that she had not always been faithful to Stephen. Her affair with his groom, Gareth Davis, had lasted undetected until the latter's violent death in an accident. However, the feeling was shortlived. Her secret was safe and she quickly pushed it back into the deepest recesses of her mind.

'I'm quite happy, Mama, honestly,' Victoria assured her. 'I loved Thomas deeply, but I am getting over the loss. Obviously, I wish I could have kept Tommy with me, but at least I know he's safe with Gertie. Perhaps one day, when I'm a middle-aged old maid, she may come back to England and I could adopt him.'

Although this statement was accompanied by a smile, Tamar knew that the hope was genuine. 'Gertie will regard him as her own,' she cautioned. 'I think you should put the hope of seeing him again out of your mind.

Victoria smiled sadly. 'I suppose you're right,' she replied.

'Anyway,' her mother went on, 'Francis hasn't been snared yet. He's kept that little chit Caroline Chelton dangling for over two years now, and she still hasn't got him to the altar. I hear her mother's casting about for bigger fish.'

Victoria was thoughtful. 'I suppose I felt hurt that he didn't wait for me,' she reflected. 'But to choose such an empty-headed, immature creature in my place was adding insult to injury.'

'There's one thing certain,' Tamar said, fondly assessing Victoria's looks, which were still as outstandingly striking as they had ever been. 'If Mrs Chelton doesn't get Caroline married off soon, she'll be left on the shelf. She's no good bone structure to speak of. Her prettiness depends on her colouring – and she'll fade early.'

A few weeks after this conversation, when Hodgetts brought the post to the breakfast table, Tamar was surprised to receive a letter from Canada in a hand she did not recognise.

'This isn't from Joe,' she said, slitting the seal. After the first line or two, she looked up. 'Listen to this!' she exclaimed.

'Dear Madam,

'I am the pastor of Portage la Prairie and I am writing to you on behalf of Mrs McDonald, who was, I understand, in your employ before coming to Canada. Her husband has been killed in an accident and she is left with no means of support for herself and her imbecile child . . .'

Tamar's voice died away. 'Imbecile child?' Her tone was disbelieving, as they looked at each other in horror.

'He can't mean Tommy,' Victoria gasped.

Tamar looked down at the letter and continued,

' . . . I am, therefore, writing on her behalf to ask if you are able and willing to do anything to help her, as she has no family of her own.

'I am, madam, your obedient servant,

John McCormick.'

The three seated at the table were devastated. Victoria began to weep.

'I can't believe that Tommy's an idiot. He was only a

couple of months old when I left him, but he seemed normal. He gurgled and laughed as babies do.'

Tamar was stunned. Tommy was the child of an incestuous relationship and she assumed the whole blame for this dreadful outcome. Her only grandchild was tainted through her own affair with Sir William Forster, who had seduced Tamar when she was an ignorant country girl, and left her pregnant. Stephen had married her and adopted the child, Victoria, only later coming to know her true parentage. Tamar could never reveal to Victoria that Tommy's father was her own half-brother. 'The sins of the mothers are visited upon the children,' was the thought that sprang sadly to her mind. Thomas Forster had died after learning the truth of his relationship with Victoria.

At that moment, Tamar wished vehemently that she could live her life over again.

Stephen looked at his wife's stricken face. 'This is a blow, but we must do our best for the boy,' he stated. 'And for Gertie, of course,' he added. 'She's been a faithful servant to us and we must do all we can in her hour of need.'

Victoria looked at him pleadingly. 'Oh, Papa, can we bring them back? I never thought to see Tommy again, but he must come home to us. He must!'

Stephen was thoughtful. 'There's a lot to be considered. If they come back, you can never acknowledge him as your child. In addition, he will be constantly before you, as a reminder of your lapse. His presence will make life difficult for you, my dear.'

'I don't care. I don't care!' She broke into sobs once more. 'I feel that this is Fate, giving me a chance to have him back.'

Tamar added her weight to the argument. 'Number thirteen in the village is empty,' she reminded her husband. 'We could furnish it and settle them there.'

Although, lawyer-like, Stephen tried to assess the options dispassionately, Victoria and Tamar were insistent that Tommy and Gertie should be sent for, so he eventually agreed and sent a banker's draft for Mr McCormick to make the travel arrangements for Gertie and the boy. Any surplus money was to be used as a donation to his church.

'I wonder why Joe didn't write and tell us?' Tamar mused.

Realising that her mother could have no idea of the vast distances of the prairies, Victoria explained, 'Joe's place is a long way from Portage la Prairie, which is the only settlement for hundreds of miles. When Gertie got married, she moved as far the other way from the Fort.'

The negotiations took several weeks, but eventually all was arranged and Tamar and Victoria set off for Liverpool to await the ship's arrival.

Hilary, who was home from school for the holidays, was at a loss to understand all the fuss. 'Why does Gertie want to come back? According to Uncle Joe, Canada's the land of opportunity. I'd have thought she'd be better off there!'

'No land offers many opportunities for a widow with a child,' his father replied. 'Gertie has served us well since Victoria was a little girl, and we owe it to her to do our best now that she's left in difficulties. One day this estate will be yours and you must learn to care for it. Our greatest asset is our workers and you must remember to look after their welfare. A contented worker serves his master best.'

Victoria and Tamar stood on the quayside, eagerly straining for their first glimpse of Gertie and the child. As the throng of passengers jostled down the gangplank, they caught sight of the familiar figure, shabbily-dressed and with a pathetically small bundle clutched in one hand, a little boy astride her hip.

'Gertie! Gertie!' Their voices rang out in unison above the surrounding hubbub and, as Gertie's eyes scanned the crowd on the dockside, their frantic waves caught her attention. Breaking into a smile, she waved back, saying something to Tommy and pointing.

When the two groups came together, there was the merest fraction of embarrassment, each unsure of how to greet the other and then Victoria threw her arms round the maid, kissing her cheek. Hungrily she looked at the child, searching his features for some trace of either herself or Thomas.

There was none. The child who peered at her shyly from Gertie's shoulder resembled neither of them. His hair, which was still in the ringlets of babyhood, was mid-brown with golden lights, while the grave eyes which stared at them solemnly, were large and hazel.

'Tommy.' As she breathed his name, Victoria held out her arms, but he was overwhelmed by the strangers and turned his face into Gertie's bosom.

They had moved into a small hotel for the night, so as not to make Gertie feel uncomfortable in the grand surroundings of their previous accommodation. Both Tamar and Victoria were entranced by Tommy who, rather than being slow-witted, appeared to be a child of high intelligence.

This was confirmed by Gertie. ''E's bright as a button, Miss Victoria,' she affirmed. Make no mistake about that, no matter what anybody says.'

'Why doesn't he speak?' Tamar asked. 'He's not deaf, so why is he mute?'

''E wasn't mute, until 'is dad was drownded,' came Gertie's reply.

They had no real knowledge of what had happened, so Gertie settled down to recount the whole tale.

'Ben McDonald was a good man, and he took to Tommy as if 'e was 'is own,' she began. 'One day 'e took t'little lad out wi' 'im, collecting fallen trees along t'lakeside, to saw into logs. While 'e was busy loading t'cart, Tommy wandered on to t'lake. The ice was breaking up.' She paused for breath, her eyes far away, obviously affected by the memory of that day. After a while, she continued, 'It was 'orrible. Aah saw it all from t'cabin. Ben ran out on to t'ice and grabbed Tommy and threw 'im clear. At that very moment it cracked and broke, just where poor Ben was standing. He went down, right in front of Tommy's eyes and t'bairn 'as never spoke since.'

Her listeners were silent. Even though Gertie's range of vocabulary was limited, the stark simplicity of the tale conjured up the scene vividly for them.

Tamar was the first to break the silence. 'I'm sorry,

Gertie.' She placed her hand on the maid's and squeezed it. 'Until then, did Tommy seem normal?'

'Normal? 'E was as right as rain. 'E could say a lot of words and was beginning to string 'em together an' all.'

They sat in thoughtful silence, each going over Gertie's tale. While Gertie was obviously still affected by the memory of her husband's death, the other two were absorbing the news about Tommy.

'If he's talked once, do you think he could talk again?' Victoria voiced both her own and Tamar's hopes.

'I can't see why not,' replied her mother. 'We must do our best for him.'

Gertie looked from one to the other. 'Thoo won't tek 'im from me, will you, Miss Victoria?' Her voice was husky with emotion and her eyes were tear-brimmed. ''E's all Aah've got left, now.'

Before Victoria could answer, Tamar spoke for her daughter. 'Of course not, Gertie. You took Tommy for us and, as far as anyone is concerned, he's your son. Nobody but us knows any differently, apart from my husband.'

'Oh, thank thoo, m'Lady.' If either Gertie or Tamar noticed the shadow of disappointment which crossed Victoria's face, it was ignored. Turning to her, Gertie burst out, ''Ere, Aah'm calling thoo "Miss Victoria" an' thoo's probably Mrs Sturdy by now.'

'No, Gertie, I'm still unmarried,' answered Victoria. 'Mr Sturdy had chosen somebody else when I reached home.' She smiled wryly at the maid's astonished expression.

'Why, Aah thought at least thoo'd be betrothed, if not married,' she exclaimed. ''E pledged ti wait.'

'We all make promises we don't keep I'm afraid, Gertie,' Victoria answered sadly.

Gertie and Tommy were soon established in the cottage prepared by the Lassiters about halfway down the village of Thorsbury, next to the church. Compared with her Canadian log-cabin home, the two-bedroomed cottage of honey-coloured stone was snug and cosy.

'Aah can't tell thoo 'ow grateful me and Tommy is, m'Lady,' she often told Tamar.

'Nonsense, Gertie. It's the least we can do.' Tamar considered that it was they who were in Gertie's debt.

Tempy, who had been in service with Gertie at Stephen Lassiter's Helmsley home when Tamar had been his housekeeper, was delighted to see her old friend back in England and came up the village to visit her.

'By gum, thoo's fallen on thi feet!' was her exclamation, upon looking round Gertie's house. 'Sir Stephen and Lady Tamar 'ave certainly looked after thoo.' She stared at Gertie curiously. 'They paid for thoo ti come back and furnished this place, didn't they?'

'Aye, they did an' all.' Gertie nodded.

Tempy was still not entirely satisfied. 'What made 'em do that?' She pushed for more information.

Gertie considered before replying. 'Well, it was the pastor in Canada who wrote a letter to 'em when Ben, mi 'usband, was killed. A pastor's like a vicar,' she explained. 'T'next Aah knew, Sir Stephen 'ad sent t'money and all was arranged.'

'Aye, they're a grand family ti work for. Aah don't know of any other that would be so kind.' Tempy was quite satisfied with Gertie's explanation. 'What's up wi' t'little lad, then?' she asked, nodding towards Tommy, who was playing on the hearthrug.

'T'shock of seeing 'is dad drownded took 'is speech,' Gertie replied.

So, in due course, her story circulated round the village and all the estate employees agreed that the Lassiters were grand folk to work for.

Tamar and Victoria talked at length as to what they could do to help Tommy to speak again.

'Why don't we go to the healing well in Sleightholmedale?' Victoria suggested. 'We could stay for a few days with Auntie Martha and Uncle Bob.'

Tamar hesitated. She flinched from the thought of her father's penetrating gaze falling upon Tommy. On reflection, however, she was satisfied that he bore no resemblance at all to his true mother.

'It's a good idea,' she answered. 'It will cost nothing to try and people come from all over, both to bathe and to drink the waters.'

Victoria rode up the village the next day and called in at Gertie's. She dare not call too frequently, and yet she found it difficult to keep away from Tommy. He recognised her tap on the door and ran to meet her. Seeing the horse tethered outside, he clapped his hands and chuckled with delight. Swinging him up into her arms, Victoria carried him to the horse.

'Horsey,' she said, holding him up to stroke it. 'Say "horsey", Tommy.'

He fondled the creature, stroking its face and showing not a trace of fear. He made no attempt to speak, however.

When she went into the cottage, Victoria was full of enthusiasm.

'Mama is making arrangements for us to take Tommy to the healing well down in Sleightholmedale, where my grandfather lives,' she told Gertie. 'I do hope the water cures him.'

Gertie's eyes shone. 'Oh, Miss!' she exclaimed. 'Aah hopes as 'ow it works.' Turning to the little boy she said softly, 'Thoo knows what's said, love, doesn't thoo?'

His face broke into a smile as he nodded his head vigorously and pointed to his mouth.

Victoria sighed. 'He's so bright,' she said pensively. 'We must find a way to cure him.'

It was mid-June before the arrangements were made. Victoria, Gertie and Tommy travelled in the Lassiter coach to Cherry Tree Farm. Martha had fully recovered from the trauma of her miscarriage and had recently become pregnant again. Time had healed not only her physical wounds, but also the hurt and bitterness she had felt towards her niece on learning from Mary the true reason behind Victoria's visit to Canada. She was also curious to see 'Gertie's son'.

'I suppose it'll be someone for Maria to play with,' she conceded to Bob, who was at a loss to understand her slight reluctance to entertain Victoria.

As the coach trundled down the Dale, Gertie took in the views. The trees covering the steep escarpment down which the road snaked were in full leaf; in the dappled shade beneath them, among the curling fronds of bracken, was a wealth of summer flowers, while on the verges at the side of the track, the pea flowers of vetch and bird's foot trefoil struggled towards the sun from amid the grass.

'By 'eck, Miss.' Gertie's face was a picture. 'It's t'loveliest place Aah've ever seen.'

'Yes, Gertie. It is.' No matter how often Victoria came down into the Dale, she never ceased to appreciate its beauty and tranquillity.

The peace was broken, however, when they reached the valley floor. From the direction of the beck came the sound of shouting and splashing, together with the bleating of sheep.

'Stop a minute,' Victoria called to the coachman. 'We'll take Tommy across the field to see the sheep being dipped.'

Each taking a hand, they ran and swung the little boy towards the commotion. The beck had been dammed to create a deep pool, through which the sheep were being driven, before reaching the freedom of the moor that swept upwards on the far side. Tommy clapped his hands in glee, showing no fear either of the animals or of the men who drove them into the water with much yelling and waving.

Jonadab came towards them and Victoria could not help but notice how heavily he now leaned upon his stick.

'And who's this, then?' He addressed the little boy, looking down at him. Although his height and fierce expression must have appeared awesome to Tommy, the child was not intimidated.

As Victoria answered, 'This is Tommy, Gertie's little boy,' the child cocked his head on one side and gave the old man a broad smile.

Jonadab knew about Tommy's muteness and had presumed that the child was simple-minded, but now, noting the lively expression and intelligent eyes, he revised his opinion.

'Thoo's a lively lad, isn't thoo?' His face softened in a rare smile and it was obvious that there was an instant rapport between the two.

The week spent at Cherry Tree Farm was in many ways idyllic. During the long golden days, Victoria and Gertie played with the children, encouraging Tommy to help with the animals, gather wild flowers and run about the fields surrounding the farm.

Of all his new activities, however, what Tommy enjoyed most was to be led by the hand and shown around the loose boxes with their huge grey occupants, whinnying and neighing as he stroked their shaggy manes. Day after day, Victoria and Gertie would take him up the lane to Aumery Park Farm for this special treat.

'Come on then, lad,' Jonadab would say fondly, pleased to have someone who shared his love of horses. 'Let's see what yon 'osses is up ti today.'

Tommy would look to Victoria for permission, all the time unable to conceal his eagerness.

'Yes, Tommy, you can go with Mr Oaks,' Victoria would reply. 'But don't be a nuisance.'

One morning Jonadab hesitated before leading the child out of the kitchen. 'It's a load o' daft, all this "Mr Oaks" business. Let t'bairn call me Grandad, like t'rest of 'em.'

Victoria managed to hide the blush which threatened to expose the truth that the old man was, in reality, Tommy's great-grandfather. She faltered, but seeing the look of pride in Tommy's eyes, instantly agreed.

'It dissent seem right some'ow, Mr Oaks,' Gertie put in worriedly. 'It's not seemly.' Then, noticing the looks of disappointment on both Janadab and Tommy's faces, she added, 'But if thoo's sure thoo dissent mind, Aah can't see as 'ow it can do any 'arm. An' it'll be easier ti say when 'e gets 'is speech back.'

Although the time he spent with Jonadab and the animals was of enormous benefit to Tommy, the waters of the spa, alas, failed to cure him.

Upon the advice of the couple who ran the bath-house, they tried massaging his throat with the water and also, making him drink it. His first taste brought a look of horror to Tommy's face and he spat out the mouthful.

'You must drink it,' exhorted Victoria, 'it'll make you better. Come along now,' and she held the glass to his lips.

It was too much for Tommy's normally sunny nature and he dashed the glass from her hand, bursting into tears, lips tightly clenched together and shaking his head.

The bath-house attendant seized his arms while his wife nipped the writhing child's nose and poured the liquid down his throat.

'Stop! Stop!' Victoria cried. 'We can't have him upset.' As the man released Tommy, Gertie gathered him into her arms, patting him solicitously.

'There, there,' she soothed. 'No more nasty water. We'll just bathe thi throat next time.'

There was no result, however, and at the end of the week, when the coach came for them, they left Sleightholmedale disappointed and disconsolate.

'Something *must* be done,' vowed Victoria. 'He shall not be the butt of the village children's jokes.' She felt that it was Tommy's birthright to have the chance of an education and a normal life. He was after all, her son and Thomas'.

Chapter Eleven

'Who's that, Aah wonder?' Although Tommy made no effort to speak, Gertie talked to him constantly. Not only was he her one companion, unless Tempy popped in, but she chattered incessantly in the hope that, by some miracle, he would one day reply.

The crisp knock on the door had come as she was busy preparing the midday meal, one dull day in early January, half a year since Tommy's visit to Sleightholmedale Spa. Straightening her apron and smoothing her hair, she hurried to answer the door as another series of staccato raps sounded.

'All right, all right. Aah'm coming,' she muttered, lifting the latch. The man who stood there seemed to fill the doorway and, as Gertie peered up into his face, she caught her breath in disbelief. 'Ben?' She felt quite faint, but recovered upon realising that the visitor, although bearing a startling resemblance to her dead husband, could not be Ben.

'Who is it? What does thoo want?' she asked, with a tremor in her voice. The man seemed so huge that she felt uneasy.

'Let me in, Gertie,' he replied brusquely, stepping over the threshold.

Overawed by his size, she moved back and he brushed past her into the kitchen.

'This is Tommy then, is it?' He bent down and ruffled the child's hair.

Gertie felt panic rising within her. 'Who is thoo? 'Ow does thoo know us names?' Her voice was shrill, betraying her nervousness and the man's lips curved into a smile. His eyes, however, remained cold.

'A fine way to greet your brother-in-law,' he replied.

'Brother-in-law? Ben's brother?' She was incredulous. 'But thoo was in Canada.'

'Aye, and so were you,' Rob McDonald answered. 'You've taken some tracking down.'

Gertie was bewildered. She had known than Ben had a brother, the restless one; driven from place to place and job to job, always seeking his El Dorado. 'He wants something nobody sells,' Ben had often told her in his soft Scottish brogue.

Still at a loss to know how he had found her and why, she indicated a chair by the scrubbed deal table.

'Sit thissen down and 'ave a bit o' dinner,' she invited. 'There's not much, but as Ben's brother, thoo's very welcome.'

She placed a breadboard with a crusty loaf, and a knife on the table and ladled hot stew into three dishes. It contained no meat, but was thick with vegetables. Warm and filling, it was the staple diet of Gertie and Tommy. They ate in silence and it was not until the man pushed away his empty dish, sighing with satisfaction, that either spoke.

'Why . . . ?' Gertie began, but he interrupted.

'You'll want to know my business,' he stated.

Gertie nodded. 'It's very nice of thoo ti come and see me, now you're in England, but 'ow's thoo found us?' And why, she added to herself.

He nodded towards the boy, who was looking from one to the other, intrigued by the stranger.

'I've come to see my nephew – my poor, dead brother's lad.' As he made the statement, his lips curved again in a satisfied smile. 'This is your Uncle Robbie, Tommy,' he said. 'Say hello!'

''E can't talk,' Gertie flushed. Every one of her acquaintance knew of Tommy's disability and accepted it.

There had been one rather ugly incident, a few months earlier, when Victoria, riding down the village, had come across Tommy, crouched by the churchyard wall, surrounded by a ring of children. She had been horrified and distressed to see them pushing and poking him, with taunts of 'Dummy! Dummy! Cat's got thi tongue-y!'

Sliding down from her horse, she had berated them

soundly, cuffing a few ears and they, in fear of their fathers' jobs, had left him alone ever since.

Now Gertie was embarrassed, afraid that her brother-in-law would dismiss the child as simple-minded.

''E's bright enough,' she said defensively. 'The shock of seeing Ben drownded took 'is speech.'

Rob sat in silence for a few minutes. Taking a pipe from his pocket, he filled it with a plug of tobacco, pressing it down thoughtfully, before pushing a spill into the fire and lighting it. Drawing a deep breath of smoke, he looked at her.

'That won't suit the Lassiters,' he said softly. 'Having a simpleton for a grandson.'

Gertie went cold. She had heard of jaws dropping, and hers did just that. Mouth agape and eyes wide, she stared at him as if mesmerised. Recovering her wits, she turned to Tommy who was staring at his uncle, looking puzzled. Hurriedly, she pushed him towards the back door. 'Pop out into t'back an' play for a bit, love. Put thi coat on an' wrap up warm. Go on, pet.' Then, turning back to her brother-in-law, she said spiritedly, 'Whatever dost thoo mean? With Ben for 'is dad and me for 'is mam, 'ow can 'e 'ave owt ti do with t'Lassiters?'

It was a vain attempt at bluster. His eyes narrowed and his smile was cocksure.

'You don't think I'd have got the Lassiters' address from the parson at Portage la Prairie, worked my passage over to England and found this benighted hole, if I'd any doubts, do you?'

Gertie saw no point in denying it any longer. With Tommy safely out of earshot, she broke down. 'Nobody else knows.' She spoke pleadingly. 'Thoo'll not say owt, will thoo?'

His laugh was sardonic – a short, sharp bark. '*I* know; that's just the point. Ben wrote and told me the whole story when they paid him to marry you and take their bastard.'

Gertie crimsoned with humiliation. 'There might 'ave been money exchanged, but Ben loved me. We was 'appy together.' She glanced towards the back door, to make sure

Tommy was not listening. ''E doted on t'lad an' all,' she added.

Rob drew on his pipe reflectively. 'Aye, well. There'll be others that dote on him,' he said calculatingly, 'and that's why I'm here.'

As he revealed his intentions, Gertie felt her whole world crumbling.

'All my life I've been searching for my crock of gold,' he continued, looking at her with satisfaction. 'Now I've found it. The Lassiters will keep me in comfort for the rest of my life, or the whole world will know of their daughter's shame.'

Gertie could not believe that she was hearing right. She felt perspiration beading her top lip and she began to shiver uncontrollably. She had been Victoria's companion and maid since being taken from the workhouse at the age of ten. She adored her mistress and could not bear the thought of her secret being exposed.

Breaking into sobs, Gertie mumbled at him, 'Oh, thoo evil, wicked man. Ow can thoo be my poor Ben's brother? T'Lassiters 'ave done nowt ti thoo. Why should thoo persecute 'em?'

He sneered at her naivety. 'They have what I want: money! And now I've got a way of transferring some of theirs to me.' This statement was made, slowly and clearly, as though he were addressing a child.

Gertie began to cry again as Tommy lifted the latch. He ran to her, climbing on to her lap and pressing his cheek against hers, not knowing the reason for her distress, but wanting to comfort his mother, as he still believed her to be. Eventually, her head splitting with the thoughts that were chasing round it, she put the child down and, rising from her chair, gathered the pots from the table. When she had put them in the enamel bowl in the tiny scullery, she carried the kettle through and began to wash up.

What was she to do? She was sick with worry, feeling that in some way she had failed Victoria.

Upon returning to the living room, she still had no idea of what was to be done.

'Where's thoo stopping?' she asked him sullenly.

'Why, here of course,' came the reply. She blenched. How could she allow this creature of menace to share her home? Looking at his size, she knew she would never feel safe with him in the house.

'Thoo can't stop 'ere,' she protested swiftly. ''Tisn't seemly.'

'Nonsense,' he retorted sharply. 'Many a widow takes a lodger – and what's more natural than a man coming to stay with his sister-in-law? And little nephew, of course,' he added, with a wolfish grin towards the child.

The little room, with the firelight playing on the old oak beams and whitewashed walls had seemed a safe haven; now Gertie felt trapped in its confines.

Rob sat before the fire, deep in thought. 'Are the Lassiters at home?' he demanded.

'Lady Lassiter and Miss Victoria are,' she replied. 'Sir Stephen's away on business.'

'Right, you can leave the laddie here with me and get yourself down there. Tell them I've come and why. Ask one of them to come up here. I want a word with them.'

'I can't do that,' protested Gertie. 'Thoo doesn't tell t'gentry what to do.'

'Well, in this case you do! I've got the whip hand and they'd better believe it.'

Reluctantly, Gertie took her cloak from a nail behind the door and then looked uncertainly at Tommy.

'Bugger me!' Rob exclaimed in exasperation. 'He'll be all right. I'm not likely to harm my trump card, am I?'

'Aah won't be long, Tommy love,' she told the boy, going from the cottage.

It had begun to rain steadily and the afternoon was sombre under the heavy, rolling clouds. Pulling the cloak tightly round her, Gertie ran down the village street. Passing through the wrought-iron gates, she scurried to the back door of the Manor. It was opened by one of the footmen, in answer to her tap.

'Lord, Gertie! What are you doing out in this lot?' he asked as he swung back the door and let her in.

She stood for a moment with her back to the door, breathless, her hair clinging streakily to her face.

'Is Miss Victoria in?' she asked wildly. 'Aah must see 'er. It's important.' She slipped off her drenched cloak. 'Can this be put to dry while Aah 'as a word wi' Miss Victoria, please, Mrs Earnshaw?' she asked the cook. 'It's urgent,' she entreated desperately, sensing the woman's hesitation. It wasn't done to allow the lower orders the run of the house, but Gertie, like Tempy, was more than a mere employee.

'Aye, all right then,' capitulated the cook.

Gertie was relieved to find Victoria alone in the library when her tap received the command to enter. As she slipped through the door, Victoria's eyebrows rose and her forehead creased in a frown.

'Whatever's wrong, Gertie? Is it Tommy?' she enquired anxiously.

'No, Miss.' Gertie was at a loss as to how to frame her story.

'Sit down,' Victoria instructed and Gertie perched on the edge of one of the green leather chairs.

'Aah doesn't rightly know 'ow ti tell thoo, Miss,' she began tearfully. 'But Aah've brought trouble to thoo all.'

Bunching up a piece of rag which served as a handkerchief, and dabbing at her eyes and tear-runnelled cheeks, Gertie haltingly poured out her tale.

Victoria's horror grew with each fresh revelation. 'This is blackmail,' she gasped. 'You're sure he means it? He's not just joking?'

Gertie's mind recalled the cold slits of eyes and the cruel mouth.

'No, Miss.' She spoke with the calmness of despair, drained of all emotion. ''E doesn't look as if 'e's got a joke in 'im. 'E means it, all right. There's nowt so sure.'

Victoria began to pace up and down the room in agitation. Pressing her hands to her forehead, she paused. 'I must find Mama. She'll know what to do.'

As she went out of the library, Gertie thought miserably, 'We'll be lucky if anybody can do owt, except pay t'sod!'

When Victoria returned accompanied by her mother, Tamar's normal vivacity was absent. Looking soberly at Gertie, she said, 'Now, begin at the beginning and tell me every word that was said.'

As Gertie obliged, Tamar's face became more grave, while Victoria's vivid beauty faded, as her face paled and her nostrils became pinched. As the story unfolded, the two women exchanged looks of consternation.

'Oh, Mama, what are we to do?' Victoria's voice trembled.

'We certainly can't have him disclose what he knows,' asserted Tamar. 'There's not only your reputation at stake, but the Lassiter name and Hilary's career.'

Hilary was now almost sixteen and university material. With his brains and the Lassiter money, a brilliant future lay ahead of him: there was no way his mother would allow that to be jeopardised. Gertie made a tentative suggestion.

'Wouldn't it be better for Sir Stephen ti see 'im, m'Lady? Mebbe 'e'd 'andle it better . . . bein' a man.'

Tamar pressed her hands to her aching head. 'No. My husband would call in the police. He would never countenance paying blackmail. He is a trained lawyer and would never condone a crime.' Besides, she thought grimly, I'm a match for any man!

A sudden thought struck her like a hammer blow. If the story ever came out, her own family knew the name of Victoria's true father. Putting two and two together, they would learn that Victoria's son was the product of an incestuous relationship. Her stomach knotted up into a tight ball and she felt sick at the thought of their reaction, especially her father's. And Victoria must never know.

Glancing out of the window, she saw that it was almost dusk, the dark dreary day drawing early to its close.

'Go home, Gertie. Miss Victoria and I will follow shortly. We'll let it get a bit darker, first. We don't want tongues to wag.'

When, after a perfunctory interval, they entered Gertie's kitchen, it was to find the stranger occupying the only comfortable chair beside the fire, while Gertie sat at the table, Tommy upon her knee. The child's face lightened as Victoria entered and he proudly held up the picture he had drawn with wax crayons.

'Lovely, Tommy,' she praised, and forced a smile.

The man made no effort to rise, merely eyed them coolly over the fumes of his pipe.

'I think it's time Tommy was in bed,' Tamar announced crisply.

Picking up the child, Gertie hurried up the steep stairs, glad to be away from the heavily-charged atmosphere. Although she dallied over undressing the boy and putting him in her own bed, she could hear no voices from down below and realised, with a sinking heart, that the discussion would not start until her return.

She gave Tommy a kiss, tucked the bedclothes round him and reluctantly descended the stairs. The room was as she had left it. Rob McDonald leaned back almost placidly in the fireside chair, puffing away at his pipe, while the two women sat at the table in silence, arms on it, faces set.

Looking across at her brother-in-law, Gertie marvelled. It could be a larger edition of Ben seated there and yet, how different he was! Ben had been a kind and gentle man, whereas who knew to what depths his brother would stoop.

'Sit down, Gertie.' Tamar indicated a chair. Turning to McDonald she said curtly, 'Well?'

He looked across at the Lassiter women admiringly. They were a couple of beauties, and no mistake. Seeing Tamar's narrowed, feline eyes glowing in the lamplight, the thought crossed his mind, 'I bet the mother's a hard bugger.'

'I expect Gertie's given you my message, or you'd not be here,' he said aloud. 'Well, eventually we all pay for our sins and the time has come for you, young lady, to pay for yours.'

'And what about yours?' flashed Tamar. 'You'll burn in Hell for eternity, when the time comes!'

A glimmer of amusement crossed his face, although his eyes remained cold and fathomless. 'The day my time comes, I'll have had a dammed good life – with your help, of course. I shan't care what happens next. I don't fear the afterworld – there isn't one. When you're six foot under, you're six foot under, and that's that! It's up to every man to get what he can in this life.'

'Cut the cackle!' Tamar's carefully disciplined years of making herself a lady were being peeled away, like layers of onion. 'Spit it out!'

Victoria's eyes widened. She had never heard her genteel mother use such phrases. Still he did not speak. He eyed them calculatingly, trying to assess what they were worth. Their clothes were expensive and Tamar's throat wore the milky translucence of pearls. He had not yet seen Thorsbury Manor. The village street curved below Gertie's cottage and the house was out of view, so he had no idea of its size and splendour.

He weighed things carefully in his mind. He wanted to screw them for as much as they could afford, and yet he had no desire to ask for more than they could meet, otherwise it might prove a job for the police. 'Never mind,' he told himself, 'I can always come for another bite at the cherry.'

Tamar's voice interrupted his debate. 'How much?'

'How much do you value your daughter's honour?' Glancing across at Victoria, he gave a suggestive smirk. 'Not that she has any left.'

Victoria flushed hotly and looked away from the eyes which raked her.

He went on, 'I've no idea why Tommy's father didn't marry her. It might have been a tumble in the hay with one of the grooms, for all I know. I only know that her bastard's been farmed out and you'll be set to foist her on some unsuspecting nobleman as pure and untouched. To further that plan must be worth quite a bit.'

Victoria had lain her head in her hands on the table, scarlet with humiliation and sobbing quietly. Her love affair with Thomas Forster had been wonderful and this obnoxious creature was making it feel dirty and sordid.

Her mother's voice cut through her thoughts. 'Pull yourself together, Victoria. Don't let this toad upset you.' Turning her blazing eyes on McDonald she repeated, 'How much, I said?'

'Give me twenty pounds to be going on with. I'm about broke.' Tamar's eyes widened in surprise and relief, but his next statement caused her heart to plummet. 'And then I want five thousand pounds – and soon. I don't want to stay in this dump any longer than necessary.'

Tamar was shaken. Although Stephen was generous, never begrudging money for clothes for her or Victoria, she had no real funds of her own; just a few hundred pounds from her allowance, which was paid quarterly into the bank at Malton. True, Stephen had settled some shares on her upon their marriage, but she had no idea how to sell them. Besides, Stephen's stockbroker was in Leeds and a visit to the city would need to be explained.

Frantically, she searched her mind for a solution. Bringing her thoughts back to the present situation, she decided to tackle one problem at time.

'I've brought no money with me,' she said, 'but Gertie may come down to the house tomorrow and I'll send you twenty pounds. That must suffice for the time being. As for the rest, I don't know how I can meet your demands.' She thought it best to lay her cards on the table. 'I have no money of my own. My husband supplies all my needs and I don't know how I can lay my hands on such a large sum.'

The light from the fire played on his expression, which was ugly. 'Find it you will, Lady Lassiter. I've not come here for no recompense. This is my chance to start a spread of my own back in Canada, and I'm determined to take it. Your husband's got a pile.'

Tamar's lips compressed in a hard line. 'If a whisper of this reaches my husband, he'll bring in the police and be blowed to the consequences,' she retorted.

Victoria made a low moaning sound. 'Oh, no,' she breathed.

Tamar's heart bled for the girl, who was suffering because she had inherited her own passionate nature. No matter how she did it, she was determined to save her daughter from public disgrace. The girl was a replica of herself in every way, and she would fight like a tiger to save her.

Taking Victoria's hand and giving it a squeeze, she turned once more to McDonald. 'I shall find some way of raising the money,' she told him, with a confidence she did not feel, 'but you must give me time.'

'I'm not giving you much bloody time,' he threatened. 'I can't see me stopping down here for long. What anybody finds to do here, God only knows – there's no pub, no shops, nothing.'

Tamar had had time to recover her spirits and now the steely core, which she hid so well, was once again in evidence.

'If you want the money, you'll have to wait,' she snapped. 'I can't work miracles, but I've said I'll get it and get it I will.'

With this he had to be satisfied, and she and Victoria took their leave of Gertie by the door.

'Will you be all right?' Victoria whispered, indicating McDonald to show her meaning.

'Aah don't know, Miss,' Gertie mouthed back, looking fearfully over her shoulder at the man who was staring into the fire.

Squeezing her hand, Victoria said, 'I'll be back in the morning,' and followed her mother into the night.

Neither spoke until they reached the privacy of Tamar's bedroom. Once there, Victoria broke into a torrent of tears.

'Oh, Mama, I'm sorry. I seem to have brought you nothing but worry.'

'Nonsense!' Tamar was brisk and businesslike. 'It's no use crying over spilt milk. What's done is done and we must find a way of coping.'

Raising tear-filled eyes, Victoria blurted out, 'But how are we to raise such a large amount?'

Tamar did a mental inventory of her jewels. The most valuable were kept in the bank vault and she knew that the topaz set, bought for her by Stephen on her betrothal, were not worth such a great sum.

Sighing deeply, she made no reply for the moment. Then, an idea began to form in her mind. Victoria was William Forster's daughter, as well as her own. It was about time he did something for his child. Apart from Stephen, he was the only person who knew of the affair between Victoria and her half-brother, and even he had no knowledge of Tommy's birth.

Tamar's expression was ironic. She and William shared a grandchild that neither could acknowledge. She wondered what would be his reaction when he knew.

Turning to the daughter who was so dear to her, she placed a comforting arm round her shoulders. 'Don't worry, love. I think I've found a way out. It's a good thing your father is away. I hope we can keep the whole business from him. He has such high moral standards, I know he'd bring a prosecution if he found out.'

'It's such a large sum. However are you going to raise it without Papa knowing?'

Tamar's smile was quite cold and her tawny eyes bleak. She would enjoy taking Sir William Forster's money. He had not wanted to know her when she was expecting his child, but surely he could not refuse her request.

'Least said, soonest mended,' she replied. 'It's best that you don't know. Suffice it to say that I shall get it, don't worry.'

Chapter Twelve

Tamar's letter to William Forster was written with speed and dispatched the following day. She made no requests. It was a demand. She knew that, despite his excesses, Forster was still an exceedingly wealthy man, far richer than Stephen.

She wrote:

The affair between your daughter by me, and your son by your legal wife, resulted in the birth of a son. I am now being blackmailed by a scoundrel who has discovered the truth and threatens to reveal it to the newspapers.

'I have no need to emphasise the effect these disclosures will have, not only on our daughter, but also upon your wife. Until now, you have not helped Victoria in any way, even though she is your flesh and blood.

'I am now calling in the debt you owe us. I need five thousand pounds to pay off the blackmailer and I beg of you to send a banker's draft for this amount.

'I dare not tell my husband. You are my only hope. Victoria has your blood in her veins. Please help us.

Tamar Lassiter

All that could be done now was to await his reply and hope that McDonald contained himself in patience for a few weeks. The days seemed interminable. Sir William could of course, be out of the country for the winter months – she had no way of knowing. She had sent the letter to his seat in Leicestershire but, if he did happen to be abroad, would it be forwarded to him, or would it lie around, awaiting his homecoming?

Victoria grew pale and lost her sparkle. She even declined invitations to winter balls. Having once more been reunited with her child in the summer, she had regained much of enthusiasm for life, and had been enjoying the winter season – until a few weeks ago.

Stephen was concerned. Neither of his womenfolk seemed in their usual frame of mind. Victoria was lethargic and had no interest in anything, while Tamar was edgy and cantankerous.

'What's wrong with you both?' he queried.

Tamar looked out of the window. The day was dank and miserable, with a gusty wind and squally showers.

'Victoria worries about Tommy,' she replied. 'As for me,' she laughed evasively, 'this weather's my trouble. If only I could get out for a brisk ride, no doubt I'd feel better.' With that, Stephen must needs be satisfied.

Gertie's visitor had created quite a stir in the village. It was a tight-knit community, all the cottages housing either estate-workers or those living on the small pensions provided by Stephen. Strangers were rarely seen and for a newcomer to be living among them caused a ripple of excitement.

When Gertie went a few doors down to visit Tempy, the latter bombarded her with questions.

'Ow long's 'e stopping?' she asked.

Gertie wished she had never come and yet, to sit in the house with her brother-in-law once the daily work was done, was out of the question. She was terrified of him and her fear was almost a physical thing, like a rabbit before a stoat. When he raised his head and sniffed the air, she was certain that he could smell the terror which emanated from her.

'Aah dissent know. Aah 'asn't asked 'im,' she replied defensively.

Tempy sniffed. 'Well, thoo should. Does 'e pay any board?'

'Well, 'e 'asn't up to now. Aah 'asn't asked for any.' Gertie thought that she had better vouchsafe a little more information. ''E's Ben's only brother and, as 'e'd to come over ti England, 'e thought 'e'd come ti see us, and get ti know Tommy.'

'Is 'e married? 'As 'e any family?' Tempy wanted to

wheedle all she could from Gertie about the intriguing stranger.

Gertie began to get exasperated. '’E dissent say much. Aah've no idea.'

'Aah just thought as 'ow 'e might leave your Tommy a bit o' brass, if 'e's no other kin,' was Tempy's response.

The two had been friends for most of their lives. Gertie had gone to Stephen's house in Helmsley as a ten-year-old, to take charge of the two-year-old Victoria when Tempy, the housemaid, was fourteen. They were as close as sisters and yet Gertie could not confide in her.

True to her promise, Tamar had sent Rob McDonald the twenty pounds. Now, with money in his pocket, he took to walking most evenings the two and a half miles to the pub at Barton, the next village.

This increased Gertie's tension. She had noticed the way McDonald eyed her and was acutely conscious of her lack of protection against his lust. She fervently wished that she had a lock on her bedroom door, for she feared him all the more when he was drunk. As the days went by and Tamar had failed to obtain the larger sum, his temper was on a short fuse. At the beginning of his stay, he had made quite a fuss of Tommy, taking him on his knee and telling him enthralling stories about the animals and Indian tribes of the Northern Territories.

The child was fascinated. His days were normally dull and monotonous, with only his mother for company. He had no companions of his own age; the village children, although they no longer taunted him, still regarded him with mistrust. When the weather permitted, he would wander down to the buildings, watching the blacksmith or fondling the horses which he loved, but while the weather was unsettled, he was confined to the house.

However, at the beginning of Rob's stay with them, his uncle enlivened his days with the adventurous tales he told, and with the little figures and animals that he whittled out of wood. Lacking men's company, Tommy basked in the unaccustomed maleness of his uncle's presence, soon forgetting the fear which had emanated from his mother on the day of the man's arrival.

No matter how hard Gertie tried, there was no way she could encourage Tommy to speak. Although lively and intelligent, he remained mute. As the days dragged on and there was no communication from the Manor, Rob became more taciturn and brooding and Tommy's inability to answer him seemed to annoy him more each day.

'Aah'm getting afeared of 'im, Tempy,' Gertie confided to her friend one day. 'When 'e comes 'ome from Barton of an evening, 'e's often blind drunk – cussin' and swearin' till Aah shivers in mi bed.'

'Go down to t'Manor and tell Sir Stephen,' advised Tempy. ''E'll 'ave 'im chucked out. Aah've 'eard 'e's not too chuffed that 'e's 'ere.'

Sir Stephen's intervention was the last thing Gertie wanted. Absolute secrecy had been impressed upon her by Tamar. She was, however, uneasy to hear that Sir Stephen knew of Rob's presence and objected to it. He was, after all, her landlord and benefactor.

'Aah wish summat 'ud 'appen. Aah can't go on much longer,' Gertie thought to herself. ''Ow long's Lady Lassiter going ti be, afore t'money comes? She dissent 'ave 'im ti put up with!'

When McDonald came home from the inn that night, she lay in bed, listening to him pottering about downstairs, singing to himself as he made a pot of tea and got his supper.

''E'll eat me out of 'ouse and 'ome,' she thought, tensing herself in bed. The creak of the fifth stair came to her ears and she held her breath, waiting for the sound of his bedroom door. The click of the latch, when it came, was ominously close.

Although no chink of light came through her door, Gertie could smell the tobacco smoke that permeated her brother-in-law's clothes and knew that he was in her room, feeling his way towards her bed. That he was in his stockinged feet there was no doubt, as there was no sound, although she knew he was drawing closer.

Her body was rigid with apprehension and she felt the sweat trickling down her forehead and coursing between her breasts. The smell of drink on his breath was suddenly all around her. Slipping a hand under her pillow, she seized the rolling pin which she now placed there every night. As his strong hands grasped her shoulders, she brought it down with all her might. The weight of his body landing on her knocked the breath out of her, but she pushed the senseless hulk on to the floor and frantically scrabbled for the matches of her bedside chest. After a couple of attempts, she managed to light her candle with shaking hands.

Her plan had been formulated some days ago, when first she had seen the look in his eyes as they passed over her body. 'Aah knowed it in mi bones that this was coming,' she thought. 'Thank God Aah was prepared.'

Tommy was still sleeping peacefully in his little nest in the feather mattress, next to her. His face was cradled on his hand and he was undisturbed by the thud of the falling body. Working with feverish haste, Gertie seized McDonald under the armpits and began to drag him, heels trailing, over the bedroom floor. He was even heavier than she had expected and she was dreading that he would come round, before she had him secured. Pulling and tugging, she strained with all her might until, at last, he was out of her room and into his own.

Here she bundled him through the door, her heart racing as he began to groan.

'Oh, God help me,' she prayed. Running back to her bedroom, her bare feet soundless, she seized the coil of strong twine which she had put on the chest of drawers. Upon returning to where he lay, she rifled through his pockets and removed his knife. Closing his door, she threaded the twine through the latch-hole, across the yard-square landing and through the same aperture on her own door. Pulling it taut, she tied it tightly round the knobs of a heavy, mahogany five-heights chest.

'There! That should 'old 'im,' she breathed, as she climbed into bed and turned to blow out the candle. 'No. Aah'll leave it lit. Expense be blowed,' she murmured to herself. She heard a few more moans and groans from the other bedroom and then the sound of him struggling to his feet. As he rattled his door, hers rattled in unison, but the twine held.

'Let me out, you bitch!' his voice roared through the house, causing her to quake. Thank God, the foot-thick walls would contain the noise, she thought. Eventually, the violent threats and curses stopped. There came a creak of bedsprings and before long, the sound of his snores reverberated through the cottage. Closing her eyes wearily, Gertie fell into a nightmare-filled sleep.

The following morning, she rose early before Tommy could wonder what was afoot, and undid the cord. Winding it round her hand, she popped it into the top of the chest of drawers. After riddling the grate and polishing it with black-lead, she banked up the fire and went to waken Tommy.

She knew that Rob would lie abed late after his night's carousing so, after a hasty breakfast, she wrapped Tommy warmly, gathered her cloak round her and hurried down to the Manor. Upon ascertaining that Victoria was still in bed, she scuttled up the back stairs. A quick tap and she was inside the room, to find Victoria sitting up in bed sipping her cup of tea. A glance round told her that Victoria was alone.

'Oh, Miss. When's t'brass coming?' she gasped.

'I've no idea,' Victoria replied. 'I don't even know where Mama's going to get it from.'

Gertie recounted her tale in graphic detail, her obvious fear conveying the night's events vividly to her mistress.

'Oh, Vicky!' Gertie was transported back to the easy familiarity of their days at Helmsley, in Victoria's childhood. 'Whatever am Aah ti do? Aah'm that scared.' Tommy sat wide-eyed at the foot of the bed, looking from one to the other. He understood his mother's story, but could not believe that his nice Uncle Rob had intended to kill her.

'It surely can't be long, now.' Victoria was shocked that her old friend had been put in such danger. It was all her fault. 'You must take a knife up, tonight. In fact, carry one with you at all times.' Sliding out of the high bed, she went over to the dressing table. From one of the drawers she brought out a jewelled stiletto.

'It's really a paper-knife,' she said. 'It came from Italy.'

Gertie felt the blade gingerly. 'It's very sharp!' she exclaimed.

'Keep it in your apron pocket,' Victoria advised her. 'If he attacks you again, plunge it between his ribs. If you kill him, Papa will get you off. It will be self-defence.'

Gertie was not reassured by this statement, although Stephen's kindness to her had given him God-like status in her eyes.

'Aah'll nivver dare use it,' she protested.

Victoria, however, was adamant. 'Nonsense! If he attacks you again, you'll use it.'

As she ran back up the village, Gertie was forced to admit that the feel of it on her thigh, through her apron, was a great comfort.

When they arrived home, Rob was already downstairs in his customary chair by the fire. He was ladling porridge from the pan she had left on the hob into a bowl.

He did not look up as they came in and Gertie sent Tommy into the stone outbuilding, with a bowl.

'Go and bring Mammy some potatoes from the sack in the shed.' She pushed him out and shut the door.

Going back into the room, she faced her brother-in-law with a steadiness she did not feel.

'Next time, it'll be t'carving knife.' She said the words with no emotions; it was a bare statement of fact.

He looked up over his porridge bowl, regarding her wryly.

'Our Ben never said what a fire-brand he'd got.' The words were spoken almost with admiration. 'I like a woman with spunk.'

'Well, Aah dissent like thoo, so keep away from me,' Gertie retorted.

'When Ben and I were lads,' he said reflectively, 'we were dragged off to church three times on a Sunday. I always understood that a man owes it to his dead brother to take his widow and beget children by her.'

Gertie's eyes widened. 'God strike thoo dead for saying such an unchristian thing!' she ejaculated.

'No, it's in the Bible,' he replied.

'Aah dissent believe it. Thoo's a liar,' she answered, her tone shocked. He made no reply, but merely smiled his wolfish smile into his porridge.

'Anyroad,' she cautioned, 'let last night be a warning ti thoo. One foot over my threshold again and thoo'll get a knife in thi ribs.'

The incident was not referred to again by either of them. Rob's impatience for the money, however, was becoming increasingly obvious.

By early February, it was apparent that the belated winter was about to descend upon them. The air became crisper and the rain dried up. A couple of bright but bitterly cold days lulled them into a false sense of security.

'Spring's going to come early,' said Victoria the following morning as she and her mother rode round the estate. Tamar cast a countrywoman's eye over the skies.

'I don't think so, dear,' came her reply. 'It's drying up for snow.'

Once out of the village, they slowed to a walk and turned their conversation to their problem. 'I can't understand why the money hasn't come.' Tamar's voice filled with anxiety and her brow furrowed. Gertie's struggle with McDonald had caused her great distress. They could never repay her for all she had done for them. Then Tamar dismissed the thought. None of this would have come about, if Gertie had not continued to deceive them over Victoria's trysts with Thomas Forster. She sighed deeply. If only the money would come . . .

When they reached home for luncheon, her suspense was ended. On a silver salver on a side-table in the Great Hall lay a letter bearing a Leicester postmark. Quickly seizing it, she hurried up the staircase, with Victoria close on her heels.

Rushing into her room, she tore it open. Inside there was no letter, but a bankers' draft fluttering to the floor. Stooping quickly she picked it up.

'Five thousand pounds!' She savoured the words as she spoke them aloud. Her shoulders straightened and relief flooded through her. 'Oh, Victoria. Thank God!' The load which had oppressed her was lifted and the joy she felt was akin to sexual rapture, so heady and breathless did she feel.

'If only it had come earlier, we could have taken it when we went for our ride,' Victoria said regretfully.

Tamar's golden eyes had narrowed, giving her face a cat-like expression. Her smile was long and slow, her lips curling back in anticipatory pleasure.

'No.' Her reply was breathy and drawn out. 'Let him stew,' she answered softly, and then a little louder, 'let the blackguard sweat!'

Victoria's face registered disappointment. 'But Mama, he's becoming impatient. Gertie's terrified of him and, besides, he's said he won't wait much longer.'

'He'll wait.' Tamar oozed confidence. William had come up trumps and the problem was solved. Prolonging McDonald's uncertainty gave her the thrill she derived from the hunt. Waving the draft she proclaimed, 'If he turns nasty, he can be paid immediately, but until then, we can keep him dangling a few days longer.'

Before their dinner guests arrived that evening, the snow had begun, as Tamar had predicted. Those seated round the dining table at Thorsbury Manor had no knowledge of the conditions outside. The fire roared and blazed, the table shone with silver and crystal, and good food and wine were impeccably served by Hodgetts and his staff. Stephen was relieved that Tamar and his daughter had recovered from their ill-humour, whatever its cause. Both were radically sociable and it was obvious that Sir Bramley and Lady Wheatcroft's son was captivated. His eyes followed Victoria's every movement and, if she turned to exchange conversation with either of his parents, he almost drooped with dejection.

Tamar was despairing of Victoria ever choosing a husband, and watched the couple hopefully. She knew little about the Wheatcrofts, who had recently moved into the area, Sir Bramley having lately come into his inheritance.

However, the boy seemed smitten and Victoria was at her most charming.

While the dinner-party pursued its merry course, the threatened snow began to fall. At first the florin-sized flakes floated lazily, firmly clinging to the frozen ground. It no time at all there was a covering and, as the wind began to rise, whipping and whistling through the skeletal branches, so the snow became more and more intense, until it swirled in an impenetrable curtain, blotting out the landscape like a bridal veil before the wedding.

The inhabitants of the village, too, were snugly cocooned indoors, warm and cosy in their ignorance of the wild conditions beyond their doors. They heard the wind, which rattled their latches and crept through chinks with icy fingers, but were unaware of the burden of snow which it bore.

When the Wheatcrofts were preparing to leave, Hodgetts glided towards his master.

'Excuse me, Sir Stephen, but I am informed that a blizzard has been blowing for several hours now. The wind has caused heavy drifting and I understand that the road out at the top of the village is completely blocked.'

Stephen's eyebrows rose. He looked towards the heavy velvet curtains which clothed the windows in muffling drapes.

'We had no idea,' he answered. 'See that the guest-rooms are prepared and fires lit.'

He explained the situation to the others and, after offering them another drink and light refreshments, settled them round the fire until their rooms were ready.

Gertie lay in bed listening to the howling of the elements, clutching at the handle of Victoria's dagger beneath her pillow. Although convinced that she would never be able to bring herself to use it, the very feel of the ornate handle under her fingers gave her confidence. Strain her ears as she might, though, she caught no sound of her brother-in-law's return.

'Aah 'opes as 'ow 'e's took a room at Barton pub, because o' t'blizzard,' was her last sleepy thought.

Unlike the occupants of the Hall, Gertie was fully aware of the wildness of the night. At bedtime, she had peered through the flimsy curtains and seen winter's fury hurling the snow at the village.

Upon waking she hardly dared poke her nose from under the bedclothes, so piercing was the cold. Even the tumbler of water, placed by the bedside in case Tommy woke in the night with a thirst, bore a thin film of ice.

Her priority was to blow the sleeping fire downstairs into flame with the bellows, before riddling and feeding it with plenty of logs. Once the porridge was thickening, she called up to Tommy.

'Come on, love. Bring thi clothes down and get dressed by t'fire. Thoo'll be withered up yonder.'

Breakfast over and the bowls and spoons washed, she peered cautiously out of the front door. The village street was a stretch of crystalline dunes, some as high as a man's chest.

'We're blocked in!' called her next-door neighbour. 'Is there owt thoo wants?'

'Nay,' she replied. 'Aah've plenty o' flour for bread and vegetables for soup. We sh'll manage.'

Her summer evenings, like those of all the village women, were spent in the woods, gathering dead wood for kindling and fallen branches to be sawn into logs. Her time in Canada had made her self-reliant, so that she could handle a logging saw as well as any man and had an outhouse packed to the roof with a winter's supply of firewood. A glance at the garden showed her that the snow had drifted, leaving an almost clear path to the well.

'We're as snug as bugs in a rug, Tommy,' she told the child. 'Your uncle must 'ave stopped at Barton, so we're shut of 'im until t'road's cleared.' Thank God, was the thought that flew through her mind.

Although Sir Stephen set men with shovels, accompanied by teams of heavy horses, to work to clear a road from the Manor up through the village and towards the main highway, it was several days before they managed to complete the task.

The longer the Wheatcrofts remained at the Manor, the more impressed Stephen and Tamar were with the son, Hoyland.

'He and Victoria seem to have a lot in common,' Tamar remarked to her husband the following evening.

He considered for a moment. 'Yes, they certainly get on well together. In fact, she seems livelier with him than she has been with anybody since young Forster. And he seems quite taken with her – if I'm not mistaken,' he added.

Tamar stared at her reflection in the dressing-table mirror and smiled at his image, looking over her shoulder.

'I hope it comes to something,' she sighed. 'Time is passing and I want to see her settled.'

'He seems a good chap, so we can but hope.'

' "Them as lives in 'ope, dies in despair", is what my father always says,' she answered with a smile.

Three days of hard weather kept their guests at the Manor and the longer they stayed, the more hopeful Tamar became. Hoyland was obviously enchanted by Victoria, and both sets of parents made their approval apparent. Surely she had had sufficient time to recover from Thomas' death and Francis Sturdy's rejection, was the thought that crossed Tamar's mind with great frequency.

Every moment which could be spared from tending the stock saw the estate-workers toiling on the snowdrifts. The hard-packed snow, with its coating of ice, proved a bigger obstacle than Stephen had anticipated.

Suddenly, with no prior warning, the thaw began. What had one day been an unyielding barrier swiftly turned to slush, and this was shovelled to the side of the street away from the houses, great, dirty, melting heaps.

The Wheatcrofts left, with promises from the Lassiters to repay the visit before very long.

Gertie was puzzled when, even though the road between the villages was re-opened, there was no sign of her brother-in-law's return.

'Maybe he's changed his mind and gone on to either

Malton or York,' suggested Tempy. 'There's nowt ti keep 'im 'ere, now 'e's seen that thoo and t'lad's fit and well.'

Gertie was noncommittal. If Tempy only knew, there was plenty to keep Rob in the village – a fortune, in fact.

Her conundrum was solved a couple of days later, when she opened her door to a knock. There stood a policeman. Gertie's eyes widened with shock and her hand strayed involuntarily to her throat.

'Mrs McDonald?'

'Aye.' Her mouth was suddenly parched and her heart thumped.

'May I come in? It's bad news, I'm afraid.' Once inside, he looked at her kindly. 'A couple of farmworkers have come across a body in the ditch between here and Barton. From documents found on the body, it appears to be a relative of yours.'

'My brother-in-law.' She managed to force the words out without releasing the inane grin which was struggling to paste itself all over her face.

Taken to the mortuary in Malton to identify Rob's body, she stood looking down upon him. Rigid and composed, with the pallor of death, there was little resemblance now to Ben. 'Oh, thank you God,' she found her mind repeating, over and over, like the beads of a rosary.

''E must 'ave tried ti reach 'ome,' she said aloud. 'Aah thought 'e'd stopped at t'inn, but 'e would be drunk and slipped in t'blizzard.'

Upon reaching Thorsbury, she went straight past Tempy's cottage, where Tommy waited, and down to the Manor. Tamar and Victoria were together in a small sitting-room, busy with their needlework.

Without any preamble, Gertie burst out. 'Rob's dead!'

They were utterly aghast, demanding all the details. When the whole story was out, Victoria turned to Tamar with shining eyes.

'You can repay the loan, Mama.'

Tamar remained silent, until Gertie had left. 'It was not a loan; it was a gift,' she replied cryptically. 'I shall not return it. It will be placed in a bank account, in Tommy's name. Your child shall have a decent start in life.'

Chapter Thirteen

Although the incarceration of the population of Thorsbury by the blizzard, had been of relatively short duration, the remote vale of Sleightholmedale was cut off from the outside world for over two weeks.

The track between Aumery Park and Cherry Tree Farm was opened up by the constant passage of plodding teams of great shire-horses, which patiently trod down each new snowfall, but there was no way out of the valley into the outside world. While they were almost self-sufficient and stocked up well in advance of winter with items they were unable to provide for themselves, Jonadab Oaks was nevertheless impatient for it to be gone.

'Aah've t'threshing machine due in three weeks,' he grumbled, at the first heavy fall. 'If Aah misses 'im, 'oo knows when 'e can come again. 'E's booked solid, most of t'year.'

Since Joe's suggestion, the threshing machine had visited Aumery Park Farm the previous year and Jonadab was bound to admit, albeit reluctantly, that the innovation was money well spent. If the machine was unable to reach the valley and they had to revert to flailing, it would certainly be a retrograde step.

Sarah's 'new house' baby had been another girl, Hannah. This caused Edward to feel even more isolated. Freddie's death had changed him for good, and he had developed into a quiet, studious boy. His schooling, like all the children of the moorland valleys, had been haphazard but there was now a school at Gillamoor so that, whenever it was possible, he rode the three miles up through Fadmoor, carrying his lunch tied in a snowy white cloth.

One of the benefits of school, as far as Edward was concerned, was the company of other boys. He had been disappointed when his mother had presented him with a second sister and, once school was over and during the holidays, he spent most of his time with his father, absorbing George's knowledge of the valley and its wildlife, in addition to the skills of the farm. He was a small boy for nine, but had a whip-like strength that belied his years.

When the family was confined to the valley, as they were now, Edward was quite happy to sit reading the few books which his father and grandfather possessed.

Kitty had reached the age of nineteen and was a capable and dependable help to Sarah, coping with the girls and much of the housework, leaving her free to deal with the eggs and the dairywork. The two Jersey house-cows provided sufficient milk, butter and cheese, both for their household and for Lydia, who supplied lodgings for the workforce.

When they sat round the table for meals, Jonadab constantly carped and grumbled about the weather.

'I'm sick of his chuntering,' George confided to Sarah. 'We can't alter this weather and we must put up with it.'

Each mealtime, George slumped wearily in his chair, too tired, until after a sustaining meal, even to untie the drenched sacking that was supposed to protect his legs from the worst of the snow. He and Bob Lamb worked full days of endless toil. Although the sheep were down from the high moors, the shelters were scattered and the two shepherds spent their days trudging over the snow-covered fields foddering the flocks. No sooner were feet towelled, clean woollen socks donned, and wet boots exchanged for those drying in the hearth than they were out again, shadowed by their faithful dogs.

George's legs ached from lifting them high to make his way through the snow and his shins were raw and chapped from the constant chafing of his wet trousers and leggings.

'Is there any sign of a thaw?' Jonadab demanded, every time George returned to the house.

'No, Faither. When there is, you'll know it as quick as me.' His voice reflected the tiredness of both body and spirit that was his constant condition in the winter months.

He had come to accept that, although now in his mid-seventies, Jonadab would never totally relinquish his authority over the farm, and there were still occasions when he smarted and bucked against his father's dominance.

When it came, the thaw was rapid, leaving the ground squelchy and the road-side dykes full. In a farewell gesture to winter, gusts of wind chased squalls of rain over the valley, causing Jonadab to fret and worry as threshing-time grew closer.

'Whatever are we ti do?' he asked petulantly. George caught sympathetic glances from his wife and mother. Annie was now very frail, needing a helping hand to reach the table or her bed, but her mind was still, at times, needle-sharp.

'We must do as best we can,' George retorted. 'We spend our lives pitting our strength against Nature, but there's really nowt we can do to win. If She makes up her mind that we're to be the losers, then the losers we shall be.'

These philosophical sentiments from the placid George drew a 'Humph!' from his father as he took himself off to the stables and his beloved horses.

His worries were groundless. Within a day or two, it was as if winter had never gripped the valley. The trees were whipped by a gusty breeze, tossing the few early hazel catkins and drying the land. The beck sparkled with silvery trout and the slow, flapping flight of the herons could be seen as they returned to their nests among the reed-beds.

'Another lucky year,' Annie observed, when her little namesake ran to tell her that the elegant birds were back. It was a deep-rooted but unwarranted fear of hers that, if there came a year when the herons failed to return, it would augur ill for the Oaks and their farm.

As the last dull remembrance of winter faded, Jonadab's spirits brightened and, consequently, so did those of the rest of the family. Such was his strength of character, even in old age, that every nuance of his temper influenced those around him.

There was great excitement among the children when the threshing set was due. For once, Edward did not resent his little sisters' company. Taking one by each hand, he led them into the road, to watch. Just before five, their patience was rewarded. The sound of hooves came from the entrance to the valley and the cavalcade soon emerged into sight. The first pair of heavy horses drew a flat dray, on top of which was fastened a steam engine. Following this, trundled the threshing machine itself. Its colour was the dusky pink of faded cabbage roses but, to the children, it was impressive in its size.

They followed it into the stackyard where, after much manoeuvring to the owner's instructions, it was eventually positioned within easy access of two stacks. When this was done the owner, Wally Heward and his son Jack, joined the Oaks round the table for tea. They would be back early next morning to start the steam engine and get everything ready before once more taking their places at breakfast.

The fact that all meals must be provided for them was a sore point with Jonadab.

''E must be coinin' brass,' he complained to all who would listen. 'What wi' what 'e charges and then 'is missus only feeds 'em at weekends, it's money for old rope.'

When the children were in bed and Edward, who had achieved his ambition of sleeping in the 'lads' room', had exacted the promise of no school tomorrow, the adults sat round the fire, chatting in a desultory fashion.

Jonadab's eyes were closed and the others presumed that he had nodded off. Beneath the resting lids, however, his brain was working at full speed.

'Aah wonders what they cost?' The question came out of the blue.

'What?' George looked up from where he was chatting to his wife.

'Threshing machines, o' course,' retorted his father. 'If we got one, it 'ud be practically all profit. We'd need two extra men, but they'd get their feed for nowt and we'd get oor own corn threshed free.'

George laughed. 'Oh, Faither, do you never give up? We've two farms as well as a flourishing horse trade and you still want another sideline!'

Jonadab was indignant. 'Thoo's no cause ti laugh,' he

said sharply. 'As long as a man 'as breath in 'is body, 'e must strive ti improve 'is lot in life. 'Oo's ti tell what's round t'next corner? Look at t'potato famine in Ireland and there's places in oor own country where t'crops 'as failed from time ti time. We can't 'ave too many irons in t'fire.'

'Well, let it rest for now,' pleaded George. 'There's threshing tomorrow and a busy time ahead. What with harrowing to make the land ready and sowing spring corn, then lambing'll be upon us, we shall hardly have time to draw breath.'

Jonadab merely grunted. Once the seed was sown, his mind would nurture it and he was determined to bring the idea to fruition. For those of his acquaintance who stagnated, rather than progressed, he had an uncompromising indictment. ''E's squandered t'seed corn wi' no thought for tomorrow,' was his summing up. If foresight could avoid it, the Oaks would never place themselves in such a position.

The Hewards arrived the following morning at the crack of dawn. Whenever did they sleep, Annie wondered. The boiler fire of the threshing machine had been damped down overnight, leaving the first task of the morning to be the riddling of the fire-box and the opening of the air-intake. While his father tended to this, Jack Heward topped up the boiler with water and adjusted the belts of the thresher. With this done, and while the boiler was getting up steam, the two men joined the Oaks at the breakfast table.

No ordinary breakfast would suffice on threshing days. Every farmer's wife was honour-bound to try to win the accolade for the finest table and the best food at lunch and 'lowance times. Now the Hewards were plied with thick slices of pink and succulent ham, a couple of fried eggs and lashings of fried bread and homemade sausages.

All this was shovelled down at breakneck speed by the threshing team, and before anyone else at the table was ready, Heward senior pushed back his chair and gave a great belch.

'That were grand, missus,' he congratulated Annie, never questioning that the old woman might not have been the one responsible for the spread. Then, consulting his pocket-watch he ordered, 'Come on, then. Time ti start. Time's money!'

Jonadab was affronted at anyone else giving orders in his own house, but the threshing master's word was law. George followed, cramming the last of his breakfast hastily into his mouth as he dashed after the Hewards. His father took his time over going to the stables, where his help was needed to release men for the threshing.

Once the table was cleared, the women began to work with frantic speed. Martha had come up to help, so too had Ann Butler, although her assistance was becoming limited as age took its toll. Kitty took all the young children off to collect the eggs, while the other women started on the mid-morning allowance. For each man there was a large bread-cake the size of a dinner plate. This was split, buttered and filled with slices of boiled ham. Once ready, they were placed in flat baker's baskets and covered ready to take out with a bucket of tea and a large, sliced fruit cake.

When these were stowed away in the cool dairy on a stone slab, they started on the noon lunch. Each man was allocated a hefty meat pie and an apple turnover, the baking of which occupied them for the rest of the morning. The mid-afternoon snack was to be the same as the mid-morning one.

When Jonadab called in on his way from the stables to the stackyard, the kitchen was unbearably hot and the women round the table had flour-dusted, rosy faces. Annie and Ann Butler were seated away from the direct heat of the fire, paring apples, allowing the curls of peel to fall on the newspaper at their feet.

Jonadab frowned round at the hive of industry. Although he often told anyone who would listen, 'A man can't work on an empty belly,' the thought of these great amounts of food being prepared for the threshing gang was anathema to his Yorkshire thrift.

'Whatever's this lot costin' mi?' he demanded testily, of no one in particular.

'Nay, Jonadab. It was practically all in t'larder,' reasoned Annie.

'What goes into their bellies, doesn't go into ours,' came his reply. 'Aah've already 'ad ti fork out t'brass for a quarter ton o' coal, as well as half a day for a man ti fetch it from Kirkby.'

Annie's eyes met Ann Butler's across the kitchen. He'd never change!

When Jonadab arrived at the stackyard he had to admit to himself that the whole operation was running smoothly under Wally Heward's direction. In addition to the Hewards there were five threshing tramps, as they were called. These were men, often Irish, who followed the threshing machines and offered their services for a day's wage. They augmented the number of men who could be spared from the daily running of the farm.

The stationary steam engine chugged away quietly, consuming Jonadab's coal. 'Bought wi' mi 'ard-earned brass.' he thought balefully, watching Jack Heward jump down and feed the monster with yet another couple of shovelfulls of fuel.

Two of Jonadab's own men were on the corn stack, forking the sheaves down to Wally and Jack, who cut the straw bands and fed the corn down into the gaping jaws of the threshing machine. Here, as Edward watched in fascination, by some apparently miraculous means, all were separated. The golden grains of corn were spewed out of one opening at the other end into a waiting sack, while the loose stalks of straw were taken from the rhythmically moving machine by three men, who forked them into a straw stack, working easily, tossing the straw from fork to fork. The chaff was allowed to fall on to a large sheet. When the pile was sufficiently big, the four corners were seized by the chaff-carrier, who heaved it over his shoulder, depositing it in a loose-box, especially cleaned to accommodate it. This would be mixed with the horses' feed, not only to eke it out, but to provide roughage.

Corn-carrying was the most strenuous job and commanded the highest wage, so there was no way that Jonadab was going to pay over the odds for that. George and Bob Lamb were delegated to do this. While it was a source of pride, as this was proof of their superior strength, it meant that their day would be ended in a state of utter exhaustion, often with chafed and bloodied shoulders, especially if the crop was barley.

Jonadab prowled about the yard for a while and then sat down beside his grandson.

'I'm going to be a corn-carrier when I grow up,' boasted Edward, eyeing his father and uncle with pride.

'Thoo'll 'ave ti grow a bit, methinks.' Jonadab took in the slight frame.

'Well, anyroad, I'll not be a chaff-carrier. That's for t'weedy ones,' Edward retorted disdainfully. In a way this was true for, although the bundles of chaff were bulky, they were comparatively light.

George and Bob had neither the breath nor the time to join in the banter which was tossed back and forth among the other workers. It was a long carry, at the end of which there were the granary steps to mount, before the sack could be emptied with a whispering sigh on to the growing pile of grain. Backwards and forwards they went, passing each other midway, shoulders bent and eyes down under the weight of their burden. No sooner were they back than the sack which had replaced the previous one was full, providing no respite from their toil.

When the whistle blew and the women bustled among them with refreshments, George and Bob threw themselves down at Jonadab's feet.

'Well, that's half the stack threshed. We sh'll finish this 'un by dinnertime. Then t'other'll be done this afternoon.'

'Ye's not wacked already?' one of the Irish threshing tramps laughed. 'To be sure, oats is nothing' but twelve stone a bag. Just wait till ye've carried beans at twenty, sor.'

George and Bob exchanged glances. Thank goodness they didn't grow beans!

Jonadab limped towards the Hewards. 'By gum, it's a grand machine, Wally.' He cast an admiring glance over the rig.

'It is an' all.' Heward was complacent. 't'best money

Aah've ever laid out,' he boasted. 'Aah've more work than Aah can manage.'

'Is that a fact?' Jonadab was gently probing. 'Wherever did it come from?'

Subtlety was not Wally's strong point, and he could not see where Jonadab was craftily heading.

'Malton,' came his reply. 'T'best that money can buy.'

Jonadab stored the information away in his mind and, after chatting about mutual acquaintances on whose farms the Hewards had threshed, he returned to his seat, satisfied with the results of his enquiries.

Edward moved from group to group, listening to their boasts of loads carried and stacks shifted in a lifetime of work. He was drunk with pride to be among the men and part of the scene. If only he could be part of the action, too! He felt far superior to his sisters.

They in their turn were blissfully happy following Kitty, hand in hand, while she milked the cows, washed the eggs and worked in the dairy. Like Edward, they were effortlessly absorbing the skills which would, at some future time, enable them to make efficient and diligent farmwives.

Exactly on the quarter-hour, Heward's inexorable whistle sounded and the men rose to their feet, wiping dusty, sweat-stained foreheads with equally grubby arms. They returned to their labours knowing full well that there would be no further let-up till noon.

By the time the second stack was threshed, they had had enough. The Hewards damped down the boiler fire, harnessed up their horses and moved in stately procession on to yet another gargantuan meal at another farmer's table. The thought of this was enough to make up Jonadab's mind.

Before the evening meal, while George stripped off his shirt and had a thorough wash at the sink, he sat staring thoughtfully at the dull glow of the fire which, now that the baking was over, was damped down under turves.

Edward was boasting to little Annie and Hannah about the noise, the steam and what were to his young eyes, the marvels of the day.

Before they sat at the table, George knelt down at Sarah's

feet, his head in her lap, while she gently smoothed soothing salve into his raw and tender upper back. Once he had donned a clean shirt, they drew their chairs up to the table.

During a breather in the bustle of the day, she had taken the opportunity of a quiet word with Martha.

'I'm afraid your mother's failing,' she had said, her voice laced with sympathy.

Martha's startling blue eyes met her brown ones, brows lifted in surprise.

'Oh! I was trying to pluck up the courage to say the same about yours,' she answered.

Annie Oaks felt content. She had enjoyed Martha's presence in the house. It had seemed like old times. Ann Butler's visit gave both old ladies the opportunity to wallow in memories of Joe and Mary. Neither really knew why these two children of theirs had curtailed their stay in England, but nobody else seemed inclined to discuss them at length, so their mothers found great solace in these chats.

Once all were seated and Grace had been said, Jonadab looked across at George.

'Aah've made up mi mind,' he announced. George was too bone-tired to show his resentment that his father had once more assumed full control of farm matters. Jonadab's sharp eyes, however, intercepted the quick glance of frustration which George threw at Sarah. 'That's if thoo's in agreement, when we've discussed it,' he amended hastily.

George smiled across at him. The old beggar was learning, even if the progress was slow.

There was nothing to discuss, in reality Jonadab's plan had been formulated during the day. 'We'll go over to Malton and 'ave a look at them machines. Both of us,' he added, to win George over. 'When we've got one and tried it at 'ome, we'll get a couple o' men at Martinmas and, after that, it's nearly all extra profit. It'll soon pay for itself.'

'Why do you want more profit for at your age, Faither? You never spend any money.'

Jonadab's amazement was mirrored in his face. 'Aah've built this farm up from nowt,' he explained, as if to a doltish child. 'When others went under, Aah went into t'eavy 'osses.

Many a man thought Aah was mad, but they sank while Aah swam. Now there's big changes in farming methods and we must be in first, if we're ti tek advantage of 'em.'

George nodded. Even in his old age, his father was more adventurous and more modern in his ideas than many others. And he himself had always thought the machines far better than the old method of flailing.

Jonadab's face softened. 'We must think o' t'land, George. Thoo'll come after me and then t'lad,' with a nod towards his grandson, 'after thoo. All us Oaks must repay this farm for all it's done for us. If we don't progress, we sh'll go backwards.' With a look round the table, he ended his homily. 'Man was born ti struggle and improve 'is lot, and don't forget it!'

George smiled wryly at Sarah. 'I've struggled enough today to last me for weeks,' was his thought. If the plan came to pass, he knew that he would be the one to relinquish his beloved sheep to another shepherd and become the threshing master. For a moment his heart failed but, on talking it over in bed with Sarah, he decided that it might be a change that he would like.

'I'd really be t'boss then,' he smiled confidently. 'All that's needed is for me to learn how it works and then I'd travel round in charge.'

'What about me?' Sarah was uneasy. 'You'd be away from dawn to dusk, all day and every day.'

George pulled her close and nuzzled her loosened hair. 'Come on, love,' he whispered. 'I'll be home every day after tea and all day Saturday and Sunday. We shall be better off, all round. After all,' he added, 'we've Edward to think of, and there's more to farming than just sowing and reaping and tending t'stock.'

Chapter Fourteen

Tamar Lassiter looked up from the letter she was reading.

'You'll never believe it!' she exclaimed. 'Father's bought a threshing set.'

Stephen shared her surprise. 'Who's going to run it?' he asked. 'It isn't really something to be left to others.'

She read on a little. 'George!' She was incredulous. 'Steady old George! Fancy him having anything to do with machinery.'

Stephen was thoughtful. 'If he can master it, it'll be one of the best things that can happen. It will bring him out from your father's shadow. Once he can do something that the old man can't, he'll truly be the master, in his own right.'

Tamar was pleased for George, who had written so proudly of the new venture. It was high time Jonadab allowed him to stand on his own two feet and this would be one aspect on which his father's dominance could not encroach.

Rob McDonald had been buried in the pretty little churchyard at Thorsbury and there were those in the village who thought Gertie unfeeling; she never tidied the grave, nor laid flowers there. ''Er own brother-in-law an' all,' the women who were her neighbours gossiped behind her back. 'And 'im come all t'way from Canada ti see 'er and t'lad.'

Victoria had felt that perhaps there was something immoral about not returning the blackmail money, but Tamar had quelled her misgivings.

'No one knows anything about it. The person who gave it will think it's been paid and really, it's the only thing that we are able to do for Tommy.'

Her daughter eventually accepted that this was for the best and the matter was rarely referred to again.

Later that summer, Hoyland Wheatcroft asked Stephen's permission to court Victoria. There was no stammering or embarrassment on his part, as there had been with several young men who had approached Stephen on the same errand.

'It must be obvious to you that I'm head over heels in love with Victoria,' he said directly, his clear blue eyes fixed on Stephen. 'She's perfect in every way in my eyes, and I can think of nothing that would make me happier than to have her as my wife.'

Stephen did not answer immediately. There was no doubt in his mind that the young man was a good catch. Since first noting how the land lay, Stephen had made discreet enquiries and could find nothing to Hoyland Wheatcroft's detriment. He came from a good family with plenty of money: his character was as equable and agreeable as it appeared on the surface and there was no breath of scandal associated with him – no gambling, women or heavy drinking. 'Almost too good to be true,' he had commented to Tamar.

Bringing himself back to the present, he looked into the anxious eyes which were searching his face.

'Is it that you don't think I'm good enough for her?' His tone was disconsolate.

Stephen was hasty to reassure him. 'Not at all, Hoyland. You would be the perfect husband for Victoria, and I'm sure Lady Lassiter would be the first to agree with me. I just don't want you to be hurt. I must warn you that several young men before you have paid court to Victoria, with no success. There was a young man about six years ago, but he was killed in a riding accident. It was a great shock to my daughter, but I hope, for your sake, that she's over it by now.' He looked at the earnest young man with a smile. 'I can say, with all honesty, that there's no one we would rather have for a son-in-law.'

Hoyland's face was wreathed in a smile of delight. Seizing Stephen's hand, he shook it warmly. 'Thank you, sir. I shall do my best to win her. I shan't rush her. I'll take my time.'

When this conversation was relayed to Victoria, she met it with a protest.

'Oh, no! Surely he's not going to spoil everything!'

Tamar was exasperated. 'You get on well, don't you?'

'Yes, of course.' She frowned slightly. 'But really, only as brother and sister.'

Victoria was Tamar's favourite child. In her, she could see herself as she had been in her youth and wanted the best for her girl. Now, however, she was short with her.

'Well, consider him as a future husband,' she almost snapped, and Victoria's eyes opened wide. 'It's no good looking at me like that. Heaven knows, you've thrown away enough chances and there aren't going to be many more. You must look to the future.'

Victoria's bottom lip came out. 'I've told you, Mama. I want a marriage like yours and Papa's.'

Tamar took her hand. 'I'm going to tell you something that I've never admitted before.' She spoke seriously, hesitating before proceeding. 'When I married your father, I didn't really love him. He was kind and considerate and he loved me. In the beginning, I married him to escape to a better quality of life.'

Victoria's eyes reflected her disbelief. 'But you must love him! You always act as though you do.'

Tamar smiled. 'It isn't an act. I do love him, dearly, but my love grew after our marriage. If you give Hoyland the chance, your love could develop as mine has.'

Victoria was thoughtful. When Hoyland next called, she spoke frankly to him.

'I can't promise anything,' she told him. 'When Thomas was killed, I thought my life was ended.' Wisely she made no mention of Francis Sturdy. 'I couldn't imagine loving anybody else. However, I do like you better than almost anyone I've ever met, and I will try to love you.'

His relief was obvious; his smile brilliant. This was more than he could have hoped for, after his talk with her father.

'Take all the time you need.' He felt confident that he could win her. 'I'll wait for ever, Victoria.'

She was reminded of the time Francis Sturdy had made

the same declaration to her parents. She snatched her hand from Hoyland's grasp. At his look of astonishment, she composed her features into a smile, hoping that she had not betrayed the quick stab of bitterness she felt.

'I'm sorry, Hoyland.' She tilted her head to one side and gave him a winsome smile. 'I didn't mean to do that, but you did say you would be patient.' And with that, he had to be content.

When Hilary came home for the summer holidays, Victoria found that they had more in common than they had ever had. The puny child had developed into an active and fit young man. Because of his weak chest, Tamar had been over-protective and he had been late going away to school. Obviously, the régime and the games had been of benefit and, although he had his father's tall, slim frame, he had lost the pigeon-chest of the chronic bronchitic and now stood tall and straight. He had inherited Stephen's silvery, ash-blond hair, but his slight tan and clear blue eyes took away any hint of femininity.

Although he studied for part of each day, Hilary often rode out with Victoria and provided a welcome change from having only her mother for company.

'I'll gradually take you all over the estate,' she told him. 'You were too delicate as a child to go very far afield.'

He gave a deprecating laugh. 'I wasn't delicate,' he protested. 'Merely over-mothered.' Remembering his sudden fevers and the nights that their mother and Tempy had sat up with him in turn, Victoria made no reply.

'Anyway,' she reflected, 'one day it will all be yours, so you'd better get to know it thoroughly.'

As one shimmering day followed another, they visited the different farms on the estate. Victoria rode with him along the open trails which dissected the dense Thorsbury woods, explaining how the timber was harvested and replacements planted. They visited the saw-mill where the foreman gave Hilary a more detailed explanation of this lucrative part of the estate business. The real money, of course, came from the woollen mills in the West Riding, in which Hilary's grandfather had wisely invested.

It never occurred to Victoria that she was usurping their father's place. By the time Stephen was free to ride out beside them, there was no part of the estate that Hilary had not explored with his sister. Stephen masked his twinge of disappointment well. It was pleasure enough to see the two of them getting on so famously together, he thought, eyeing them appreciatively, the one so dark and the other so fair.

Hilary noted that Victoria called on Gertie each time their rides took them up the village. His quick intelligence also told him that it was not Gertie who concerned her, but the dumb child, Tommy.

'Why are you so besotted with Gertie's boy?' he questioned one morning, when she had spent a quarter of an hour playing with the boy.

He watched with clinical detachment the flush that started in her neck and rose rapidly to suffuse her whole face. Why should this question embarrass her?

Victoria bit her lip, to stem the hot denial which was her natural reaction. After a moment of consideration she answered, in an even tone.

'Gertie has cared for me since the age of two. I have, really, no other friend. I am extremely fond of her and visit her as often as I can, now that she has fallen on hard times.'

No more was said on the subject, but Hilary stored it away to ponder on, later. He supposed that Victoria's maternal instincts were frustrated, but after all, she'd had plenty of offers of marriage and had cast them aside. He hoped that when he came into his inheritance, she wouldn't expect him to provide for a widowed maid and her child, as well as a spinster sister.

The faithful Hoyland Wheatcroft seemed to be forever calling and, though Victoria would walk with him in the garden, if he ventured to take her hand, she removed it as soon as she possibly could without giving offence. She was trying hard to love him, she told herself, but so far there was no spark there.

'You're a ninny,' Hilary told her. 'You should marry for love, but love where there's money. When I leave Oxford,

I shall choose a girl with looks, but her father's bank account will be the prime consideration.'

Victoria saw her brother in a fresh light. How cold and calculating he seemed. 'Although you look like Papa, you're as different as chalk and cheese,' she said. 'If he'd had your attitude, he would never have married Mama – and look what a good marriage they've got.'

They rode in silence for a few minutes, and then she said tentatively, 'If I don't accept Hoyland, when you inherit Thorsbury will you promise to allow me to stay on here? I could live in the Dower House with Mama.'

'Don't be a fool,' was his noncommittal reply. 'Grab him while he's still on offer. He won't wait patiently for ever.'

'No, I'm sure he won't.' Victoria's tone was bitter as she thought of Francis Sturdy.

The women of the village rarely left it, apart from at the Martinmas Hirings when Stephen provided wagons and carts to take everybody into Malton for the festivities. However, it would soon be the Michaelmas Fair and Gertie had been saving a tiny amount each week, determined to buy a small Christmas gift for Victoria to show her gratitude for their support.

'We'll cadge a lift on t'carrier's cart into Malton, Tommy,' she told him. 'Thoo'll like ti see t'shops and t'market, won't thoo?'

He nodded his head and smiled broadly. She sighed as she looked at him. She had long ago come to the reluctant conclusion that he would never speak again, and worried as to what would become of him.

Tommy, however, had no such qualms. He had an inborn affinity with animals and wanted either to work with horses, or with Mr Baggot, the gamekeeper. Miss Victoria would arrange it all. He would be all right. He looked fondly at his mother. How he wished she could read and write. Tommy was desperate to acquire these skills. However, there was talk that Lady Lassiter was going to start a school in the village and Tommy, whose intelligence far outstripped that of the majority of the children there, was hopeful that he would receive the education he craved.

Meanwhile, there was the excitement of the trip to Malton. Sitting between his mother and the carrier, he avidly took in the views over the heavily wooded, rolling countryside.

When they reached the town, he was awed by the hordes of people thronging the market and the main shopping streets. The carrier had arranged to meet them at four o'clock.

'Aah'm only goin' back as far as Barton,' he told Gertie. 'But thoo can walk t'last couple o' miles.'

The Michaelmas Goose Fair was in full swing and Tommy's head swivelled from side to side, wide eyes taking in the excitement. In addition to stall after stall, groaning under displays of pink, succulent-looking, dressed geese, there were rows of pens of snowy geese to be sold live. Poor Tommy strayed too close to one pen, to find that a gander's long neck snaked out with the speed of a striking cobra and seized his trousers in a vice-like grip. No matter how the boy struggled, he could not free himself.

He let out a shriek, whereupon Gertie rushed over and began to lay about the gander with her umbrella, forcing him to let go.

After this shock, they sat on a wall by a tea stall and had a cup of tea and a mutton pie. As Tommy gazed round at the fire-eaters, jugglers and acrobats, he felt that nothing could ever surpass the happiness of this day.

Seeing that the rest and snack had calmed him down, Gertie brushed away the crumbs and they started to wander down the aisles of general stalls, pausing where the stall-holders called their wares with a string of patter and jokes.

'They're called "barkers",' Gertie explained. Some even juggled with whole tea services in breathtaking fashion.

As well as the present for Victoria, Gertie had made a mental list of a few modest household items that she needed. They paused by a stall where a barker was holding up a huge, oval platter, large enough for the biggest goose. He had started off at a shilling and by the time Gertie and

Tommy reached the stall, had reduced the price to sixpence. Still the crowd stood unmoved. His broadly accented West Riding voice was beginning to sound desperate.

'Come on, then, fourpence,' he pleaded. Silence! 'Twopence, then, an' I'm losing money!' Still the crowd were silent.

Gertie hesitated. It was certainly a bargain. The man was not done, however.

'Come on! Who'll take it off mi 'ands for nowt?'

The crowd was incredulous, but Gertie's voice rang out, 'Aah will!'

The man looked at her and then tossed the meat dish to her.

''Ere, and I 'opes you smashes it on t'road 'ome,' he called after them as they turned away, Gertie clutching the dish to her chest.

Wriggling through the throng, Gertie found a quiet corner and, taking off the shawl she wore under her cloak, bundled the platter in it, tying the corners across it. There was no way it would fit into the calico bag which she had brought for her shopping.

'That mun be a bargain, Tommy. T'price is just right,' she smiled and the boy threw back his head and laughed aloud. 'We'll get Miss Victoria's present first, then Aah'll do t'rest o' mi shopping. Then it'll be time ti go to t'Green Man and meet Carter Johnson,' she listed, leading the way to a row of stalls dealing with linens of all kinds.

'Aah thought as 'ow we'd get three nice embroidered linen handkerchiefs,' she said, stopping by a stall. Rifling through the pile, she looked admiringly at the fine needlework. 'Thoo 'ave a choose, then thoo can choose t'last.'

Tommy examined the squares of linen carefully. The man came down the stall towards them.

'Pure Irish linen.' His tone was proud. 'Fancy-worked by nuns.'

The boy laid aside one delicately embroidered with a rose. Gertie quickly chose a forget-me-not. At Tommy's second turn, he triumphantly produced one with brown and gold pansies. Pointing to his eyes, he laughed.

'Clever boy!' exclaimed Gertie. 'They're the same goldie-brown as 'er eyes.'

The temperature had dropped considerably by now, and the crowds were clustered round the chestnut-seller's braziers. Gertie stopped and peered into her purse.

'Aah thinks we can afford a penn'orth between us. They'll keep us 'ands warm on t'cart.'

They had not been travelling long when a steady drizzle began to fall. Gertie pulled her hood well forward and held her umbrella over Tommy. When they left the carrier's cart at Barton, the fine drizzle had turned to a steady downpour.

'We could 'ave done wi'out this,' Gertie muttered in exasperation, raising her eyes to the elements. Kneeling before Tommy, she turned up his coat collar and pulled his cap well down to cover as much of his hair as possible.

Cursing the giant meat-dish, which had become a real encumbrance as the day had gone on, she took the child's hand and they resolutely began to trudge through the curtains of rain that almost obscured the road ahead.

By the time they reached home, they were both on the point of exhaustion. To add to their troubles, although Gertie had banked up the fire with slack coal before setting out that morning, it had died out and the grate was cold.

Tommy pushed her into a chair and scurried about collecting kindling, logs and a small amount of coal. He soon had a cheerful blaze going, with the kettle swinging over it. Gertie removed her cloak and, after shaking it, hung it behind the door.

'Aah reckons we've got some bargains today, Tommy,' she announced, as she set the table for tea. 'Aah'll wash that girt dish and put it in t'top o' t'cupboard, after tea. Then Aah'll iron Miss Victoria's kerchiefs.'

Taking a deep swig of tea, she paused. 'Aah feels a bit off it,' she told him. 'Aah 'opes as 'ow Aah 'asn't got a chill. Aah'll tek a dose of 'ot 'orehound an' 'oney tonight.'

Taking a couple of hot bricks out of the oven, she wrapped them in flannel and went up and popped them into the bed. When she came down, she pulled her chair up to the fire.

'Come on. Mammy'll tell thoo a story while we get warmed through. Then we'll 'ave an early night. Blow t'dish and t'ironing. Aah dissent feel fit ti do 'em.'

Chapter Fifteen

Gertie managed to struggle through the following day although she felt wretched. Her throat resembled sandpaper and there was so little room between her tonsils that it was difficult to draw breath. By Monday, when Tommy awoke, he was unable to rouse her. Climbing on a stool, he hooked her cloak off the back of the door and spread it over the bed, for extra warmth.

He then ran down to his Auntie Tempy's and, taking her hand, indicated that she was to come with him. Tempy took one look at Gertie and her heart sank.

'Oh, my God!' she exclaimed. Turning on her heels, she made for the Manor as fast as she could.

Tamar was sitting up in bed with a cup of hot chocolate. Her eyebrows rose when Tempy hurled herself into the bedroom.

'Whatever is wrong?' she demanded.

'There's an epidemic of Dip in Malton and it looks as though Gertie's brought it into t'village. She's bad, m'Lady.'

'Dip?' Tamar looked blank.

'Diphtheria,' Tempy explained.

'Oh, my God! It could sweep through the village in no time. What about the boy?'

''E seems all right, m'Lady. Up to now, anyroad.'

'Ring the bell and I'll get dressed while you go and tell Miss Victoria,' ordered Tamar.

Victoria was still asleep, sprawled in a tangle of silken sheets. Tempy shook her awake and when her lashes swept open, she said, 'Miss Vicky, Gertie's ill. Very ill. I think you should come.'

Victoria's reactions were instantaneous. She swung her legs to the ground, passed a damp cloth over her face and threw on some clothes. By the time Tamar and Tempy reached Gertie's cottage, Victoria was already there, kneeling by the bed, bathing Gertie's forehead with a cloth wrung out in a basin of cold water and vinegar.

Tamar raised her to her feet. 'You cannot stay here, darling. The only thing we can do for Gertie is to make her comfortable. I'm afraid there's not much hope.'

Victoria clung on to the bedpost, refusing to allow her mother to tear her away.

'I will not leave Gertie. I insist on staying to nurse her.' Her face was despairing as she looked down upon the maid. Gertie's skin was putty-coloured and beaded with sweat, while her shallow breathing rasped in her throat.

Tamar caught sight of Tommy. The capable little boy had lit a fire in the bedroom and now crouched beside his mother, clutching her hand and sobbing quietly. Inspiration struck her. Taking his hand, she placed it in Victoria's.

'You can't leave the child here.' She leaned towards Victoria and almost forced the words into her ear whilst giving her shoulder a sharp tweak, to bring her to her senses.

'Your Mama's right, Miss,' urged Tempy. 'Think o' t'laddie. T'longer 'e stays 'ere, t'more danger 'e's in.' As she spoke, her eyes encountered Tamar's above Victoria's shoulder, her fear naked in her eyes.

Between them, they convinced Victoria and she allowed them to bundle her and her child, unprotesting, from the cottage.

When they were alone, Tamar asked Tempy, 'Is there anyone who can nurse her?'

'Nobody in t'village will want ti tek it on. They've all got families. 'Owever, there's old Grannie Topliss. She 'as a cottage in t'woods. She gathers and sells 'erbs and meks potions. She'll nurse owt and nivver seems ti catch it.'

Tempy sent her eldest boy scampering through the woods to fetch old Mrs Topliss. When she arrived, the stink of the crone caused Tamar to take a step back.

'Ah, Mrs Topliss,' she smiled. 'We think Mrs McDonald has diphtheria. Will you be able to nurse her for us?'

'Aye. Aah sh'll be all right, m'Lady,' the woman assured her. 'Aah've nursed all sorts o' fevers and Aah nivver gets between t'patient and t'fire. All t'germs rush straight towards t'fire and Aah've nivver caught nowt yet.'

Tamar was only too thankful to leave her in charge. 'Do your best for Gertie. She has been my daughter's companion and friend since she was two. You'll not be out of pocket, I promise you.' With a smile, Tamar hurried from the house.

'Aye, thoo'll pay me ti tek risks thoo wouldn't tek, m'Lady.' The old woman's voice followed her from the cottage.

Granny Topliss set a pan of carefully chosen herbs on the downstairs fire and then carried several long branches up to feed the bedroom fire. This way, she could push them between the bars of the grate, from a distance, to avoid passing between the bed and the fire.

The old woman had considerable knowledge of herbs, gleaned through years of woodland life. She used various combinations to bathe Gertie's burning body, others to dose her and yet others to poultice the swollen throat. Despite all her ministrations, however, she had been called too late to help Gertie. After struggling for two days, Mrs Topliss lost her patient; an event which damaged her considerable pride.

After laying Gertie out, the old woman walked down to Tempy's to make her report.

'Aah were called too late,' she informed Tempy. 'If there's any more cases, and Aah should think there will be, see that Aah'm called straight away.'

''Ow much does 'Er Ladyship owe thoo?' Tempy wanted to know.

'If it's payment by results, she owes me nowt,' answered the crone. 'But tell 'er ti give me whatever she thinks.' With that, she made her way through the woods back to the cottage.

Before going down to the Manor to break the news of Gertie's death to the Lassiters, Tempy slipped up to Gertie's cottage. She was surprised to see that not only had Mrs Topliss laid out Gertie's body, but the whole house was spotlessly clean and strewn with sweet-scented herbs.

'Why on earth doesn't she do t'same for 'erself?' she muttered, and then burst into tears.

Gertie's death posed more than one problem for the Lassiter family. The first hurdle was the funeral. Both Tamar and Victoria considered that, taking into account Gertie's special place in the family affections, Stephen himself should be present. It was, however, his custom to attend only the funerals of male servants and leave his wife and daughter to go to those of the womenfolk of the village.

Despite their pleas, he insisted on sticking to his decision. 'You must realise that everything we do is examined and criticised,' he said. 'In a small, gossip-hungry community like this, our tenants are only too eager to look for favouritism – even after death.'

So it was agreed and, on the day of Gertie's funeral, Tamar and Victoria attended, with Tommy between them, wearing a black armband. This had caused another argument when Victoria had been insistent upon taking him to Malton to buy him a black suit.

'It is unsuitable that we should do so.' Her father would not be moved. 'After the funeral, we must have a family conference and decide what is to become of Tommy.'

Victoria did not like the sound of this and seized Tommy's hand, which she held tightly throughout the service. When they left the church, Tempy served tea and funeral cakes in Gertie's cottage. The village women were impressed with how clean and fragrant Grannie Topliss had left the premises.

'She knows what clean is,' said one woman. 'Why can 't t'mucky old cow keep 'ersen clean?'

'She did well for Gertie,' defended Tempy. 'If there's any more cases, she wants sending for straight away, to give 'er a chance to cure 'em.'

To Grannie Topliss' amazement, Tempy was sent to her by Tamar with a leather drawstring bag containing ten pounds.

'This is not just for Gertie, but any other of t'villagers who might need nursing,' she explained to the old herb-gatherer.

'God bless 'Er Ladyship,' the old woman replied. 'Aah'm afeared there'll be others, don't thoo fret. If Aah gets 'em early enough, Aah reckons Aah can 'eal 'em.'

The evening after Gertie's funeral, dinner at Thorsbury Manor was a very solemn and quiet affair. Each member of the family was thinking about Tommy. Victoria was anxious to know what her parents had meant and could see no problem about him staying with them.

After the meal, Tamar said, 'We'll take our coffee in the library, please, Hodgetts.'

Once settled round the fire, there was silence for a few minutes and then Victoria burst out, 'I don't know what you mean when you said we must discuss what was to become of Tommy, Father. He's here – with us! That's what's become of him.'

Stephen sighed patiently. 'As with the funeral, the whole village will watch to see what is our attitude to the child. They will expect us to treat him as we would one of their children left an orphan. No better, no worse.'

Victoria burst into tears. 'I was forced to leave my baby in Canada to be brought up by Gertie,' she sobbed. 'I never expected to see him again and yet God brought him back to me. I've had to treat him like any village child, when I've wanted to cuddle him and love him. Now, poor Gertie has paid with her life – and for what? Why, to give my child back to me.'

Tamar bit her lip. 'This is impossible talk,' she insisted. 'There is no way that you can acknowledge Tommy as your own child. You would be the scandal of the whole county.'

Stephen intervened. 'We've been through all this before, Victoria. You agreed with us then and you must agree with us now, that for the sake of your own reputation and the family name, you must make no claim upon your child.'

Rising quickly to her feet, Victoria crossed to the window. There she stood with unseeing eyes, twisting and untwisting the gold threads that acted as tie-backs.

'It seems that Fate has decreed it,' she sobbed. 'God seems to have worked to give Tommy back to me.'

'You must pull yourself together and realise that God

would not take Gertie's life, to give you possession of your illegitimate child.' Tamar was quite harsh.

Stephen looked shocked. 'Now, Tamar,' he remonstrated.

Tamar drew one or two deep breaths to steady herself. 'There is no way that you're going to keep him and acknowledge him as your own child,' she stated. 'There! That's one possibility disposed of!' With a warning look at her husband, Tamar hardened her voice again. 'Many parents would not hesitate to put the child into an orphanage.'

At Victoria's gasp, she shook her head. 'Don't worry. Tommy is our grandson and we love him. I'm only pointing out the possibilities before presenting my own idea, which I hope you'll accept.'

Tamar's plan was simplicity itself. Tommy would be provided with a room in the servants' quarters, on the top floor. This, he would keep clean himself. Tamar would begin the school she had planned for the village children, in the old schoolroom, which could be reached by the back stairs.

She intended to order sufficient desks from the estate joiners to furnish the schoolroom completely and, apart from a teacher whom Tamar hoped to bring from Malton, all would be ready very shortly.

'So you see, darling,' Tamar went to the window and put an arm round Victoria, 'Tommy will be under our roof. He'll get the chance of the education he needs and yet nobody can turn round and say he's getting preferential treatment.'

Victoria's tears cleared in an instant. 'Thank you, Mama. I should have known better than to doubt you.' Her face was rapturous with gratitude. 'You manage to deal with all my problems.'

Tamar gave a little sigh and replied, 'There's one problem your father and I cannot help you with.'

Victoria bit her lip. 'I know. It's Hoyland Wheatcroft, isn't it? I do think of what you told me, but there's no spark there.'

Stephen interrupted. 'It is becoming embarrassing, Victoria. The Wheatcrofts are good friends of ours now and constantly expect an announcement.'

Still she would not commit herself, much as she wanted to please her parents. She was reluctant to take the final irrevocable step, but did not know why she held back.

Granny Topliss was called to two more cases of diphtheria, but arrived in time to save each patient. This success was a great boost to her trade and she found the local girls and women treading a path to her cottage door, to buy love potions, chest lotions and all manner of medicines. This ensured that she had a better living coming in than ever before and for this, she blessed Lady Lassiter.

Once Tamar had finally made up her mind about the school, she set to work with a will. Victoria and Hilary's desks were transferred to the estate workshop to be copied in various sizes, to fit from a five-year-old to an eleven-year-old. A Miss Jewson was engaged as the governess but before she took up her duties, she and Tamar compiled a list of what needed to be bought, from a register to pens, ink and chalk. Miss Jewson also advised on primers, reading books, atlases and any other necessary equipment.

Stephen Lassiter was pleased that Tamar had at last made a start on the school about which she had talked for so long.

'It will be a great benefit,' he commented. 'It means that eventually, all the tenants and workpeople will be able to read and write, which will upgrade our workforce. I'm a great believer in education for the masses. The more a man knows, the better he can do his job.'

The Sunday before the school was to open, Stephen had the vicar make an announcement from the pulpit, asking all the villagers to attend a meeting in the Long Room immediately after the service.

Once they were gathered together, Stephen stood to make his announcement.

'Her Ladyship and Miss Victoria have opened a school and all children between the ages of five and twelve will attend on each weekday.' He then went on to introduce

Miss Jewson, the new schoolteacher. 'Miss Jewson will keep a register and I shall want a good excuse for any absentee,' he said firmly.

The first morning, the children shuffled and giggled as they queued through the kitchen and up the back stairs. Once inside the schoolroom, however, they were so impressed by the light and airy surroundings that all silliness was forgotten.

Tamar and Victoria stayed for the first couple of days and made it quite clear that they would drop in from time to time. Although she had great confidence in Miss Jewson's ability as a teacher, there was no way Tamar was going to allow the older ones to get out of hand. The threat that she could pop in at any time would keep them on their toes.

Miss Jewson proved a real treasure. She was thrilled to have charge of her own little school and encouraged the pupils to bring acorns, autumn berries and other nature specimens with which to decorate the room.

As Victoria had hoped, Tommy showed that he was highly intelligent. In fact, when the slates and pencils were first given out, to the amazement of the three women, he proudly wrote, 'I can read.' They hurriedly gathered at the other end of the room, to discuss his statement.

'He must have taught himself to write! And how can he read when he is unable to talk?' demanded Tamar.

'Think how little of our reading is done aloud,' replied Mary Jewson. 'I will give him a passage to read and answer comprehension questions on. That sorts out the true readers from those who repeat parrot-fashion.'

By the time the rest of the children had mastered the alphabet, Tommy had answered the set questions, proving that not only could he indeed read, but also understood what he read. There was no doubt that he was Miss Jewson's star pupil.

It seemed that providing him with writing materials had proved the catharsis Tommy had needed. He now felt equal to anybody and would write to anyone who had the time or ability to read his messages.

Chapter Sixteen

It was the custom in Thorsbury to auction off the contents of any cottage whose tenant had died. However, as Gertie had died of diptheria, no one would want to buy her possessions, so Stephen sent for a dealer from Malton to empty the house.

The day he came with his flat cart, Tamar asked Tempy to negotiate with him, as she would have more idea of what Gertie's bits and pieces were worth.

'Do your best for Tommy,' she said. 'It will go in the bank for when he's older.'

Before the second-hand dealer left, Tempy went down to the schoolroom to where Victoria was giving Miss Jewson a hand.

'These were in a drawer, Miss,' she said, handing over the three linen handkerchiefs.

Seizing his slate, Tommy wrote, 'Christmas' and pointed to Victoria.

'Oh, how lovely! Thank you, Tommy,' she enthused.

Tempy took them from her. 'Better ti be safe than sorry,' she said. 'It was getting these as cost Gertie her life. They'd best go down ti t'laundry and be boiled, Miss.'

Victoria was startled. 'I never knew the reason Gertie had been to Malton,' she said sadly.

Over breakfast the next morning, Stephen discussed the meagre amount they had been paid for Gertie's possessions.

'It's not a great deal,' he said, 'but it will grow in the bank for when Tommy starts work.' He did not notice the silence between his wife and daughter, as their eyes met guiltily, each thinking of the five thousand pounds invested in Tommy's name.

When Hodgetts brought in the post, Stephen shuffled through his pile. 'These are all business letters, nothing urgent. Put them in my study, please. I'll deal with them later,' he instructed.

Victoria read hers, wrinkling her nose as she did so.

'Who's yours from, dear?' her mother asked.

'Hoyland Wheatcroft,' she answered. 'He wants me to be his partner at the Sinnington Hunt Ball.'

'Jolly good,' commented Stephen, looking towards his wife for support. Tamar, however, was frowning over her letter.

'It's from Sarah. She sounds anxious. She says that Mother's ill,' she said in a worried tone.

Stephen was instantly alert. 'What is it? What does she say?' he wanted to know.

'She gives no details. Apparently a few months ago, she and Martha told each other that they were worried about the two mothers.' She paused, thoughtfully. 'I suppose it's odd, really, that they each look after the other one's mother.'

Stephen considered the news. 'I think we had better go down to Sleightholmedale on Sunday,' he said, 'and find out exactly how things are. Sarah must feel that things are serious, if she's taken the trouble to write especially.'

Tamar had read on. 'No, that's only part of the letter. Joe is sending Georgie and Jeanette and Jeanette's new husband on a honeymoon trip.'

'It's a wonder he hasn't written to you,' Stephen mused.

'He will, but letters take so long to arrive. I expect Joe will want them to stay here,' she smiled. 'He was most impressed with our home.'

'And rightly so.' Stephen gave an answering smile. He was justifiably proud of his family home.

It was with mixed feelings that Victoria approached the trip down to Sleightholmedale the following Sunday. While she loved the picturesque valley, she was also worried at leaving Tommy alone so soon after Gertie's death. There would be no school that day to occupy him and she wondered how the child would pass his time. However, Mary Jewson was so intrigued and delighted with Tommy's progress that she was only too happy to take him for Nature walks and to set up a Nature Table in the classroom for him.

When the coach turned right at the top of the steep drop into the valley, the broad-leaved woodland that clothed the valley sides was a riot of autumnal colours, while the squirrels scuttled along the branches, gathering their winter stocks of acorns and beechnuts.

As they reached the valley floor and came in sight of the long, low, thatched farmhouse, even Stephen had the feeling of coming home. Although they loved their own elegant mansion, this quiet vale and the homely farm held a special place in their hearts.

They had called for a meal at the King's Head at Kirkbymoorside, so as to avoid encroaching on the Oaks' dinner-time.

They arrived just as the pint mugs of tea had been passed round after the meal. The adults were by the fire while Edward and Annie sat drawing at the table and baby Hannah played with the cat on the rug. Kitty stood by the sink washing up and, as they entered, quickly poured out three more pint pots, while the Lassiters took their places at the table.

'This is a surprise,' said Jonadab Oaks. 'What 'ast thoo come for?' He had not been in the front row, when tact was handed out.

'We came to hear about Gertie and Jeanette's visit,' answered Tamar. 'And do I understand that Jeanette is married?'

'Aye, she is an' all,' replied Jonadab. 'To a Canadian man at that.'

As her father spoke, Tamar took the opportunity to study her mother and was disturbed at what she saw. There was nothing tangible; merely a blurring of the outlines, as though her mother had become a shadow of her former self. As the afternoon wore on, it became very obvious to Tamar, also, that her mother's memory was badly impaired. She frequently repeated herself and asked Tamar questions to which she had only just given the answers.

When the mugs were cleared away, Jonadab rose swiftly to his feet.

'Come along, Stephen. Aah've a few good foals Aah'd like thoo ti look over. Then Aah'll show thoo t'threshing set.'

George's eyes met Stephen's as his father went towards the door. He smiled shyly. No matter how his father showed off the threshing machine, only George could work it; this was a source of great satisfaction to him and one of great irritation to Jonadab.

When his grandad and uncle went out, Edward packed away his drawing and began to fidget.

'We are off, aren't we, Dad?' he questioned. Just then a pony trap drew up outside. 'Here's our Maria. She expects to go,' he pressed.

Tamar looked curious. 'Where are you going?' she asked.

'Our Dad shows us the secret places of the woods,' answered Edward impressively.

George smiled, sheepishly. 'Perhaps your Cousin Victoria would like to come? Unless she's too grown up,' he added.

'No, I'd love to come, Uncle George.' Victoria gave a conspiratorial smile. 'It sounds intriguing.'

The steep hillsides of the valley, before they gave way to the heather-clad moors further into the vale, were clothed with seemingly impenetrable woodland. To the casual observer, the trees were so densely packed that there was no apparent way in. To the Oaks of George's generation, however, when every childhood moment stolen from their father's stern gaze and injunctions to work was precious, they presented a different story. Each secret little trail was familiar, every one leading to its own hideaway, be it an open glade, where the sun dappled through as the trees thinned a little, or secret grottoes and caves hollowed out of the fragrant bracken. Here they could lie, luxuriating in the silence and solitude, oblivious of the consequences of their return to the rigours of the adult world.

This was the secret kingdom that George was revealing to the new generation – not theirs for a few stolen moments, but to enjoy as a right of childhood.

Bringing up the rear of the Indian File, as it snaked through the undergrowth, ankle-deep in crisp leaves of russet and gold, or burrowing through the bracken which here, and under the trees, was still green and sweet-smelling, Victoria too, recaptured her childhood. The outside world and its pressures became remote and she realised for the first time what a sensitive and thoughtful man her Uncle George was.

While her husband and daughter were each enjoying themselves in a different way, Tamar settled down for an afternoon of chat with George's wife, Sarah and her own sister, Martha, who had come down from Cherry Tree Farm.

While the two old women dozed by the fire, the three younger ones discussed them anxiously. Tamar recalled the days when she had lived at Cherry Tree Farm, when Victoria was a baby. Mrs Butler had been a forceful and dominating woman in those days, constantly struggling to exert pressure on George and his first wife, her daughter Elizabeth.

Now, to quote a saying of Jonadab's, she'd 'gone into t'little room.' Not only had she shrunk, but she had become pathetically dependent, needing constant reassurance. In fact, Martha and Bob were thinking of employing a girl especially to look after her.

'It's hard to believe,' said Martha, 'that she took charge completely when my legs were burnt and I lost the baby. It's less than four years since, and yet look at her now.'

Before Tamar could ask for more details of her own mother's condition, however, Annie Oaks started into wakefulness.

'Beth! Beth! As thoo turned them cheeses today?' she demanded.

Her daughter Beth had been married for twenty-six years, so the listeners were distressed at this large gap in her memory.

'We've talked it over with Kitty as to whether she would rather look after Ma,' said Sarah, 'and get another girl in for the housework. Anyway, she says she would rather look after your mother, as Mrs Oaks knows her and will take better to her than to a stranger.'

Annie had now settled into a fitful, twitchy sleep.

'She's very difficult to control,' Sarah told Tamar. 'She wanders about, even at night-time. The other night we found her going across the meadow towards the beck, looking for Maria.' This was the child of Annie and Jonadab, who had been drowned at the age of ten, over twenty years ago.

Tamar rubbed her eyes and then rose to her feet and began to pace the kitchen floor.

'I'd no idea,' she apologised. 'Surely there's something we can do. We can provide a trained nurse. Two, in fact,' she added, turning to her sister, Martha.

'Nay. You know Faither would never allow it. He'd consider it charity,' smiled Martha. 'But thank you all the same, love.'

'Besides,' Sarah broke in, 'I think it's better if their lives remain much the same. It's less disturbing for them.'

Before any more could be said, George arrived back with Victoria and the children. All were flushed and giggling and, although they had done their best to tidy themselves up, twiglets and fronds of bracken clung to their hair.

'Where on earth have you been?' asked Tamar, but Victoria merely smiled and shook her head, while Edward replied, 'Secret places,' laughing up at his father.

What a difference between George's relationship with his children and Jonadab's with them, Tamar thought. How easy it would have been for George to have been forced into the same mould as Jonadab, but thank goodness, he had had the strength of character to be his own man.

'Come on, son,' he said to Edward. 'Let's go and show Uncle Stephen how the threshing machine works.'

Edward was now almost eleven and George was determined that he should master the machine and add another string to his bow. Edward had already amassed as much farming knowledge as many a man, simply through trailing round after his father from earliest childhood and constantly asking questions. George treated him as an equal and answered all his queries in full detail, rather than keeping him under his thumb, as Jonadab had done with his own sons. Now, it did Tamar's heart good to see the boy take his father's hand and go out laughing.

'It's grand to see them together,' she smiled across at Sarah. 'Especially when you think how scared we all were of Father.'

Just then, her mother's voice rang out. 'Oor Tamar's afeared o' nobody. She'd tek a stick ti stir mud up in t'clearest pool.'

Tamar smiled wryly, her lips quivering. 'She always said that,' she explained. 'I must have been a great trial to her.' She dabbed her eyes with a lace-edged handkerchief and then saw nothing incongruous in helping her sister and sister-in-law to lay the big pine farmhouse table for Sunday tea.

Normally they ate from the scrubbed pine surface, but on Sundays the table was spread with a huge, white linen cloth.

Outside, in the stackyard, George was climbing over the giant threshing machine, explaining how the cut sheaves were fed in and how the machine separated them, sending them out at the far end as straw, grain and chaff.

Stephen was intrigued. 'I wonder if it would pay me to invest in one?' he mused.

'Well, you need about thirteen men to run one,' George replied, 'but labour would be no problem to you. You employ plenty of men. What you need to weigh up, is whether or not the initial outlay would be recouped on your own farms or whether, in the long run, you'd be more in pocket employing a threshing contractor.'

'You're right, of course.' Stephen answered. 'I'll get my Estate Manager to sort out some figures, and see what we think.'

Jonadab had brooded about the stackyard, like a child with its nose out of joint, ever since George and Edward had joined them. It was bad enough to have their George lording it over him, knowing how the thresher worked, but now that Edward understood the workings of it too, it was even more humiliating. If it were not such a profitable venture, he would have regretted investing in it.

Try as he might, he could not bring the conversation back to his own domain. As the group headed towards the farmhouse, he made one last attempt.

'Thoo thinks as 'ow Aah'm into a good streak wi' me breeding, then?' he pressed Stephen.

'Yes, indeed, Father-in-law,' he answered. 'You've kept the colour true and yet I think there's more strength at the shoulder.'

'Aye. Aah 'ave that.' Jonadab was just going to elaborate on the good features of his new strain of foals when, to his incredulity, Stephen turned away again to George.

'I'd like you to give me a list of the rough cost of the day-to-day running expenses, such as coal,' he suggested.

'Of course,' George replied, as they re-entered the kitchen. Here the table groaned under the usual Sunday tea. In front of Jonadab's place was a huge pink succulent ham, with the carving knife and fork at hand. To accompany it was a selection of Sarah's pickles and chutneys with homemade bread and golden butter.

To follow, there were blackberry and apple pies, various cakes and scones with homemade strawberry jam to spread.

'By Jove!' Stephen rubbed his hands appreciatively. 'There's no food to compare with Sleightholmedale victuals.'

'Aye,' Jonadab replied, as he took his place. 'Mother's allus kept a good table.'

'Aah does mi best,' Annie smiled proudly. Tamar caught Stephen's eye. Neither of her parents, it seemed, realised that it was Sarah who was responsible for the excellence of the food. It was, Sarah had confided to her, several months since Annie had baked or cooked at all.

'I've been thinking, Stephen,' Tamar commented. 'It's been such a good year that we're never going to manage to get through all the fruit in the greenhouses. Perhaps Mother, Mrs Butler and the children would enjoy some grapes and peaches.'

Jonadab glowered across the table suspiciously, intent on

refusing this offer of charity. Stephen, however, forestalled him.

'What a good idea,' he answered. 'I hate waste and that would stop good food being thrown away. We'll send Robert down next week.'

With a grunt, Jonadab was forced to give in, although he could not help feeling that somehow he had been tricked.

After the meal, when they were all sitting around the fire in the parlour, Martha brought out Mary's letter to Ann Butler.

'I have no doubt that our Joe will be writing to you, Tamar,' she said, 'but this is what Mary has said to her mother.' Looking round to ensure she had their attention, she began:

Dear Mam,

I hope you are keeping well. I'm writing to tell you that our Jeanette has got married to a very nice young man, whose father has the farm nearest to ours.

Joe is paying for them to take a trip back home, our Georgie as well. They'll arrive in Liverpool at the beginning of April so that they are in England for the prettiest months. I have sent a wedding picture.

Your affectionate daughter,

Mary

While they digested the sparse contents of the letter, the photograph was passed round. It showed a couple, with the wife seated on a chair and the husband standing behind her. The thing that struck them most was Jeanette's startling resemblance to her mother. Indeed, the picture could have been of Mary at the time she had left for Canada.

On the way home, Tamar snuggled up to Stephen.

'What's your opinion of Mother?' she asked.

He hesitated. 'You must remember that she is in her seventies, which is a very great age,' was his reply. 'I feel that both she and Mrs Butler are dying, but I don't think it will happen soon. For one thing, I think the prospect of a visit from their grandchildren from Canada will give them sufficient boost to see them through most of next year.'

She sighed. 'Well, at least we are warned in advance. It must be dreadful to lose someone like they lost John Butler,' thinking of Ann's husband, who had suddenly dropped dead.

'No matter how long we have to prepare, it's always a shock,' warned her husband.

The rest of the journey was passed in animated conversation about the Canadian guests.

Fortunately for the two old ladies down in Sleightholmedale, the winter was reasonably mild, so that they did not have the cold to contend with. Also, there was no chance of the farms in the valley being cut off by snow, so that the doctor was always available should he be needed. Stephen's prediction proved correct and there was no deterioration in the condition of either of them. The forthcoming visit of their grandchildren provided a much-needed stimulus and they discussed it incessantly with anyone who would listen.

Victoria had become more and more involved in her mother's school. She and Mary Jewson had become friends and Victoria spent much of her free time teaching the younger children.

In vain did Tamar argue with her on the subject of marriage, but there was no way she would be moved.

'You are no longer a girl, Victoria. Don't think Hoyland Wheatcroft will wait for ever upon your whim! His father wants him married and an heir provided. Although they considered you the ideal choice, it's obvious now that they are growing impatient with your perverseness.'

Victoria's expression was mulish. 'I have no wish to be married, Mama, as I'm tired of telling you,' she maintained. 'I've tried and tried to love Hoyland, but there's no way it can come. Next time he asks me to marry him, I shall refuse him and free him from his obligation.'

Tamar was nonplussed by the finality of this declaration. 'Please, Victoria, don't be hasty,' she pleaded. 'He's the last opportunity you're likely to get. Whatever will become of you?' She looked at her beautiful, wayward daughter, for whom she had hoped for so much, then with a sudden insight into her daughter's obstinacy, she flashed, 'I hope you don't still entertain some foolish fancy about young Sturdy!'

Victoria shot her a glance of unrepressed fury.

'I can assure you, Mama, that there is nothing either foolish or fanciful about my decision!' Seeing the reproach in her mother's eyes, she calmed herself, and before Tamar could speak, she continued, 'I have been talking to Mary – Miss Jewson,' she corrected herself, 'and she had explained a great deal about education. Things I had no idea about. It seems that since the Education Act in Parliament in 1870, the government has begun to crack down. The Act has been in force for several years now and yet many schools, including ours, do not comply. You see, Mama . . .' Her eyes were bright with enthusiasm as she continued with the lengthy preamble to the point she would eventually make. 'We only require the children to remain in school until they are twelve, but the government has raised the upper age limit to thirteen. It will no longer be satisfactory for them to leave on their twelfth birthdays.

'This means there will be more children on the roll. Far too many for Mary to manage on her own.' Tamar's eyes narrowed warily, as her daughter continued, 'She'll need help, either from me or another paid teacher, so I have made a decision. I shall devote my life to teaching!'

Tamar groaned aloud. 'You can't want to develop into a middle-aged drab like Miss Jewson!'

Victoria bridled. 'I admire Mary more than anyone I've ever met,' she retorted. 'I should be proud to be like her.'

Tamar tried another ploy. 'What about Hilary?' she demanded. 'He will marry a suitable girl and how is she going to accept a middle-aged spinster as a sister-in-law?'

There was silence for a moment, but Victoria was defiant. 'She would have to accept me. This is my home.'

'No, Victoria. It is only your home for as long as you stay unmarried or your father remains alive. After that, it is Hilary's home. He and his wife will decide whether or not they wish you to stay here. Think about your position very carefully, before you close any doors.'

Victoria did not accept many invitations over the winter but, those she did accept, she went to as Hoyland Wheatcroft's partner. Tamar saw that no expense was spared on the cost of her gowns and accessories, so that she was outstanding. She put on a good show for Hoyland, laughing up at him and teasing, until he was once more besotted with her.

'She's a little minx,' observed Stephen. 'She brings him on and off the boil as she likes, but Bramley's getting annoyed.'

'It's too bad of her,' Tamar agreed. 'They are accepted as a couple, although no announcement has been made. If she cries off now, she'll make him look such a fool.'

Just as there had been no real winter, so its end, when it came, was imperceptible. The lowering skies broke up, to be replaced by shafts of blue and the children at Thorsbury school brought bunches of hazel catkins and pussy willow for the Nature table. Tamar realised that March was upon them already and that Joe's family would be arriving in early April. She was determined that this visit was going to be more successful than Joe and Mary's had been.

'We don't know why their visit went wrong,' she said one breakfast-time, 'but part of it was our fault, at this end. We just expected them to come back here and fit in, taking their places as though they'd never been away. We must make more effort to entertain the younger ones.'

Stephen folded up his paper. 'You mean plan out the time that they're staying here with us? Find out what's on and get invitations for them to garden parties and spring balls?'

Victoria leaned forward excitedly. 'We can take them to the Theatre Royal in York and the York Spring Race meeting.'

'I'll go down to Sleightholmedale and tell the family that we'll keep them here for April and arrange a full programme for them. Then they can have them for all of May, when it's the prettiest period in the valley.' Tamar said.

'In June,' cut in Stephen, 'they can visit their Butler relatives in Leeds and Middlesborough.'

'Oh, how I wish we'd put ourselves out for Joe and Mary.' Tamar was not to know that it was Joe's own character which had caused the failure of their visit.

Chapter Seventeen

As the date of the arrival of their young guests drew near, Tamar began to feel qualms as to their tact and dependability.

'I do hope we can rely on their discretion,' she tackled Stephen in a worried tone one morning.

'You were anxious when Joe and Mary were coming,' he reminded her, 'and not a breath passed their lips.' Neither Tamar nor Stephen was aware of how Mary had blabbed Victoria's secret to Martha, and in ignorance of this, he went on, 'I'm convinced that we can rely upon their children.'

Victoria caught the end of this as she entered the room.

'Your mother's worried about Georgie and Jeanette, hoping that we can depend on them to say nothing about Tommy,' he informed her.

'I'm sure they'll be fine,' she replied. She was quite pensive for a moment. 'They are a really grand couple and I've often thought that I wasn't very nice to them, when I was over in Canada. I was far too wrapped up in myself and my own troubles. I must make it up to them now.'

It had been arranged that the Lassiters should be in York to meet the train in which their relatives were arriving from Liverpool. Victoria thought back to her own journey over the same route when she had left Tommy with Gertie. What a lot of water had passed under the bridge since then, she mused.

They had booked into their usual hotel in York, a discreet and luxurious one, close to the Minster, where they were well known. York was looking at its best. Although it was only the first week in April, the huge dome of the sky was a deep cerulean blue, stretching from horizon to horizon. The Minster stood in its gleaming glory against the blue of the sky, while the city walls snaked from the station towards the spires that shone in the sun.

Victoria was quite excited as they went towards the station. She had built up her expectations of Georgie and Jeanette coming over to England and was looking forward to seeing her cousins again.

They stood in the station which was like a wind tunnel, even though it was such a warm day outside. When the train drew in, in a cloud of steam, and the passengers alighted, looking towards the bridge, Victoria saw them crossing over and waved vigorously. She shouted with a smile, 'There they are!'

Catching sight of her, they waved back, pointing out their aunt and uncle to the other young man who accompanied them. When they met up, Victoria kissed her cousins and was introduced to Jeanette's husband.

Stephen competently organised the luggage and they drove in the Lassiter coach to the Hotel. Here the three young Canadians were obviously impressed by the high esteem in which the staff there held the Lassiters.

As they sat in the lounge over afternoon tea, Tamar said, 'We have booked to stay in York for a week. This evening we'll just have dinner in the Hotel, so that you can have an early night after your journey. Later in the week we have booked for the Theatre Royal. That's a comedy, so you should enjoy it.'

Jeanette laughed. 'As we've never even seen a theatre before, I'm sure we shall enjoy it!' She looked at Tamar and Victoria. 'Dad's given us some money and asks that you help us to choose suitable clothes for the kind of functions we shall be attending.'

Remembering Joe and Mary's unsuitable clothes, Tamar and Stephen were grateful that Joe had shown sensitivity over this aspect of their visit.

They found all three young people charming. They were frank and open and got on well together, as well as making a fuss of Victoria, so that she thoroughly enjoyed their excursions round York.

Tamar and Stephen watched fondly at the way Victoria relaxed in Georgie's company. He treated her with an old-fashioned courtesy and charm, to which she responded happily.

'It's a pity they're cousins,' Stephen remarked. 'She seems more at ease with him than any chap she's met for years.'

Tamar frowned. 'It isn't the fact of them being cousins that worries me – I don't think that matters nowadays. I just don't want them to fall in love, because I'm sure that Victoria would never be happy in Canada. She hated the time she was there.'

Stephen spoke again, after a few moments thought. 'Of course, Georgie knows about Tommy. It's something we have learned to live with and never even think about: it would probably make a difference to his feelings, however.'

Meanwhile, the four young people filled their days with trips on the river, walks on the walls and shopping expeditions. Jeanette and Ned seemed to accept company on their honeymoon and enjoyed every moment of this new standard of living, far removed from the rigours of the prairies.

The highlight of their stay in York was to be a visit to the races, followed by the spring ball that evening, in the Assembly Rooms.

The day of the races was bright and clear and Tamar noted how well the two girls looked together. Victoria had chosen a two-piece of deepest rose-pink velvet, which set off her dark beauty, while Jeanette wore a similar outfit of softest powder blue, her dainty fairness providing the perfect foil for Victoria's striking vividness.

The three Canadians were overwhelmed by the jostling crowds and excitement of the occasion, never having encountered horse racing before.

The Lassiters joined friends for a champagne reception and it was brought home once again to their guests what wealthy and influential people they were. Their companions were knights, baronets and earls, and the party also included two Members of Parliament.

Seeing Victoria at her most vivacious, Tamar regretted

that Hoyland Wheatcroft never seemed to inspire such liveliness in her.

Before explaining to the young ones the intricacies of betting on the runners, Stephen had a serious word about losing money.

'Make up your mind how much money you are prepared to lose,' he cautioned, 'both on each race, and on the whole afternoon. Don't forget that the favourite is the horse which most people expect to win and there are reasons for this. If you back the favourite in most races, you are far more likely to win but, on the other hand, you won't win much. It will be more exciting for you to choose a horse in each race which you fancy and only put on it what you are prepared to lose.'

All this seemed complicated to his listeners but, as the time for the first race approached, they grew more excited. They went to the paddock to see the runners parade and admire the brightly coloured silks of their jockeys. The two girls made their choices according to what they thought were the prettiest outfits, while Georgie and Ned summed up the quality of the horse-flesh, as though they were experts.

Eventually, their bets were placed and they took their places in the stand to watch the progress of the race. When the horses came within sight of the winning post, Victoria could hardly believe her eyes. Her horse, Bonnie Blue, was in the lead, although being hard-pressed by another horse.

Forgetting her upbringing, she began to jump up and down, yelling its name at the top of her voice.

'Come on, Bonny Blue!' she almost screamed. Tamar could not believe that this was her daughter, acting in such an uncontrolled fashion in public. She had not seen her so deliriously happy for many years.

There was a great groan when it seemed that Bonnie Blue would be overtaken and Victoria covered her eyes for a moment. As she dared to look again, however, the jockey spotted the danger, applied a couple of brisk touches of the whip and Bonnie Blue surged forward, to win by half a length.

Among the surrounding crowds who smiled in amusement to see this lovely girl so carried away by her win, was Francis Sturdy.

Like Victoria, he had taken little part in public life since he had allowed himself to be beguiled by Caroline Chelton, rather than await Victoria's return from Canada. He had soon seen Caroline for the empty-headed girl she was, and it had taken a lot of ingenuity to avoid being bamboozled into a proposal of marriage by her very determined mother. He had spent long periods abroad after that and when, on his return, he had seen Victoria at various social functions, she had been on the arm of Hoyland Wheatcroft and had greeted him with no more than an occasional circumspect nod of acquaintance. He had thought, with disappointment, that he had missed his chance.

It was pure coincidence that his parents had persuaded him to accompany them to the York races that day. Now, seeing Victoria again, so obviously happy and as lovely as he ever remembered, he stopped short, searching for her escort. Unable to see young Wheatcroft, he hardly dared to hope that she had broken off the relationship.

As he stood, undecided about whether or not to approach her, a young man ran up to her and taking her round the waist, swung her round, laughing.

'Congratulations, Vicky! You've won!' he exclaimed. Another young couple joined them and all four went in a laughing, singing group towards where the bookmakers' stands were.

Francis felt sick. For almost six years he had cursed himself for allowing Victoria to slip through his grasp. When his cousin, Thomas Forster, had been killed, Francis had pledged himself to care for Victoria when she came home from Canada, where her parents had sent her to recuperate from the shock.

He had been young and insecure, and the loss of his cousin and best friend had been a bigger shock than he had realised. Victoria had been whisked away by her parents just when he needed someone to hold on to.

Now, for a few wild moments he had thought that she

was within his reach again. Seeing her there, he was determined to seize a second opportunity and speak to her.

At the very moment of his happiness, his hopes were dashed once more, to see Victoria embraced in public by a young and handsome man. Such behaviour could only betoken an understanding and he turned away, sick at heart.

The rest of the day at the races was equally thrilling, but, Victoria's was the only win. None of the young people lost much, however, being content to take Sir Stephen's advice.

They all piled into the coach back to the Hotel, where the men sat over drinks in the lounge while the women went to lie down in their rooms, to rest before dressing for the ball.

Victoria had only just removed her two-piece and lain down on the bed, when there was a tap on the door. To her surprise, her mother came in. She had expected Jeanette, coming for a chat about the events of the afternoon.

'Hello, Mama,' she smiled, as Tamar came and sat on the bed. 'What a lovely day out it's been, hasn't it? They all enjoyed it thoroughly and so did I.'

Tamar hesitated, unwilling to cast a cloud on Victoria's happiness. 'Yes, darling, but your Papa wants me to have a word with you. Their ways are not our ways and you must discourage your Cousin Georgie from embracing you in public. It gives a wrong impression. It may be quite acceptable in Canada, but it certainly is not done in England.'

Victoria's face was downcast. 'I'm sorry, Mama. We were all so excited that there seemed nothing wrong in Georgie giving me a hug.'

'We'll say no more about it. Just remember not to let it happen again,' Tamar smiled. 'Get some rest now, and look as lovely tonight as you did today.'

When they assembled in the Hotel lounge, waiting for the coach to pick them up, the three men looked appreciatively at them, convinced that they would be escorting the three most beautiful women at the ball.

Stephen had ordered corsages for the ladies and it was a merry party which set off for the Assembly Rooms.

Unfortunately, Francis Sturdy had also decided to go on to the ball with his parents. When he saw the Lassiters' party arrive, his heart seemed to beat in his throat. Victoria, by some strange coincidence, was wearing exactly the same shade of gold satin that he remembered so clearly from the days when he and Thomas had vied for her affections. It suited her colouring perfectly, showing off her unusual tawny eyes, with their golden lights.

Francis debated with himself whether or not he dare pluck up his courage to ask her for a dance, but his heart quailed at the thought of presenting himself in front of Sir Stephen and Lady Lassiter. He remembered the fervour with which he had assured them that he would wait for ever for Victoria, and recalled how shallow his vow had been. His resolve was strengthened when the party was joined by the same two young men who had accompanied them to the races that afternoon. The one who had been so attentive, embracing her in public, made straight for her with a most proprietary air, taking the seat next to hers.

Seeing the way they laughed together and really seemed to enjoy each other's company, Francis gave up hope. He decided that he had left things too late. He ought to have apologised to Victoria as soon as he had finished with Caroline Chelton. Perhaps then, she would have given him another chance. Now, his fears of the afternoon were confirmed. She had found someone else.

There were a couple of occasions when Victoria thought she glimpsed Francis dancing, but the floor was so crowded and she was having such a good time, that she could not be sure. She must be imagining things.

Jeanette, like Tamar, was beginning to be worried about her brother's attitude to Victoria. While dancing with her husband, she confided to Ned, 'I do hope George isn't falling for Victoria. She comes from such an entirely different background and she hated it in Canada.'

Ned looked over to where his brother-in-law was dancing with Victoria. 'He's all right. They're cousins and get on well together. That's all there is to it,' he assured her.

The ball was the highlight of their week in York and

the following day they travelled to Thorsbury. The bright weather still held and they exclaimed at the freshness of the rolling fields of bright green spring grass. As well as clutches of thicker woodland, the fields themselves were also scattered with trees, veiled with the verdant green of their burgeoning leaves.

As they drove into the sweeping main drive, the Manor looked at its most imposing. The sun from the west lit up the east front with its many sparkling windows. Backed by the dense trees of Thorsbury Woods the Manor stood out almost like a fairy castle.

The three young visitors had been impressed by the standard of luxury at the Hotel in York, but to find the same standards in a private house was more than they could have ever imagined, even though Joe had never stopped boasting about the magnificence of his sister's home.

All three were good riders and Stephen chose mounts to suit them all, so that they could explore the countryside in Victoria's company. Although it was a quieter time than the week they had spent in York, they were entranced by the countryside which was rich and luxuriant, especially compared with the rolling landscape of the prairies back home.

On the last Sunday of their visit to Thorsbury, they were all going together for a grand family reunion in Sleightholmedale.

Tamar warned them before they set off, 'You'll find your Grandma Oaks and Grandma Butler both rather frail, but they are looking forward so much to seeing you. You, of course Jeanette, they have never seen, but Georgie was almost two when he left for Canada.'

Jeanette laughed. 'We notice you all call him Georgie, but at home we call him George. Georgie sounds a bit babyish for a grown man, don't you think?'

Tamar smiled. 'Yes, I suppose so, although I'd never thought about it. He was called "Georgie" as a child to avoid confusion. There was my brother George and my father's brother, our Uncle George. So you see, we've always called him Georgie!'

The visitors were just as impressed by the journey down

into the valley as was everyone who first saw it. The trees were just unfurling into full leaf, with the fresh, tender green of the beech trees acting as a foil for the rich, deep purple of the bluebells which carpeted the woodlands. Nearer the road, the verge was studded with clumps of primroses and delicately pale violets peeping from behind their dark green, polished heart-shaped leaves.

Jeanette leaned first from one side of the coach and then from the other. 'Look at the steepness of the hillside!' she cried, peering up at the tree-covered escarpment, which filled the window and soared upwards towards the sky.

Crossing again to the other window of the coach, she looked out into what seemed to be a tree-lined abyss. From her position, she could not see the road and felt that the wheels were going straight over the edge.

'Oh, Ned!' She covered her eyes and crouched close to her husband, who placed an arm protectively round her. Looking over her head he felt rather squeamish too as the ground seemed to fall away for hundreds of tree-clad feet.

When they reached the base of the hill, Stephen tapped on the coach roof. 'Stop here for a moment, please, Robert.'

The coach stopped. They all got out and Tamar pointed ahead.

'There's Aumery Park Farm, your Grandad's home,' she said.

Down the road, next to a small pond, snuggled a long, low thatched farmhouse.

'It's just like a picture book,' breathed Jeanette, as they looked back towards the sheer drop and then forwards again towards the farm.

'We'll get back into the coach. They'll be waiting for us,' Tamar said.

'We can walk down from here,' urged Victoria. 'Let Robert take the coach down and see to the horses and we'll walk the last half-mile.'

So they set off to walk towards the farm, where Jonadab Oaks was awaiting them.

Chapter Eighteen

Jonadab grew more impatient with old age and, although he would admit it to no one, his patience was stretched to the limit as the morning wore on. Those around him could show their excitement at the thought of this visit from Joe and Mary's family, but Jonadab refused to regard it as anything out of the ordinary.

'Aah dissent know what all t'fuss is about,' he grumbled to himself, as Sarah and Martha bustled about preparing a gargantuan meal.

The two grandmothers sat by the fire. Winter or summer, this was their favourite spot: the perquisite of old age. Now they chatted in quiet anticipation, recalling anecdotes of Georgie's childhood, before Mary and Joe's departure for Canada.

Although Jonadab refused to acknowledge any excitement, for the whole of the previous week the entire farm and buildings had been subject to the most rigorous tidying and cleaning, until it was almost possible to eat off the washed cobblestones.

'Anybody'd think t'Queen were coming,' complained one of the men, who had been called upon to redo a piece of work which did not meet with Jobadab's exacting standards.

Now George and Bob Lamb were supervising the last-minute grooming and brushing of the in-foal mares and those in the loose-boxes who had foals at foot. All the rest of Jonadab's considerable number of shire-horses were out in the fields, where they made a fine sight, grazing in the sunshine.

He was determined that the first sight of his heavy horses should impress. Try as he might, he could not avoid taking out his gold turnip watch with great regularity, flicking open the lid to consult the hour.

'It's time they were 'ere,' he grumbled. 'After all t'work

thoo lasses 'as put into t'dinner, we don't want it spoiled. There's nowt worse than Yorkshire pudding what's flopped.'

His daughter and daughter-in-law smiled at each other.

'They won't flop, Father,' Martha said, keeping a straight face with difficulty. 'Tamar knows what time we eat and they'll be here by then, don't worry.'

'Aah'm not worried,' Jonadab asserted stoutly. 'It's all t'work thoo's put in as Aah'm thinking about.'

Just then the Lassiter coach passed the window, but instead of stopping, went on towards the yard.

'Where's 'e off ti? Why 'asn't 'e stopped ti let 'em out?' Jondab limped over and threw open the door, peering both ways. 'They're up t'road, walking down! 'Oo's daft idea is that?' he frowned.

He stood by the door, peering up the road at the six figures who were strolling down towards the farm, Tamar obviously pointing out items of interest such as the heronry at the other side of the beck.

Unwilling to appear to be waiting for the guests, Jobadab came back into the kitchen. 'If they 'ad ti walk, they wouldn't want ti,' he chuntered. 'Folks is never right.'

By the time George and Bob had come in from the buildings and washed their hands at the kitchen sink, Tamar and Stephen opened the back door and led the guests inside.

Tamar introduced her parents first and then Ann Butler. After that, she worked down in ages from George to little Louisa Lamb, Martha's daughter.

After kissing their grandparents, much to Jonadab's embarrassment, there was a moment or two when the visitors stood about, feeling uncomfortable and not knowing quite what to do or say.

'Come on,' he ordered. 'Sit yourselves down and get a bit o' dinner stuck under your belts.' So saying, he directed them to places round the table while the five children were seated apart at a separate little table by the window.

'Edward, thoo's in charge there,' his grandfather commanded. 'See that t'lasses behave and we don't want any spill, oor Louisa.'

Suddenly, everybody felt comfortable.

After he had said Grace, Jonadab doled out Yorkshire pudding and onion gravy. Although their mother, Mary, often made Yorkshire pudding in Canada, it didn't taste anything like these and the guests tucked in with relish.

'It's probably different flour,' Sarah explained tactfully.

Once these were devoured, Jonadab carved a huge joint of beef, which came with creamed and roast potatoes and tureens of spring vegetables. When it seemed impossible for another mouthful to be consumed, fruit pies were placed on the table, with lashings of cream.

Jonadab had put Jeanette and Georgie one on each side of him so that he could monopolise their conversation. Ned was placed down at the other end of the table, so that everyone got some chance to talk to the visitors.

Georgie reminded Annie of Joe, when he had been young. Or indeed, he could have been his Uncle George's son, having a similar chestnut tinge to his hair and the same steady brown eyes. Ann Butler could see Mary in Jeanette and took on a new lease of life, chatting to her granddaughter.

Although they had thoroughly enjoyed their month at Thorsbury Manor, it had been like a novelty, really, not like real life to the Oaks from Canada. Here they felt completely at home. There was nothing pretentious about Aumery Park Farm. Georgie was particularly thrilled to find that he was to sleep in 't'lads' room' with Edward. He recalled his father's tales of his youth spent sleeping in the room with his brothers.

After the midday meal was over, Jonadab let the visitors out to look round the farm. The whole concept of the farm was now geared towards the breeding and breaking of grey shire-horses. It was his boast that stock of his breeding was instantly recognisable by those in the know.

Now that the running of the threshing machine took up most of George's days, he was unable to devote as much time as was necessary to breaking in the horses. Consequently, a new shepherd had been taken on, thus releasing Bob Lamb to learn to be a horse-breaker.

Jonadab set great store by the gentleness of his stock and, although some young foals were sold unbroken, he preferred to sell them older and ready broken in for work. That way, he could guarantee that they would work willingly and with no vices.

His grandchildren, for he regarded Ned as one, were greatly impressed by the whole operation. The fields had been subdivided by wooden fences and seemed to be filled with dozens of the great, gentle beasts, in addition to those under cover, awaiting foaling or being newly foaled.

Discussing the farm later, Ned and Georgie were amazed at the value of the horses possessed by Jonadab.

'I bet he doesn't know what he's worth,' Ned commented.

'That is what Dad said,' answered Georgie. 'They live as they've always lived, frugally. Nobody seems to realise how the money mounts up.'

'I expect they could almost live at the level of your Aunt Tamar and Uncle Stephen if the old man would loosen the purse-strings,' Ned went on.

Nevertheless, they were thoroughly enjoying the experience of staying down in Sleightholmedale. They explored the whole valley, going down to the healing spa behind Cherry Tree Farm and partaking of the waters, even though they had no ailments.

'Ugh!' exclaimed Jeanette. 'Fancy people coming all the way down here and paying to drink that. It tastes like rotten eggs!'

They rode up on to the moors, from where they could see the whole tiny Dale laid out below them. Hodge Beck ran the length of the valley, gurgling over its stony bed, with silvery trout lurking in the deeper pools. The water fowl darted from the shelter of the beckside reeds, followed by a trail of young ones, to hide further along in another safe haven of rushes.

Further down, almost opposite Aumery Park Farm, they could see the herons launching themselves lazily into the air on their huge wingspan, quartering the beck, ready to pounce on any unsuspecting fish.

They sat astride their horses in silence, unable to find words to express what they felt about the beauty which was spread out below them.

Turning to the moors, which stretched towards the horizon for mile upon undulating mile, they found this view more reminiscent of the prairielands at home. There were few trees, and the fresh spring green of the new heather, among which unfurled the fronds of young bracken, gave the same unbroken view that was more familiar to them.

As well as exploring the close environs of Sleightholmedale, they ventured further afield and Georgie persuaded his Grandmother Butler, frail as she was, to go with him in a pony trap up to Fadmoor. Jeanette and Ned rode beside them and the old lady pointed out what had been the Butlers' farm, where Georgie had lived with them when he was a child. He found this going back to his roots fascinating. Both Jeanette and Ned had been born in Canada, but Georgie felt somehow different, perhaps even superior, to think that he had been born in the Old Country and knew the very house. He was determined to go across the moors to Whitby and see the spot from which he had emigrated. This trip, however, would have to wait until a plan of their grandad's had been put into operation.

The sale of young horses and older broken mature ones was an ongoing process during the spring and summer, and it occupied a great deal of Jonadab's time. While he enjoyed bantering and haggling with the buyers, he felt that his time could be better spent.

Consequently, he had arranged with the local auctioneer to advertise a sale of surplus stock, when he hoped that all prospective buyers would congregate on the farm, see the various horses paraded and bid against each other for those they fancied.

He realised that he was taking a risk. There would be the auctioneer's fee to meet and some of his regular customers might object to bidding on the open market. However, Jonadab was always one to take a chance, even though he was now in his late seventies.

'What we lose on t'roundabouts we sh'll gain on t'swings,' he told George. 'Nowt ventured, nowt gained. We can but try it,' he said philosophically.

George and Bob had discussed the plan between them and did not consider that it would be a success. However, George was the first to admit that he was unadventurous, especially compared to his father, so was quite happy to let the old man have his head.

The farm was once again tidied up and everything made ready for the sale a good week before it was due to take place.

'Aah wants it all well-fettled up,' Jonadab announced. 'Folks'll see 'ow a well-run farm should look.'

About three or four days before the sale was to take place, Bob Lamb was awakened just after dawn by the sound of heavy horses galloping. He lay for a few seconds trying to decide what on earth it could be, before jumping out of bed and running to the window. To his horror, he caught sight of two or three of his father-in-law's heavy shire-horses galloping round the corner, behind the farm, up towards the moors.

Almost as he rubbed his eyes, not believing what he saw, another two galloped past, skittishly kicking up their heels.

As Bob dragged his trousers on, he woke Martha and told her what had happened. He then dashed from the house and rode the pony, bareback down to Aumery Park.

Fortunately, there was no need to lock the doors, so he was able to run straight in, through the house, and up to George and Sarah's bedroom. Here, he knocked urgently on the door.

'George! George!' he called, in a hoarse whisper, unwilling to awaken anyone else just yet.

George flung open the door. 'What's up?' he demanded.

Bob had seen enough on the way down, to know what had occurred. The horses tended to lean against the fence-posts and rub. Obviously, several of them had chose the same post, which had gradually become weakened and then snapped. The crack of the breaking post had, no doubt, frightened the shires, which were just as excitable as lighter-built animals. Trampling down the fence, they would have milled around for a time and then followed the most adventurous of the group out of the field and away to freedom.

George brought his trousers, stockings and boots out on to the landing, while Bob poured out his tale. They slept in their shirts, so that saved a few moments.

'We'd best saddle up a couple of decent horses. Them shires can cover some ground when they're that road out,' said George.

'What about your father?' asked Bob. 'Should we wake him or not?'

George considered for a few seconds. 'I'll leave him a note,' he decided. 'He'd only insist on coming and it'll be too much for him. We'll call at Toby and Lydia's and collect some of the men. Mebbe our Georgie and Ned could com an' all. It'll take a fair number of us to round 'em up, if they're up on t'moors.'

Once a group of about seven or eight were saddled up and ready, it was easy to follow the trail of the runaway shires. There were about twenty of them and the track down the valley was flattened from hedge to hedge, showing how they had surged along the trail.

The path of the horses was clearly seen passing round the back of Cherry Tree Farm, down to the back and up towards the moor.

George groaned. 'If they've got spread out over the moors, it'll take us all day to round 'em up.'

Going down behind Cherry Tree Farm towards the beck, they came across the first casualty. Hearing a pathetic whimpering, slightly off the track, one of the men cut aside towards it and found a yearling foal writhing, wild-eyed in the hedge-bottom. To his distress, it had a leg almost severed, wrapped round by a piece of wire.

'Boss!' he shouted to George, who came back quickly.

'Oh, no,' he groaned, his heart overwhelmed by the pitiful sight. Seeing the wire wrapped so tightly round the fetlock, he frowned. He knew his father's opinion of wire blocking gaps in the hedges. In Jonadab's eyes it was not only unsightly, but dangerous.

Bob came riding back, full of apologies. 'I'm sorry about the wire, but I'm always short of time,' he tried to explain.

Fond as he was of his brother-in-law, George could not help but hold him responsible for the foal's accident.

'You'd better go and fetch your gun and put it out of its misery,' he said shortly, then turned to rejoin the others.

Once they reached the high moor, the grey shire-horses could be clearly seen, browsing in twos and threes, spread over a large area.

George marshalled his men and sent them in pairs, each couple to round up a specific group and escort them down and back to Aumery Park Farm. Once they had expended all their energy, they should be reasonably placid and easy to manoeuvre. Georgie and Ned found the episode thrilling, and rode off across the moor in pursuit of their designated horses with a great sense of excitement.

George himself set out after a group of three who were tossing up their heels playfully on the horizon. He had heard the sound of Bob's shotgun and knew that he would soon be up to give him a hand.

Looking round to see that all the other groups were moving sedately towards the moor edge, he spotted Bob making his way towards him. Raising a hand, he waited for his brother-in-law to catch up. He was fond of Bob, who had taken the place of his own two brothers. Nevertheless, he did wish that he would not take so many chances. There had been the episode when he had got drunk with Joe and now this laxity in filling the gap in the hedge with wire, rather than planting in-fill hedging. Jonadab was strict, and although George did not believe that his father would dismiss Bob, he was determined that he would speak up on Martha's husband's behalf.

When they drew level, George pointed to the three horses in the distance.

'There's just them three,' he said. 'All t'rest is on t'way back. They seem to 'ave settled down.'

'We'll just amble slowly towards 'em and keep 'em quiet,'

suggested Bob. 'Then, if we split up and approach 'em from each side, we should manage 'em all right. 'Ow's t'Canadians getting on? Can they manage, d'you think?'

'Oh, aye. They're good horsemen,' commented George, 'and we needed every extra hand we could to handle this lot.'

The two men slowly guided their mounts towards the least three stray horses, but were disturbed to see that they were by no means settled. Their eyes were still rolling while their ears twitched and they snickered to each other in nervous apprehension.

'Take it steady,' said George. 'We mustn't upset 'em.'

Speaking soothingly, they drew nearer to the horses, but the beasts remained twitchy and nervous. Before George and Bob could get close enough to usher their own horses flank to flank with the runaways, to bring them under control, they threw back their heads, tossed up their heels and with a whinny, set off at full speed.

The two men started up in pursuit, hoping that their faster horses would soon overtake them. However, before the strays had gone half a mile, the lead horse launched itself in the air with a shrill scream, and leapt over a sharp drop, down into a deep ravine. The following two horses came upon it too suddenly to halt and overbalanced, landing in the base in a tangle of broken limbs.

With a sharp, 'Whoah!' George and Bob steadied their own mounts and peered down on the scene below them. The first horse appeared to have survived the fall, scrambling terrified over the twisted limbs of the other two.

'It's another job for t'gun, Bob,' said George, heavily.

While Bob rode back home for his gun, George made a detour round the ravine and put a halter on the wild-eyed, trembling animal, then led it down off the moor, passing a dejected Bob coming back on his errand of mercy.

Jonadab was heading towards the moors when he met George coming down. He drew up and looked soberly at his son.

'What's t'score, lad?' He spoke in a depressed tone and his brow was furrowed in pain.

'Three to be put down, Faither,' George answered. 'Bob's seen to them.'

'No 'ope of saving 'em?' Jonadab had no real expectations when he asked.

'No.' George had no wish to go into details. 'Broken legs. Nowt can be done.' To his relief, Jonadab asked no more, being quite satisfied to accept George's judgement.

'Aah never learns, George. Aah sets missen up above mi station in life, but t'Lord allus 'as summat waiting ti put mi in mi place. What 'E tells us in Proverbs is a lesson ti us all. "Pride goeth before destruction and an 'aughty spirit before a fall".'

He rode on, brooding, alongside his son, his face gloomy and looking his full age. 'Every so often, Aah thinks as 'ow Aah can do nowt wrong; that every decision Aah meks is bound ti be right. Then t'Lord brings some calamity ti show mi who's t'boss.'

George realised that his father must be lifted out of the trough of despondency in which he was wallowing. He was too far advanced in years to regain his optimism easily, without help.

'This is nonsense, Faither.' He spoke firmly. 'I am a joint partner in this business and if I'd disapproved of the idea of the sale, I'd have said so.'

Jonadab listened, apparently digesting his son's words, but made no answer.

'Just because we have a natural disaster, which can happen to anybody who keeps animals, there is no way that you can hold yourself to blame.'

Jonadab would not at first be consoled. 'There was t'moor fire, when we lost them fields o' oats we was depending on,' he reminded his son.

George contained his impatience. It would not help if he antagonised the old man. 'All farms pass through bad patches. We've lost three shire-horses out of goodness knows how many. It's very unfortunate, but if they'd got out and none had been lost, you'd have thought no more about it.'

Jonadab allowed this to simmer in his mind for a few moments and then he brightened up. 'Perhaps thoo's right, lad,' he conceded. 'Aah've got t'fence mended already while thoo and t'rest was roundin' 'em up. We'll put it behind us, and get ready for t'sale. Aah 'opes as 'ow t'Lord sees it in 'Is way ti mek it a success.'

As well as the thrill of the round-up, the three young Canadians were fascinated by the preparations for the sale, being under the impression that this was the customary way of selling livestock in England.

The day of the sale could not have been more perfect. The sun shone and the number of prospective purchasers who poured down into the valley exceeded all Jonadab's expectations. There were plenty of viewers who had heard of the Oaks shire-horses but who had never taken the trouble to approach Jonadab with a view to buying. Now that there was a definite day set aside and they knew that, in competition with other purchasers, they would pay a fair price, they treated it as a day out.

Sarah approached Jonadab. 'Should we give them refreshments, Father?' she enquired. 'Not all of them will have brought food.'

'Give? What does thoo mean, give?' Jonadab looked askance. 'Thoo and oor Martha could put a table outside and sell 'em some buns or summat. Thoo could mek that big urn full o' tea an' all, and sell 'em cups. But thoo dissent mek brass through giving stuff away.'

Sarah felt embarrassed at the thought of charging money, but Jeanette and Victoria thought it a huge joke.

'We'll stand behind the counter, Grandad,' Victoria laughed. She had come down with Stephen, who was insistent that he wanted no favours. He would bid for what he wished to buy along with the other buyers.

Tamar spent the time in the farmhouse kitchen, chatting to her mother. She could not help but note that the visit of their grandchildren had brought a new lease of life to both her own mother and Ann Butler.

While Victoria and Jeanette did a brisk trade in slices of cake, scones and buttered tea-cakes, Martha and Sarah blew up the fire with the bellows and set to work to bake more supplies.

'It's as bad as Threshing Day,' laughed Sarah.

'It's better,' giggled Martha. 'We sh'll be paid for this!'

At the end of the day, when all was totalled up and the auctioneer had taken his commission, Jonadab found that the day had paid off far better than he had ever anticipated. He sold every horse put forward for sale and, in the face of competition, they had raised more money than he had hoped. It could not be an annual event, but it had been a most successful way of disposing of all his surplus horses. He could now concentrate on breeding and rearing for a few years.

''Ow about thoo lasses?' he questioned Sarah.

'Yes, thank you, Father. We had a good day,' she replied, giving no details. He was nonplussed for a moment, obviously expecting her to hand over the takings from the sale of food. She kept him waiting for a minute or two and then added, 'I shall share our profit into four and we shall have a quarter each.'

Jonadab's eyebrows bristled and his blue eyes were sharp. 'Oor Victoria dissent need any,' he argued.

'How do we know?' Sarah retaliated. 'She's no income of her own and she's worked hard today for this. It's only fair she should have her share.'

With a sniff of disgruntlement, he went on his way, overseeing the tidying up and supervising the collection of the last horses.

On his way back to the house, he caught up with Victoria and Jeanette.

'Where's yon dumb little lad o' Gertie's?' he demanded. 'What's 'appened ti 'im since she died?'

Jeanette went quiet. She remembered that Gertie had taken Victoria's child, but knew no more.

Victoria hesitated. 'He lives in the servants' quarters at home, Grandad,' she replied. 'Mama and I have started a school since the Education Act came into force. He goes to the school with the other village children.'

''E won't be at school now,' Jonadab said. 'Why didn't thoo bring 'im with thoo?'

Victoria looked embarrassed. 'I didn't think of it.'

'Well, think on it now. 'E's a grand, bright little chap, poor mite. It 'ud do 'im good ti come down 'ere occasionally and play wi t'other bairns an' t'animals.'

Victoria was thoughtful. 'Thank you, Grandad,' she said. 'I'll do that in a few days' time.'

Chapter Nineteen

Victoria had been aware of her cousin Jeanette's curiosity when Jonadab had mentioned Tommy, so that, although the other girl had asked no questions, she waited until the three guests had moved on to stay with Mary's sister, their Aunt Christiana in Leeds, before accepting her grandfather's invitation to take Tommy down to Sleightholmedale at the end of the May holiday.

She could not understand why it had not occurred to her before to take the child down to Aumery Park Farm. There she could be with him without causing gossip, and her young cousins were far kinder to him than the village children.

Before the first visit, Sarah and Martha each had a word with their own children.

'Just because Tommy can't talk, doesn't mean that he isn't bright. He's just as clever as any of you and you must be kind to him,' said Sarah.

'I bet he doesn't know about threshing machines, like I do,' boasted EDward.

'There's more to life than threshing machines,' she corrected sharply. 'And don't forget – just because he can't speak, it doesn't mean he can't hear. So watch your tongue.'

Although Tommy enjoyed playing with the other children, his favourite occupation was to slip his hand into Jonadab's and go round the horses with him. Jonadab talked away to the boy, as though oblivious of the fact that he could not answer.

There was only time for one short visit before all the children were due back at school, but Victoria was determined that in the long summer holiday she would bring him down more often. She was convinced that Tommy gained from the companionship of her little cousins.

She herself missed the companionship of the three young

Canadians and realised how she had deprived herself by cutting down her social life. However, she told herself that to devote her time to Tommy and the school was worth any sacrifice.

She and Mary Jewson were very proud of the progress the children were making under their tuition. The parents too, were less resentful of the school when they discovered that children at state schools must be paid for and Sir Stephen provided a much better standard of education free. Even when the state education became free, they still appreciated the facilities provided by the village school. Tamar would have liked to see it moved out of the Manor, but no building in the village could provide the necessary size and scope.

One morning in early June, they were at breakfast when Hodgetts brought in the post. Of the two letters handed to Victoria, one was from Hoyland Wheatcroft, arranging to call on her later in the week. The second was an official-looking missive and she turned it over with curiosity, before opening it.

When she began to read the contents, she gave a little gasp, half-disbelief, half-pleasure.

'Whatever's wrong, darling?' Tamar asked solicitously. Looking more closely, she saw that her daughter was utterly colourless. Even her lips were drained of all colour.

Taking out her smelling salts, she held them under Victoria's nose, while Stephen chafed her hands. She stirred and pushed them away.

'I'm all right, thank you. It's just the shock.'

'What is the letter?' Stephen asked her.

She picked it up and smoothed it out, giving a glance towards the butler.

'Would you leave us for ten minutes please, Hodgetts?' Stephen requested and when the door had closed on him, both her parents turned to Victoria.

'Well?' they asked in unison.

Looking down at the letter, Victoria realised that it was shaking in her hand. 'It's from a firm of solicitors in Leicestershire. Sir William Forster has died and left me twenty thousand pounds in his will.'

There was a stunned silence. Stephen held out his hand for the letter. 'May I read it, Victoria? Do you think you can have made a mistake?'

Upon reading it, however, he shook his head. 'No, you're quite correct. He has left you a fortune.'

'She'll not accept it! I won't have her take a penny from that man, dead or alive.' Tamar's eyes were flashing with golden lights against the stark pallor of her face.

Victoria faced her with incredulity, while Stephen thought how much alike they were.

'Whatever do you mean, Mama? The money has been left to me and I have every intention of accepting it!' In the short time since she had first read the letter, although the enormity of the sum had not really made full impact, she realised that it would give her the independence she craved.

Stephen intervened before Tamar could say something she would regret for the rest of her life.

'Tamar, you know nothing of Sir William Forster, apart from the fact that he was Thomas' father.'

Tamar bit her lip. So great was her loathing for the man who had seduced her and who had been Victoria's real father, that she had almost blurted out the truth. If ever Victoria discovered that her lover, Thomas Forster had, in reality, been her half-brother and that her beloved Tommy was the child of an incestuous affair . . . Tamar could not imagine what her reaction would be. She had no doubt that Victoria's feeling for her would turn to hatred and she could not bear the thought of this happening.

Stephen spoke calmly. 'Now this has been a shock to all of us,' he said placatingly. 'We must consider very carefully what is to be done. To begin with, Tamar, I see no reason why Victoria should refuse this bequest. It is a great deal of money, but Forster was a very wealthy man and, after all, Thomas was his only child. What is more natural than that he should wish to provide for the girl who would have been his daughter-in-law, had Thomas lived.'

Tamar grasped at this lifeline. 'Of course,' she breathed,

on a sigh of relief. 'This is why he will have left it to you, darling. Because of Thomas.'

'What other reason could there be?' Victoria asked, innocently.

Tamar hesitated. 'There is no other motive for him to leave you a legacy. The reason I felt you should refuse it is because he had a bad reputation where women are concerned and I didn't want strangers lumping you with females of ill-repute.'

Victoria threw back her head and laughed aloud. 'I couldn't care less what strangers say about me or think about me. We all know why he left me the money and I have no compunction over accepting it.'

Stephen undertook to do all the negotiating with the solicitors for her and said that he would invest the money to the best advantage.

'I want a certain amount available to be able to use it as I wish,' she insisted, but would give no details of what she intended to do with the money.

In the excitement of the news of her legacy, Victoria had forgotten the letter from Hoyland. Now she re-read it and noted that he was calling the following day to discuss a visit to a summer ball, for which he wanted her to be his partner.

Victoria spent a sleepless night trying to come to a final decision about Hoyland. She knew that she could never love him and the money from Sir William's will removed the necessity for her to marry at all. Despite this, she had no wish to hurt the young man, who had been faithful and patient throughout her whims.

When he was announced the following day, Victoria suggested that they should go for a stroll up the Walks. Here they would be private and she could make her decision clear to him.

It was obvious that Hoyland took this to be a favourable sign. The little paths that wound through the trees were edged with wild strawberries, mostly still in flower, but occasionally in early fruit. Between the trees hung draperies of wild dog-roses, ranging from almost white to the flush of deepest pink.

As they ambled through the dappled shade, he took her hand in his and gently stroked it. 'Dear Victoria . . .' he began.

She disengaged her hand and said firmly, 'Please Hoyland. I have something I wish to say.' The gravity of her expression and the seriousness of her tone warned him that what was to come was not what he had hoped.

By now they had reached the summerhouse at the furthest extent of the Walks. Here they sat down and Victoria drew a deep breath, both to steady her voice and to give herself the confidence to say what she must.

'There's no beating about the bush, Hoyland. Although I respect you and am very fond of you, I cannot love you as a wife should love her husband. I feel that the only fair thing for me to do is to release you from your pledge to me, so that you may look for someone else to become your wife.'

His face was stricken. 'Please, please, Victoria, don't say that! I don't mind how long you take, as long as you give me the hope that one day you'll be mine.'

She was quite firm, however. 'I'm sorry, Hoyland. It isn't fair to you. I don't suppose I shall ever marry and it's wrong of me to keep you hanging on.'

Eventually, he was forced to accept her decision. 'Is there someone else?' he asked.

'No. I can truthfully say that there is no one else,' she assured him. 'It's just that I want to fill my life with the school and the village children.'

'What a waste!' he said bitterly. 'You're such a lovely girl. You'd make an ideal wife and mother.'

'Well, I'm afraid it's not to be,' she smiled wryly, and then kissed him on the cheek. 'Goodbye, Hoyland. Please don't think too badly of me.'

He turned away abruptly and went to the stable block for his horse.

Victoria said nothing to her parents of her final rejection of Hoyland. The acquisition of such a large amount of money, even though she had not yet actually received it, had changed her whole attitude to life. For the first time, she felt that she was a person in her own right – not her parents' daughter, nor her brother's sister, but Victoria Lassiter, lady of private means.

She called at her father's study one morning a few days after she knew that all the negotiations were completed and that the money was invested in her account. Stephen looked up in surprise.

'Now, darling,' he said. 'It can't be business, surely, that brings you to my study?'

'It is business, Papa,' she replied. 'I need your help.'

He laid down his pen and smiled across at her. 'I'm at your disposal,' he offered. 'What can I do to help you?'

Victoria hesitated, then burst out, 'I want to take Tommy to Harley Street or some other medical centre. I am convinced that as he has spoken once, he can speak again, given the correct medical help. Now that I can afford to pay for him to see a really good specialist, I feel that I must do so.'

Stephen hesitated. 'What are people going to think? Ostensibly, Tommy is your late maid's child and it's going to look odd if you take him to London for treatment.'

Victoria's eyes flashed. 'I don't care what anybody thinks,' she retorted. 'Tommy is my child and I shall do my best for him. This is all the money means to me. I would willingly spend the whole twenty thousand pounds, if it enabled him to speak. Think how you would feel, if Hilary were in the same situation.'

Stephen frowned. 'It's hardly the same thing,' he objected. 'The circumstances are different.'

'In what way are they different?' she demanded. 'Tommy is my child, just as Hilary is yours. Tommy will inherit anything I leave and, as far as I'm concerned, it might as well be spent on helping him now.'

Stephen realised that Victoria was now a far cry from the girl she had been before her inheritance. She had a new firmness and determination, that he rather admired. He suddenly capitulated.

'I'll make enquiries from friends in London and see who is the best man in that field, then we'll arrange an appointment for him to see Tommy. I think it would be more discreet if you and your mother took him and stayed in an hotel, rather than open up the London house, so that the servants know our business.'

Victoria felt that, at almost twenty-seven, she could have gone without her mother, but was aware that the stand she had made was enough of a shock for her father, without pushing her new-found independence too far.

Once Stephen realised how determined Victoria was to do her best for Tommy, he worked quickly on her behalf and, within a couple of weeks, had made arrangements for her to take the child to a throat and speech consultant in Wimpole Street.

Before setting off, Victoria talked to Tommy explaining why he was going to see the doctor but that no one could guarantee success. She was afraid that the disappointment would be too acute for him to accept. However, he nodded cheerfully and smiled at her explanation.

The journey by train from York to London was an exciting adventure for Tommy and they were booked in at a quiet hotel, not far from the doctor's consulting rooms.

When they arrived to keep the appointment, Victoria was pleased that she had Tamar with her. She felt that 'Lady Lassiter' commanded more respect than plain 'Miss Lassiter' would have done. Tamar explained exactly how Tommy had come to lose his speech.

'He's a bright child,' she explained. 'He taught himself to read from only three books that were in the house. One was a picture book, with things like "A for acorn" in it, and yet by using that and practising with the other two books, he achieved what very few people could manage to do.'

After a thorough examination the doctor said, 'There is no physical reason why he should not speak, Lady Lassiter. There is nothing wrong with either his tongue or his throat. This leads me to believe that his dumbness is psychological, brought on by shock. I am afraid that I can offer no advice as to how he can recover his speech. It will do no harm for him to practice sucking and blowing, to keep the throat muscles active, but I can offer no practical help.'

Victoria was despondent. Her one thought, when she had inherited the money from Sir William Forster's will, had been that this would enable her to pay for Tommy to be cured. Now it seemed that there was no hope.

While the women were in London, Sir Bramley Wheatcroft paid a visit to Thorsbury Manor.

'What's this about Victoria giving our Hoyland the push?' He came out with it without any preamble.

Stephen was taken aback. 'I know nothing about it,' was his reply. 'It is true that he called on Victoria a week or so ago, but I am not aware of what transpired between them.'

'To put it bluntly, she said she could never love him and he'd better look for somebody else.'

'I had no idea. I'm so sorry.' Stephen was apologetic. 'I do hope it will make no difference to our friendship.' He and Tamar regarded the Wheatcrofts as good friends and enjoyed their company.

'She's kept him dangling for so long. She's made the lad look a fool!' Sir Bramley was quite irascible.

'I don't think so.' Stephen spoke placatingly. 'There's never been an announcement and very few people accept them as promised. I'm sure Hoyland will find an equally desirable girl and make a good marriage.'

'She told him there was nobody else,' Sir Bramley pressed.

'That is quite correct,' answered Stephen. 'Victoria has become very strong-willed recently, and does not consult us about the decisions she makes. However, there is no other young man in the offing.'

Eventually, he smoothed the other man's ruffled feelings and they agreed that the broken romance would make no difference to their friendship.

Upon Victoria's return from London, Stephen sent for her. 'Why did you not tell us that you had broken off with Hoyland Wheatcroft?' he asked.

She raised her eyebrows. 'I'm sorry, Papa, but I didn't consider it was anybody's business but mine and Hoyland's.

If he's been round whingeing to you to intervene on his behalf, he's gone down in my estimation.'

'It was Bramley who came to see me,' answered her father. 'He was most distressed and thought that you had treated Hoyland shabbily.' He paused for a moment and then added, 'As do I, Victoria!'

She had suffered a great disappointment in London and to return home to criticism from her father was more than she could bear. To Stephen's consternation, she broke down in tears.

'I never encouraged Hoyland,' she sobbed. 'I have been quite open from the beginning and told him that I didn't think I could love him. Be honest, Papa, you and Mama encouraged him because he's a nice man and a good catch.'

Stephen was about to protest, but upon reconsidering, was bound to admit that she was correct.

Victoria dried her eyes. 'I'm independent now, and have no need to marry just so that I won't be a burden to Hilary. So, you see, I didn't consider it anybody's business but mine and Hoyland's. However, now you've pointed it out to me, I realise that it was only courtesy to have told you of my decision and I do apologise.' She looked across at her father and smiled, lips quivering. 'I'm afraid the money went to my head, Papa,' she admitted. 'I felt that it gave me the power to do anything I wanted to. Anyway I've come to my senses now.'

'Your mother and I must learn to stop treating you as a child,' Stephen smiled. 'But our children will always be children to us, no matter what their age.'

Chapter Twenty

A few weeks later, Victoria received another letter which gave her cause for thought.

Her parents were together in the small sitting room, when she took it in to show them.

'This arrived for me this morning,' she said. 'It's from Lady Rowena Forster. Sir William's widow.'

Tamar was disturbed, remembering the five thousand pounds which Sir William Forster had provided, to pay the blackmail money to Gertie's brother-in-law, Rob McDonald. Was there any way his widow could have traced the sum to her and Victoria? If so, could she demand the return of the money? Various thoughts chased through her mind.

'What does she want?' The words came out in an almost churlish tone.

'She's staying at the Towers, Sir James Sturdy's home, and she would like me to call and see her,' replied Victoria.

'You won't go, of course.' Tamar spoke decisively.

Victoria looked enquiringly from her mother to her father.

'I see no reason why not,' Stephen answered.

'She may be intending to contest the will and rob Victoria of what is rightfully hers,' Tamar protested.

Stephen hid a smile, remembering how vehemently his wife had opposed Victoria accepting the bequest in the beginning.

'She can't do that, darling. Probate has been granted and the money is in Victoria's possession. It cannot be reversed now.'

'I think she has every right to be curious as to what kind of person her husband bequeathed such a large sum of money,' Victoria said. 'For my part, I would like to meet Thomas' mother.'

'Then I shall come with you,' asserted Tamar. Not only did she want to be present at the interview, so that she knew exactly what passed between Victoria and Lady Rowena, but she herself, wished to satisfy her own curiosity as to what kind of woman William Forster had married in preference to her.

Knowing the truth about Victoria's parentage, Stephen was well aware of the turmoil that Tamar's thoughts would be in. Catching Victoria's look of pleading, he again intervened. 'We tend to forget that Victoria is no longer a child, Tamar.' he reminded her. 'She is a grown woman and quite capable of conducting her own affairs.'

Tamar took a breath to argue, but he held up a hand to forestall her. 'There is something else which you haven't considered,' he added. 'Lady Forster's invitation is extended to Victoria, and to Victoria alone. She would have every right to take exception if she turned up with her mother in tow.'

Tamar rose to her feet and flounced from the room. 'Thank you for wording it so tactfully,' she threw back over her shoulder.

'Thank you, Papa.' Victoria was delighted to have had his backing. 'I hope we haven't upset Mama too much.'

'I'll talk her round,' he said confidently. 'What you must do is to write and thank Lady Forster for her invitation and suggest a date when you can call. Make it early next week and you can go in the coach.'

Victoria did as he suggested and the following Tuesday found her heading for the Towers. She was rather apprehensive, both at the prospect of the interview with Lady Forster and additionally, in case she should encounter Francis Sturdy. It was, after all, his home and she debated with herself as to how she should react if they met. If she was strictly honest with herself, it was on the chance of meeting Francis that she was wearing the rose-pink velvet outfit which she had worn for the visit to York Races. Her Cousin Georgie had made it obvious that she looked beautiful in the costume, so she felt at her best as the coach entered the drive of the Towers.

The house was not as large and imposing as Thorsbury Manor, but on each side of the drive were large banks of rhododendron bushes. Although well past their flowering time, it was obvious that, in their season, they must be a glorious sight.

When the coach drew up by the front door, Victoria was a moment or two screwing up her courage, before allowing Robert to hand her down. She rang the bell and explained her errand to the butler, who conducted her to a pretty little sitting room, before announcing her.

'Miss Victoria Lassiter, m'Lady,' he said as he ushered her in.

The woman who looked up as she entered was about her own mother's age, but was now frail and delicate-looking. She had obviously been pretty, but was faded and had an air of sadness. No wonder, thought Victoria, having lost her only son and then her husband in such a few short years.

When she looked up and saw Victoria, her eyes widened in surprise.

'Do sit down, Miss Lassiter.' She spoke quietly, indicating the chair opposite hers.

Victoria took the seat and looked expectantly at her hostess.

'I hardly know where to begin.' Lady Forster seemed uncomfortable. 'You are not really what I expected when I asked you to call,' she said.

Victoria hesitated. It was not her place to take the initiative, but Lady Forster seemed to be in a quandary.

'Is it, perhaps, that you wished to know why your husband left me such a large legacy in his will?' she prompted.

The older woman appeared surprised at her openness. 'Why, yes. As a matter of fact, that is the reason,' she replied. 'But I must admit that you are not at all the type of person I had expected.' She studied Victoria carefully. The girl was obviously a lady and far too young and beautiful to have been one of her husband's paramours. Could she be one of his love-children, she asked herself. 'Who are your parents, my dear?' she asked. 'If you don't think it rude of me to enquire.'

'Not at all,' Victoria reassured her. 'They are Sir Stephen and Lady Tamar Lassiter.'

That settled that, then! She had a father, thought Lady Rowena. 'May I ask how you came to know my husband?'

'I had never met Sir William,' answered Victoria. Again, she was so transparently honest, that the other woman felt bound to believe her. 'The bequest came out of the blue and I could think of no reason why he should leave me anything,' Victoria continued. 'However, upon discussing the matter with my parents, we came to the conclusion that Thomas must have confided in him about me.'

'Thomas?' Lady Rowena turned quite pale. It was clear that she had never recovered from the tragic death of her son.

'Yes,' Victoria continued sadly. 'He had asked for my parents' permission to court me and, if it had not been for the accident which took him from us, he and I would have been married.'

'Oh, my dear.' She rose from her seat and came and put her arms round Victoria. 'To think that I had no idea. You would have been my daughter-in-law, had Thomas lived.'

They chatted for about half an hour and Lady Forster asked Victoria to keep in touch with her, for Thomas' sake. Victoria felt tempted to disclose to her that she had a grandson, but thought the better of it. She would wait and see how their friendship developed. She and her parents had managed to hide Tommy's existence for almost seven years and she felt that she owed it to them to keep the secret.

Francis Sturdy came round from the stable block to the front of the house, to see the Lassiter coach standing by the front door. Unable to believe his eyes he strode round and inspected the coat of arms on the door. Looking up at the coachman, he said: 'This is Sir Stephen Lassiter's coach, is it not?'

'Yes, sir,' came back the reply.

'Who is calling, may I ask?' Francis could not understand how the coach came to be at his home. When the reply came, he was incredulous.

'Miss Victoria, sir.' The coachman was impassive, seemingly unaware of Francis' astonishment.

He could think of no reason why Victoria should call at his house, but was determined that, if at all possible, he would seize the opportunity he had missed at York Races and at the Grand Ball which had followed. 'Third time lucky,' he murmured to himself. 'After all, I've nothing to lose.'

He entered the house and was standing indecisively in the hall, wondering whether or not he had time to go up and change, when the butler appeared, making for the little sitting room, which his Aunt Rowena was using during her stay.

'Brook,' he hissed. 'Is it Miss Lassiter you're going to show out?'

'Yes, sir.'

'Would you ask her to step into the library?' Francis was desperate to talk to Victoria in privacy. 'Don't tell her I'm in there,' he insisted. 'Just ask her to step in.' With that, he darted into the library to wait for her arrival.

'Show Miss Lassiter out please, Brook,' Lady Forster said. Then, turning to the girl, she embraced her. 'Please write to me. Keep in touch. I don't want us to lose contact now, since we've found each other.'

When she was once more in the hall, Victoria turned towards the front door, but the butler spoke.

'If you would just step this way, Miss Lassiter, please,' He ushered her down the hall and towards another door.

Victoria hesitated in the library doorway, but he bowed her in and closed the door behind her. The room was quite dark, as walls which were not book-lined were oak-panelled. She peered uneasily into the gloomy room and then saw Francis Sturdy standing by the fireplace. He leaned against the carved black marble, looking far more relaxed than he felt.

She gave a start, then turned back towards the door.

'Please stay, Victoria,' he pleaded. 'Please give me a chance to talk to you.'

Victoria's heart seemed to be racing in her throat and

she felt quite faint. She groped for a chair which was close to her and lowered herself into it. There she sat for a few minutes and there was silence in the room.

She was still half-inclined to leave and refuse to either listen or talk. However, she told herself, she might as well stay long enough to hear what feeble excuse he could concoct, to account for his neglect of her.

He crossed over to her and crouched by the chair. 'Please, Victoria, give me a chance to explain my actions when Thomas was killed.'

She refused to look at him, keeping her face turned away. He took her hand, but she snatched it from him, as though his was red-hot.

'When I was at my uncle's in Canada, recovering from the shock of Thomas' death, your offer to wait for me was a great solace.' Her voice was barely above a whisper, but once her silence was broken, the words came out in a torrent and she was unable to stem the flow. 'When I first met you and Thomas, there was little to choose between my feelings for you. I found you equally attractive. It was just that, as I got to know Thomas better, we seemed to have so much in common that he was the one for whom my love developed.'

She paused, unwillingly to reveal how distressed and humiliated she had been when, on her return to England, she had discovered that he had not waited for her as promised. As she turned her face away from his, he saw the tear which crept down her cheek.

'O Victoria, I could kill myself,' he groaned. 'Will you allow me to say a few words in my own defence?'

'I suppose so.' she said reluctantly.

'Please remember that, although we felt sufficiently mature to ask for your hand, both Thomas and I were not long out of school. When he was killed, I lost not only my cousin, but my best friend as well. Then, when your parents sent you to Canada my only sheet anchor was removed.' He drew his hand across his forehead and was deep in thought for a moment or two.

'My parents thought it would be good for me to go on

the Grand Tour, which had been arranged for me and Thomas. As it turned out, it was the worst thing I could have done. I drifted aimlessly round Europe, not being able to communicate with you. For all I knew, you could have disappeared from the face of the earth. I felt bereft and was fair game for Mrs Chelton to foist Caroline on me. She appeared so sweet and kind and, of course, she was available, whereas you were not. These are not excuses, Victoria. Nothing can excuse the way I treated you. I'm merely trying to explain the reasons for what I did.'

They sat in silence, each unwilling to break it. Francis was the first to do so.

'And now, of course, it's all too late. I should have approached you as soon as I realised what a mistake I had made over Caroline. I should have called on you with my apologies, but I simply had not the courage.' He sighed deeply. 'Now, of course, I've missed my chance. It's too late.'

Victoria had listened intently to what he had said. Now, she turned and looked at him. 'What do you mean, it's too late?' she asked.

'You've found someone else,' he answered, in a surprised tone. 'I saw you at the York Spring Race Meeting. You looked so beautiful and the young man who accompanied you was so obviously head over heels in love with you that it only remains for me to offer my congratulations.'

He was surprised at the peal of laughter which rang out as she threw back her head. 'That was my Cousin George from Canada,' she explained. 'I'm merely his relative. There is nothing between us whatsoever. It was a honeymoon trip for his sister and her new husband, so George came along to visit his birthplace.'

There was a long silence, as each digested what had been said. Victoria looked at him shyly.

'There is no one else in my life,' she whispered and then bit her lip in case she had been too forward.

'Have you received an invitation to the Morleys' ball in July?' he asked.

'Yes, but I was not intending to accept,' she replied.

'Nor was I,' he smiled. 'But if we both accept, may we take up our friendship where we left off?' On seeing Victoria hesitate, he continued, 'It may not develop as we expected it to last time, but at least we could be friends and companions.'

She looked at him with a smile. 'We shall not refer again to what has happened in the past. Let our friendship start again from new.'

A shadow crossed his face. 'What about your parents?' he asked. 'They are hardly likely to greet me with open arms, after what has happened.'

She smiled. 'We are no longer children, Francis. My parents know better than to interfere with my way of life. I'm twenty-seven now and your uncle, Thomas' father, left me twenty thousand pounds in his will, which gives me independence.'

Francis' face was a study. 'He left you twenty thousand pounds? Did he know you?'

'No, I presume that Thomas had told him that he wanted to marry me.'

'He left me the same sum, so he did us both a good turn!' he smiled.

He escorted her out and handed her into the carriage. 'You will go to the Morleys' ball, won't you, Victoria?' he urged. 'Even though I let you down when you came back from Canada, you won't let *me* down, will you?'

'Of course not,' she said gently. 'I shall be there, don't worry. I think we've managed to sort out our problems now, and all will be well with us from now on.'

As the coach drew away, she leaned from the window, returning his wave. Sitting back against the upholstery she realised that she felt happier than she had since Thomas had died, and wondered if this could be the beginning of a new and better life for her.

When she reached home, Tamar was impatiently awaiting her return.

'What a long time you've been,' she said, a question in her voice. Victoria had debated with herself on the way home whether or not to tell her parents of her meeting with Francis Sturdy. Upon consideration, she had decided against it. If he went to the July ball and asked her, quite naturally, for dances, it could develop from there, but if she confided in her parents and something prevented his attendance at the ball, not only would she appear to be let down, but Francis would plunge even lower in her parent's estimation.

'Your father is anxious to hear what has happened, as I am, of course,' said Tamar, with an air of nonchalance which thinly disguised her raging curiosity. 'Come into Papa's study and tell us all that took place.'

Victoria smiled. Tamar's disappointment on being overruled in her decision to accompany Victoria to the Towers would be alleviated by hearing the whole story – the thread through the needle, as she herself would phrase it.

When they were all seated. Victoria told them every detail of her interview with Lady Forster. 'She is so sweet,' she said. 'She looks so frail and delicate and obviously still misses Thomas. When I explained that had he lived, Thomas and I would have been married, she asked me to keep in touch with her. She wants us to correspond and for me to visit her whenever she is staying at Sir James Sturdy's home.'

Victoria was at a loss to understand her mother's reaction to this statement. It was almost as though Tamar felt jealous of Lady Forster and yet, Victoria wondered, on what grounds?

'You won't follow it up, of course.' Tamar spoke as though it was an understood thing that Victoria should reject the older woman's invitation.

'Why, of course I shall. She is so lonely and such a sweet person that I shall be only too pleased if I could bring a little happiness into her life.' retorted Victoria. 'Her home in Leicestershire is entailed and she is looking for a smaller place, somewhere in North Yorkshire, close to the Sturdy's.'

Tamar bottled up her anger. She dared not allow it to show, but she feared that this woman who had taken William Forster from her, was now going to take her daughter.

Yet in her heart of hearts she knew that there was no truth in her supposition. William would never have married her, Tamar. She was not his class, but she had always blamed Rowena Sturdy, considering that the other woman had stolen him.

If she acknowledged the truth, she could not have had a better husband than Stephen, who had given Victoria his name and raised Tamar to the status of Lady. In holding a grudge against Sir William's widow, she was merely being perverse.

However, she decided to allow things to take their course. She had learned better than to try to interfere in Victoria's life.

'The only thing that worries me,' Stephen said thoughtfully, 'is that if you visit Lady Forster while she is staying at the Towers, you are bound eventually to encounter Francis Sturdy. Don't you feel that you may, perhaps, feel embarrassed by such a meeting?'

'No, Papa,' she answered easily, marvelling at how calmly she could, if not actually deceive her parents, at least mislead them. 'A lot of water has passed under the bridge since Francis and I were friends. I think we are both sufficiently adult to cope with such an eventuality.'

Upon discussing the issue later, both Stephen and Tamar decided that Victoria had matured in a most satisfactory way.

Chapter Twenty-One

Victoria Lassiter found herself looking forward with excitement to the Morleys' ball. By cutting herself off from much of her social life over the past few years, she had been living an unnatural life, she realised. Although she still enjoyed helping at the school, she was beginning to find Mary Jewson rather too earnest and even dreary, for a constant companion.

The three young Canadians had left Sleightholmedale at the end of May, to spend part of June with Mary's sisters, Christiana in Leeds, and Jane in Middlesborough. From Middlesborough they would sail back to Canada and Victoria knew that she would probably never see them again.

When they had left, it was brought home to her how much she had enjoyed their company, especially that of her Cousin Georgie. She had basked in his obvious admiration, which he had made no attempt to hide, although she regarded it as no more than a light-hearted flirtation. The fact that Francis had presumed there was more to the affair than that, had caused her both surprise and amusement.

While Jeanette and her husband had enjoyed their visit, storing up memories of a different way of life and the magnificent scenery of the North Yorkshire moors and the little dales which ran between them, Georgie felt more personally involved. The scattered village of Fadmoor was not just a pretty village to him; it was his birthplace. He often rode up and stood looking at the farm where he had first entered the world. Leaving Jeanette and Ned to their own devices, he sometimes rode through the picturesque village of Gillamoor, with its cottages of honey-coloured stone and wide grass verges, starred with daisies and the sky-blue of speedwell. At the far end of the village he would enter the church and sit there, imagining his parents' wedding and his own baptism.

This visit back to his roots had had a profound effect on Georgie. The slower pace of life and the way that, after the wide expanses of his homeland, everything was on a miniature scale, was endearing to him. He had been charmed by the horse sale and excited by the incident with the escaped horses, interpreting them as just two of the many varied facets of life in England.

On the journey up to Middlesborough, they had stayed overnight at Whitby for Georgie to see the site of his emigration. His Uncle George had described the day to him as vividly as if it had only just occurred. It still stood out, in fact, in George Oaks' mind as one of the most memorable days of his life. Although he was not really an articulate man, he made the event live for his nephew, describing not only the sights and sounds of the busy little port, but both families' feelings to be losing, as they thought for ever, three members of their family.

The visit to Whitby proved traumatic for Georgie. He could feel the acute sorrow of the Oaks and the Butlers, and found himself regretting that the decision to go to Canada had ever been made.

The landscape and the small villages were attractive to him and he found the idea of staying in England very appealing. It was unlikely, however, that it would have occurred to him to put off his return to Canada, if things had gone as planned and their stay in Middlesborough had culminated in them sailing back to Canada.

As things turned out, they were called back to Sleightholmedale unexpectedly. Both Annie Oaks and Ann Butler had improved in health during the visit of their grandchildren but, although Annie Oaks' improvement was sustained after they had left, their leaving seemed to remove from Ann Butler all reason for living. She took to staying in bed all day and had no interest in life.

One clear day in late June, Martha drove up to Aumery Park Farm. Sarah was aware that her mother seemed to be gradually fading away and, each time she saw Martha's pony and trap heading up the lane which wound between the two farms, she feared the worst.

'How's things?' she asked as her sister-in-law came in.

Martha hesitated. 'I don't know whether or not it's too late,' she replied. 'She feels that she hasn't long to live and wants Georgie and Jeanette to come back from Middlesborough. She wants to see them before she dies.'

Sarah frowned slightly. 'Their passages are booked and they were going home at the end of the month. I don't know whether we can catch them in time.'

The message did reach them however, and the three managed to arrive back in Sleigholmedale in time to sit with their Grandmother Butler and talk to her again about their home and their life there.

'What about our Jack?' She spoke faintly of the son who had run away to follow Joseph and Mary.

'We don't see a lot of Uncle Jack,' answered Jeanette. 'When he first came over to join Father and Mother, he took up trapping to earn fast money, while Father built up the farm. He likes the life better than farming and he's away most of the year in the wild lands of the north, trapping animals for their furs.'

'He never married?' Ann Butler was eager for knowledge of her only son, even though she had heard it all before. Jeanette hesitated. She still could not tell her grandmother that, as far as they knew, Jack was a squaw-man, having taken an Indian woman as his wife. They had never seen the woman. It was only hints dropped by their parents; they themselves knew nothing definite.

Ann Butler smiled. 'John, your Grandad, would be glad that he's happy,' she said.

Their visit seemed to bring comfort to their grandmother and she drifted out of life, a day or two later, in her sleep.

It was the middle of hay-time on the Oaks' farms and, although he would not have voiced his thoughts, Jonadab could not help but feel that Ann Butler could have hung on a little longer, until all the hay crop was in.

Meadow hay was a vital part of the winter feed for the horses and he was anxious that it was safely gathered in before the weather changed.

Georgie was particularly intrigued by this facet of farm

life which he had not encountered before. The rhythm of the reapers, as they strode in unison across the field, every sweep of the scythes cutting a swathe of the fragrant hay, fascinated him. He found the strokes mesmeric and would have liked to have taken part. He realised, however, that there were years of practice behind the seemingly easy movements and satisfied himself with using the large wooden rakes to gather the cut hay into windows. These stretched across the mown fields, to catch the sun and the breeze and ripen the grass into sweet hay.

Aware that the family must attend Ann Butler's funeral. Jonadab strode round the hayfield, leaning on his stick and constantly consulting his watch, urging the workers on to greater efforts.

'Nay, Faither, you can't make t'sun work any harder and t'hay will only make it t'weather's right,' George remonstrated.

Jonadab was all for Ann Butler's coffin being carried up to Gillamoor Church on a freshly-scrubbed farm wagon, drawn by two of his best grey shire-horses.

'Nobody could want for better.' He made the statement as though defying anybody to argue.

Sarah, however, was adamant. She remembered her father's funeral and was determined that her mother's should be in no way less impressive.

'George is Mother's executor,' she told her father-in-law, 'and he will go up to the lawyer's tomorrow. I'm quite sure he will find that she has left sufficient money to pay for a good funeral. He'll call at the undertaker's while he's there and make the arrangements.'

Jonadab was surprised to know that George had been chosen by Ann as her executor. It was proof of how her opinion of him had undergone a dramatic change since he had first married her daughter, Elizabeth. But then, he thought, she only needed to get to know George to realise what a grand, dependable chap he was.

George was amazed at the amount of money Ann Butler had left.

'Of course,' he said to Sarah, 'she would spend very little

after selling the farm and the stock. She's lived first with us and then with Martha and Bob, so she's spent hardly anything.'

Sarah was quiet for a moment. 'When she and I lived with you and Elizabeth, didn't she pay anything towards our keep?'

'Of course not,' he answered. 'We would not have taken it, even if she had offered.' Not for the first time did Sarah marvel at what a kind and selfless man she had married. He had inherited none of his father's pride and dominant personality, and for this, she thanked her lucky stars.

During the mid-morning break in the hay-field, Jeanette sat, leaning against a hay-cock, between her husband and brother. Georgie was thoughtful for a while and then broached what was on his mind.

'The way of life, here in England, appeals to me, Sis,' he confided. 'So much so, that I'm considering staying here instead of going back to Canada.'

His two listeners were disbelieving.

'Oh, George! You can't make a decision as important as that, without a lot of thought and discussion.' Jeanette was horrified.

'I've thought about it, deeply,' he assured her.

Ned intervened. 'Think of your parents, George. Your Dad has been over twenty years building up the spread, especially for you to inherit. You can't leave him in the lurch.'

'Think of Mother, too. You must come home with us.' Jeanette was even more distressed.

Georgie bit his lip. 'I feel that Grandma Butler's death was a sign. It stopped us going home to Canada when we'd booked. Postponing our passage gave me time to think again. I want to stay in England.'

Before they had any more time to try to dissuade him, Jonadab's whistle sounded out as he called them back to work.

That night, in the privacy of their bedroom, Jeanette sobbed in her husband's arms at the thought of Georgie remaining behind in England. 'We must talk to him, Ned,' she said. 'I can't bear the thought of him staying here. How shall I ever face Mother and Dad?'

The following day they were needed again to give a hand with the hay-making, while Martha came to help Sarah to bake for the funeral, which was to take place the next day.

Jeanette and Ned stuck to Georgie like limpets, determined that when the time came for the mid-morning 'lowance, they would be close enough to tackle him again regarding his decision.

When they sat down with their tea and pie, Jeanette turned to her brother. 'George,' she began.

At the same moment, he said to her, 'Jeanette.'

'Have you changed your mind?' she pleaded.

'No. I've reached another decision,' he said. 'If Victoria comes to Grandma's funeral, I shall take that as another sign and ask her to marry me.'

Jeanette could not believe her ears. 'But George,' she expostulated. 'What about the baby?'

Ned looked from one to the other. 'What baby?' he enquired.

Jeanette looked round, then leaned closer to her husband and, lowering her voice, whispered, 'Victoria came to Canada to have an illegitimate baby, so that nobody here would know.'

Ned looked incredulous. 'Victoria? It can't be true!' he exclaimed.

Georgie glanced round uneasily, anxious to verify that they could not be overheard. 'Knowing her as I do, I am convinced that it could not have been her fault. She must have been taken advantage of.'

'But besides that, you've got nothing in common,' Jeanette objected.

'We have everything we need. I love her and I believe she loves me.'

Jeanette was becoming exasperated. 'You're talking like a love-sick youth, not a grown man. Look at it logically; what can you offer Victoria? You haven't even a job here in England and she's been brought up in luxury.'

'I'll get a job. Uncle George will employ me in some capacity. Of that I'm sure.'

At that moment, they were called back to work, raking the rest of the windows into haycocks.

There was no question of Stephen Lassiter attending Ann Butler's funeral, as he would be away on business. Tamar, however, was insistent that both she and Victoria must go.

'I hardly knew her, Mama,' objected Victoria, who disliked funerals and clutched at any straw to avoid going.

'When your real father died.' Tamar explained, 'you and I lived with Uncle George and Aunt Elizabeth. Mrs Butler and Sarah lived there too and she was kind to us. Suffice it to say that I want you to come with me.'

Victoria had been fed the myth ever since she was tiny, that her real father had died in a farm accident, and left her mother a penniless widow with a child to support. She had no reason to question the story and indeed, Tamar almost believed it herself, except when some ghost from the past presented the truth to her.

'And besides,' added Tamar, 'you will have a chance to see your cousins for one last time.'

With that Victoria grudgingly agreed to attend.

The day of the funeral dawned as crisp and fresh as a newly-starched sheet. Although almost July, the landscape had not faded into the blowsiness which often characterised the month. Apart from the sere écru of the newly-mown hayfields, the grass was still green. The hedgrows were colourful with foxgloves and white and red campion.

When Tamar and Victoria arrived in the Lassiter coach, Jonadab's brows drew together.

'They should 'ave come in summat a bit less conspicuous,' he grumbled.

'Nonsense,' smiled Sarah. 'Mother would have revelled in the tone it lends to the cortège.'

When they returned to Aumery Park Farm after the funeral in Gillamoor, Jeanette hung close to Georgie, determined that, if she could help it, he would have no chance to speak to Victoria alone.

In the end, although he was normally of a sunny disposition, he became quite short-tempered. Pushing his way through the crowd of people, he went to where Victoria was talking to her aunt, Ann Waind from Bransdale.

'Excuse me, Victoria. May I have a word?' he interrupted.

She turned in surprise. 'Of course, Georgie,' she smiled in welcome. 'I haven't had a chance to speak to you yet. I'm so sorry about your Grandma, but perhaps it was a blessed release.'

Before she could say more, he took her elbow. 'I want to speak to you in private. Please come outside,' he said urgently. She accompanied him, feeling intrigued as to what he could possibly want.

As Jeanette saw them making for the door, she caught her husband's eye and motioned with her head. Ned darted after them and caught up with them by the door.

'George,' he began, unsure of what to say.

Georgie was brusque. 'Not now, Ned,' he threw over his shoulder, as he steered Victoria through the back door.

Neither spoke as they crossed the sunlit road to stand by the spring, which was the only source of water for the house. It trickled down through the woods, to pour in a crystal cascade into moss-encrusted stone trough.

Still Georgie was silent, as Victoria trailed her fingers in the icy cool water. At last, the silence became unbearable and Victoria turned to look at him.

'Well, George. What is it?' she prompted.

He could think of no way to introduce his request tactfully. 'Will you marry me, Victoria?' he blurted out, unable to face her.

It was the last thing she had expected and she could not reply, not knowing what to say. Her mother had been correct when she had warned her that Georgie's feelings for her were deeper than the casual flirtation that Victoria had presumed.

Receiving no answer, he looked at her appealingly. 'I'm not asking you to come to Canada,' he answered her earnestly. 'I'm determined to stay in England and make my home here.'

Feeling that she must say something, Victoria raised her eyes to his and he saw that her normally light topaz eyes were now deep amber and tear-brimmed. He could read her answer in her expression and pleaded his case more desperately.

'I love you more than I can ever say. I'm willing to leave my family and change my whole way of life, just for you. Please say that you'll marry me, my darling.'

Victoria held up her hand and the tears brimmed over. 'Please stop, Georgie,' she begged. 'I can't bear to hear any more.'

He was devastated. 'You can't mean that you don't love me!' He was incredulous.

She shook her head, too overwhelmed to speak for a moment. 'Dear Georgie,' she whispered when she had composed herself. 'I love you as a cousin, but not as a husband, I'm afraid.'

He swallowed. 'I was so sure that you would say yes,' he protested. 'We seemed to get on so well.'

'Marriage needs more as a base than getting on well, Georgie,' she said, gently. 'I'm truly sorry if I've misled you, but although I've thoroughly enjoyed our relationship, what I feel for you is not the true love that marriages are made of.'

He shook his head numbly. 'It isn't your fault, Victoria,' he murmured. 'I haven't had much to do with young ladies and, just because I love you, I took it for granted that you loved me in return. Please forgive me. I've been a fool.'

'There is nothing to forgive. You've paid me the greatest compliment a man can pay a woman and I'm only sorry that my answer has to be no.'

They remained by the spring until each had recovered their composure, then moved as if by mutual consent back to the house.

As Victoria entered the kitchen, Jeanette came towards her through the funeral guests, who were beginning to make their farewells.

'Congratulations are in order, I take it?' she said coldly.

Victoria looked at her blankly, her mind still on Georgie's

distress. 'What?' she queried and then, as the meaning of Jeanette's words dawned on her, she answered distractedly, 'Oh, no,' before passing across to her mother.

Jeanette went over to Georgie, who had come into the house a little way behind Victoria. One look at his set face confirmed what Victoria had said.

'She didn't refuse you?' Jeanette had never envisaged this reaction from their cousin and took it as an insult that she should reject her brother's offer of marriage. 'Who does she think she is?' she hissed. 'She's nothing but . . .'

'Leave it!' He almost snapped the instruction to her. 'Forget it, Jeanette. Make yourself pleasant to those who are leaving. We'll as likely as not never see them again.'

'No doubt she thinks she can hunt around for bigger fish. Well, with her background, she should be grateful for what she can catch!' Jeanette hissed.

'You mention one word about Victoria, and I'll never forgive you!' Georgie threatened, then smiled and nodded in his uncle's direction. so saying he masked his feelings and passed among the guests, smiling his goodbyes and shaking hands.

Victoria found Tamar talking to Annie Oaks.

'Hello, Grandma,' she said. 'You're looking better.'

Annie peered at her. 'Now, Victoria,' she said. 'No sign of a young man yet?'

Victoria smiled. 'No, not yet,' she replied. Turning to Tamar, she whispered. 'Are you ready to go?'

Her mother eyed her closely. 'Is anything wrong?' she queried.

'I want to go, if you're ready,' was the only response she could elicit.

Squeezing the old woman's hand and kissing her cheek, Tamar said, 'We must go now, Mother. We'll be down again before long.'

'All being well, I'll bring Tommy down to play in a week or two,' promised Victoria.

They passed among those in both the parlour and the kitchen, saying goodbyes. To Victoria's surprise, Jeanette merely proffered a cool cheek for her kiss, although both Ned and Georgie were quite natural.

Tamar's sharp eyes missed nothing and, as soon as the coach drew away from the farmhouse, she tackled Victoria.

'What has happened?' she demanded. 'What was wrong with Jeanette?'

Victoria was unable to control her tears. 'You were right about Georgie. He proposed to me this afternoon,' she sobbed. Pouring out the whole incident, she finished up, 'I don't know what has upset Jeanette. Whether she's annoyed that he proposed or that I refused, I don't know.'

'Why did you refuse?' Tamar wanted to know, feeling that perhaps any husband was better than none. 'If he was willing to stay in England, couldn't you have married him?'

Victoria sighed. 'Oh, Mama. You don't understand me at all. I did not love him.' She enunciated the words clearly and slowly. 'It's the same reason for my refusal of Hoyland and Wheatcroft's proposal. I can't marry a man I don't love.'

'Then I'm afraid you'll remain single for the rest of your life,' her mother retorted.

'If that's what it's to be, so be it!' was Victoria's reply.

Chapter Twenty-Two

As July progressed, the fresh greenswards faded until the tips of the grasses were bleached to the colour of straw. The field flowers of summer were over, leaving the hedgerows a mass of meadowsweet scenting the air with its soothing perfume, interspersed with the deep carmine spears of foxgloves.

Victoria found the July ball filling her thoughts, to the exclusion of all else. On more than one occasion, she had thought deeply about her Cousin Georgie's proposal and asked herself whether or not she would have accepted his offer, if she had not met Francis Sturdy again. She told herself that she was expecting nothing from her forthcoming meeting with Francis and yet her heart raced when she thought of it.

For the last few years, she had greeted each invitation with indifference and was now afraid that her enthusiasm would betray her feelings to her parents. Her mind was in turmoil and she constantly wondered whether Francis was thinking of her as much as she thought of him and whether or not, after such a long gap, they would be able to resume their relationship where it had been left off.

Tamar's astute eyes noted her daughter's restlessness and discussed it with Stephen. 'I do hope that she isn't regretting turning down Georgie's proposal.' She was heartfelt in this hope. 'They could never have been happy together – their backgrounds are so different.'

Stephen comforted her. 'She's basically sensible and I'm quite certain that she has not regretted her decision. She's probably unsettled since Georgie, Jeanette and Ned have gone back to Canada, but I'm sure there's no more to it than that.' He smiled at her teasingly. 'She's like her mother – an irresistibly beautiful woman. I've seen the way men look at you both when we're in company. She will always attract men, darling, and we must wait until she meets one who attracts her in return.'

Although Victoria intended to take Tommy down to Sleightholmedale three or four times during the August holidays, she made up her mind to have a day there with him beforehand, to break up the waiting time before her planned meeting with Francis. Not only did she relish the change, but she felt that she wished to be away from her mother's watchfulness. She sensed that Tamar was aware of the tug of war which was going on in her mind between anxiety and anticipation.

She ordered the coach early, hoping to deter her mother from accompanying them. Since Annie's deterioration in health, Tamar visited her mother fairly frequently. She was acutely aware of the worry she had caused her parents and regretted the anxiety she had brought to Annie when she was younger.

Had she but known it, the fact that she had made such a good and successful marriage and that Victoria had been legitimised, more than compensated, in Annie's eyes, for the trauma of Tamar's seduction by Sir William Forster.

Although Tamar had toyed with the idea of going down to her parents' farm with Victoria and Tommy, Victoria's stratagem in ordering the coach early served to put her off.

'I want a good long day there,' Victoria explained. 'It's been a long time since Tommy's been out, and he doesn't get a great deal of fun.'

He was to have more fun than they had anticipated, however. When they arrived at the farm, Edward ran to meet them.

'T'chimneys is going to be swept,' he laughed in high glee.

'It's a good thing you've arrived early,' her Aunt Sarah said. 'Tommy will enjoy the chimney-sweeping. Edward, lend him a pair of your threshing overalls to cover his clothes. You'd better borrow a big pinafore of mine, Victoria. And also, cover your hair.'

Victoria was puzzled. When the chimneys were swept at

the Manor, the sweep and his boy came and the family neither knew nor saw anything of what went on.

To her surprise, all the furniture in both the kitchen and the parlour was draped with old sheets, while others were fastened over the empty fireplaces. Annie Oaks' rocking chair had been carried out into the garden at the front of the house, where she sat sunning herself, rocking rhythmically and dozing.

The children gathered outside in the lane, excitedly watching as one of the farm-men propped a ladder up the side of the house. From the top of the ladder, he had a much lighter one leading up the thatch to the chimneys.

'Come on, Tommy. Help me to catch a couple of 'ens,' Edward called, running to where there were a few hens scratching in the hedge-bottom. Stealthily creeping up behind one, he pounced and grabbed her, before she could escape. Tucking her head under her wing, he gently cradled her in his arms and rocked her to and fro. To Tommy's surprise, this put the hen to sleep.

Passing it to him, Edward said, 'If she starts to struggle, give 'er a rock and she'll go back to sleep.'

Tommy held the hen lightly, giving her a rock whenever she stirred. He gently stroked the feathers, revelling in their softness.

Edward caught another hen and they took them to the man who was waiting at the foot of the ladder. Edward handed his hen over, magnanimously allowing Tommy to continue to nurse his.

'Here you are, Billy,' he said. Billy tucked it securely under his arm and, speedily mounting the ladder, climbed up the roof-ladder over the thatch. He then popped the hen quickly down the chimney.

Tommy's eyes widened and he clutched his own hen tighter, in a protective gesture. Edward, however, took it from him and gave it to Billy's mate, who stood at the foot of the ladder, ready to hand it to Billy, when he came down to take it up to the parlour chimney.

Taking Tommy's hand, Edward ran with him into the kitchen, where the hen could be heard, squawking and clucking as it flapped its way down the chimney, its wings sweeping the soot from the sides as it fell.

When it landed in the kitchen, Edward drew the sheet to one side and scooped up the bird. Her lovely dark brown feathers were soot-coated, but another gentle rocking settled her to sleep again and, apart from the soot, she seemed none the worse for her adventure.

Before Edward could run outside with her, they realised that the parlour chimney was the next to be done and the children ran into the room to witness the same thing happening once more. Tommy's eyes filled with tears as Edward pushed the soot-encrusted hen into his arms and prepared to catch the next unwilling chimney-sweep.

'It doesn't hurt them, Tommy,' laughed Sarah. 'A good shower of rain and they'll be as clean as a couple of whistles. You soon won't be able to tell these two from the rest of the hens.'

The two farm-workers came in with shovels and sacks, to clean up the thick of the soot, which had been contained in the grate by the confining sheets. Sarah swept up the remains with a goose-wing brush and then Kitty washed both ranges and the hearthstones. All the other sheets were carefully removed and both rooms thoroughly dusted, but the smell of soot clung to everything, choking in their throats.

While Kitty lit the kitchen fire and Sarah began to prepare dinner, Victoria had a word with her grandmother and then strolled with the children across the fields, which were now denuded of their hay-crop, to walk along the banks of Hodge Beck. Although it had happened several years before she was born, she knew that ever since her grandparents had had a little daughter drowned there, the children were not allowed to go near the beck without an adult. Because of this they enjoyed lying looking at the speckled trout, which lurked among the pebbles, and dabbling their fingers in the cool clear water. Tommy was the exception to this pastime. He would not lie on the bank, gazing into the water with the others, but sat about a yard from them, watching, obviously anxious. No amount of cajoling would persuade him to move any closer to the water.

'What's up wi' 'im?' asked Maria Lamb.

''E's a scaredy-cat,' Edward said dismissively, making an unsuccessful grab at a trout which lingered in the shallows, close by.

Victoria sprang to Tommy's defence, unwilling for the other children to think badly of him.

'Tommy saw his father drown,' she told them. 'This is why he doesn't like to go too close to the water.'

They stared at him and he gazed back at them solemnly and nodded his head.

They went back in time for the midday meal, which the children ate in silence and during which the adults spoke very little, conscious of Jonadab's ever-watchful eye. 'God's good food needs no conversation,' was one of his maxims and any child who dared to speak was told, 'Let your meat stop your mouth.' If George or Bob Lamb were working close enough to the farmhouse to join the rest of the family at the table, however, Jonadab himself was quite likely to talk for the duration of the whole meal.

After dinner, he took Tommy by the hand. 'Come on, lad. Thoo'll enjoy looking at t'osses.'

Tommy was a comfort to the old man. Edward's interest in farmwork was now channelled into helping his father with the threshing machine and all Jonadab's other grand-children on the two farms in the valley were girls, whose place, according to their grandfather, was in the house, learning to be good farmers' wives. Tommy's interest in and affinity with animals appealed to Jonadab and the child's visits to the valley brought him much pleasure.

Hand in hand, they made their way to the stables, where Tommy was fearless among the huge shire-horses. Sometimes Jonadab would lift him on to the back of one and he fondled its ears, stroked its mane or caressed its head. Despite his disappointment that Edward showed little interest in the horses, Tommy's enthusiasm for the great beasts created a bond between the old man and the boy which the lack of conversation did nothing to lessen.

'So thoo's scared o' watter, ist thoo, Tommy?' Jonadab questioned. The child turned his blushing face away and nodded. 'We sh'll 'ave ti do summat ti cure that, next time thoo comes,' the old man said gently, but Tommy merely looked nervous.

The visit down to her grandparents' home had provided the calming influence needed by Victoria. Tommy, too, although unable to express his appreciation in words, made it clear that he loved his trips down to Sleightholmedale, where there always seemed to be something interesting going on.

As the date of the ball approached, Tamar became increasingly exasperated with her daughter.

'She's refusing to have a new gown!' she told Stephen. 'The Morleys live far enough away to draw on guests we haven't met before and there will be young men who have not seen her. I want her to create a good impression.'

'Whatever she wears, she'll look beautiful. Don't worry,' he soothed.

'She says she'll wear what she wore for the Race Ball in York,' Tamar complained.

'And lovely she looks in it, too,' her husband replied. 'If you're not careful, my darling, you'll develop into a typical Mrs Chelton; pushing your daughter at every eligible bachelor.'

Tamar bit her lip. She was bound to acknowledge to herself that his criticism contained some truth.

'I'm beginning to doubt that she'll ever find a suitor she feels she can accept,' she rejoined.

'Victoria will be all right,' he comforted. 'She has her mother's determination. Sir William's legacy has ensured her independence so, if she feels that she has no need of a husband, we must respect her wishes.'

Tamar leaned over his shoulder and rubbed her cheek against his. 'She's inherited something else from her mother, too – a passionate nature,' she smiled.

He swung her round into his arms and kissed her hungrily. 'For which any husband would be grateful,' he laughed.

Hilary was home from Oxford for the long summer

vacation and when they were ready for the ball, the Lassiters made a striking quartet. The two men were equally tall and slender, with hair of a silvery sheen. It was difficult to tell whether or not Stephen still retained the ash blond of his youth or whether he had crossed the line to the silver of middle age.

Tamar had chosen a black moiré taffeta gown, which rustled and gleamed with every movement. Together with the raven blackness of her hair, it threw into relief her creamy shoulders and the still impressive beauty of her face. With nothing to detract from them, her strange tawny eyes shone with an almost feline glow.

Although she had refused a new gown, Victoria looked more lovely than ever. No matter how she assumed an air of indifference, her inner anticipation lent a sparkle which had been missing for some time.

'You look lovely, darling,' her father commented, as she came downstairs.

'Thank you, Papa. I'm looking forward to this. It seems a long time since I've had any excitement – not since our relatives went back to Canada,' she reminisced.

'Well, it's been your own fault,' Tamar chided. Upon this note, they made for the coach.

They had never before been to Lawnscome Hall, the Morleys' seat, and were most impressed. Coaches and carriages queued to deposit their passengers at the grand double stairs that led to the open front door. The sound of the orchestra met them as they entered and there was already a good number of guests dancing in the magnificent ballroom.

Hilary's glance roved over the young females present. Unlike his sister, Hilary's attendance at social functions was specifically targeted at finding a suitable bride. He was an ambitious young man, conscious of his good looks and with an outstanding university record. He was determined to marry a wealthy, well-connected wife. If she possessed good looks, so much the better, but that was not the main criterion. He was impatient with what he considered to be

Victoria's finicky attitude. She had had offers which most girls would have grabbed and yet still remained unmarried.

Her eyes swept the ballroom, taking in the number of withdrawing places where she could be out of her parents' gaze with Francis, if he turned up. She noted the number of seats hidden discreetly behind potted palms and the huge conservatory, where dozens of couples could talk without being overheard. The great double doors at the other end of the ballroom, opened on to a terrace, which was most inviting on such a balmy night. Satisfied, she crossed the floor and took her place with her parents and brother.

Hilary was not with them long. His gaze having swept the room and made his choice, he left them to put his name on the cards of the girls of his first selection. He wisely left blanks in case he heard any background details which made some young ladies particularly interesting. Several young men came to claim dances from Victoria, although she obviously refused to give up the supper dance. Tamar too, was claimed by several of the older men, though Stephen, who was proud to show off his wife, had signed up for more than half of her dances.

Victoria was dancing with a very amusing partner when, in the middle of a laugh, she caught sight of Francis across the room. When her partner returned her to her seat, she panicked for a few moments. What if he made no attempt to speak to her? How would he approach her, if her parents took their seats again?

Stephen and Tamar were caught up in conversation further down the ballroom and Victoria sat alone, willing Francis to come while she was by herself. To her surprise, he made no attempt and she promised another precious dance, this time to Hoyland Wheatcroft, who begged for the supper dance, upon seeing that it was unclaimed.

'No, Hoyland. It's already promised to an old friend,' she said. 'This is how I regard you, too. Please respect my decision.'

He sighed. 'It's very difficult, Victoria, but I do know it's over between us.'

'It was never really on,' she replied gently.

Stephen and Tamar made their way over to join her and her heart began to race as she saw Francis begin to cross the floor, coming purposefully towards them. 'Oh, no,' she breathed to herself, having hoped that he would approach her when she was alone. Francis, however, was no longer the callow youth that he had been at the time of Thomas' death.

He bowed to Tamar. 'Lady Lassiter,' he greeted her. She made no reply, merely inclined her head, frigidly. 'Sir Stephen.'

Stephen did go as far as nodding his head and replying, 'Sturdy.'

Francis could not for the life of him remember Hilary's name. It was obvious that he was the brother, but Francis had hardly encountered him all those years ago and contented himself with bowing.

Ignoring Tamar's baleful glare and the general air of hostility, Francis bowed to Victoria. 'If I may have the pleasure, Miss Lassiter,' he smiled, holding out his hand for her programme. To Tamar's chagrin, he signed up for every vacant dance, including the supper dance.

As he left them, Tamar let out her pent-up breath in a burst of fury. 'How dare he!' she fumed. 'I'm surprised at you, Victoria, after the way he treated you.'

'As I told you before, Mama,' she answered, 'a lot of water has flowed under the bridge since then. Francis was little more than a child; only just out of school. He's a man, now, and cannot be held responsible for what he did then.'

'The child is father to the man,' her mother retorted ominously.

'And we learn from our mistakes,' replied Victoria. 'Give Francis credit for having learnt from his.'

Hilary knew nothing of what had happened all those years ago. He had been a child and only recalled that a beau of Victoria's, a relative of Sturdy's, had been killed in a riding accident. Why Sturdy was in his parents' black books, he had no idea. All he could see was that the chap was pleasant, eligible and obviously head over heels in love with Victoria. In his parents' place, he would have grabbed him.

As the evening proceeded, even Tamar was forced to reluctantly admit that, when Victoria danced with Francis, she was radiant. When she, herself, was dancing with Bramley Wheatcroft, he was rather cool.

'Victoria has not been entirely open with Hoyland,' he tackled her. 'She told him there was no one else, but you've only to see her with that chap for it to be obvious that they're besotted with each other.'

Tamar looked across and to her dismay, had to acknowledge that it seemed to be true. 'I can assure you, Bram,' she replied, 'that she has barely set eyes on Francis Sturdy for six or seven years, although she did know him many years ago. In fact, she was engaged to his cousin.' It was a half-truth, and it came out glibly.

'The cousin was killed in a riding accident and she hasn't seen Sturdy since,' she added. With this he had to be satisfied, although he was disgruntled that this ordinary-looking fellow could kindle such a spark in Victoria when Hoyland had failed.

When the supper dance came, Victoria was warm and elated. Her evening had been far more enjoyable than she could ever have anticipated. She basked in the admiration of several new young men and, to crown all, her evening with Francis exceeded all her expectations.

'Shall we supper on the terrace, since it's so warm?' he asked.

'Oh, yes.' Victoria would have agreed with whatever he had suggested.

He found a secluded wickerwork sofa, discreetly hidden behind a high, foliage-covered lattice screen, and left Victoria there while he went to fetch supper.

When he returned, he also brought two glasses of champagne. 'I hope these aren't inappropriate,' he said pleadingly, as he handed one of the crystal flutes to her.

Unwilling to commit herself, but brimming over with happiness, she cast her eyes down and made no reply. However, he saw the smile and when he raised his glass, with the toast, 'To us,' she touched hers to his and drank.

They sat in silence for a few moment and then, putting

down his plate, he took her hand. 'Victoria, it's all right, isn't it? I've been through hell all these years without you. You're so incredibly beautiful. I was sure some lucky man would have grabbed you and that you'd be married long before now.'

'I refused them all, Francis.' She spoke shyly, not giving any reason.

'I love you, Victoria. I've always loved you.' His voice was hoarse with sincerity, then it rose with self-reproach. 'I don't know what came over me with that . . . that nitwit, Caroline Chelton. She can't hold a candle to you!'

She placed a hand over his lips. 'Don't let's talk of love yet, please Francis,' she whispered. 'I was very hurt and let down when I came back from Canada and I want things just to take their natural pace. Don't let's rush things.'

'I suppose I must beard the lions in their dens,' he laughed, 'and ask permission to call on you. I wonder how your parents will react? This evening has been enough of a shock to them.'

Victoria hesitated, still unwilling to commit herself. Then, gathering her courage, she looked deep into his eyes. 'I don't care what they say, Francis. I want you to call. I want us to resume our relationship.'

While Stephen and Tamar were eating supper, Tamar's eyes raked the ballroom, as they had done the dining room, where the lavish buffet was laid out. 'I can't see Victoria anywhere,' she complained. 'That Francis Sturdy has whisked her off somewhere, to be alone with her.'

Stephen sighed. 'You're building this up out of all proportion to what it really is,' he remonstrated. 'I've watched them together and Victoria is obviously happier with him than with anyone else. After all, every dog is allowed one bite and every man one mistake. He's patently explained his actions to Victoria's satisfaction and that's all that should matter to us.'

Tamar remained unmollified. 'She's behaving like a lovesick girl,' she objected.

'Oh, for heaven's sake, Tamar. Isn't this what you've wanted all these years?' He was unusually short with her.

'We know the Sturdys. He's eminently suitable. If she's willing to forgive what was, after all, a boyish weakness, who are we to stand in the way of her happiness? It may come to nothing, but I feel we should give it every chance.'

After the last dance, Francis brought her back to her parents and, with a humble bow to Tamar, said contritely, 'Sir Stephen and Lady Lassiter, I realise that you have every reason to think badly of me. My only excuse for my treatment of Victoria was that I was young and foolish. The many years between have been spent despising myself and feeling too ashamed to approach her again.' He paused, but neither Tamar nor Stephen spoke, each determined not to ease his task. With an audible gulp, he went on, a note of desperation in his voice. 'I have come to ask your permission to call on Victoria.'

Looking at his daughter, Stephen saw the glow of inner radiance, which had been lacking for so long. If Sturdy made her feel like this, as far as Stephen was concerned, his attentions were welcome. Glancing at Tamar, who refused to meet his eye, he smiled at the young man and put him out of his misery.

'It would be our pleasure for you to call on our daughter,' he said. 'May I ask your intentions?'

Francis smiled at Victoria. 'Eventually, matrimony, sir,' was his firm reply.

Victoria blushed with pleasure and even Tamar softened. Having declared himself so openly, he would not dare let Victoria down again.

Chapter Twenty-Three

Over twenty years earlier, when Stephen Lassiter had given up his law practice in Helmsley and taken over the family estate upon the death of his father, the farming side had been very run down, owing to his father's years of ill-health. The estate was subsidised by the woollen mills, which his father owned in Leeds and Bradford. It had taken many years of hard work on Stephen's part to get the farms back on a successful footing, but now he often congratulated himself on the smooth manner in which things were going at Thorsbury. There were three farms, all with efficient managers in charge and the very extensive Thorsbury Woods provided a good source of income.

The trees were treated as any other crop, being harvested and replanted in rotation and the saw-mill ran at a good profit. Softwood was sold for immediate income, but the hardwood was sawn into planks of various thicknesses and stacked for seasoning, most to be sold to the furniture trade, for although foreign woods were becoming more fashionable, there was always a demand for good English oak.

Stephen was, therefore, very upset when Percy Holden, the manager of Paradise Farm, dropped dead at work. He was only in late middle-age, and in addition, was a dependable farm manager. Although Stephen offered his widow Gertie's old cottage, which was still vacant, she chose to go and live with a married daughter.

When Stephen interviewed for Holden's replacement, one man called Jethro Smith had outstanding references although Stephen, for some reason, found himself disliking the man. Chiding himself for allowing personalities to influence him, he decided that he could not overlook the man's credentials and so appointed him.

For the first few weeks, he made a point of riding out to

Paradise Farm, which was quite a long way from the village. Although he found himself unable to like the man any better, he could not fault Smith's running of the farm, and so felt satisfied that he had made a good choice.

In the months that passed, Francis Sturdy called regularly on Victoria and often the couple attended the theatre in York, chaperoned by one or other set of parents. Before allowing her to stroll in the Walks with him alone, Tamar had a serious talk with her daughter.

'After what happened with Thomas, I hope there is no need to warn you about your behaviour with Francis,' she said.

Victoria flushed, hotly resentful and yet acknowledging that her mother had every right to caution her.

'Thomas and I were very young,' she protested. 'Francis respects me too much not to wait for marriage. Don't worry, I've learnt my lesson,' she added.

Tamar thought bitterly, 'Thomas possessed his father's lustful blood.'

One day when Victoria went to help at the school, Tommy handed her a note, placing a finger to his lips. Upon opening it, Victoria's brows rose in disbelief. '*Jimmy Smith's Dad hits his Mam*,' Tommy had written. At her astonished look, he nodded his head vigorously.

When she returned to the Manor, Victoria showed her mother the note. Tamar sent a message that one of the scullery-maids should run up the village and ask Tempy to come down. When she showed her the note, Tempy frowned.

'Aah 'aven't heard owt,' she said, 'but she nivver comes into t'village. There's three kiddies, but only Jimmy is old enough for school and 'e comes on 'is own. Don't worry, m'Lady. Aah'll keep mi ears skinned,' she assured Tamar.

Stephen was most perturbed. His mistrust of the man appeared to be justified. 'No doubt the child told Tommy, believing that as he can't talk, he can't communicate,' he speculated. 'Being new to the school, he wouldn't know how bright Tommy is. He probably just wanted to confide in somebody whom he thought couldn't make trouble.'

The following morning, Stephen called at Paradise Farm at an hour when Mrs Smith would be busy in the kitchen. Making no attempt to locate her husband, he knocked at the door. It was opened by Jimmy.

'Good morning, young man. Is your mother in?' he asked, walking past the child and straight into the kitchen. Mrs Smith was at the kitchen table, rolling out pastry to cover a meat and potato pie. She was quite a pretty woman of about thirty, but one of her eyes was badly blackened.

'Good gracious, Mrs Smith,' Stephen exclaimed. 'Whatever has happened to your eye?'

'I caught it on t'cupboard door, sir,' she replied, evading his eyes.

'That isn't the truth. You know it and I know it. Finish making your delicious-looking pie while I sit here and wait for your husband.' He spoke kindly, but firmly. The children looked at him in awe, fully aware that he was their father's boss. When she had put the pie into the oven and made a few jam tarts with the trimmings, Mrs Smith began to sob quietly while the children looked on, wide-eyed.

'Oh, sir, please don't say owt to Jethro,' she begged. ''E'll kill me.'

'Oh, no he won't,' Stephen assured her. 'Depend on me.'

At that moment the door was flung open and Jethro Smith walked in. Upon seeing Stephen, he halted and looked from his employer to his wife.

'Good day, Sir Stephen. Is there owt I can do for you?' His tone was deferential, almost ingratiating.

'You can get off my farm,' Stephen replied. 'I will not employ a man who abuses his wife.'

'What I do in my own home is my business,' the man blustered.

'What goes on in *my* property is *my* business,' Stephen informed him curtly. 'I'll give you fifteen minutes to collect your clothes and get off my land.'

Smith turned to his wife with a snarl. 'When I get you away from here, I'll teach you to keep your bloody mouth shut,' he threatened.

Stephen controlled the rage he felt. 'You're merely wasting your time with your idle threats. I told you to get off my land but your wife will not accompany you, unless she wants to.' Turning to the cowering woman, he spoke kindly. 'Do you wish to go with your husband, Mrs Smith?'

'I've nowhere else to go,' she whispered, avoiding her husband's glowering look.

'I shall find you and the children accommodation if you wish to stay. Now, do you wish to accompany your husband?'

'No, sir,' she mumbled, darting a terrified look at the brooding Jethro.

'Then take your pie out of the oven and wrap it in a cloth,' Stephen said. Going to the door, he called a couple of the farm labourers. 'You men, bring a horse and flat cart to the back door,' he ordered.

By the time Jethro Smith came downstairs, carrying a bundle, the kitchen table and chairs were already loaded on to the cart, together with his wife and children, with their dinner pots and cutlery, packed into baskets.

'If you're seen on my land again, you'll either be jailed for trespass or shot as a poacher,' Stephen warned Smith in reply to a mouthful of curses. 'And you'll feel my whip, if you use language like that to me,' he added.

By the time Smith's wife and family had eaten their dinner in number thirteen, Gertie's old cottage, the men were back again with the rest of her furniture.

Stephen rode up the village later in the day, to call and see that she was safely settled.

'I don't know how to thank you, Sir Stephen.' She had tears in her eyes as she spoke.

'Until the two youngest are old enough to go to school, I shall make you a small allowance,' he reassured her. 'After that, we'll find work for you at the Manor – perhaps in the laundry.'

Telling Tamar and Victoria of the incident that evening, he summed up by saying, 'I didn't really fancy Smith when I employed him, but his references were excellent. Upon looking back, it's a blessing for his wife that I did. At least it's saved her from a life of misery.

A few weeks after the incident with Jethro Smith, Victoria was looking through the *Yorkshire Post*.

'Have you read this, Mama?' she enquired.

'What's that, darling?' asked Tamar.

'At the Leeds Theatre, there's a mesmerist next week.' To Tamar's surprise, Victoria sounded excited.

'Well, I suppose it could be quite interesting,' Tamar answered, 'but it isn't my kind of thing. I prefer musical comedy.'

'It's not the show itself. It says he does healing. I wondered about taking Tommy.'

Tamar looked up from her needlework. 'Oh, darling! Will you never accept that he can't speak and there's nothing that can be done?'

'No! I can't accept it and never will. I want to try anything – anything that offers hope of any kind.' As she spoke, her eyes filled with tears.

Seeing her distress, Tamar patted her arm. 'We'll go, even if it's only the two of us who take him. I don't think your father will be interested, but Hilary might enjoy the show.'

'Francis might like to come with us,' Victoria suggested.

Tamar hesitated. 'Won't he consider it odd for you to go to such lengths for a servant's child?'

'No. Gertie was more than a servant to me. She was my friend and companion since I was a little girl. It's only natural that I should want to do my best for her child.' Victoria, it was obvious, was set upon taking the child so, with a sigh, Tamar set about making the arrangements.

As she predicted, Stephen declined to join them, but Hilary seemed quite enthusiastic. Francis would meet them at Leeds and return to spend the weekend at the Manor.

Despite her previous misgivings, Tamar found herself enjoying the show. The first half of the programme consisted of two good singers, a comedian and a chorus of dancing girls. Tommy's amazement and delight at this completely new experience amused them all and Tamar privately decided that the trip had been worth it, even if the venture was unsuccessful.

After the interval, the whole of the second half consisted of Khalib – The Great Mesmerist. To the fascination of the audience he took volunteers from amongst them and had them doing various things, of which they had no recollection once he had snapped his fingers and awoken his victims.

When the show was over, the four of them went backstage and requested a private meeting. Inside the dressing room, Victoria explained Tommy's story to Khalib.

Standing the child in front of him, the performer said, 'Look into my eyes, Tommy. Deep, deep into my eyes.' Tommy went rigid and the mesmerist said, 'When I count five, raise your arm.'

The four onlookers watched in fascination as Tommy's arm shot into the air. The hypnotic voice went on, slowly and persuasively. 'You can speak, Tommy. You can speak. When I count to five you will speak to me.'

Again came the slow, deliberate count. At the end, Tommy was ordered, 'Speak to me, Tommy. Speak!'

Tommy's throat began to work and his eyes opened wide. Suddenly coming as a shock to them all, his voice rang out, loud and shrill.

'No! No! Water!' and then, still in a trance, he burst into tears.

Again the mesmerist spoke. 'Hush, Tommy, don't cry.' Tommy's tears immediately ceased. The persuasive voice droned on. 'You *can* speak, Tommy. Speak to me, Tommy. You are able to speak.'

There was no reply from the child and while he was still in a trance, the hypnotist told them sadly, 'He undoubtedly still has the ability to speak, as you see, but the shock which robbed him of his speech was so traumatic that nothing will break through it. If even I cannot bring it back, then no one can. When I bring him round, he will know nothing of this. Allow him to think he has been brought backstage just to meet me.'

'How much are we in your debt?' Tamar asked, but Khalib held up his hand. 'I feel that I have failed the little boy. There is no charge. I am only too sorry that I did not succeed.'

Tommy soon fell asleep on the way home, conscious only that he had had a wonderful evening, concluding in meeting the Great Khalib in person. The rest of them discussed the show in detail, all having been greatly impressed by the mesmerist. Although Victoria was comforted, in some measure, that Tommy was still able to talk, she was depressed and frustrated that the hypnotist had been unable to provide the key to release the imprisoned voice.

Although they had been to the first house at the theatre, it was growing late so they stopped at an inn on the way home for a meal.

'Cheer up, darling,' Francis said to Victoria. 'We've had a most enjoyable evening and nobody is any worse off.'

She smiled. 'You're right, I suppose – and it certainly was a good show.'

As the coach pulled into the drive of Thorsbury Manor, the coachman tapped on the roof with the handle of his whip.

'M'Lady! Master Hilary! There's a fire!' he exclaimed. They looked from the window, but could see nothing. From his elevated position on the driving seat, Robert had a much better view. 'It's somewhere in the woods, m'Lady.'

'Drop us at the house, and go and ring the alarm bell in the buildings,' Tamar ordered.

They gathered on the steps, impatiently waiting for Hodgetts to answer the doorbell. Francis was holding Tommy, who was still fast asleep, while Tamar and Victoria drew their cloaks round them against the chilly, freshening wind.

Once they were admitted, Tamar said, 'Rouse the menservants, Hodgetts. There's a fire in the woods.' She then ran to Stephen's study, where he was taking the opportunity to work late. She burst through the door, but before she could say anything, the tolling of the alarm bell in the buildings rang out through the silence of the night.

Stephen sprang from his desk. 'Whatever's wrong?'

'There's a fire in the woods,' she said. 'Robert saw it as we came along the drive.'

While Francis carried Tommy up to bed, the rest of the menfolk rushed through the woods to the source of the fire, which was the sawmill and the adjoining woodyard.

Stephen groaned. The stiff breeze was whipping up the flames into a roaring fury.

'My God! We'll not save any of it!' He was desperate. The fully-seasoned wood was tinder-dry and burnt with a ferocity which prevented them from even approaching the stacks.

'Excuse me, Sir Stephen.' The manager of the sawmill approached him. 'T'greenest wood is nearest t'river. Mebbe we can run a bucket chain and give it a good drenching.'

'Thank you, Ward,' he replied, 'but for God's sake don't let any of the men slip into the river. It's treacherous. We lost our head groom that way a few years back.'

'Aye, sir. Don't worry, there's enough light from what's afire for 'em to see all right.'

When Francis had watched Victoria undress Tommy and pop him into bed, he joined the rest of the men at the scene of the fire.

The heat was so scorching that they were forced to protect their faces with their forearms. The fully-seasoned oak burnt fiercely and showers of sparks flew towards the surrounding woods so that, while Ward directed more than half the men with the chain of water from the river, damping down any stacks of wood which were not yet alight, Stephen organised the other men with shovels to beat out any fires which the flying sparks ignited among the growing trees.

It was dawn before the best wood was sufficiently burnt out, to allow them to quench it completely with water from the river, and all the secondary, minor fires were extinguished.

Stephen led the men back to the kitchen in the Manor, where Tamar had organised the kitchen staff to prepare food and ale for the weary men.

'This isn't enough for the way these men have toiled tonight!' Stephen exclaimed. 'Bring some brandy, Hodgetts, and give every man a stiff drink,' he ordered, ignoring Hodgett's disapproving look, as he turned to obey.

Stephen looked round at the exhausted men with their smoke-blackened faces and clothing.

'Thank you all,' he said to them. 'I'm most grateful for the way you have responded. Eat and drink your fill. There'll be a good bonus for you when you're paid at the year end, at Martinmas.'

As he turned to follow Hilary and Francis from the kitchen, Ward called him back.

'Excuse me, Sir Stephen,' he said.

Stephen turned back. 'If it's your job you're worried about, Ward, you have no need to be.' Looking round he spoke to them all. 'All who work in the saw-mill will be retained. Mr Ward will find work to keep you in employment until the mill is fully operational again.'

Ward coughed. 'No, sir, although thank you, Sir Stephen, for your consideration. It's just that I couldn't understand 'ow it started. None of my men smoke at work and it was all t'best wood that 'ad been burning t'longest. Anyroad, I 'ad a scout round afore we left and all best wood 'ad a smell of lamp oil round about it. I reckons it were done a purpose.'

Stephen was stunned. 'You mean it was arson?' He found it difficult to believe.

'Aye, sir, somebody with a grudge.' The manager was insistent. He was sure of his facts and wanted no blame to fall on him or his men.

The next day, Stephen accompanied Ward on an inspection of the damage.

'It's put us back at least a couple of years, sir,' Ward said.

When planked up into varying thicknesses, the wood was stacked up, one plank above the other, with small pieces of wood holding them apart, so that the air could get all round and season them fully. Once fully seasoned, no movement would occur when the wood was used by joiners or cabinet-makers. The stacks which were totally destroyed had been those fully-seasoned and ready for selling.

Stephen spoke to the family over luncheon. 'I can't minimise the seriousness of the situation,' he told them, looking round the table. 'We are insured, but that only covers the actual cost of the timber we have lost. A good proportion of our income came from the seasoned timber and we shall have none to sell for three or four years.'

'Oh, Papa. Whatever shall we do?' Victoria asked.

'For one thing, we can thank our lucky stars that you chose last night to go to the theatre, or we'd have lost the lot.' He was thoughtful for a moment, then turned to his daughter. 'I take it you had no luck with the hypnotist, or someone would have told me.'

'Tommy *can* speak. We all heard him,' she replied sadly, and described their encounter with the Great Khalib. 'Anyway,' she concluded, 'that doesn't seem important now, compared with the fire.'

'A child being able or unable to communicate is of very great importance,' he chided. 'You must not give up hope, Victoria.' He smiled round at their doleful faces. Even Francis was looking downcast. 'Don't worry! We shall not be destitute – nor anywhere near it. There'll still be plenty for pretty gowns, so cheer up.' He was almost teasing, cajoling them out of their depression. 'It's just that I like every enterprise to be self-sufficient. It has taken me many years to get the farms and the timber business to be paying propositions. My father was too ill to bother and my elder brother was only interested in the army.' He paused, his eyes far away, while he took a sip of wine.

'The farms are all running well. I've put Sellers, the foreman, in Smith's place, and he seems not only capable but popular with the men.'

'Smith!' exclaimed Hilary.

'What about him?' asked Stephen.

'Someone with a grudge, Ward said. Well, Smith bears you a grudge.'

Stephen pondered. 'I have sent for the police, as well as the insurance assessor. Perhaps it would do no harm to mention the episode with Jethro Smith.' After a moment's thought he went on, 'I warned him to keep off my land, but he wouldn't expect to be seen in the night.'

'He wasn't seen,' Tamar interrupted, 'but I'd like to bet it was him.'

'No stranger would know about the timber and the sawmill,' put in Victoria.

When the police sergeant came from Malton, Stephen sent for Ward to take him to the scene of the fire and show him which parts smelt of lamp oil.

Upon his return to the house, the sergeant said, 'I'm afraid it does look like arson, Sir Stephen.'

Stephen recounted the whole episode regarding Jethro Smith and the policeman shared his suspicions.

Sure enough, a couple of days later the man was arrested in Malton on a charge of being drunk and disorderly. His clothes had a strong smell of lamp oil and, when charged with arson, he was so drunk that he not only admitted the crime but boasted of the way he had got even with his ex-employer. When brought to court he received a sentence of ten years. This was a great relief not only to his wife, who felt safe at last, but also to Stephen, although it was no consolation for the damage Jethro Smith had caused.

Chapter Twenty-Four

Sarah Oaks was not entirely happy with her life at the present time. She loved George dearly and had done so since she was a young girl and he had been courting her elder sister, Elizabeth.

Since the buying of the threshing machine, however, there were many weeks when she saw practically nothing of him, apart from Saturdays and Sundays. He would be up before dawn, to have his breakfast at the farm where the threshing was to be done that day, and his evening meal would be taken at the following day's farm, after the machine had been moved and set up there.

When he had been occupied at home with farmwork, even if he was up on the high moor amongst the sheep, he usually managed to be home for his midday meal and was always with them at the tea-table.

Nowadays, once she had got Edward and Annie off to school at Gillamoor, she was left to the company of little Hannah, two maids and her mother-in-law, Annie Oaks, who dozed by the fire for most of the day.

At mealtimes, she was joined by her father-in-law, Jonadab Oaks, whose conversation was limited to his horses and the running of the farm.

She tried to express her frustration to George when they were alone in bed, which was really their only opportunity to talk privately.

'Don't worry about silly little things, love,' he comforted her. 'We've a good life. I'm always here at weekends, to take you shopping in Kirkby or to go for a walk.'

'I wish the threshing machine had never been bought,' she cried in a petulant outburst.

George was aghast. He considered the threshing machine the best thing that had ever happened for him.

Sitting up in bed, he lit the candle and looked at her

tear-stained face. 'Poor little love,' he said, kissing her gently. 'Things are just getting too much for you, that's all. Is it Mam being poorly, that's getting you down?'

'No.' She sat up as well. 'It's not just that, George. I married you because I love you and I want to be with you – not just at weekends and in bed, when you're usually too tired even to talk.'

He tried to express in words what a difference the threshing machine had made to his life. 'Here on the farm, no matter what Faither says, I'll never be the boss while he's here. Out there, with the set, I'm in charge. It's summat I can do that he can't.'

'I know.' She was contrite, and kissed him tenderly. 'It's brought you out of the old man's shadow and I'm a pig for resenting it. After all, you're not threshing every week of the year.'

'No, and I'm not too tired tonight for talking – or owt else,' he laughed, blowing out the candle and taking her in his arms.

A few weeks later, she was sure that she was again pregnant. She was not altogether happy at the realisation, although George was delighted.

'Mebbe it'll be a little lad. Then you'll have one of your own,' he enthused.

'I *have* one of my own. I've brought Edward up since babyhood and regarded him as mine. He's as precious to me as the girls,' she said, quite truthfully.

For her part, she felt that she was nicely getting the children off her hands. Little Hannah would soon be going up to Gillamoor school with the others and she felt that she did not really want to be bothered with another baby. She did not believe in the large families such as her mother and mother-in-law had had.

Her sister-in-law, Martha, down at Cherry Tree Farm only had the two girls and there were no signs of any more, although she knew Bob Lamb would like a son.

However, she wisely kept her thoughts to herself, and smiled tolerantly at George's pride and delight. A week or two later, her father-in-law looked at her quizzically one dinner-time.

'Thoo's looking a bit peaky, lass. What's up?' he demanded.

'I'm expecting.' She was embarrassed at having to tell him. It should have been George's job, but she had wanted to keep the secret for a while. Perhaps she had hoped against hope that she had made a mistake, but knew by now that it was true enough.

'Good!' exclaimed Jonadab. 'That's what women were bred for. To look after their menfolk and give 'em sons.'

Sarah was livid at his narrow and intolerant attitude. Although she normally got on reasonably well with the old man, there were times when his rigid and unyielding view of life annoyed her. Times were changing, but Jonadab Oaks could not change with them. His standards were those of the beginning of the century and he would consider that he was lowering them if he deviated from his chosen path. Jonadab's view was that man was made in God's image and that he, personally, was made more in His image than most of his fellow men.

Sarah felt wretched, almost from the beginning, with her third child. Whereas with the two girls she had bloomed with a matronly glow and felt fit and well throughout her pregnancies, now she suffered dreadfully from sickness and her constant tiredness drained her so that her pallor and the lines of strain on her face reminded George, terrifyingly, of when Elizabeth had been pregnant.

'Would you like to drop a line to our Jonna and Maisie and ask 'em to tea one Sunday? It'll make a change for you and it's time Jonna saw Mam,' he suggested.

'Yes, I'll do that.' Sarah liked Maisie, Jonna's wife, who had produced two little boys, much to Jonadab's satisfaction. 'Two more Oaks to farm in this area,' he had said with pride.

Jonna, himself, although a younger edition of his father, had been out of favour since he and Joe had tried to persuade the old man to sell up and split his money four ways.

He and Maisie had been over twice since Joe's departure

for Canada – once to meet Joe's family and once to Ann Butler's funeral. Each time there had been family occasions, contact between Jonadab and his youngest son had been minimal. Now, however, they would have a full afternoon and a meal-time together. Sarah could see the afternoon being a strain, but consoled herself that Jonna and Maisie's children would provide a distraction.

By the time the invitation had been dispatched, accepted and a date arranged, summer had passed its peak. Harvest was over and the Mell Supper had been held at the Oaks' farm. Summer had slipped, unnoticed, into autumn. The lush green of the valley had faded and the grass was sere, bleached to almost the shade of parchment. The amethyst sweep of the moors was now muted and dark, but the trees surrounding the little Dale had erupted in the fiery colours of autumn. They seemed almost ablaze with the orange, gold and even red tints of summer's end, giving the whole Dale a radiant and breathtaking beauty.

Driving down into the secluded valley, Jonna caught his breath. He still looked back with nostalgia to his childhood and was bound to confess to himself that Sleightholmedale was one of the loveliest places he'd seen.

The stubble fields were full of Sarah's geese feeding on any spilt grain to start the fattening-up process, some for the Michaelmas Market in late September, the rest for Christmas.

Jonna admitted to himself that the whole farm looked neat and prosperous. However, he thought with satisfaction, Len Brayton, Maisie's father, owned his farm and it would one day belong to Jonna, whereas George would always be a tenant farmer. He noted, but did not comment on, the row of circular corn stacks, or pikes, all neatly thatched. Traditionally these stood alongside the road, if well built, for passers by to admire. George could still best his younger brother at this skill, so Jonna ignored them and made no comment.

On the whole, the visit went well. Sarah had also invited Martha and Bob Lamb, so that there were plenty of children to play with Maisie's two, Richard and Albert.

The menfolk spent the afternoon walking round the farm, discussing the stock and chatting amiably about general farming topics. Jonna was interested in the threshing machine and, although he did not commit himself, the others got the impression that he would be using it that year. What he did not tell them was that the decisions made at the farm were still his father-in-law's. Although Jonna would one day inherit Len Brayton's farm, he was, in reality, merely the foreman, although he gave a very different impression to his family.

Sarah discovered during the afternoon that both Martha and Maisie envied her in her pregnancy. Maisie wanted a little girl and Martha longed for a boy. Sarah felt a vague disloyalty to George that she could not feel more enthusiastic over the coming child.

When tea was over and the visitors had gone, George smiled at Sarah.

'That was a nice change, wasn't it, love? And you put on a good spread,' he added.

'Yes, I enjoyed it,' Sarah replied. 'I think we sometimes get stuck in a rut, when a bit of thought would provide us with a change.'

'Oor Jonna's done well,' Jonadab said proudly.

'*We've* done well too, Faither,' George pointed out. 'We've built this up from a moor-end farm. Brayton's farm was thriving when Jonna went there.'

'Aye, thoo's right,' his father admitted. 'What we've got we've worked for, wi' no 'elp from any man.'

A few days after the tea party, Sarah had another brush with her father-in-law. George was working at home, helping to salve the sheep, and was back for the midday meal.

'I shall be glad when our Edward leaves school and can come fulltime on t'threshing machine with me,' he remarked. ''E's as good as any man and better than most.'

Sarah hesitated. This had been something she had wanted to talk over with George privately, but some strange feeling of perverseness drove her to bring it up in front of his father.

'I don't want Edward to leave school.' She spoke almost rebelliously.

Before George could answer, his father butted in. 'Not leave school? Whatever dost thoo mean? Of course 'e'll leave school.'

George saw by the mutinous set of his wife's lips and the over-bright eyes that this was something she cared deeply about. 'Wait a minute, Faither,' he interrupted, as Jonadab took a breath, ready to continue. 'What is it, love?' he said to Sarah.

'I'd like to pay for him to go to a private school in Kirkbymoorside, until he's sixteen,' she said.

'Sixteen!' Jonadab exploded. 'Dost think we're made o' brass?'

'Hilary is still being educated and he's a grown man,' she said defiantly.

'Stephen an' oor Tamar's got more brass than brains!' barked back her father-in-law.

George was becoming exasperated with his father. 'Will you let me get a word in, please, Faither,' he almost shouted.

'Humph!' Jonadab was offended.

'Now, love. Go on,' George encouraged.

'He's a bright boy.' Sarah hesitated. How could she say that she considered him too bright for farming, when his father, grandfather and all his relatives were farmers? 'There are other jobs besides farming,' she concluded lamely, realising that she stood no chance.

'It's all Edward's ever wanted to do.' George spoke patiently, believing that this was some whim due to her pregnancy. 'He's always wanted to farm and, since we got the thresher, he's wanted nowt else but to work on that.'

'Because he knows nothing else,' she reasoned. 'He could work in a bank, or all kinds of different jobs.'

'Would 'e mek as much brass?' demanded Jonadab.

She could have screamed with frustration. 'What good is your brass to you? What benefit does it bring you? What do you ever do with all your precious brass?'

'Why, put it in t'bank o' course,' he said in amazement.

'If there'd been no brass in t'bank, there'd 'ave been no threshing machine, for one thing.'

Still she argued, stubbornly, although she realised that the odds were stacked against her. 'There are other, more secure types of work.' She spoke wearily, her head pounding with the argument. 'Farming has its ups and downs. You have good years, then you have bad ones; you lose crops, stock dies or storms wreak havoc. It isn't all rosy.'

George placed an arm around her shoulders. 'That's what makes it so fulfilling, love.' He spoke gently. 'It's us against Nature. Sometimes she wins, sometimes we win, but it's never boring.'

Shaking his head at Jonadab, who was preparing to speak again, he continued, 'Edward will be fine. He understands machinery. He's growing up with it. There's more and more machinery coming into farming and what we are putting into the bank will buy Edward his own farm one day. Don't worry. I shall see that it happens.'

With this she had to be content, but she felt that in some way she had failed Edward. Although she knew that he would be blissfully happy in his chosen life, she felt he deserved better.

Later that night, as he undressed, Jonadab told Annie, 'It's all that gallivanting off ti Leeds them Butler lasses did. It's given 'em ideas above their station.'

The following Monday, Sarah was up early, thankful that it was a bright and breezy washday. Kitty had been up since five to light the fire under the boiler in the wash-house. All the water to fill the boiler had to be brought from the spring and this George had done the night before, as he did every Sunday evening.

Washday was the hardest work of the week. Once the beds were stripped, the sheets and pillowcases from five beds were boiled in the copper. This had a fire beneath, which must be kept alight. Once sparkling clean, the linen was lifted out with what was known as a copper-stick and transferred to one of the two wooden tubs for rinsing. After this the items passed through the huge, wooden-rollered mangle; one person fed the sheets through, while another turned the handle. When all the surplus water was removed, the linen was shaken and folded before going a final time through the wringer, to make it straight and easier to iron.

Once the sheets were blowing on the line, the rest of the washing was tackled, being 'possed' in a tub with a posser. This was like a three-legged stool at the end of a long handle, which was vigorously pushed up and down and rotated, to keep the clothes moving in the water.

The flagged floor of the wash-house was always puddled with soapy water and the place was full of steam, so that the women's clothes clung to them wetly and their faces ran with perspiration.

When the copper fire had died down and the water had cooled somewhat, Sarah often popped little Hannah in for a bath, after which the hot water was used for floor washing. Today, however, she decided that she did not feel well enough to bathe the toddler. Perhaps Kitty would do it, although she had no wish to ask the girl to do another job on top of having to wash the floor and empty the tubs.

As Sarah bent over the tub, rubbing clothes vigorously on the rubbing board, she began to sense that the ache in her back was not merely from stretching. As she straightened in alarm, a searing pain ran round from her back to her front, causing her to cry out.

'What's up, missus?' asked Kitty.

Sarah bit her lip to stifle further cries. 'I think it's the baby,' she said. 'I don't know what to do. There's no one here to help me.'

Kitty was now nearly twenty and, although she had never assisted at a birth, she was resourceful and plucky. She reassured her, 'Don't worry, missus, there's me 'ere. I'll 'elp.'

Before Sarah reached the bedroom, she was on her hands and knees, leaving a trail of bloodstains in her wake. The beds had not yet been remade with clean linen, so Kitty laid a double sheet on the floor and rolled Sarah on to it.

'Thoo'll not mek it to t'bed,' she said, raising her mistress' head and giving her a sip of water. She had no idea what to do to help Sarah, if there was anything to be done.

She thought of Annie Oaks. Was she too far gone in senility to help? She decided that something must be done and went and fetched the 'old missus', as she was known.

At the sight of her daughter-in-law in agony on the floor, Annie seemed to shed years. 'Run ti t'buildings and send a man ti ride up ti Kirkby for t'doctor and another ti run down and fetch Mrs Lamb from Cherry Tree,' she said, 'and get back as quick as thoo can.'

By the time Kitty returned, it was all over. Indicating what looked like a red blob amongst the blood, Annie said, 'Wrap it in a towel and save it for t'doctor ti see.'

Kitty was apprehensive, but used the towel to pick up what, on closer inspection, bore some resemblance to a baby, though horribly deformed.

'Put a towel under 'er ti catch any afterbirth,' directed Annie. 'T'doctor'll want ti see that, an' all.' When this had been done, she seemed to slump. 'Tek me back ti mi chair, lass,' she said, 'then clean 'er up and give 'er a cup o' tea.'

Martha did not arrive until Kitty was attending to Sarah, so she immediately offered assistance to the girl, who was obviously upset by the whole episode. Together they made up the bed and gently lifted Sarah into it. Her eyes were closed and her breathing was shallow, so that they could not tell whether she was unconscious or asleep.

'Poor Sarah,' sighed the tender-heared Martha, who, believing that Sarah's pregnancy had been a welcome one, could not imagine that her sister-in-law would be any less distraught than she herself had been when she had miscarried several years previously. It would never occur to Martha that Sarah had not wanted the baby, and that the loss of it would be a relief.

When the doctor came, Sarah had recovered consciousness.

'It's a blessing, Mrs Oaks,' he comforted her. 'The child would have been deformed had it gone full term. Nature knows what she's about.' He hesitated, before delivering what he expected to be a further blow. 'I'm afraid there'll be no more children, Mrs Oaks. This has put an end to increasing your family.'

Sarah's eyes closed whilst the doctor and Martha stood in silent sympathy. Her prayers, however, were prayers of thankfulness.

When George came back, quite late in the evening, after a day's threshing, he was distraught. 'We'll get rid o' t'thresher!' he pledged. 'It's not right for me to be away all these long hours, when I should be at home.'

'No, George. After what you've said about Edward having his own farm, I'm determined that we're going to earn and save as much as possible. I've even wondered about taking a stall at Kirkby market like your mother and Elizabeth used to do. I'd get more there for my poultry and dairy produce than I do from the huckster. I'd cut out the middle man.'

George shook his head. 'There's no need for that, love,' he said. 'We earn plenty, without you working.' He smiled at her and confided, 'Nobody knows how much money I have put away in the York Union Bank. Before Elizabeth died, we'd saved enough for a little farm of our own, but every time it came to it, I wouldn't leave Faither. We've added to it over the years, apart from my share of this farm. So you see, my love, we're far from penniless.'

Sarah was impressed. 'So there's every chance that Edward will have a farm of his own one day?'

'Take my word for it, love,' George replied. After a moment, he suggested, 'If time hangs heavily, why don't you start a proper garden at the front? I loved gardening when we lived at Cherry Tree, but I've never bothered here. If one of the men does the rough digging, we can both work on it at weekends and we can get seeds and plants in t'market.'

'I'd love that,' Sarah smiled, surprised that she had never thought of it herself. As George was leaving the bedroom, she called him back. 'I was ashamed, because I never wanted that baby, George,' she confessed, 'but perhaps, deep down, I knew there was something wrong.'

He came back to the bed and kissed her. 'You concentrate on getting well, love. We've a grand little family – three healthy bairns and that's all that matters.'

Chapter Twenty-Five

Sarah took longer to recover from her miscarriage than she had expected. Without her to preside as hostess, Victoria was unable to bring Tommy down to Aumery Park Farm for a further visit. And so the rest of the year passed.

The two families did not exchange Christmas visits as they usually did, as Sarah still felt unable to cope with many guests and Annie was not fit to make the journey to Thorsbury.

The Oaks and the Lambs spent Christmas together instead, the five children having an exciting time. They hung up their stockings, although Edward was sceptical. His father, however, had a strict word with him and he kept his doubts to himself, and was as eager as the rest to explore the contents of his stocking, from the toy at the top, through the apple, orange and chocolate bar, right to the shiny new penny at the tip of the toe.

On Christmas Eve, the Lassiter coach had driven down with a toy for each child and a soft, knitted jacket for Annie. Tamar had learned her lesson and no longer tried to give what her father regarded as charity.

The Lassiters, although Jonadab had no means of knowing this and would have been amazed had he done so, spent Christmas night with the Sturdys at the Towers. There had been no official betrothal announcement, but both families accepted that the couple would eventually marry. They had hoped that Christmas would bring a naming of the day, but Victoria still appeared to be reluctant.

The winter was really too cold for much snow. Although there were odd periods of snow flurries in the early part of the year, in Sleightholmedale, for day after day, the ground was iron-hard. The men trudged to their work under layers of clothing, stamping feet and blowing on hands in order to keep going. Their breath hung around them in clouds, lingering on the bitterly cold air. The trees bore a tracery of rime for weeks on end, giving the lie to Jonadab's oft-repeated piece of folk-lore: 'Three hoar frosts are followed by a thaw.'

'Aye, but it doesn't say how long afterwards,' laughed George.

Martha had always driven Maria the mile up the lane to go to school with Edward and Annie, but this winter, she and Sarah took it in turns to drive the children all the way to school and collect them at home-time. There was always a good fire in the schoolroom, but they had no wish for the children to become chilled on the journey home.

In February, back came the herons, with their slow, flapping flight, to the heronry on the far side of Hodge Beck. They were some of the earliest birds to nest and, once he could see both parents taking it in turn to incubate the eggs, Jonadab became impatient.

'When's oor Victoria bringing yon little lad o' Gertie's?' he frequently asked.

George looked at the turbulent sky, its lowering black clouds blotting out the moors. The icy hand of winter still held the land in its grip while the trees stood grim and bare in dark, forbidding ranks.

'Nobody wants to come down here yet,' he chided his father. 'She's all the summer to bring him down.'

'Aah've summat in mind for that young man and Aah wants 'im down 'ere while t'herons is still nesting.' More than this Jonadab refused to say.

With March came a change. In a farewell gesture to winter, the breeze whipped gusts of squally rain across the valley and the fitful sun began to struggle through. Work on the land started in earnest. The fields that had been laboriously ploughed earlier now needed breaking down into a finer tilth. Jonadab was anxious for the harrowing to get under way.

'Get them 'arrows working,' he urged George. 'We'll 'ave ti get yon spring corn in soon.'

'It will all get done, Faither,' George reassured him. 'We've had no real snow to speak of, so the land's not sodden. That frost has broken it up nicely – it's good for summat, after all.'

Although Jonadab Oaks' life had been spent on this land, and he knew it like the back of his hand, each year he became more fretful and impatient that they would not get through the work.

'Any lambs we're sellin' wants sorting out before t'lambing season starts,' he reminded his son.

'It's in hand, Faither.' George was hard put to keep his patience. 'Jim Dale's on with it, now.'

Jonadab looked puzzled.

'We have got another shepherd, now that Bob spends his time breaking in the foals. Jim Dale – remember?'

'Aah knows, Aah knows,' the old man almost snapped. 'Aah's not doity yet thoo knows.'

To Bob, George commented privately, 'If he doesn't stop nattering, he'll drive *me* doity.'

The winter had taken its toll on Jonadab. The thigh he had broken several years earlier, now gave him a lot of pain, making him even more short-tempered. The doctor had told him that it was rheumatism, thereafter referred to by Jonadab as 'mi screwmatics'.

Eventually, he was so impatient for Tommy to come down that he asked Sarah to write to Victoria. Both he and George were able to read and write, but writing did not come easily to them, so Sarah usually dealt with any family or business communications.

When she received the letter, Victoria was intrigued.

'Grandfather wants me to take Tommy down, before the end of March if possible,' she told her parents. 'I can't understand his urgency. I know he's fond of Tommy, because Tommy likes his horses, but he has all the children down there if he wants young company.' After consulting her diary, she said, 'It will be towards the end of the month before I can manage it.'

Since her relationship with Francis Sturdy had been resumed, her diary overflowed with social engagements and she was enjoying life as she had not done since her very first season, when she had met Thomas Forster.

It was a crisp, bright day when Victoria eventually drove down to Sleightholmedale with her son. The sky was a clear cerulean blue with fluffy white clouds chasing each other across it. The haze of fresh green which mantled the trees was burgeoning in places, as the leaves unfurled in the strengthening warmth of the sun.

The air was full of birdsong, for nesting was in full swing and the lapwings were disputing their territories with shrill, piping cries. Among the celandines and dead-nettles of the verges were, here and there, clumps of pale yellow wild daffodils, or Lenten Lillies, as old Annie called them.

They arrived just in time for the midday meal, although George was not present. Jonadab held forth at length about Victoria's delay in bringing the child down.

'There's summat special Aah wants ti show 'im,' he said, but would divulge no more.

Sarah took Victoria out to the garden she was creating at the front. 'What do you think the old man's got in mind?' she asked her niece.

'Goodness knows,' answered Victoria. 'He's quite old and old people sometimes get strange whims.' After admiring the garden, she went on, 'How's Grandma?'

'She gets no better; yet she gets no worse,' replied Sarah. 'Some days she's as lucid as you or I, and yet at other times she's way back in the past.' After a pensive pause, she added thoughtfully, 'She took complete charge when I lost the baby, mind. The years just rolled away.'

What Jonadab had planned for Tommy was, in his mind, quite simple. Tommy loved horses – therefore he would take Tommy for a ride on his horse. The child was afraid of water, so he would ride with him along Hodge Beck, showing him the delights of the stream from the safety of the horse's back.

Jonadab had reconnoitred the beck on various occasions in preparation for this excursion. In addition to the nesting herons, whose young were still nestlings, taking seven weeks before they were fully fledged, he had noted several other points of interest for the boy.

The beck, which twisted and chuckled through the vale,

was teeming with fish, from tiddlers and sticklebacks to trout, lurking in the deeper pools among the stones. He had spotted where a mallard was nesting and knew that, by now, she would have ducklings in tow. There were also several nests of coots and water hens among the rushes which fringed the banks of the beck. To the old man's naivety, all these delights would intrigue Tommy so much that he would forget his fear of the water.

Consequently, once dinner was over he took Tommy's hand and said, 'Come on, mi lad. You and me's going somewhere.'

His intention was to ride down the lane to Cherry Tree Farm, cross the beck behind the farm and go slowly along the edge of the water, pointing out to Tommy all the interesting sights he had in mind. Then they would re-cross the water close to the stepping stones near to Aumery Park Farm. He was convinced that, from the height and safety of the horse, Tommy would feel secure. In this way, he hoped to cure the boy's fear of water for good.

Tommy clapped his hands and laughed with glee when Jonadab lifted him on the back of his own horse, Peggy, and then mounted her himself, behind the boy. Tommy knew that Edward had a pony of his own and often wished that he could have one, too. However, this was a ride on a proper big mare – much better than a little pony.

Jonadab walked the horse slowly down the lane, pointing out to Tommy the cock pheasants strutting proudly across the track, eager to attract a mate, and rabbits scuttling about on their courtship ritual.

When they came to Cherry Tree Farm, Jonadab steered the reins to the left, behind the buildings, and took the track which led to the spa. The path was much narrower here and the encompassing hedges higher, until they were in what was really a grove of trees, with the lane only the width of a carriage and pair.

They came upon the stream without prior warning, and Tommy wrapped his fingers in the horse's mane, his eyes widening in fear.

The ford was deeper than Jonadab remembered, the

channel having been cut by the passage of horses and carriages carrying those who wished to bathe in or drink the waters. There was a small island in the middle, only big enough to hold one tree and a few shrubs, but it divided the beck into two narrower, faster-flowing arms. This rushing water had scooped out deeper pools downstream of the island, so that in trying to cross there, Jonadab was attempting to ford a spot that was more treacherous than he realised.

Feeling the boy stiffen and recognising the tension in him, the old man patted his shoulder. 'Thoo's all right, laddie. 'Ave faith in old Jonadab. Aah'm 'ere and Peggy won't let thoo near t'watter.'

Had Tommy been able to speak, he would have protested. As it was, he closed his eyes tightly and clung with desperation to Peggy's mane.

On the brink of the stream, Peggy hesitated, deterred by the swiftness of the current. A frightened child was enough for Jonadab, without a nervous horse as well. He dug his knees into Peggy's flanks and said firmly, 'Goo on!'

She took a tentative step forward, nervous both with the dim light under the dense trees and the sound of the swiftly-rushing water. Unfortunately, the edge of the bank was soft and gave way under her weight. She teetered for an instant and then recovered her balance, but it was too late for Jonadab.

He had been riding the ambling horse with the reins held loose in his hands, confident after a lifetime in the saddle of his ability to control her. Now, he lost his grip and was catapulted down into the turbulent stream, landing winded in the torrential rush of icy water.

Tommy, aware of the sudden loss of security afforded by the old man's body behind him, and hearing the splash as he fell, opened his eyes in alarm and saw Jonadab lying, as he thought, drowned in the beck. To begin with, he screwed his eyes tightly shut again, trying to blot out his greatest fear. But, when he opened them once more, Jonadab was still in the water, eyes ominously closed.

The little boy's throat worked convulsively and then, in

panic, desperation and grief-stricken memory of his father's death, a high-pitched scream rang out.

'Grandad!' he cried. 'No, Grandad! No! No!'

The years of frustration and silence were dashed away as he sat, watching history repeat itself.

'Grandad!' he called again, tears teeming down his pale and horrified face. Then, seeing that he had failed to arouse the old man who meant so much to him, and who had in the past shown him such consideration and compassion, he screwed his courage to the utmost and slid down what seemed to be a great height from the horse's neck. Taking the reins, he pulled her towards the water. 'Come on, come on.' The words were slow and unsure, but words they were, and he uttered them continuously as he clicked his tongue to persuade the skittish mare to approach the brink of the beck.

Gathering his courage again, he swallowed hard and stepped into the icy torrent. To his surprise, it was not as deep as he had thought and he tried at first to raise Jonadab, but the old man was too heavy. He did, however, lift his head clear of the water, and reduce any further damage of him slipping into the flow.

Looking around for a source of inspiration as to how to help the man he loved so much, he was struck with an idea. Undoing Jonadab's broad leather belt, he slipped the reins through it and re-fastened the strong, brass buckle.

Jonadab was soaked through and chilled to the bone and even the young child realised that he must be got out of the water as soon as possible. To his consternation, the horse was too big for him to remount her without assistance. However, by dint of climbing on to a tree stump he managed to scramble across and into the saddle.

As the reins were tied to Jonadab, he was now in a quandary as to how to make the horse go back.

'Back! Back!' he shouted, but she ignored him. Still Jonadab did not stir. The child's mind raced. The memory of his own helplessness on seeing his father fall through the ice, all those years ago, flooded over him. He would not let it happen twice.

Cautiously, he wriggled up on to Peggy's neck, then leaned precariously forward and grasped the reins close to the bit at each side of her mouth.

'Back! Back, girl!' he screamed, pulling on the bit as he did so.

To his relief, the horse slowly began to move backwards, dragging her master from the stream and up the bank. Once Jonadab was safely clear of the water, Tommy freed the reins and fastened Peggy to a nearby tree. Then he ran as fast as his legs would move, back to Cherry Tree Farm.

Bob Lamb had been working up at Aumery Park Farm, helping Jim Dale with the lambing. He had been kept late dealing with a difficult birth, and was in the middle of his dinner when Tommy knocked on the door.

When Martha opened it, a breathless Tommy, soaked up to his waist, stumbled over the threshold, gasping, 'Drown-ded! Grandad, drownded!'

The enormity of the fact that Tommy had spoken did not register with Martha and Bob. The latter leapt from his chair and shook the boy, saying, 'Where? *Where*, for heaven's sake?'

'Beck,' replied the white-faced child, pointing in the direction of the back of the house. Bob ran from the kitchen, taking the right path more out of good fortune than cer-tainty.

When he caught sight of his father-in-law, lying in a soaking wet heap on the bank, his heart almost stopped. Jonadab certainly looked to be dead. However, when Bob reached him, he was definitely breathing; in fact, his teeth were chattering, even though his eyes were closed.

It took a great deal of effort for Bob to raise him from the ground and hoist him on to Peggy, where he slumped across her neck. Bob mounted behind him, and though he felt like galloping at full speed, walked the horse gently back to the farm.

When they arrived, Martha had undressed Tommy and rubbed him dry. He now sat by the hearth, wrapped in a warm towel.

'Come and give me a hand with your father, can you?'

said Bob. Together they carried the old man in. 'Put him on the hearthrug, by the fire,' Bob instructed. 'Then go and pop a couple of oven shelves in t'spare bed.'

Martha wrapped two of the shelves from the oven in old pieces of blanket and ran up to put them in to the bed. While she was upstairs, she fetched a couple of towels and one of Bob's shirts and placed them to warm on the oven-shelves in the bed.

When she went downstairs to help her husband to carry the old man into the bedroom, she said, 'It didn't dawn on you, did it? It certainly didn't dawn on me at first.'

'What didn't dawn?' he enquired, as they manoeuvred Jonadab up the stairs.

'Tommy spoke,' she replied.

The amazement on Bob's face was a picture. 'By gum, 'e did an' all. I was too worried about your dad to notice.'

Martha left Bob to towel the old man dry and put him into the clean shirt and warm bed. She returned to the kitchen, to prepare some hot milk and treacle for both the child and old man.

'Here you are, Tommy. This'll warm the cockles of your heart,' she said, holding out the mug.

She watched as his throat worked, silently at first, then he managed, 'Fank you.'

She could scarcely believe her ears. 'When did you first speak, Tommy?' she asked gently.

'Water. Him drownded.' His eyes filled with tears.

'Jonadab's not drowned,' she assured him softly. 'I don't know what happened, but you must have saved his life. He's upstairs, asleep in bed and I'm just going to take him some hot milk, like you've got.'

The child wiped his tears and managed a vague smile before staring into his mug, reflectively.

Martha put his wet clothes through the mangle, to squeeze out as much of the water as possible, then arranged them over the fireguard to dry. After doing this, she took up the mug of hot milk to her father.

Upon entering the bedroom, she was relieved to see that

Jonadab was lucid and sitting up in the warm, feather bed. His first thought was for young Tommy.

'Where's yon lad?' he demanded fiercely. 'Is 'e all right?'

'Aye, he's downstairs by the fire,' Bob reassured him. 'What I want to know is, what happened over there?'

'T'stupid 'oss missed 'er footin' on t'bank,' Jonadab grumbled, omitting to say that he had chosen the deepest part of the beck to cross, instead of the shallow part above the island.

'Yes, but then what? What exactly happened?' asked Martha.

'T'last thing Aah remember is landin' in t'watter, until Aah woke up in bed 'ere,' her father told her.

'Well, we shall never know how you landed on the bank, but it's a blessing you did,' observed Bob.

'Of course we sh'll know,' Martha reasoned. 'Tommy is able to write. Even if he can't talk very well, he can write it down and tell us exactly what happened.'

'What dost thoo mean, "can't talk very well"? 'E can't talk at all,' put in Jonadab.

'Oh yes he can, Father. It was Tommy who came and told us you were hurt. He only used single words, but he spoke quite clearly.'

Jonadab smiled as he digested the information. 'Well, by gum! That's a bonus,' he chuckled. 'Aah was tryin' to cure 'im of being afeared o' watter, but if Aah got 'im ti talk an' all, that's just grand!' He spoke smugly, taking all the credit for the mircale which had restored Tommy's speech.

Sipping the hot milk, he looked round. 'Aah'm not stoppin' 'ere. Aah wants ti be back in mi own 'ome,' he grumbled. 'And anyroad, there's not need for me ti stop in bed – there's nowt wrong wi' mi!'

Martha sighed in exasperation, but was still too much in awe of her father to argue with him.

'I'll take Peggy back home,' said Bob, 'and see how we can get you back up there. Your clothes are sopping, so you can't get dressed!'

When he arrived at Aumery Park Farm, he took Peggy straight to her stable and told Toby to give her a good rub down and feed of oats, to settle her. He had not wanted anyone from the house to see him riding her, not wishing to alarm them.

Upon reaching the house, he hesitated as to how to break the news. Victoria was growing impatient, wanting to set off on the long journey home.

'You haven't seen Grandad and Tommy, have you, Uncle Bob?' she asked him. 'They rode off towards Cherry Tree Farm, ages ago.'

'Aye, they're down at our house,' he said.

'I wish they'd get back. I'm anxious to be off,' she complained, glancing at the long-case clock in the corner.

'Well,' he paused, 'there's a bit of a hitch, really.' He looked at Sarah. 'T'old man's met with an accident. We've got him in bed at our house.'

'What kind of accident?' Sarah may have had her ups and down with her father-in-law, but basically she was fond of him.

Bob explained as best he could. He hesitated about telling Victoria of Tommy's restored speech, as for one thing he did not want to raise her hopes in case it should prove to be an isolated incident and secondly, he felt that the accident was enough of a shock for the time being. 'Anyroad,' he concluded, 'he's set his mind on coming back home, but how we're to manage it I don't know.'

'That's easy,' Victoria told him. 'We'll fetch him in the coach.'

Bob was dispatched to get Robert, the coachman, who spent his time at Sleightholmedale in Lydia and Toby's cottage, where Lydia always provided him with a meal.

Jonadab was swathed in a goose-down quilt to keep him warm and made a very undignified progress down the stairs and out into the coach.

'Such namby-pamby goings on,' he complained bitterly. 'Fancy me ridin' in one o' these contraptions!'

Upon reaching home, he peered all ways, to convince himself that none of the workers could see him in his quilt and bare legs. Only when he was completely satisfied, did he allow Bob and Robert to help him into the house. Tommy trailed behind, still garbed in his towel.

Once Jonadab was safely in bed, Sarah said, 'I'll look for some of Edward's old clothes which might fit Tommy. They'll do for him to go home in. His own are still wet.'

When the boy was dressed, she laughed. 'They fit where they touch. But at least they're warm and dry.'

Tommy smiled. Looking at Victoria, he said, 'Miss Vitty.'

Victoria felt her jaw drop open with amazement. Her eyes met Sarah's, which were equally disbelieving.

'Tommy?' Victoria's voice was a question. 'Tommy, say it again.'

'Miss Vitty,' he said and then, pointing round the room said, 'Clock. Table. Cat.'

The emotion of the moment was too much for Victoria. All her hopes for the child had come to fruition and she burst into tears, taking him in her arms and hugging and kissing him. 'Oh, darling Tommy!' she cried. 'I never thought the day would come.'

Sarah, too, was overcome and felt tears of joy running down her own cheeks.

Drying her eyes, Victoria explained shakily, 'We've had so many disappointments; first the doctor in London and then the mesmerist in Leeds. And now, in some miraculous way, it's happened,' she said. 'I can't really believe it.' Turning to the child, she pleaded, 'Say something else, Tommy. Let me just hear your voice, please.'

With a beaming smile, he did his best to oblige. 'Rug. Fire,' he pointed. The words were guttural and enunciated with difficulty, but they were recognisable, and to Victoria's ears, as sweet as music.

When they went up to say goodbye to her grandfather, Victoria asked, 'How did it happen, Grandad?'

'Aah dissent rightly know,' he confessed, 'but Aah set out ti cure 'is fear o' watter, and Aah's finished up gettin' 'im ti talk. Not bad for an old man. Come 'ere, young 'un an' let mi shek thi 'and.'

Tommy stepped forward, his young eyes bright with pride

and admiration for his friend. Stretching out his hand he shook the old man's, beaming as he did so.

'Fank you,' he said, then drew himself across the old man's chest and hugged him tightly.

Jonadab chuckled as he ruffled the boy's hair affectionately. 'Eeh, we're a matched pair, thee an' me. A right matched pair!'

With that self-satisfied statement, he closed his eyes and went to sleep.

Chapter Twenty-Six

On the way home, Victoria questioned Tommy, pointing out objects from the carriage windows and asking him to name then until his eyelids drooped with the effort of speaking and the excitement of the day. Finally, he fell into a deep sleep.

It was late when they arrived back at Thorsbury Manor and Tamar was beginning to worry. 'Whatever has happened that it took you so long? I expected you back a couple of hours ago!'

'Oh, Mama! I'll tell you all that's happened over dinner, but the important thing is that Tommy can speak again!'

Tamar sat down abruptly, her eyes searching Victoria's face. 'This isn't a joke, is it? You wouldn't joke about something as serious as this.'

Victoria was bubbling over with happiness. 'No, it isn't a joke. I can hardly wait to tell you and Papa all that's happened, but I must get ready for dinner. Be patient, Mama, and I'll tell you both together.' So Tamar needs must contain her impatience.

Over the meal, Victoria told them the events of the day, or rather, as much as she knew of what had actually happened.

'Grandfather had decided that he could make Tommy overcome his fear of water, if he took him across the beck on horseback, high above the stream,' she explained.

'Only somebody as stubborn and as cocksure as your father would concoct such a wild scheme,' Stephen remarked to Tamar.

'Well, it worked!' Victoria told them triumphantly. 'When something went wrong and Grandfather ended up unconscious in the beck, Tommy went into the water and saved him. We don't know exactly what happened, but no doubt Tommy will write it all down for us tomorrow.'

'Plucky little chap,' Stephen commented, full of admiration.

'I couldn't believe it, when I heard him actually say words.' Victoria's eyes were full of tears and she blinked them away rapidly. 'It's silly to cry about it,' she smiled tremulously, 'but it's a thing of such of such immense happiness to me.'

'What does he say? Does he speak normally?' Tamar wanted to know.

Victoria hesitated, trying to assess how near to normal Tommy's speech was. 'He doesn't speak in sentences,' she admitted, 'but he can name almost anything. He calls me Miss Vitty, by the way. I suppose he speaks as he did when he lost his speech – like a toddler.'

'He'll soon learn to string sentences together, once he's regained the ability to formulate words,' observed Stephen.

Victoria thought for a moment then said, quite firmly, 'I want to employ someone to teach him to speak properly. I don't want him to grow up speaking like one of the village children. I want him to talk like a gentleman.' Her voice held a small quaver, as she looked pleadingly at her parents.

Stephen demurred. 'We must not make him unsuited for his station in life, my darling,' he said gently.

'He is my son and his father was a gentleman,' she said fiercely. 'I want to educate him according to his birthright. We can see, as he grows up, what he makes of himself.'

Stephen's lips tightened, but she could tell by her mother's expression that the unconventional Tamar agreed with her.

The following morning her mother accompanied her to the schoolroom, where they asked that Tommy should write an account of the events of the previous day.

Tamar looked round the overcrowded room. There had been more newcomers than leavers in recent months and now that they were required by law to send their children to school, few parents kept them at home to help.

When they returned to their own quarters, Tamar said thoughtfully, 'I haven't been into the schoolroom for several months, so I hadn't realised how overcrowded it had become. There's that piece of spare land, between number eight and nine in the village. I'll ask your father about building a school there. It could have a cottage attached for Mary Jewson. I know that the kitchen staff object to the children trailing through their quarters to reach the schoolroom.'

'If you did that, Mama,' Victoria's eyes were shining, 'could I have the schoolroom for Tommy and hire a tutor for him? I'd pay him myself, of course.'

Tamar hesitated, unwilling to commit herself to something she feared would meet with Stephen's disapproval. 'We'll see, darling,' was all she would say. 'But it will be some time before the new school is built, anyway.'

With this, Victoria had to be satisfied, although she made her plans and dreamed her dreams.

Francis Sturdy, meantime, was becoming impatient with Victoria's refusal to name a date for their wedding, or to accept a betrothal ring.

'I know I let you down once, my darling,' he admitted, 'but I do truly love you and I want us to be married as soon as possible.'

Still she hesitated. 'I feel that I'm unworthy of you,' she said diffidently, looking into his blunt features which, though not strictly handsome, were open and kind.

His deep, grey eyes looked into her golden ones as, with a quick glance to make sure they were unobserved, he swept her into his arms and kissed her with a passion and intensity which left her trembling. To his surprise, after a momentary hesitation, she returned his kisses with an ardour which shook him. Before he could tighten his hold, however, she drew back, placed her hands on his chest and pushed him away.

'No! No more,' she whispered huskily, an expression of panic on her face.

Francis laughed exultantly. 'Your love for me is as strong as mine is for you,' he claimed. 'When can we be married, my little love? I can't wait much longer.'

'You must wait,' she insisted. 'I do love you, dearest

Francis and I long to be your wife, but you must give me a little longer.'

His disappointment was so severe that he turned almost churlish. 'I consider that I've waited long enough,' he said shortly. 'If I hadn't experienced the passion of your response to me just now, I would feel that you were amusing yourself with me – as you did with Hoyland Wheatcroft,' he added.

She gave a gasp of disbelief. 'Oh, Francis, how could you? I was not amusing myself with Hoyland. I always discouraged him and made it clear that I didn't love him.'

Francis was not to be placated, however. He was bitterly disappointed in her reaction to his constant proposals and stayed away for the next two weeks, until Victoria began to fear that he would not return.

Before the situation could be resolved, however, news came which shattered the whole Oaks family as nothing else had done. Annie Oaks slipped out of life, as quietly and with as little fuss as she had lived it.

Jonadab awoke one bright June morning to find her lying peaceful and still by his side, in the bed which had been their marriage bed. His first emotion was one of disbelief, resentment even, that she had gone before he was ready to go with her.

'Oh, Annie. Thoo could 'ave waited, old lass,' he murmured sadly, as he stroked the long silver plait which trailed across the flannel night-gown and rested on her wizened and motionless bosom. 'Thoo could 'ave waited.'

Kneeling beside the bed, he prayed for his wife and then, placing his face into the down of the mattress, wept as he had never done in his life. Silently, in the privacy of his room, Jonadab Oaks cried his heart out for the woman who had shared his life for over fifty years.

'Thoo's been a grand wife and mother, Annie,' he whispered; a tribute which he had never thought to pay in her lifetime. Jonadab had never felt so alone. He was, he realised, the last survivor of his generation.

The whole Oaks family was desolate. Those closest to Annie had noted how much her condition had deteriorated, but the shock was greater to the scattered family, many living on isolated farms in distant dales. The only times they could manage the journey to Sleightholmedale were on special occasions, but the ties which held them as a family were strong.

Although Jonadab prided himself upon his firm hold on his family, it was in reality Annie who had bound them together. Many problems had been ironed out round Annie's kitchen table. She would listen without interruption to two differing points of view, and then give a balanced judgement.

Although she would never have claimed to be clever and was willing to defer to Jonadab in most things, her countrywoman's love and skills, passed down from her mother and grandmother, had been handed on to her own girls, fitting them for their roles as good farmers' wives.

This, with the exception of Tamar, whom Annie had often thought must be a changeling, so unlike her siblings was she, in both appearance and temperament. Yet Tamar was the one most affected by her mother's death. Her own escape from the type of life led by her sisters brought home to her what a life of unremitting hard work, even drudgery, Annie had lived until her old age.

When the family gathered on the day of the funeral, it was clear to each of them, that with Annie gone, the magnet which had drawn them home had been removed. They respected their father, but they had loved their mother. The love which Annie had given so unstintingly to her family, accepting their weaknesses and forgiving their frailties, was returned devotedly by each one. Even Jonna, as self-sufficient as his father, was moved to tears by his mother's death.

The day of the funeral was glorious and golden, although Jonadab would have preferred rain, to echo the desolation of his feelings.

In keeping with his belief, there was no 'bought' funeral for Annie. Jonadab's newest flat cart had been scrubbed and newly varnished and his biggest and most impressive pair of matched greys yoked up to it, to carry Annie up to

Gillamoor Church. The coffin, upon which Jonadab had not spared a penny, lay on the cart.

'T'best oak, wi' brass 'andles,' he had instructed the undertaker. Sarah had ravaged her newly-established garden to pile the cart with flowers, from blowsy peonies to humble stocks and asters.

When Jonadab came out of the house, with George and Sarah on either side, even Tamar was touched by his appearance. The once ramrod-straight shoulders were bowed and his face was seamed with sorrow. He surveyed the cart and the two patient shires that stood waiting to draw it, and nodded with satisfaction.

'Aye, that's 'ow it should be,' he said. 'No fancy flummeries. Just a man's own best 'osses and a good, plain cart.'

This was all he said. At the graveside, however, Jonadab, who had buried his parents, his only brother, and one of his children, with no alteration of his normal stoical expression, showed the depth of his distress at the loss of his wife. As he bent over the open grave, to toss the first symbolic handful of earth on to Annie's coffin, a solitary tear coursed its way down his grief-furrowed cheek and his shoulders slumped in dejection. He remained, bent and desolate, staring forlornly into the open grave, until George and Sarah led him away.

The Oaks were valued and respected tenants so, as his father was away in London, Francis Sturdy had been delegated to attend the funeral as his representative. When he saw Victoria in deepest black among the family mourners, his brow furrowed in puzzlement. Seeing the look of questioning in his face, Victoria realised that he would have had no way of knowing, nor could he have imagined, that the Oaks were her mother's family.

Normally, after the actual burial, the gathering afterwards is lighter and freed from restraint. When Annie and Jonadab's children, grandchildren and great-grandchildren gathered at Aumery Park Farm after Annie's funeral, however, there was still an atmosphere of gloom. All there knew that this was the end of an era and, without Annie to draw them together, few would visit Jonadab's home. Tamar would still come. She and George had always been close, there being only a year's difference in their ages, but the deep affection in which Annie's descendants held her was not mirrored in their feelings towards Jonadab.

They conceded that he was a grand old man; they admired his principals; he earned their grudging respect for his business acumen, but his children feared him, rather than loved him. Each knew, with a feeling of disloyalty, that he or she would not make the effort to come again to the farm which had been their home.

The next time Francis Sturdy called to see her, Victoria arranged with her mother to be alone with him, in Tamar's own little sitting room. His first remarks were to express his surprise at seeing her at 'old Mrs Oaks' funeral'. Victoria explained the relationship and although he was too polite to comment, he was even more surprised to learn that Tamar was Jonadab Oaks' daughter, considering her to be more ladylike than much of the real Quality.

Today, Francis seemed ill-at-ease. He stood with his back to Victoria, looking out of the window, then he moved to stand by a small table, sniffing deeply at the bowl of roses that stood on it.

'Is there something wrong, Francis?' Victoria was vaguely uneasy at his behaviour. It was so much at odds with his normal frank and open character. Perhaps he was ashamed because her grandfather was a tenant farmer? Perhaps he no longer thought she was good enough for him? Victoria's heart fluttered like a captive bird, as she recalled how often he had begged her to marry him and she had refused to say yes. She could have been safely betrothed, or even married to him, long before he found out her relationship to Jonadab.

She repeated her question. 'Is something wrong?'

He came and took the chair opposite, looking faintly incongruous in the delicate crinoline chair. For a moment he studied his hands, as though they were of the utmost importance. Then he raised his dark, almost smokey grey eyes to hers.

'Victoria,' he began and then halted. He cleared his throat and began again. 'Victoria, I have made a decision. I have come today to ask, for the last time, if you will marry me.'

Her heart went cold when she heard the words, 'for the last time'. She realised how much she loved Francis; how much she had come to depend upon him.

'Well, Victoria? Remember, this is the last time I shall ask. Will you marry me? Will you name a date?'

He dabbed his upper lip with his handkerchief and she noticed that his forehead too, was beaded with perspiration.

Suddenly, she recognised how dear he was to her. She was afraid of losing him and yet still she held back. 'I can't commit myself to set a date, while we are in mourning for my grandmother,' she heard herself say.

His face was strained and tinged with grey despite his normally healthy tan. 'So, that's my final answer, is it? Another rebuff.' His tone was bitter as gall, as he leapt to his feet. 'At least I know where I stand.'

The eyes which she raised to his were tormented and dark. Her voice was low, scarcely more than a whisper.

'I do love you, Francis. Believe me! There's nothing I want more in this world than to be your wife.' It was obvious that she was struggling maintain her composure.

He placed a hand across his brow, in a gesture of bewilderment. 'If you love me, as you say you do, what is the obstacle? I love you dearly. I want you for my wife and you say that you want to be my wife, so I can see no problem. What is holding you back? Am I not worthy of an explanation?'

Victoria's efforts to keep control of her feelings proved to be in vain. Throwing herself into a chair, she laid her head on her arms and began to cry. Gradually, the tears engulfed her and she became totally incoherent, sobbing and hiccupping together.

Gently, he patted her and rocked her in his arms. Leading her to a sofa, he sat down and drew her on to his knee. Tenderly wiping her eyes with his own handkerchief, he soothed her until her weeping had subsided into the occasional sob.

'Now, tell me what is the matter,' he prompted, when she seemed calmer.

She turned her face away, unwilling to meet his questioning eyes. Taking her chin in his hands, he turned her back towards him.

'You are the most beautiful creature I have ever seen, as well as the sweetest-natured,' he told her. 'I want to marry you, as soon as it is possible.'

Her eyes, when they met his, were deep amber with anguish. 'Oh Francis,' she spoke sadly. 'I am unworthy to be your wife. I am unfit to be the wife of any decent man.' She began to sob again, this time with a quiet dejection.

His gaze was intent and he saw that she was in earnest. 'Victoria, my darling, my own true love, if you told me you had committed murder, I would still want you for my wife,' he told her, trying to penetrate her sadness.

But Victoria would not be comforted. Holding his hands tightly in hers, she fixed her eyes on his, her face strained and pale. 'Thomas Forster and I were lovers,' she confessed.

Francis sighed with relief. 'I presumed as much,' he said, with a smile. 'Your confession comes as no surprise to me. Thomas and I were very close and, although he never betrayed your secret, he was so desperate if he could not ride over to see you, that I realised it was more than just a mild flirtation.'

She held his hands even more tightly and closed her eyes for a moment. Taking a deep breath, she opened them and fixed them intently upon his.

'That is not the worst.' Her voice was so faint that he had to lean close to her, to catch what she said. Her brimming eyes overflowed once more, and the tears rolled silently down her cheeks.

Gently wiping them away, he murmured, 'Go on, darling. Tell me what it is that's causing you so much distress.'

She appeared to be reluctant to say more, but then she gathered her courage and blurted out, 'Tommy is my son! Mine and Thomas'.' Drawing a deep, shuddering breath, she said, 'There! Now it's out. You must understand why

I cannot bring myself to marry you. I thought at first, that I could marry you and leave Tommy here at Thorsbury with Mama and Papa. But I realise that I can't. I thought I'd lost him once, when my maid, Gertie took him as her own, but he was brought back to me. I couldn't do it again. He means everything to me. I'm sorry, but at least you have your explanation.'

His face paled. This news was obviously a shock to him. After sitting for a while, digesting what Victoria had said, he turned to her once more, his face drawn and serious.

'Is this why you were sent to Canada, so quickly after Thomas' death?' he queried.

Mutely she nodded, unable to bring herself to speak and not daring to look at him. The gravity of his tone sounded knell-like to her ears.

'If you left him in Canada with your maid, how did he come to be back in England?' Francis asked her.

She gazed at him for some moments, gathering her thoughts. Then, haltingly at first, but gaining in confidence as she went, she poured out the whole story. 'My cousins must have thought I was too stiff-necked and unfriendly to mix with them, but I was wallowing in shame and self-pity,' she confessed.

She went on to tell how Gertie had come to be in England and even of Rob McDonald's blackmail attempt.

When the tale was done, she dared not raise her eyes to his, afraid of what she would read there. She sat, lips drooping and eyes downcast, awaiting Francis' words of rejection.

He had been deeply touched by her confession. 'Oh, my poor little love,' he said, drawing her into his arms. 'After all that you've been through, don't you think you deserve some happiness?'

'I'm glad there are no secrets between us,' she admitted. 'I've wanted to tell you for so long, but I was afraid of losing you.'

'Not only do I intend to marry you, but I shall adopt Tommy as my own son, and give him my name. It's the least I can do for Thomas. He was my best friend as well as my cousin, after all. We'll ask your father's advice about the legal side.'

Her face was radiant. 'Oh, thank you, Francis. I have hated these past few months, when I thought I should have to choose between you. I love you both so much, but I could not bear the thought of leaving Tommy behind again.'

'What could be more natural than that you should want to care for your faithful maid's orphan?' he asked. 'And now, what about a date for our wedding?'

'I had never expected that this day would come,' she admitted, still trembling and on the verge of tears. 'I could not marry you without telling you the truth and yet, when you heard it, I thought you would turn from me in disgust.'

Smiling, he placed his hand caressingly over her lips. 'Don't say another word, unless it's a date for the wedding,' he insisted.

'Easter, next year?' Her brows rose questioningly.

'Next Easter!' he demanded incredulously. 'I can't wait until then.'

'I shall be in full mourning for my grandmother until almost Christmas,' she reminded him. 'And we don't want to be married too early in the year. If there's snow, it will make travelling difficult for the guests.'

'So, I'm getting a practical wife as well as a beautiful one, am I?' he teased. 'Come along then, darling. Let's break the news to your mother. I'm sure she'll be pleased that we've set a date. I know that my parents will be.'

As he took her hand to lead her to the door, she tugged him back. 'Wait,' she begged. 'There's something else.'

'Now what is it? Not another snag?' His brow furrowed and his normally clear eyes clouded over with renewed doubt.

'No.' She hesitated for a few seconds. 'I've often thought that I'd like to tell your aunt, Lady Forster, that Tommy is her grandson. I would not wish her to think badly of either me or Thomas and have tried to weigh her opinion of us, against the pleasure of knowing that Thomas left a child – her own flesh and blood.'

Francis stood, debating with himself for a while. 'It's a

very sweet thought, my dearest, but we'll think about it carefully and do nothing until after we are married.'

Tamar had been restless all morning. When Victoria had asked her permission to see Francis in the privacy of her sitting room, she knew that a final decision was imminent. Victoria was so much like her: just as she had not been able to marry Stephen without telling him the truth about Victoria's illegitimacy, so Victoria would feel bound to confess the secret of Tommy's birth to Francis. Tamar could only hope that his love and understanding would be as strong as Stephen's had been.

When they appeared in the grand hall, hand in hand, faces radiant, she uttered a silent prayer of thankfulness.

'I've at last got a date out of this stubborn daughter of yours, Lady Lassiter,' he announced with delight. 'Can you arrange a wedding for Easter?'

Tamar kissed them both. 'I'm so happy for you,' she smiled. 'Congratulations. We must go and break the news to your father at once.'

Stephen rose from his desk, smiling broadly and shook Francis by the hand. 'May I say how pleased I am. I wish you every happiness!' he exclaimed.

'There is just one thing you can help us with,' Francis told him, when the congratulations were over. 'Can you tell us just how Victoria and I go about adopting Tommy?'

Stephen's face was shadowed and his lips were set. 'I think that would be a grave mistake,' he told them. 'The boy is all right as he is. In any case, we don't want tongues to wag.'

Francis, however, was not to be intimidated by the older man. With a grim set to his jaw, he replied, 'I think you are over-sensitive on the subject of Tommy, sir. Why should tongues wag? Victoria has every right to care for the orphan child of her faithful servant.' He looked from one to the other. 'There is one other thing which none of you seem to recognise. Tommy is related to me by blood and I want the best for him.'

Stephen was forced to capitulate. 'Very well, my boy,' he

said, 'I shall do my best to facilitate the adoption proceedings.'

That afternoon, Tamar wrote to her father, wishing to tell him the news herself, before he read the announcement in the *Yorkshire Post* or *Malton Messenger*.

Jonadab laboriously read her letter and then re-read it.

'Well, if this dissent beat hen-racing bi candlelight!' he ejaculated. 'Aah'm gobsmacked!'

'What is it, Faither?' asked George.

'Oor Victoria's goin' ti marry young Sturdy.' Jonadab's amazement was manifest in his tone.

'Good for her!' exclaimed Sarah. 'The Sturdys are nice folks.'

'That's as mebbe,' the old man admitted, 'but thoo sees what it means.'

'What's that?' asked George.

'We sh'll 'ave ti look for a farm ti buy.'

George looked amazed. 'I thought you never wanted to leave Aumery Park?'

'That Aah dissent. But Aah can't 'ave a grandson for mi landlord.'

George and Sarah caught each other's eye and both burst out laughing.

'Oh, Faither,' George chuckled. 'Sir James is not much more than my age. Barring accidents, you'll be pushing daisies up long before young Francis inherits.'

'It's still summat ti be borne in mind. Things is better done early than late. As soon as Aah'm gone, look for a place ti buy.'

Although he would never have admitted it, Jonadab was impressed and flattered when the invitations arrived. When Sarah tentatively suggested a new suit for the occasion, however, he was outraged.

'A new suit? Thoo must be mad! Mi Sunday best's as good as new.'

'Oh, Father,' she remonstrated. 'It's more than fifty years old – you were married in it! You can't show Victoria up. You must buy a new one.'

'Aah'm not spending good brass on a new suit at my age.

Aah'd get no wear out of it. Look after t'pence and t'pounds'll look after themselves.'

'I suppose the next one will be "This best friend is thi pocket"?' Sarah laughed.

'Aye, it is an' all. What's so funny about that?' he demanded.

So Jonadab took his place at the wedding in the seat of honour beside Tamar in the front pew – of equal importance with Sir James and Lady Sturdy across the aisle. Tommy was beside him, his hand firmly grasped in the old man's. Even in his Sunday best, old and out of date as it was, Jonadab was an impressive figure. When they rose to greet the bride, a vision of exquisite loveliness on her father's arm, he straightened his back and squared his shoulders, regaining for a time the upright stance of his youth, making his family look upon him with pride.

Jonadab Oaks might not inspire deep affection in his family, but they were all proud of this dour and God-fearing dalesman.

Tamar smiled a wry, wistful smile to herself, as she surveyed her family, gathered together in the Great Hall of Thorsbury Manor for the wedding breakfast. Her father, old now, but nonetheless a bold and steadfast figure, talked to Sir James Sturdy with ease, showing no sign of intimidation nor inferiority. Sir James, for his part, treated the old man with the deference and respect worthy of one of the old breed of Yorkshiremen. Her father was a true patriarch – head of his family, obstinate and wilful in his beliefs and yet, Tamar acknowledged, it was those same qualities, inherited from him, which had made her what she was today.

She looked across at her brother George, kind and considerate but lacking the confidence – conceit, almost – of his father and she sighed, sadly. George reminded her so much of her mother.

How proud Annie would have been, she thought, to see them all there, farmers and gentry alike, spanning the chasm between landlord and tenant. How she wished her mother could have hung on just a little longer.

Stephen took her arm. 'A penny for them,' he smiled.

'I was thinking about Mother,' Tamar confessed. 'I wish she could have been here.'

Leading her towards the long banqueting table, he spoke softly and comfortingly. 'She is – and always will be, in spirit. But she would not wish us to dwell on the past. Your mother had a good life. We have all benefited from her wisdom and I, in particular, have more than most to thank her for. Without her, I would not have my beloved wife – and daughter,' he added, nodding in the direction of Victoria, vibrant and happy on the arm of Francis.

Tamar smiled, grateful for his understanding.

'Yes,' she agreed. 'We have a great deal to thank her for. There's a little part of her in all of us, and will be for many a generation,' she added, smiling fondly at the small boy clutching Jonadab's hand. 'She once said to me, when I was going off to Helmsley, "As one door closes, another opens. Make the most of life's opportunities", and you know, my darling, I think we are about to walk through another door right now.'

So saying, she slipped her arm through that of her husband and they walked together to join the rest of their family in their celebrations, happy in the knowledge that Victoria, like her mother before her, had at long last made the most of life's opportunities.